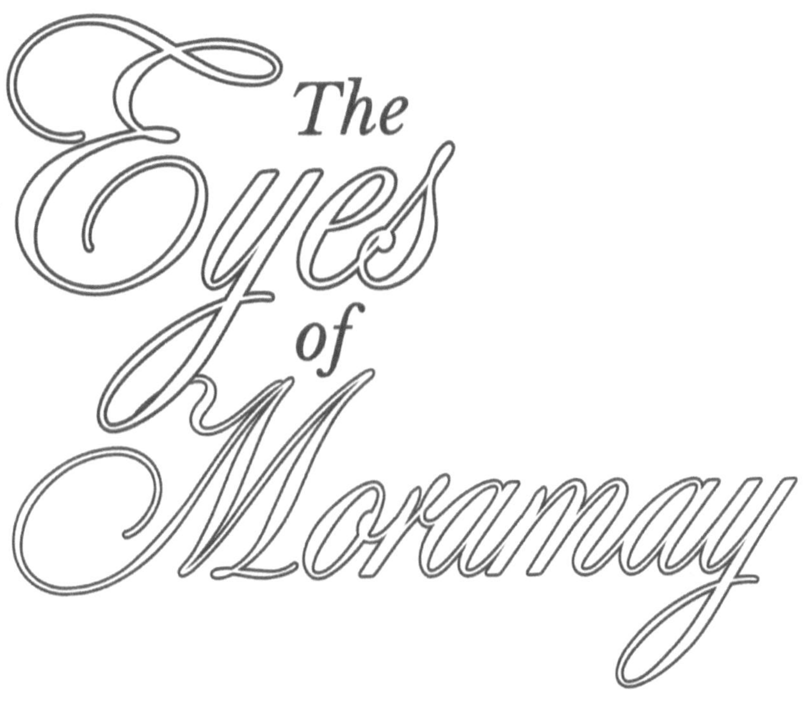
The
Eyes
of
Moramay

The Eyes of Moramay, 1st Edition.

This work is an adaptation of *Lo Que Dios Ha Unido* by Hugo Wast originally published in 1945, and which currently has no copyright in the United States of America.

Cover design © 2025 Kapena Ornellas.

Editing, print preparation, formatting, back cover summary, and final cover design © 2025 Sloane Hybarger and Staback Author Services.

Books may be ordered through popular, online retailers, Page Turner Books, Inc.'s online store, or by contacting the publisher at:

Page Turner Books, Inc.®
170 S. Green Valley Pkwy., Ste. 300
Henderson, NV 89012-3145

Visit our website at www.ptbooksinc.com or contact us via email at contact@ptbooksinc.com. Page Turner Books, Inc.'s name and logo are copyright of Page Turner Books, Inc.

Audiobook ISBN: 978-1-967289-12-7   Hardcover ISBN: 978-1-967289-14-1
iBook ISBN: 978-1-967289-13-4   Paperback ISBN: 978-1-967289-15-8

Printed in the United States of America. First Printing: March 2025

Adapted from a novel by Hugo Wast

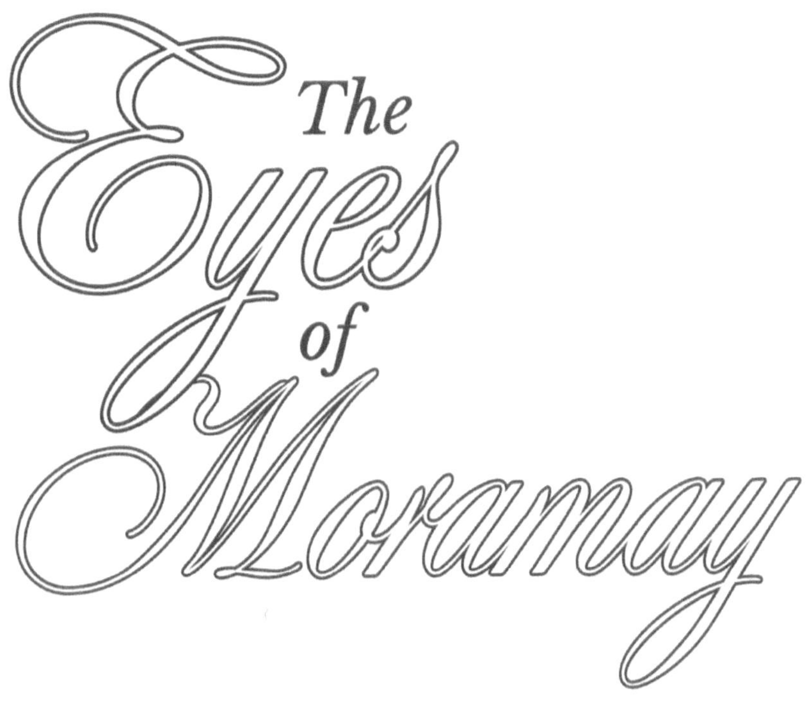

Leanne E. Staback, Ph.D.

Henderson, NV, USA

For my friend, Moramay Moses,

whose mother named her after Moramay in this story.

Thank you for introducing me to the literary world of Hugo Wast.

It has been a thoroughly captivating experience!

Table of Contents

Chapter 1: Written on the Heart

That year, Corpus Christi—a sacred feast that moved with the Church's calendar—fell on June 8th. Though winter was still nearly two weeks away in Buenos Aires, the city shivered under the coldest day of the year. By six a.m., as the Eastern Catholic Missionaries gathered for their first Mass, the temperature had plunged to seven degrees below zero.

They had settled into their new home—a former military barracks, now painstakingly restored into a convent. In the heart of the city's southern district, they had built their church, its spire rising defiantly into the frozen morning air.

At the helm of this growing mission stood Father Gazapo, a man whose vision stretched far beyond the city limits. For years, while living in Shanghai, he had nurtured an audacious dream—to plant missions in Buenos Aires and Rio de Janeiro, twin beacons of faith in the Southern Hemisphere.

Now, that dream had become reality. Both missions flourished—their schools filled with eager students, their congregations expanding with renewed devotion.

That morning, as Father Gazapo stood in the icy courtyard, rubbing his hands together for warmth, a rare smile crossed his face. Turning to a young priest, one he had personally ordained in Shanghai, he spoke in a low voice, his breath rising in a mist.

"One day, I will send you and a few others to start a new mission—perhaps in Chile," he smiled. "It is only the beginning."

That morning, long before dawn and well before the community bell roused the missionaries, the telephone beside Father Gazapo's bed rang with relentless urgency.

He jolted awake, blinking against the darkness, and fumbled for the receiver.

Pressing it to his ear, he croaked out, "Yes?"

"There's a young man here asking to see you, Father," the doorman said.

Father Gazapo frowned, still groggy.

"A young man at this hour? For heaven's sake! Does he think I'd rather have a conversation than sleep? I barely got to bed after midnight. Those Brazilian priests kept us up half the night with all their news from Rio…"

"Yes, Father, I know," the doorman interjected, trying to keep him focused.

Still trying to wake up, Father Gazapo continued, "They went on and on, and now…"

"Yes, Father Superior, I know," the doorman interrupted again, more firmly this time. "But this young man isn't here for a social visit. He needs a priest for a heart whispering its final beats."

That snapped Father Gazapo fully awake.

"Well, why didn't you say so from the start, Brother in Christ?"

"Because, Father, you didn't let me!"

After a brief silence the old priest sighed and swung his legs out of bed.

"Alright, alright, don't get upset, son. I'll throw on my trousers and cassock and be down at the lodge before you can say 'cock-a-doodle-doo.'"

He yanked on his clothes, keeping the receiver in his hand, still muttering at the now-dead line. When he finally realized he was arguing with no one, he let out a long sigh, crossed himself, hung up the phone, and hurried to finish dressing for his early visitor.

"Brrr…what a bitter night!" he grumbled as he pulled open the door.

He shivered violently as he was hit by an icy gust of wind that sliced through the open-air gallery like a knife.

"This feels more like the mountains of Guadarrama! And they told me it would be hot here? *Ha!* Buenos Aires *wishes* it could boast fifty degrees in the shade like my beloved Shanghai!"

Unwilling to risk catching a cold he went back to his room, grabbed a scarf, and wrapped it snugly around his neck. Then, gathering his resolve, he strode toward the doorman's lodge, his heels clicking sharply against the frozen tile, each step echoing in the silent corridors punctuating the sharpness of the frigid air.

Inside the small room—dimly lit by the embers of a crackling stove—Father Gazapo found the doorman warming his hands, his breath rising in faint wisps.

Beside him stood the visitor. The young man was tall and lean, his skin darkened by the sun, like a soldier returning from war. Yet, despite his rugged appearance, there was something refined about his features. His black eyes, deep and solemn, carried a quiet sadness, and the furrow in his brow hinted at the weight pressing on him.

For a moment, Father Gazapo simply observed him. The silence stretched between them—the doorman rubbing his hands near the flames, the young man standing tense by the wood stove, the night's chill still clinging to him.

Shaking off his hesitation, Father Gazapo greeted the young man with his usual flair, his voice ringing through the chilly room like a trumpet call.

"You're all so quiet! Why did God give us tongues, if not to praise Him? As Saint Paul says, 'Every tongue must confess God.' Come now, my son, why the silence? What brings you here at this unholy hour?"

The young man hesitated for only a moment before answering, still caught off guard by the priest's energy.

"I'm here to ask you to visit someone who is seriously ill."

Father Gazapo studied him with interest. The flickering light of the stove cast shadows across the young man's lean, sun-darkened face. Despite his solemn expression, there was a quiet strength in him, something steady and unwavering.

"A sick person, eh?" the priest echoed, his thick brows lifting. "Tell me, are you sure they're still sick and not already dead? These days, people seem to forget about priests and sacraments until the poor soul has already thrown in the towel—so to speak—and is bargaining with Saint Peter at the gates without even a ticket in hand."

"She's not dead, Father," the young man assured him. "But she's very ill... critically ill."

"Ah! So, it's a woman. Your mother, perhaps?"

"No, Father."

"Your sister? Your wife? Your daughter? No, not your daughter, you're far too young for that!"

Even as they spoke, Father Gazapo had already started moving toward the door, his thick boots clicking against the floor with purpose. As he stepped outside, a vicious wind whipped through the streets, carrying the biting chill of the mountains straight into his bones.

"All for the love of God," he muttered, tugging his scarf tighter.

He fought the urge to let loose one of the colorful expletives that had made him legendary back in Madrid.

Luckily, the young man had come prepared. A hired car stood waiting at the curb, its engine purring softly in the cold. They climbed inside, and at once, the warmth wrapped around them like a heavy cloak, chasing away the winter's bite.

Father Gazapo, momentarily robbed of speech by the cold, let out a satisfied grunt as he thawed. Then, regaining his voice, he turned to his companion with curiosity.

"Tell me, son—how did you know to come find me, of all people, without even knowing me?"

The young man met his gaze.

"The lady told me," he replied simply. "She said, 'Call the Father Superior of the Eastern Catholic Missionaries—I belong to his parish.'"

"Ah!" Father Gazapo's chest swelled with a quiet satisfaction.

He hadn't been chosen by chance. He had been sought out! Father Gazapo turned to the young man with newfound interest.

"It does my heart good to hear that this sick woman—whose health I am already praying for—knows of the Eastern Catholic Missionaries and is familiar with our church. Is that true?"

"Yes, Father. I believe she has attended Mass at your convent more than once."

"Wonderful! I like that," Father Gazapo said, a smile curling his lips. "And why don't you come yourself? Now, I say this with no vanity—because that has no place here—but, my son, the Eastern Catholic Missionaries are truly among God's favored sons. We've stepped onto the world stage at a time when priestly vocations are needed more than ever. The Lord's vineyard is vast, and the laborers are few."

His sharp eyes studied the young man for a moment.

"How old are you, son?"

"Twenty-five, Father."

"A perfect age to enter God's service..." Father Gazapo muttered, almost to himself.

Then, fixing his gaze on the young man, he asked, "Do you know how many people live in this world?"

"No, Father."

"A little over eight billion. And tell me—don't you think the greatest joy a man can have in this troubled life is dedicating himself to saving souls and leading them to the true worship of God? Wouldn't you agree?"

"Yes, Father."

Father Gazapo nodded, satisfied.

"Well, I can see you're on the right path. Even at twenty-five, there's still time to join the Lord's work. You wouldn't be the first worker to arrive late, and you certainly won't be the last. You'd be coming in around noon, let's say. But if you put your hand to the plow and never look back, by the time night falls—the night of death that comes for us all—you will have done just as much as any of us. It's not about age or knowledge, my son—it's about spirit. As the Gospel says, 'The Spirit blows where it wills.'"

Then, with a knowing smile, he asked, "Have you ever felt called to the priesthood?"

"No, Father," the young man answered humbly.

"What's your name?"

"José María..."

He didn't get the chance to finish before Father Gazapo cut in excitedly.

"Ah! What two great protectors you have in your name! Entrust yourself to them, my son. Ask for their guidance. Who knows? Perhaps God has a vocation waiting for you, one you haven't felt yet but might still discover. Sometimes, life surprises you when you least expect it. Like me for example! I never imagined becoming a priest until—"

"Father," José interrupted gently, "I'm married."

Father Gazapo froze.

"Well, that's unfortunate for you!" he blurted out.

Then, realizing how that sounded, he quickly backtracked, clearing his throat.

"I mean—why didn't you tell me that sooner, for heaven's sake?"

José, calm as ever, simply shrugged.

"Because you never asked, Father."

"Well, that's fair enough! As Saint Paul said, 'It's better to marry than to burn with passion.' Want me to say it in Latin? Do you know Latin? Not that it matters much if you're not going to be a priest! Anyway, tell me, son, what do you do for a living? Now you can't say I didn't ask!"

José hesitated before answering—a brief pause that felt like an eternity to Father Gazapo, who bit his lip in anticipation, eager for an interesting response. The young man had the sharp features and sun-kissed complexion of someone from the Argentine countryside, but there was something foreign about his accent—a curious mix of English and Spanish.

As the silence stretched on, Father Gazapo pressed him again, rephrasing the question.

"You are Argentine, aren't you?"

"Yes, Father."

"Good! I'm glad to hear that. I have a deep love for Argentines. I'm certain that from this vast and fertile land, I'll inspire many vocations in young men like you, though perhaps ones who haven't yet done what you have. Well done, by the way! Marriage is a great sacrament, as Saint Paul says. But others will give their hearts completely to God."

José spoke softly.

"I *have* given my heart, Father."

Father Gazapo waved a hand.

"We'll save that conversation for another time. What I *asked*, son, is how you earn your living."

José hesitated again, but then answered, "I'm a pearl diver by trade."

Father Gazapo sat up straight, startled. He had known pearl divers in the East, but he had never imagined there were any in Buenos Aires.

Staring at the young man, he asked, "Did you say oyster fisherman?"

"No, Father… pearl diver."

"I must admit, José María, that surprises me. If that's true, I'd love to know where you practice such an unusual profession around here."

"I've been doing it for seven years, Father—but in a faraway country."

"The East?"

"Yes, Father. My mistress, the Countess, will explain the rest to you."

The car rolled to a smooth stop in front of an elegant house, its wrought-iron gate framing a meticulously kept garden that faced the quiet street.

Under the dim glow of a streetlamp, a shadow stirred among the trees—a tall, broad-shouldered figure, his presence both imposing and deliberate. Even in the half-light, it was clear he was a foreigner. As Father Gazapo stepped out of the car, the man moved with quiet precision, removing his hat in a gesture of respect. Not a word was spoken. Instead, he strode forward, unhurried but purposeful, unlocking the gate before pushing open the heavy iron front door. His every motion carried an air of silent authority.

Behind them, José María lingered for a final exchange with the driver before following inside.

The moment they crossed the threshold, warm golden light bathed the hallway, casting long, flickering shadows against the walls.

Father Gazapo took the opportunity to study his silent escort more closely. The man was built like a titan—strong, disciplined, every movement precise. He carried himself like someone accustomed to control, his presence commanding without the need for words.

This man wasn't a pearl diver—Father Gazapo could see that right away. But a sailor? Without a doubt. And not just any sailor—an officer, perhaps. It was in the way he moved, that near-imperceptible sway, like someone whose feet had spent more time on rolling decks than solid ground. A lifetime at sea had shaped him, giving him the quiet confidence of a man who knew how to command both ships and men.

Curiosity getting the better of him, he leaned toward José María and whispered conspiratorially, "I'd bet anything this gentleman is a—"

"Carpenter," José María interrupted, his voice steady, his tone absolute.

Father Gazapo raised an eyebrow but said nothing. There was more to this story, but now wasn't the time to pry.

They stepped into the sick woman's bedroom, where the hush of the house deepened into something almost sacred. She lay still, seemingly at peace, her breath steady but barely there, as if she existed in the fragile space between wakefulness and dreams.

A single electric lamp cast a muted glow, its light softened by a blue scarf draped over the shade. Shadows wavered across the walls, lending the room an almost otherworldly stillness. Against the crisp white pillow, her profile stood out—delicate yet striking.

Her bronzed skin, the color of sun-warmed sand, spoke of distant, sunlit shores, of places where the sea kissed the land in an eternal embrace. There was something about her—something both foreign and familiar, as though she belonged to a world just beyond reach. A deep purple veil covered her head, hiding her hair completely. But Father Gazapo—who prided himself on reading people—was certain that beneath the fabric, her hair must be as black as a raven's wing. Or so he imagined.

Standing beside the bed were two silent sentinels—women of elegance and dignity, dressed impeccably, their presence both protective and discreet. One was around forty, the other much younger but just as tall, their poise unmistakable. They exchanged brief, polite nods with Father Gazapo before slipping through a side door into an adjoining room, vanishing like shadows into the night.

In those few fleeting moments, he had taken in everything. *This feels like something straight out of a novel!* Father Gazapo thought, his mind racing. *Good heavens, Saint Thomas More—my patron saint— since you wrote novels yourself, guide me here! That woman is no countess, no matter what she claims. That so-called carpenter is no carpenter. And that pearl diver? Ha! If he's ever fished for pearls, I'll eat my cassock. These people are hiding something. They're Hindus, all of them. And the most mysterious of all is the one in the purple veil, covering up her black hair, black as her intentions. Well, let's see what this is about. At least it's warm in here.*

Lost in thought, Father Gazapo nearly jumped when the veiled woman stirred at the sound of his approaching footsteps. With a slow, deliberate movement, she raised a delicate hand, made a subtle gesture—then, in one fluid motion, pulled off her veil.

What he saw stunned him. Instead of the jet-black hair he had expected, a cascade of golden curls tumbled over her shoulders—wild, radiant, impossibly bright. It was the most striking blonde hair he had ever seen.

The woman rose gracefully, the veil now wrapped around her shoulders like a shawl. Though long enough to serve as a cloak, the fabric was so fine that it fit easily into her clenched fist.

Father Gazapo, who had seen every kind of veil, every shade of hair imaginable, and who was naturally suspicious of most things, couldn't help but smirk to himself.

You can't fool an old dog, he thought. *She's probably the wife of some pearl diver, dyed her hair with God-knows-what for God-knows-why. If she's not Hindu, she's Burmese.*

Yet, despite himself, his curiosity only deepened. He was about to speak when she turned to him, her golden curls catching the lamplight, and in flawless English, greeted him with a warmth that disarmed him completely.

"Good evening, Father!"

The perfection of her English, with her accent distinctly from the Basque coast, caught Father Gazapo off guard.

"More like good morning," he muttered, irritated that his carefully crafted theories were falling apart like a house of cards. His suspicion deepened.

"So, are you the sick woman who wanted to confess? Seems you won't be needing an interpreter after all. Probably for the best, since—although Canon 903 of the new Code of Canon Law allows for confessions through interpreters, when necessary, provided they maintain sacramental secrecy under penalty of excommunication—well, this certainly simplifies things."

She smiled just slightly.

"I imagine, Father, that you must be Father Gazapo."

His sharp gaze narrowed.

"And how do you know me?"

"Because of your remarkable memory. Years ago, I was told that no one in all of Spain knows canon law better than you."

What she didn't say—but what Father Gazapo instantly picked up on—was that it wasn't his legendary knowledge of canon law that had given him away. It was his nonstop talking. Still, flattered that someone, somewhere, had actually listened to him long enough to form an opinion, he leaned back, quite pleased with himself.

"Well then," he said, pulling a stole from his pocket.

He kissed it, draped it around his neck, and pulled a chair up to the head of the bed.

"Let's get down to business."

Before offering his blessing, he studied her once more, his sharp eyes taking in every detail.

"If you ask me, my lady, you don't look like someone on the brink of death."

"Thank God, Father!" she said lightly. "But last night, we thought otherwise. The doctor even warned me to prepare for the worst—that's why I sent for a priest from this parish."

"A fine parish, my child! The harvest is plentiful, but the laborers are few. I have 250,000 souls under my care. But let's focus on yours. Are you feeling better now?"

"Yes, Father; but I spent fourteen days hovering between life and death, unconscious. It was a very strange illness."

"Bronchopneumonia, perhaps?"

"I don't know, Father. A little of everything."

"Meningitis, maybe?"

"Possibly, Father. This morning was the worst of it, but the doctor just left feeling much more at ease. Still, that's no reason for me not to confess and receive Communion today."

Father Gazapo leaned back slightly, his fingers grazing his stole.

"Well then, let's find out if you need my prayers or just a good night's sleep."

Father Gazapo's entire perception of her shifted. Mere moments ago, he had suspected her of being a Hindu, a pagan—perhaps even a fraud playing games with a minister of the Church. Now, just as suddenly, he found himself believing he was in the presence of a saint—one of those rare souls who receive Communion daily, their faith as steady as the northern star. He blessed her and straightened in his chair.

"I see you're English. I see you're a devout Catholic. And I see you value the sacraments. Let's begin, then. How long has it been since your last confession, my child?"

"Seven years, Father."

If his chair hadn't had a backrest, Father Gazapo would've been flat on the floor, gazing up at the ceiling in bewilderment.

"Seven years?" he echoed, his astonishment and disappointment undeniable.

Just moments ago, he had been ready to canonize her, and now she admitted she hadn't approached the sacraments in seven years!

The woman, sensing his reaction, quickly tried to explain.

"In all these years, this is the first time I've come across a Catholic priest. I only arrived from Australia three weeks ago—on a sailing ship."

Father Gazapo's eyes narrowed.

"The *Golondrina Coast*?"

"Yes, Father."

That changed everything.

He'd seen her name—or lack of one—in the papers. A mysterious Englishwoman, arriving alone on a small sailing ship, drifting into port like a phantom. The press pounced, hungry for a story, but she left them starving. No name. No reason. No history. And just as quickly as she appeared—she was gone.

Yet now here, before him, was the ghost herself.

This was no ordinary confession. For thirty minutes, Father Gazapo listened, his expression unreadable, his questions few but razor-sharp. He had heard thousands of confessions, yet something about this one unsettled him. It wasn't just what she said—it was what she didn't. The gaps, the careful omissions, the weight of something unsaid hanging in the air like incense that refused to fade. Still, his voice never wavered. As he whispered the ancient words of absolution, he felt their weight—words so familiar to every Catholic yet truly understood by so few.

"I absolve you of your sins."

With his right hand, he traced a slow, deliberate cross over her head. Then, wordlessly, he extended his stole for her to kiss and then stood.

"Now, my child, I will bring you Holy Communion."

He quickly glanced at his watch.

"It's six o'clock in the morning. Father…"

He hesitated.

For a fleeting moment, Father Gazapo nearly spoke the name of the priest who would celebrate the six o'clock Mass. But something stopped him.

Instead, he simply said, "Mass is about to begin. I just heard the bell— it only rings once a day at this hour."

The woman, weary from their whispered conversation, had already sunk back into the pillows, her pale face blending into the white linen. Then, just as he turned to leave, her eyes opened again, sharp and searching.

"What's the name of the priest who says the six o'clock Mass?"

Father Gazapo hesitated—just for a fraction of a second, but he felt it. He never liked talking about that young priest. The one who had become his shadow, his most trusted, most relentless worker. Tireless, disciplined, impossible to ignore—yet determined to remain invisible. No recognition. No praise. No name. So instead of answering, Father Gazapo did what he did best. He changed the subject.

"My grandmother," he said—perhaps a little too quickly, "had a deep devotion to the church bells in her hometown. She always said they inspired her best thoughts."

A faint smile curled on the woman's lips.

"Mine too. That bell brings me comfort… but also longing."

Father Gazapo nodded.

"That part's not so good, daughter. My late grandmother used to say the same thing."

The woman didn't laugh. She wasn't interested in his grandmother's musings. Instead, her voice came quiet but firm.

"Why is the bell only rung once a day?"

Father Gazapo met her gaze. He didn't answer right away.

Finally, he said, "That is a long story."

The woman said nothing. She simply waited. Father Gazapo wasn't ready to unravel that mystery. Not yet.

"For now," he continued, "I need to bring you the viaticum."

He paused as if recalling something.

"Oh, you mentioned your husband isn't in Buenos Aires?"

"That's correct, Father. He's not here."

"Where is he, then?"

She turned her face away, sinking into the pillow, silent.

Father Gazapo had already taken note of her careful restraint. No matter how subtly he tried to steer the conversation, she revealed only what was absolutely necessary—nothing more. He didn't push. Some questions weren't meant to be asked.

Still, he couldn't ignore the feeling creeping over him. Beneath the quiet, beneath the control—there was something else. Something he hadn't expected.

Father Gazapo said nothing, but inwardly, he marveled.

This woman—cut off from the world for years, armed with nothing but the remnants of her childhood catechism—had somehow grasped and applied one of the most intricate principles of Canon Law. And not just understood it—she had lived it.

No priest. No church. No guidance. Yet on a remote island, she had done what even seasoned theologians might hesitate to attempt. Not one, but two marriages, flawlessly executed. Perfectly valid. Unbreakable. As binding as if a bishop himself had stood at the altar.

It defied reason. And yet, there it was.

Good Lord, he thought, this woman in the purple veil—whom I mistook for an exotic adventurer—has applied Canon 1098 with flawless precision. That particular law, obscure even to seasoned scholars, allowed for extraordinary measures under extraordinary circumstances. Many canon lawyers would have hesitated before attempting what she had done with nothing but instinct and faith.

The carriage rattled to a stop in front of the Missionaries' church. Beside him, the pearl diver remained silent. Through the dimly lit doorway, the soft chime of the bell drifted through the air, signaling the elevation of the Host.

The six o'clock Mass was already halfway through. Father Gazapo entered the sacristy, draped himself in a white robe, and knelt at the steps of the altar. He waited, watching, as the priest before him completed the sacred act of consecration, his hands moving with the quiet reverence of one who had been anointed for eternity.

The celebrant retrieved a chalice, filled with consecrated hosts, and turned toward the kneeling faithful. When he noticed Father Gazapo approaching, he nodded and reached for the small gold ciborium—the vessel used to carry the viaticum to the sick. As the priest placed a consecrated host inside, Father Gazapo bowed his head in a silent prayer for the woman who awaited it.

He murmured the familiar words of the Psalm, the ones spoken over the sick and dying: *"My bones tremble, and my soul is in anguish."*

But why?

Father Gazapo had prayed over countless souls, watched more suffering than he cared to remember. Faces came and went, lost to time. Yet this woman—this stranger—unsettled him.

Something about her clung to him, pulling at the edges of his thoughts like a thread he couldn't quite grasp. It wasn't just sympathy. It wasn't just duty. It was something else. Something deeper. Something he wasn't ready to name.

Beyond the sanctuary, the Eastern Catholic Missionaries had transformed what was once a crumbling relic into one of the most immaculate churches in Buenos Aires. The abandoned chapel, long forgotten by its original congregation, had been little more than a skeleton of stone and dust. Now, under Father Gazapo's relentless devotion to discipline and order, it stood pristine—every pew polished, every candle perfectly placed, its grandeur a silent proclamation that nothing, not even time, could erase the sacred.

He did not tolerate slackers, constantly reminding his fellow priests, "The state of our church speaks louder than any sermon. When the holy water fonts are dry, when the sanctuary lamp runs out of oil, when the confessionals sit empty, and Masses start late—the faithful leave. And when the faithful leave, friars have nothing left to do but gossip about their parishioners' piety."

If there was one duty he valued above all, it was the confessional.

"It's far safer to reach heaven from the confessional than from a library," he often said with a knowing smirk.

"Hearing confessions doesn't take brilliance—just patience. You wait, even if no one comes. Because one day, someone will. And that someone might be as great a sinner as King David, who still became an ancestor of the Messiah. Or like Saul, a persecutor who became St. Paul. Or Angela of Foligno, who once drowned in vice but rose to sainthood. But you won't meet them unless you're there, ready. The devout will ring a bell, seeking absolution. But those who have been away for years—maybe their whole lives—won't. They'll hesitate. Linger at the church doors. Look at the confessional, then away again. They don't know how to ask for help. They don't want to be seen. And yet, they're the ones who need you most."

Among all the missionaries, there was one priest who shared Father Gazapo's quiet discipline - the priest of the six o'clock Mass. The same priest Belén had asked about—though she had never learned his name. Each morning, before the first light touched the city, he would arrive at the church doors and go straight to his confessional. If no one was waiting, he would take a seat on a nearby bench, open his breviary, and begin to pray.

He believed in presence. He knew that grace worked in the shadows, in the places where the hesitant lingered, unsure if they had the courage to step forward. He had watched them before—hovering near the dark corners of the church, glancing toward the confessional as if drawn by something stronger than themselves.

He never called out. Never gestured. He simply waited. And in time, they came.

It was always the ones carrying the heaviest burdens who hesitated the longest. Guilt turned the simplest motions—lifting a hand to the bell cord, crossing the threshold of the confessional—into impossible tasks. They lingered in the shadows, pacing near the pews, staring at the carved wooden lattice as if it might swallow them whole.

Days passed. Then weeks. Some hovered on the edges for months, drawn to the quiet figure who never left, never rushed, never judged. And then, one day, something shifted. A step forward. A breath held. A door creaking open.

And when they finally spoke, the floodgates broke.

That morning, after the hushed solemnity of the six o'clock Mass, the priest took his place in the confessional, his routine as steady as the turning of the world. Yet, for reasons he could not name, his thoughts lingered on the woman Father Gazapo had visited. A pull—subtle but insistent—urged him to pray for her.

By midday, the steady procession of penitents blurred the morning's memory. Faces came and went, sins whispered and absolved, and the weight of other souls pressed upon him. Her presence dimmed, dissolving into the stream of confessions like mist at dawn.

Father Gazapo, too, said nothing. He had met many souls in his time, heard countless stories—but something about this woman, with her violet-shrouded mystery, remained unspoken. And in the unspoken, secrets stirred.

Chapter 2: Echo of a Promise

A few weeks earlier, a ghost ship had drifted into the port of Buenos Aires, as silent and untraceable as a breath in the dark. No announcement, no escort, no watchful eyes marking its arrival—just a vessel slipping past the city's defenses, untouched by protocol.

A ship of this kind had no business crossing the ocean. Small, fragile, defiant against the logic of the sea, it should have been swallowed whole by the waves. And yet, it moved with uncanny ease, its white sails taut against an unseen force, carving through the water like something not entirely of this world.

Had anyone been watching, they might have spoken of omens, of lost souls carried in the belly of the wind. But no one saw it come. No one questioned its arrival. By the time the city woke, it was already too late—the ship was there, waiting, its mystery intact.

The ship had arrived so silently that by the time anyone noticed, it was already preparing to vanish. But more unsettling than its ghostly arrival was the eerie stillness of its crew.

Sailors, hardened by weeks at sea, should have spilled onto the docks in search of warmth, whiskey, and welcome arms. Instead, not a single figure crossed the gangplank. For three days, the ship remained sealed, its presence barely acknowledged, its purpose unknown.

Then, just as dusk thickened into night, a small boat detached from the vessel, slipping toward the shore with quiet urgency. No fanfare, no explanation—only a whispered request, an arrangement made in shadows. A woman and her companions were to step onto Argentine soil. No papers. No questions. No record of their arrival.

In another time, in the hands of a more rigid bureaucrat, the request would have been rejected without hesitation. But fate had chosen a different guardian that day.

In my experience, the official mused, twirling his pen between his fingers, *the most dangerous men always have their paperwork in perfect order. If these people have none at all... well, they must be harmless. If they were criminals, they'd probably have diplomatic passports.*

With a flick of his wrist, the papers were stamped. Permission granted. A lapse in judgment? Perhaps. But in this case, absolutely right.

What papers could possibly have proven that this woman was English, that her name was María Aguinagalde de Guernizo? That her companions were the Englishman Walter Burns and the Argentine José María Pérez—along with their wives, children, and an air of quiet secrecy that clung to them like mist?

She swore, under oath, that she had lost everything in a shipwreck somewhere in the vast reaches of Oceania. And in the absence of proof, the authorities chose to believe her.

What other choice did they have? To deny her entry? To cast her and her people back to the mercy of the sea, adrift once more upon that spectral ship, which had reached Christian shores only by what could be called a miracle?

The Director of Immigration—who ultimately decided her fate—listened with rapt attention to the tale spun by María Belén, Countess of Bazán and Marchioness of Balcázar.

She was a woman whose very life was a story fit for fiction, and she told it well.

The official, despite his years navigating the labyrinth of bureaucracy, had not yet grown into one of those men whose hearts calcify under the weight of red tape. He believed her. He believed the name she gave him. He believed the explanation for the briefcase she carried—a case filled with pearls of staggering beauty, allegedly plucked from the depths of a nameless island.

Argentine customs took their due, pocketing the necessary fees. Belén paid in crisp English banknotes. And just like that, the matter was settled.

She slipped into the city unnoticed, sidestepping the press like a shadow. The journalists arrived too late, their notepads empty, their cameras cold. Desperate to salvage their reputations, they did what they did best. They improvised.

By morning, the newspapers were filled with wild speculation. The mysterious woman—whom no one had managed to photograph—was now, according to rumor, the exiled wife of a dethroned Indian rajah, cast adrift in the remnants of a forgotten empire. It was an elegant fiction, impossible to confirm and equally impossible to refute. And like all good rumors, it burned bright, then faded, lost in the tide of fresher scandals.

Meanwhile, Belén disappeared into the city's veins. Though she could afford the finest accommodations, she deliberately sought out something lesser. A quiet, third-rate inn. A place without questions. A place to plan. She had not come to Buenos Aires to rest. She had come to fulfill a promise.

Seven years earlier, standing atop the mainmast of a ship in the middle of the boundless sea, she had spoken words that felt more like a vow than a promise.

Jorge had held her there, steadying her with a sailor's sure grip as the wind howled around them.

"There's something," she had whispered, her voice barely carrying over the sigh of the wind, "that binds me to you even more than your embrace, more than your love itself." She placed a hand over his chest, feeling the steady rhythm of his heartbeat beneath her fingertips. "Something deeper, something unshakable. The words of Jesus— 'What God has joined together, let no man separate.'"

She searched his eyes, her own shimmering with the weight of that truth. "It's not just a vow we spoke, not just a promise written in ink or whispered beneath candlelight. It's something eternal, something written in heaven long before we ever found each other in this world."

Her fingers traced the curve of his jaw, memorizing every line, as if she feared time itself might steal this moment from them. "Even if the sea should rise between us, even if the years try to pull us apart, nothing—no man, no force, no distance—can undo what was made sacred."

The night wrapped around them like a veil, the stars watching in silent witness. "We belong to each other," she breathed. "Not just in this life, but in all the ones to come."

Jorge had never forgotten that night. Nor had he forgotten the promise she made—that if fate or men ever tore them apart, she would search the world until she found him again. And before that night ended, she had made him swear—swear before the sea and the sky and the stars themselves—that if ever she came for him, he would not stand in her way.

Beneath the endless expanse of the heavens, Jorge de Balcázar y Manrique had spoken his vow, and she had clung to the certainty that God Himself had heard it. That night, she had believed in forever.

Seven years had passed since then—long, aching years of silence, of oceans and fate conspiring to keep them apart. The world had unraveled around them, time and circumstance tearing at the seams of what once had been unbreakable. Neither knew where the other was. Neither knew if the other still lived.

And yet, Belén never believed he was lost to her. Not truly.

Especially in the hush before dawn, when the city exhaled its last breath of sleep and the world stood still in that fleeting, fragile moment between darkness and light, she felt him. Not as a memory, not as a wish, but as something real. A pull in the very air around her, an invisible thread stretched across time and distance, tugging at the deepest part of her soul.

Jorge was alive.

She didn't need proof, didn't need a name on a passenger list or a letter with his handwriting. She knew it in the marrow of her bones, in the whisper of the wind, in the way her heart refused to forget its rhythm beside his.

Somewhere, in some distant corner of the world, he was calling to her. Not with words, not with letters, but with the quiet language of the soul—one that spoke through silence, through longing, through the invisible thread that bound them across time and distance. Holding her breath, she would listen. She would wait for the echo of his voice, fragile and hesitant, as if afraid to call out too loudly.

There was only one sound that never startled her, never broke her silent vigil—the deep, resonant toll of a certain bell, ringing just before six each morning. It made sense. Church bells were not mere noise. They were echoes of the eternal voices that carried through time and space. Some ignored them. Others heard them without listening. But to those who knew how to listen, they spoke.

That particular bell—cast in the eighteenth century, when Buenos Aires was still a frontier town—was far too heavy for the fragile tower of the Eastern Catholic Missionaries. Its great bronze weight strained the very bones of the structure, so much so that the city's architects had warned the missionaries that ringing it too often might bring the whole tower crumbling down.

But the missionaries could not bear to silence it; so, they reached a compromise. The bell would ring only once each day—at dawn, summoning the faithful to the convent's six o'clock Mass.

Every morning, precisely ten minutes before six, the sacristan, a man of meticulous habits, climbed the narrow stairs and, with practiced reverence, set the great bell in motion. Its deep, elastic voice rolled over the city's rooftops, a single mighty chime that shivered through glass and stone, stirring sleepers from their dreams.

The celebrant of that first Mass was always the same. A young priest. Strikingly handsome, though he paid no mind to it. From the moment he had arrived in Buenos Aires, he had requested the privilege of offering the earliest Mass—choosing solitude, choosing silence, choosing to begin each day in the hushed embrace of prayer.

He was no recluse, yet among the priests, he was the most elusive. He spent hours in the confessional, hearing the whispered burdens of others, and in doing so, earned a reputation for wisdom and compassion. Yet he never received visitors. He never allowed anyone into his quarters—not even his fellow missionaries. It was as though he were guarding something. Something sacred. Something fragile.

Father Gazapo, the elder priest who had once guided him toward his vocation, watched with equal measures of admiration and concern. The young priest was disciplined, devoted—but there was something else. A weight in his heart, invisible yet undeniable. But then again, Father Gazapo mused, who among us doesn't carry a secret?

One day, he confronted the young man with a mixture of humor and fatherly concern.

"Son! Why do you think the Lord gave you a tongue, if not to sing His praises and speak to your brothers in this world?"

The young priest didn't answer. Instead, he opened his breviary and pointed to a passage faintly marked in pencil—*In silence and in hope shall be your strength.*

Father Gazapo snorted.

"Silence and hope! As if I, who despise silence, lacked hope! And strength? By Christ, I have plenty! Tell me, my son… what hopes are you holding onto?"

The young priest only smiled, unreadable. He said nothing. Father Gazapo let it drop—for a time. But curiosity gnawed at him.

One evening, he tried a different approach. Feigning casual interest, he asked, "Remind me of that text again. Show me your breviary—toward the back."

The young priest hesitated, just for an instant. Then, slowly, he handed over the book.

Father Gazapo flipped through the pages. But when he reached the familiar passage from Isaiah, it was gone.

The pencil marks had been carefully erased.

In their place, another verse had been written, in the same hand—*In peace, my deepest bitterness remains bitter indeed.*

Father Gazapo's sharp blue eyes lifted from the page, locking onto the young priest's dark, unreadable gaze. For a long moment, neither of them spoke. There was nothing more to say. The young priest had erased his own command for silence—and replaced it with the truth.

Father Gazapo sighed, shaking his head. There was no use pressing him further. Some silences were meant to be broken. Others… were meant to be endured.

And so, every morning, with unwavering precision, the great bell in the tower of the Eastern Catholic Missionaries sent its deep, resonant toll across the city, calling the faithful to Mass. But it was more than the voice of God. It carried something else. Something human. Something warm and familiar. A message wrapped in love and trust, slipping over rooftops, through open windows, into the ears of sleeping hearts like an invisible embrace.

In the relentless clamor of the modern world—where car horns bleated, radios blared, and the streets pulsed with the restless energy of a city that never stopped—so many sounds fought for dominance. Yet fewer and fewer of them were sacred.

Many cities, in their rush to be "modern," had silenced their bells, tearing away one of the last voices that called people to pause, to remember, to listen. How much poorer they were for it. Anyone who had never heard the bells of their childhood church had lost something irreplaceable. Their ears had never known one of the sweetest melodies of a Christian life—the solemn, golden toll that once wove prayer and poetry into the rhythm of the day.

But Buenos Aires had not yet fallen completely silent. And in a quiet, secluded alley of that city, in a house with a gated garden, there was a heart that woke each morning to the sound of the great bell. And when she heard it, she smiled, because it was not just a bell. It was a voice she recognized. And no matter how many years had passed, no matter how many miles lay between them—she knew. Jorge was alive, and somewhere, he was listening too.

As the first stars surrendered to the creeping light of dawn, the great bell stirred, its deep chime unraveling the last threads of sleep. And in that fragile space between dreams and waking—where the mind floats untethered, where reality shimmers like mother-of-pearl, fleeting and weightless as the breath of angels—Belén lay listening. Sometimes, when the wind carried the sound just right, the bell's toll was so resonant, so vast, it felt as if it might wake the very stars, holding them suspended for a moment longer delaying the end of the night.

But the bellringer never lingered. He rang it as duty demanded, two or three deliberate strikes, the final call for those still lost in sleep. Then, his work complete, he released the rope, descended the narrow stair, and entered the sacristy—where the young priest already stood at the altar, flipping through the missal, preparing for Mass.

How many times had Belén felt the pull to rise before the city stirred, to step into the hush of that dawn Mass—to slip into a pew alongside the handful of elderly women and the occasional wanderer who sought not faith, but shelter from the night?

The bell's bronze voice called to her, gently but insistently; yet something always held her back.

One morning, she finally resolved to go. She rose in the pre-dawn hush, dressed swiftly, and reached for the door—then hesitated. A glance through the window stopped her cold.

The world outside lay wrapped in frost, the streets blanketed in a rare, silent snow. Buenos Aires, a city accustomed to damp winters but not to this level of bitter, crystalline cold, seemed frozen in time. As Belén pressed her fingertips to the glass, a chill spread through her—not just of body, but of spirit, a warning whispered from somewhere deep within.

She hesitated.

Then, as if surrendering to an unseen force, she stepped back from the door and returned to bed. By midday, the fever had set in.

She would later learn how close she had come to death. Days blurred into delirium, her body burning, her mind drifting between light and shadow. When at last the fever broke and she returned to the waking world, she pieced together the strange truth—she had fallen ill on the Feast of Corpus Christi.

It was no coincidence. It was a sign she could not ignore. There was a weight on her conscience, a burden only an understanding confessor could lift.

In the final days before her illness, she had made a discovery—one that now felt less like chance and more like fate. The house she had rented belonged to the parish of the Eastern Catholic Missionaries.

A spark of joy had flickered in her upon learning that it was one of their priests who had officiated her wedding to Jorge in Madrid. But what truly astonished her was discovering that the superior of the Buenos Aires residence was none other than Father Gazapo.

She had never met him. But Jorge had spoken of him often—with admiration, with warmth, with the unguarded reverence of a man who trusts another completely. He had praised his wisdom, his formidable intellect, and his rare understanding of the human heart.

And so, when the time came to request a priest to bring her the viaticum—the last sacrament, meant for the dying—she had been unwavering in her choice.

"Call for Father Gazapo," she had told José María.

If anyone asked why she had sent for him, the answer was simple: she was already his penitent.

It wasn't true. Not yet. But if she lived—if she made it through the fever that threatened to take her—she vowed that it would be.

She would make him her confessor. She would place herself under his guidance, not just in obedience to his commands, but to his counsel, his wisdom.

And so, on that fateful day, as the weight of both illness and destiny pressed upon her, Belén finally met Father Gazapo—a former militia officer from Madrid, now a man of God.

From that night on, her strength began to return. Slowly at first—an ease in her breathing, a steadiness in her hands. Within a week, the fever had vanished, leaving only exhaustion in its wake. Yet, even as her body healed, her doctors were firm: no early mornings, no braving the bitter cold. Rest was her only commandment.

Still, each morning, the great bell called to her. Its toll was more than sound—it was a summons, a whisper through the frozen air. An invitation. And every day, she resisted, bound by reason, by caution. By the knowledge that it was not yet time.

But the moment her strength was fully hers again, she did not hesitate. She wrapped herself in warm layers, stepped out into the crisp morning, and walked straight to the Missionaries' church.

Father Gazapo welcomed her without surprise, as if he had expected her all along. This was only the second time she had knelt before him, yet as she spoke, as she unburdened her soul, something in her words faltered—something he could not name. Her confession was clear, precise, yet it carried a weight beyond sin. A shadow between the lines. A hesitation that even she did not seem to recognize.

It was unusual. And it lingered.

True confession is one of the world's visible miracles—a mystery that defies human instinct. From a purely rational perspective, it seems impossible, even absurd, because it contradicts one of the most powerful forces in the human spirit—self-preservation.

Many religious writers try to portray confession as something easy, even comforting—like confiding in a trusted friend. But let's not deceive ourselves. Confession is not simply confiding.

A penitent may choose to share their thoughts and burdens, but it is not required. And how many people, eager to unburden themselves to friends, telling stories of their failures and regrets, never actually confess?

Confiding is often a pleasure. Confession never is. There is a satisfaction, subtle yet real, in recounting the past—even when the memories are shameful. A natural instinct to justify, to shape the narrative, to soften the sharp edges of guilt. Confidences can be dressed in half-truths, in exaggerations, even in vanity, as the teller unconsciously edits their sins into something more palatable.

Confiding can soothe the ego. Confession demands that it be broken.

Of course, there are exceptions. Some refuse to repent—not out of forgetfulness, but out of defiance. They are not humbled by their sins; they revel in them, parading them like medals, boasting of their transgressions as if wickedness made them interesting. Some even exaggerate their faults, desperate to appear more corrupt than they truly are, mistaking vice for grandeur.

How often do we see lost souls flaunt their supposed villainy, when in truth, they are nothing more than small, ordinary sinners, neither heroes nor monsters, just people clinging to their pride?

The difference between confiding and confessing is so profound that moralists warn against misplaced confidences—especially for those with tender hearts and restless minds. A misdirected confidence can lead one into greater turmoil, but a true confession…a true confession can set a soul free.

"Do not reveal your heart to anyone," wrote Thomas à Kempis.

And yet, in the hushed stillness of the confessional, a heart laid bare finds its truest voice. The greatest difference between confession and mere confidence is not just in their purpose, but in the force that drives them. Confession is not natural—it goes against the very grain of human instinct. It is supernatural, powered by something beyond self-interest—repentance, a longing for change, and the audacious hope of forgiveness.

Confidence, by contrast, is purely human. It is a seeking of consolation, a desire to be understood, often offered to someone who has no power to absolve, no authority to grant true peace. And sometimes, beneath the surface, it carries hidden motives, unspoken self-interest, a need for validation. Neither the one speaking nor the one listening may fully recognize this, yet it lingers in the air like a whisper beneath the words.

For those unfamiliar with the mysteries of the Catholic Church, the sacrament of confession must seem almost unbelievable.

Picture yourself stepping into the hush of a dimly lit church, the scent of aged wood and candle wax lingering in the air. Before you, a confessional stands, its dark, carved frame worn smooth by time and countless souls who have knelt there before. Inside, a priest waits.

He could be young, his voice steady but kind. Or old, with wisdom etched into the lines of his face. He might greet you with warmth, or with quiet solemnity, unreadable yet unwavering. He is human—just as flawed, just as burdened as you. And yet, in this moment, in this sacred space, he is something more.

Because the words he speaks are not his own. The absolution he offers does not come from him. What he binds on earth is bound in heaven. What he releases is released for eternity. His voice is merely an echo of something far greater. It is not he who forgives.

It is God Himself, waiting for you.

And those who kneel before him? They could be anyone. A child with an innocent heart, whispering their first timid sins. A woman burdened by years of regret. A criminal hardened by a lifetime of wrongs. A beggar or a king, a farmer or a scholar, a thief or a saint. Even the Pope himself. Yet all—without exception—must bow their heads before the same confessor. Not to boast of their virtues. Not to justify, not to embellish. But to admit, fully and without pretense, that they have fallen short. Even more remarkable is that confession is not done in secret, hidden behind closed doors like a shameful act. No— Catholics kneel before the confessional in plain sight.

In many churches, there is no secluded room, no heavy curtain to shield them from view. The faithful come forward before anyone who happens to be there, stepping into the open, kneeling before the carved lattice of the confessional—where their sins will not be confessed to the world, but in the presence of it. Others see who approaches, who kneels, and how long they remain. Not to recount their strengths, but to expose their weaknesses.

When we confide in a friend, we instinctively shape our story, soften the edges, choose our words carefully to protect our pride. We add justifications, frame ourselves in a better light, hoping—if not for admiration, then at least for understanding.

But in confession, there is no room for deception. There is no embellishment, no self-serving narrative. Here, we are stripped bare. Even the cleverest liar—the one who has spent a lifetime twisting the truth—becomes, in that moment, simple and honest. Because before God, cleverness is useless.

And when the priest lifts his hand in absolution, tracing the sign of the cross in the air, even the most powerful of men must bow their heads. Emperors have done it. Popes have done it. For all stand equally before the judgment of God.

But confession is not an end in itself. It is a preparation—a threshold to something greater. The Eucharist. For one cannot receive the Body of Christ while bearing a soul weighed down by grave sin. And so, before approaching the altar, the faithful unburden themselves at the confessional—so that, when they rise from their knees, they are newly made.

Many say they can feel it—the moment of absolution, the exact instant when grace descends. It is not merely relief. It is not just comfort. It is a miracle. A miracle hidden in plain sight.

One that defies human instinct. One that shatters pride, reshapes the soul, and leaves the penitent changed in a way they cannot fully explain. Lighter. Free. And that, more than anything, is why confession is not merely a ritual. It is an encounter with the divine.

Those who have never stepped into the luminous world of Catholic mysteries cannot begin to fathom their depth—the weight of eternity pressing upon human souls, the unseen grace woven into every sacred act.

The doctrines of the Church are not mere traditions, not relics of a bygone age. They are ancient and unshakable, forged in the fire of divine revelation and guarded for two thousand years with a vigilance that has defied kings, empires, and even death itself.

And among these, there is one law so absolute, so beyond the reach of earthly compromise, that it stands as an unbreakable fortress: the seal of confession.

It is not a guideline. It is not a principle. It is a commandment— unchangeable, binding upon every priest who has ever knelt at the altar and vowed to serve God.

No force on earth can move him to break it. No pressure, no persuasion, no fear of suffering or death. The seal is sacred beyond measure.

Not for the greater good. Not even to prevent the gravest of crimes. Not to save a life.

Because what is whispered in the confessional does not belong to this world. It is placed into the hands of God—and there it remains, forever.

The knowledge gained within those sacred walls is sealed—not only from the world but even from the priest himself. It is as if it does not exist.

This secrecy has endured unchallenged for centuries.

Even priests who have later abandoned the faith—those who have left the Church, renounced their vows, or even turned against God Himself—have never broken the seal. It is preserved at all costs, even if it means suffering, disgrace, or death.

Consider this—a bishop, having told no one, quietly decides to appoint a certain priest to a parish. If that priest, in confession, were to reveal something that made him unworthy of the role, the bishop would still be bound to proceed with the appointment.

To change his mind—even though no one else knew of his original decision—would be an indirect violation of the confessional seal.

It is this absolute, almost otherworldly strictness that makes priests cautious beyond measure—even when speaking of things that do not pertain to sin at all. Because the seal is not simply a rule. It is a boundary between heaven and earth, a silence that echoes into eternity.

And that is why Father Gazapo, ordinarily so talkative, so eager to share stories and debate theology, felt an almost visceral aversion to speaking of the penitent who had summoned him in the early hours of Corpus Christi morning.

A penitent whose tale was so extraordinary, so improbable, so utterly fantastic, that had it been told in any other setting, it would have become a story whispered over candlelit suppers, a mystery debated among scholars and priests, a legend passed through generations.

And yet—he could never speak of it.

It wasn't the sins she confessed that captivated Father Gazapo, nor was it the adventure woven through her words. It was something far more maddening—he had heard it all within the sacred confines of the confessional. And that meant it was locked away, sealed in silence, never to be spoken of again.

Yet the story burned within him. The details, the impossibilities, the sheer weight of what she had lived—it was the kind of tale that would silence a room, that would leave even the most skeptical listener leaning forward in rapt attention. It was the story of a lifetime.

And he could never tell it.

The realization was almost painful. He could already imagine the hushed, candlelit conversations it would inspire, the shock, the admiration, the disbelief. Had it reached him by any other means, he might have relished recounting it over a fine meal, savoring the reactions, watching as even the most learned minds struggled to comprehend.

How tempting it was—how very tempting—to sit with his brilliant young disciple and present him with a theological riddle such as, "Could there ever be a situation where two Catholics could lawfully marry without a priest's presence?"

He knew the young man would listen intently, with the sharpest attention, responding with theological precision, wielding Canon Law like a blade.

More than that, he knew the young priest—who rarely showed interest in mundane affairs—would be utterly enthralled by Belén's story.

And yet, Father Gazapo remained silent.

Not because it was difficult but because, in this case, silence was heroic; for once a story is heard in the confessional, it is no longer a story. It is a secret that belongs to God alone.

Chapter 3: Whisper of Doubt

Confessors follow their strictest rule with unwavering discipline. They must never dwell on what they hear in confession—not even in thought—unless reflecting on a particularly complex case of conscience. Because of this, when priests encounter their penitents outside the confessional, they are so thoroughly trained to forget that the person standing before them seems an entirely different soul from the one who once whispered secrets behind the screen.

Belén had not lied to Father Gazapo when she offered him a different name than the one she usually bore. Among the many noble names and titles inherited from her distinguished lineage were Aguinagalde and Guernizo. Nor had she truly deceived him when she allowed him to assume she would soon reunite with her husband. She had never explicitly said so. Father Gazapo had simply drawn his own conclusions. And since this was not a matter of confession, Belén—keenly aware of both her rights and obligations—let him believe whatever he wished.

After all, in a way, it was true.

Against all odds, she still hoped to find Jorge. She still dreamed of standing before him, of seeing his face light up in recognition, of hearing his voice speak her name again—not as a ghost from his past, but as the woman he had once vowed to love.

But one dawn, as the great bell of the Missionaries rang, a thought crept into her mind—one so full of sorrow that she almost staggered beneath its weight.

She remembered a dream from years ago, back on the island.

In it, she had seen Jorge building an enormous wall between them, each stone he placed widening the distance that once had not existed. Frantic, she had clawed at the cruel, heavy slabs with bare hands, her fingers torn and bleeding as she tried to tear them down. But Jorge did not stop. He worked with quiet determination, his face unreadable, stacking the wall higher and higher, until he disappeared behind it entirely.

Now, standing in the cold morning air as the bell tolled its slow, deliberate chimes, the memory of that dream returned with terrifying clarity. It was as if an invisible blade had sliced through the deepest fibers of her heart—sharp, precise, and merciless.

And with it came a thought so chilling, so unbearable, that it nearly stole the breath from her lungs.

What if Jorge, convinced she was lost forever, had returned to the path he once swore was his true calling? What if, in the hollow ache of grief, he had surrendered himself—not to despair, but to the altar?

The thought struck her like a blow, stopping her breath, stilling her very soul.

They had once laughed at the idea, dismissing it as a fanciful, impossible jest. A fleeting notion, whispered in moments of playfulness, never meant to bear the weight of reality. But now, standing on the edge of uncertainty, the laughter of the past felt distant—like an echo from another life.

Had she lost him, not to death, but to something even more untouchable?

She had teased him.

"If that ever happened, what would I do?"

Jorge, with quiet certainty, had replied, "If it did, my love, you would have no choice but to leave me in God's hands… and become a nun yourself."

She had laughed at the absurdity of it.

"A nun? Me?" She had shaken her head, her voice rich with mischief. "I know myself too well—I'd be a disaster in a convent. And if I refused? If I refused to take the veil, what then?"

Jorge had smiled, but there had been something wistful in it.

"Then I'd have no choice but to leave the priesthood and return to you."

Triumphant, she had thrown her arms around him, whispering, "I swear, if you—or the king, or even the Pope—forced me into a convent, I'd burn it down! Just imagine the scandal I'd cause within those walls."

She had pulled back, searching his eyes.

"But don't worry, my love—I would never force you. If I ever felt that you didn't want to come back to me…"

Jorge had held her gaze.

"What would you do?"

She had shrugged, murmuring, "I don't know. But I'd find a way to disappear quietly."

That was the Belén he had known—wild as the sea, stubborn as the wind, a woman who would sooner disappear into the horizon than plead for what was rightfully hers. She had never been one to yield, never one to accept defeat, never one to wait for permission to take what belonged to her.

But the Belén who once spoke of resignation, who had, for even a moment, considered stepping aside, was long gone. That woman had been tested by fire, tempered by solitude, and forged into something unbreakable. She had not merely survived—she had ruled.

For seven years, she had carved out a life where none should have existed, bending the untamed wilderness to her will. With her own hands, she had built shelter, commanded men, and defied nature itself. She had faced hunger, storms, and the weight of absolute isolation— and she had won.

This Belén did not wait for fate to decide her course. She seized it. She had returned not to plead, not to hope, but to reclaim. And no force—neither time, nor distance, nor the iron walls of the Church— would stand in her way.

The woman standing here, back on the soil of civilization, was no longer just a survivor—she was a force with a purpose. She had returned to find Jorge. She had returned to give their daughter, Moramay, the father she deserved.

And yet…

The memory of the wall haunted her. That terrible wall, rising stone by stone, widening the distance between them as she clawed at it with bloodied hands, desperate to tear it down. She had seen it before—not in waking life, but in the relentless dreams that had followed her across the ocean, whispering of a fate she refused to accept.

What if…?

No.

The thought threatened to creep in, to wrap itself around her resolve like a vine strangling the last light from a dying tree. She would not allow it. She had not come this far, defied so much, only to waver now. Fate had tried to bury her once, but she had risen. And she would rise again.

She forced the doubt aside—any hesitation that could weaken her resolve, any fear that might stand between her and the battle ahead.

Because this fight wasn't just hers. She wasn't alone.

She had a daughter. Jorge's daughter. A daughter he never knew existed because she had been born on the island after Jorge had been torn away from them that horrible day.

The night of Moramay's birth, Belén sat by the cradle that Mr. Burns had built for her out of bamboo and the softest reeds. She watched as her beautiful daughter slept peacefully, blissfully unaware as only newborns can.

The flickering candlelight cast soft shadows on her daughter's tiny face, and Belén felt the breath catch in her chest. Those eyes. Those dark, knowing eyes.

Jorge's eyes.

She traced the delicate curve of Moramay's cheek with trembling fingers, overcome by the realization that she would never truly be able to forget him—not when a part of him lived and breathed in her arms. Not when his eyes, his very soul, stared back at her each time she looked at their child.

And in that moment, her promise burned brighter than ever.

She would keep looking for Jorge no matter how many days passed. No matter how long it took.

So much time had passed since then. Moramay was now seven years old. A child with a future to protect, a name to defend. She was attending a school run by Vincentian nuns, preparing for her First Communion—a milestone Belén refused to let her face without the father she deserved.

For seven relentless years, the island had tested them—pushing them to their limits, demanding survival through sheer will and ingenuity. The first months had been merciless, every task a battle, every day a lesson in endurance. But she had endured.

Little by little, she had wrestled a life from the land, shaping a home where there had been nothing. A house of bamboo walls and a thatched roof, strong enough to withstand monsoons, to stand firm against the hammering rains. A shelter built not just with her hands, but with every ounce of determination she possessed.

But survival was no longer enough.

Now, she would build something greater. A future. A path that would lead her and Moramay back to the world they had lost. And Jorge— whether he was ready for it or not—was part of that future.

They had claimed their refuge in the heart of an ancient breadfruit grove, where twisted roots clutched the dry yet yielding earth, and a silver spring tumbled down the mountainside, carving whispers into the land. The air shimmered with the scent of ripening fruit, and the trees, gnarled and wise, stood as silent guardians of the life they nurtured.

It was here, in this untamed sanctuary, that Guazuncho—his keen eyes ever scanning the horizon—had once raised the alarm. Through his binoculars, he had glimpsed movement, a shifting blur of fiery orange. His pulse had quickened. Hostile natives? A lost tribe lurking in the wild?

But the truth was stranger than his fears.

Not warriors, but sentinels of an older world. Orangutans—brilliant, watchful, moving with a silent grace that spoke of knowledge beyond words. They were not mere beasts; they were kin to the island, bound to it as surely as the wind to the waves. Over time, they had grown close to the islanders, their loyalty rivaling that of hounds, their presence a reminder that in this forgotten paradise, nature itself could be an ally—or an enigma yet to be unraveled.

Long before Belén and her companions first set foot on the island, two figures had already made it their refuge—Kitra, a Sinhalese woman of the Rodiya caste, and her daughter, Kandy.

Ethnologists often spoke of the Rodiyas and Tahitians as among the most striking people in the world—bronzed by the sun, their features reminiscent of ancient Greek sculptures, their very presence a testament to resilience. Kitra embodied that beauty, and Kandy, her daughter, was just as breathtaking.

Kitra's story was one woven from suffering and survival. Born into a caste condemned to the harshest servitude, she had known cruelty in its rawest form. The Rodiyas, despised by the Sinhalese, were branded as untouchable, fated to a life of menial labor, forbidden from even the simplest comforts. But Kitra was never one to accept the fate others had carved for her. She had belonged to a pearl-diving family, her father a master of the deep, braving the waters off Ceylon's coast with a knife strapped to his thigh, ready to fight off sharks if needed. He had taught her everything—the art of reading the sea, of holding her breath until the ocean itself seemed to pulse through her veins, of searching for the hidden gleam of pearls nestled in the sand.

But the sea had taken him, as it had taken so many before.

Sold into servitude not long after, Kitra found herself bound to a cruel merchant, a man who saw her not as a wife, but as property. She endured, not for herself, but for Kandy, the daughter she had sworn to protect at any cost.

When the chance for escape came, she did not hesitate. A merchant ship bound for Java had docked in Colombo, and Kitra saw her moment. Under the cover of night, she and Kandy slipped aboard, stowing away in the lower hold among sacks of rice and barrels of water. Days turned into weeks, and when they were discovered, fate proved merciful—the ship's captain, an aging Dutch trader with little patience for slavers, chose to set them free on the nearest uninhabited island rather than turn them over to those who would claim them.

And so, Kitra and Kandy found themselves cast ashore on this forgotten stretch of land, left to survive or perish beneath the unrelenting sun.

They did not perish.

Kitra, with her hands hardened by labor and her mind sharpened by necessity, adapted with uncanny swiftness. She found shelter in the caves along the cliffs, wove nets from palm fibers to catch fish, and tamed the wild buffalo that roamed the island, bending them to her will with patience and an understanding that seemed almost mystical. Kandy, still a child, followed in her mother's footsteps, learning to climb trees like a creature born to the jungle, her quick fingers weaving traps, her keen eyes watching for danger.

For years, it was just the two of them—mother and daughter, building a life where none should have been possible.

Then, one day, the sea delivered something new.

A wreck. A band of survivors, tossed onto the shores by fate, just as Kitra and Kandy had once been. And among them, a woman unlike any Kitra had ever met.

Belén.

Kitra had watched her from the shadows at first, observing the way she carried herself—not as a woman defeated, but as a queen surveying her new domain. There was fire in her, a spirit that refused to break, even in the face of despair. Kitra recognized that fire because she carried it too.

It was not long before their paths crossed.

At first, it was a meeting of necessity. Belén's people needed guidance, and Kitra knew the land. But what began as an alliance forged in survival soon became something more.

Kitra, who had never sworn loyalty to anyone but herself and Kandy, found herself drawn to Belén's strength, to the sheer force of her will. And Belén, in turn, saw in Kitra something rare—someone who did not follow out of obligation, but out of choice.

To Belén, it was not Kitra and Kandy's beauty that defined them. It was their loyalty. Their quiet, unshakable courage. From the moment they became part of Belén's life, they served her not as attendants, but as warriors. Over time, they became more than allies. More than friends. Kitra became Belén's silent strength, the guardian who stood in the shadows, ever watchful, ever ready. And Kandy, quick and clever, took to Moramay as if she had been born to protect her, cradling the child in her arms as the sister she had never had.

Together, they wove a new kind of family—one built not on blood, but on survival, trust, and the unspoken understanding that they had all, in their own way, defied the fates written for them.

One of Belén's first acts on the island had been to baptize them. She had little time to teach them the deeper mysteries of the faith, but they understood she had given them a new name in the eyes of God.

When they spoke in English, soft and lilting, it was touched with the musical cadence of India. A voice that could make even the harshest words sound gentle.

Their home was simple but meticulously planned, with three rooms. There was one for Belén and Moramay, another for Kitra and Kandy, and a third for Mr. Burns and José María Pérez—though everyone still called him Guazuncho.

Beyond the clearing, they had built a sturdy corral, its thick wooden stakes bound tightly with rattan ropes. Inside, up to six buffaloes

46

shifted and snorted—their presence a testament to Kitra's mastery. She had been raised to tame them, just as she had been trained to dive for pearls. Before the Westerners arrived, Kitra had ruled this island like a sovereign, riding atop a young buffalo she had raised from infancy. But fully grown buffaloes were another matter—massive, untamable creatures with tempers as wild as the storms that lashed the island's shores. They were neither pets nor livestock; they were beasts that could kill a man in an instant.

Hunting them required cunning. With the help of Mr. Burns and Guazuncho, Kitra set traps along the narrow trails leading to the watering holes—deep pits hidden beneath layers of fragile branches. If a buffalo stepped too heavily, the earth beneath it would vanish, swallowing it whole before it could charge.

The real danger came afterward.

Startled buffaloes did not run. They fought. One misstep, one wrong movement, and the entire herd could turn on them in a stampede of crushing hooves and deadly horns. If the trapped beast was full-grown, there was no saving it. A close-range arrow through the heart was the only mercy they could offer. Its final bellows shook the trees, echoing through the jungle, its massive body thrashing until the sweet mercy of death finally claimed it.

If the creature was young, they had a chance. For days, they would leave it in the pit, offering water, bits of food. Hunger would sap its fury. Fear would dull its resistance. And when it was weak enough, they would bind it with long rattan ropes, dragging it from the earth and into the corral—where the older, tamed buffaloes waited.

At first, the young buffalo would thrash and resist, wild instincts telling it to fight. But instinct could be tamed. Surrounded by the steady presence of its older, calmer kin, it would begin to watch, to learn. The struggle would lessen. Its eyes would soften. And, in time, it would submit—not out of fear, but because it understood.

Once broken in, the buffaloes became the island's greatest allies. Under Mr. Burns' ingenuity, they pulled makeshift carts, plowed fields where no hands alone could till, and carried Kitra and Kandy across the land like queens atop their loyal beasts.

Guazuncho, however, was not about to be left behind. Determined to master the art of buffalo riding, he threw himself into the challenge with his usual reckless enthusiasm. The results were… mixed. More than once, the island rang with the sound of his body hitting the dirt, followed by a string of curses in languages no one knew he spoke. Each time, Kitra would merely watch, arms folded, her knowing laughter saying more than any words ever could.

One golden afternoon, as the tide slipped back like a curtain revealing secrets long hidden, Kitra waded into the shallows and found something extraordinary. Pearls. Scattered like fallen stars in beds of rough oyster shells, glistening beneath the water's dappled light. It was as if the sea itself had been whispering to her, calling her to this forgotten treasure.

Pearl diving had been her birthright—passed from her father's hands to hers, taught in the deep, restless waters of Ceylon. There, each dive had been a battle against the ocean's hunger, a dance between breath and silence, risk and reward. But here, in this untouched sanctuary, the pearls waited without contest, cradled in the arms of the reef, gleaming with a quiet magic that no merchant's scales could measure.

Yet in this world without markets, without kings or courtiers to covet such wonders, they were nothing more than pale stones in an unseen tide. No empire would rise or fall over them. No queen would press them to her throat and marvel at their luster.

And still, Kitra dove. Not for wealth. Not for power. But because the ocean had whispered its secret to her, and she had listened.

For three seasons, Kitra moved like a shadow beneath the waves, her fingers tracing the ocean's secrets, her sharp eyes searching for the silent shimmer of a pearl hidden in the silt. The sea, as if it knew her touch, surrendered its treasures—not for gold, not for barter, but because she belonged to it, and it to her. Some things, after all, were beyond price.

When the castaways arrived, Kitra took Guazuncho under her wing, teaching him the sacred rhythm of the dive. The stillness before the plunge. The slow inhale, the steady heartbeat, the quiet patience required to listen to the water's whispers. She showed him how to read the sea floor, to recognize the gleam of treasure tucked within the reef's ancient hands.

Guazuncho, restless and reckless as the tide itself, was quick to learn. And one day, beyond the reefs they had mapped, in waters where no other had ever dived, he found them—oyster beds overflowing with pearls, luminous as trapped moonlight, untouched by any hand before his. A fortune, hidden in the deep. Enough wealth to claim a grand estate in England or a sprawling Argentine estancia. If only they ever left this island.

"Do you doubt it?" Belén had once asked him, her voice steady, her faith unshaken. She was always the one who believed, always certain that one day, the horizon would split open and bring salvation.

At twenty, Guazuncho had no room for doubt. At that age, hope blazed like a signal fire, casting endless possibilities across the horizon. He believed in escape, in adventure, in futures yet unwritten.

Mr. Burns, however, had long since stopped scanning the sea for salvation. Unlike the others, he no longer measured time in lost years or dreamed of the world beyond the waves. The island had become his kingdom, its rhythms his own. He carried himself with the quiet ease of a man who had made peace with his exile—not because he had to, but because he chose to.

"Give me a plane, a saw, and a couple of axes," he often said with a wry grin, "and I'll build myself a world worth staying in."

And then, something shifted. Subtle at first, almost imperceptible. A quiet pull, a change in the air, like the first ripple before a tide turns.

Each morning, before the sky blushed with the first streaks of dawn, before the jungle stretched and woke with birdsong, Mr. Burns would find himself moving—without thinking, without deciding—toward the corral. Drawn by something unnamed. Drawn to her.

Kitra.

She moved among the buffaloes like something more than human, more than flesh and bone—an echo of something ancient, something untamed. The massive beasts, unpredictable and wild, yielded to her touch as if she carried some unspoken pact with nature itself. She never raised her voice, never demanded; they simply obeyed, lulled into stillness by the quiet certainty in her step.

Mr. Burns, nearing forty, often wondered if he was any different from those creatures. If she had ever turned to him, if she had ever spoken his name in a way that asked for more—he would have answered without hesitation. He would have followed without question.

But Kitra never asked.

She only called on him when Guazuncho wasn't there, when an extra pair of hands was needed, when the work required no more than his strength. Nothing more. And that, slow and creeping like the roots of the jungle, began to settle inside him—not as anger, not as resentment, but as something heavier. Something he couldn't name.

Belén, ever perceptive, noticed the shift almost immediately. Burns had grown quiet. Withdrawn. His usual easy charm had faded into something heavier, something restless. He sought solitude, his silences stretching longer, his thoughts turning inward. His roommate mentioned that Burns now talked in his sleep—muttering, uneasy, as though wrestling with something from which even the island could not offer him peace.

Belén, always practical, always intuitive, understood what was happening before Burns did.

He was in love, and it was consuming him.

As the island's self-appointed governor—its near-queen—Belén decided it was time to intervene. She confronted Burns directly, gauging the depth of his feelings and whether there was any path forward for him.

When she hinted at a possible solution, Burns, always a man of blunt truths, gave her one in return.

"This isn't something a doctor can fix," he admitted with a humorless smile. "Only a priest could do that. And the nearest priest is thousands of miles away, across an ocean we have no way to cross."

Belén thought for a moment, weighing what she knew of faith, of theology, of the Church's laws.

Then, with the quiet confidence of someone who never considered a problem unsolvable, she said, "Leave it to me. Get some rest tonight—you look like you haven't slept in weeks—and tomorrow we'll talk. With God's grace, we'll find a solution."

Burns exhaled sharply, somewhere between a laugh and a scoff.

"God's grace," he muttered. "That's the problem, isn't it? If this were up to the devil, it'd already be done."

That night, as the fire crackled low and the cool wind sighed through the trees, Belén sought out Kitra. She found her near the corral and watched as Kitra moved with quiet precision, checking the ropes securing the buffalo pen.

Belén leaned casually against the wooden fence, watching Kitra with an amused glint in her eyes.

"Kitra, I've been thinking," she mused.

"Mm…dangerous habit…thinking."

Belen laughed, "So I've been told. It's not really a thought so much as an observation about Mr. Burns. Lately, he has seemed to take an unusual interest in your whereabouts."

Kitra looked up at Belén with a flicker of curiosity and said, "Mr. Burns is a good worker. Strong hands. Steady."

"Yes, very steady," she grinned. "Although, he has spent a lot more time near the corral than necessary. I don't suppose you've noticed?"

"I notice many things," Kitra replied calmly, something unreadable flickering in her dark eyes.

"And what do you make of this?"

"You're speaking in circles, Belén," Kitra pointed out, anxious to complete her day's work so she could finally rest. "Just say what you mean."

"I mean that Mr. Burns looks at you the way a man looks at something he cannot have but deeply wants," Belén offered the words like a secret, soft but firm.

Kitra says nothing for a moment, resting her fingers lightly on the coarse rope, the wind stirring the loose strands of her hair. There is no shock in her expression. No denial. Only thoughtfulness. She turns to Belén, meeting her gaze, holding it just long enough for her comment to settle. Then, without answering, she turns back to her work, securing the last of the ropes before clicking her tongue, a signal to the buffalo. They shift, huffing softly, responding only to her.

Kitra joins Belén on the walk back to the campfire. After several moments of silence, Kitra nods.

"Yes, I've noticed," she says quietly.

"Yes. I've noticed."

"And?"

Another pause.

Then, softly, Kitra admitted, "I would never act without your permission."

The words were simple, but they carried weight. Loyalty. Deference. Something unspoken but undeniable.

Belén, watching her carefully, realized what lay beneath them. The answer had never been about whether Kitra had noticed Burns' feelings. It was about whether Kitra allowed herself to consider her own. And now, the true question remained.

Would she? Kitra thought.

She had to admit Burns was a good man. A kind man. Far better than the one she had been forced to marry. And if fate was merciful, she thought, he would make an excellent second husband.

Belén lay awake long after the fire had burned low, staring at the ceiling of the hut as the night pulsed with the steady rhythm of the waves. Sleep would not come. Her thoughts circled endlessly, like seabirds riding unseen currents, dipping close but never quite settling.

She was no theologian. She had no library of doctrine to consult, no priest to guide her through the tangled corridors of moral law. But she knew the Church's teachings on marriage. A sacrament, sacred and indissoluble, sealed before God and witnessed by His clergy. And yet, she also knew the exceptions.

In desperate times, when death loomed near and no priest could be found, the Church allowed a man and woman to speak their vows before witnesses alone. Not as an act of defiance, but as a recognition of human frailty, of love persisting even in the face of impossible circumstances. She couldn't recall the exact wording of Canon Law, but she understood its heart.

And wasn't their predicament just as dire?

Kitra and Burns had chosen each other, and who could deny them that right? There was no priest, no church, no clear path back to the world beyond the waves. Could anyone expect them to wait—indefinitely? Trapped in the prison of uncertainty? Few ships dared these treacherous waters. Belén still clung to the hope of salvation, but even she had to face the truth. Rescue might come in a year. Or ten. Or never.

Her fingers curled into the fabric of her blanket. If she was wrong— if she was misinterpreting what the Church allowed—then this was no small thing. It wasn't just a legal misstep. It was eternity.

And yet, hadn't she been given this role? Hadn't the island, this strange kingdom of castaways, made her its governor, its judge, its guide?

At dawn, she would decide. Not as a woman, not as a friend, but as something greater. The weight of it pressed against her chest, but she would carry it. She had no choice.

Belén knew Church did not turn its back on reality. It approached human matters with human understanding. Moralists taught that if a couple had searched for a priest for at least a month and found none, they could marry before two witnesses. Even those who knowingly put themselves in such a predicament—embarking on a long sea voyage without a chaplain—were granted the same right.

She was not an expert in doctrine, but knew her catechism. She trusted her judgment. And most of all, she trusted her intent. This was necessity. Kitra and Burns could marry before witnesses and God would bless their union.

At dawn, she found Mr. Burns at the corral, helping Kitra tend to the buffalo. She did not offer explanations or preambles. Instead, she asked them a single, piercing question.

"What do you truly want?"

Burns, honest as ever, didn't hesitate.

"I love Kitra more than I ever loved my pipe or whiskey," he said with quiet conviction. "I gave those up without a second thought. If I have her, I won't miss them at all."

Kitra, ever direct, considered the question.

"Mr. Burns is good with buffalo," she said approvingly. "He can walk on his hands, which I admire."

Then, with the same measured certainty, she added, "And he speaks to me with kindness. If he died, I would mourn him more than I did my first husband."

Their words were plain, but the truth beneath them rang clear as a temple bell. This was love. Belén needed no further proof. She met their eyes, her decision firm.

"Then today, you will reflect and prepare your hearts. Tomorrow, Guazuncho and I will witness your vows, and before God, your marriage will be as holy and indissoluble as if the Pope himself had blessed it."

Burns let out a triumphant whoop, flinging his hat into the air.

"God save the queen!" he bellowed, grinning. "You are our queen, Belén, and Kitra and I will be husband and wife forever—your loyal servants for life! God save the queen!"

Kitra stepped forward, her usual quiet intensity sharpened by something deeper—something ancient. In her hands, she cradled a coconut brimming with fresh milk, the liquid gleaming pale and smooth against the firelight.

She moved slowly, deliberately, as if each moment carried weight beyond the here and now. Then, with reverence, she tilted the coconut, letting the milk spill onto the earth in a thin, unbroken stream.

The ground drank it instantly.

Kitra watched it vanish, her expression unreadable. But the act spoke for her. The milk, pure and whole a moment before, now lost forever to the soil. A gift offered, with no thought of reclaiming it. A promise that, once made, could not be undone.

"I swear to God," she said, her voice steady as the tide, "to be as humble and pure as this spilled milk. To love Mr. Burns with my whole being. To bear him many children. And if I fail him, let my father's sacred kris be my judge."

The words hung in the air, as final and solemn as any vow spoken before an altar.

From her waist, she drew the blade—a Malay kris, its wavy edge gleaming with a history older than her own. It was no mere weapon. It was the last remnant of the father she had lost, the blade that had once fended off sharks in the dark waters of Ceylon. A tool of survival, of defense, now repurposed into a symbol of her surrender.

With unwavering hands, she placed it in Burns' grasp.

A gesture of trust. A silent declaration.

This was no ceremony of convenience. It was something sacred. Something binding. A covenant sealed not by ink or priestly blessing, but by earth, by blood, by the unbreakable will of the woman who had made it.

Then, overcome by something she had never felt before, Kitra—her untamed spirit suddenly soft—threw herself into Belén's arms. Belén held her tightly, feeling, for the first time, the raw and breathtaking depth of Kitra's love. There was something wild and unshaped about her, something unspoiled by the world. A beauty few would ever understand.

To track the passage of time, they had carved the days, weeks, months, and years into a bamboo pole planted firmly beside their door—a silent testament to their resilience. And because of that simple, unyielding record, they knew that Mr. Burns and Kitra were married on a Saturday.

That night, the island became something more—a place of consecration, a threshold between past and future. They feasted beneath the open sky, where the stars burned like torches over a world reborn.

Golden pigeons roasted until their skin crackled, their rich aroma mingling with the scent of sago cakes smoldering over hot coals. The dried fish, cured in salt and laced with wild island spices, perfumed the night air, each bite a taste of the land that had both imprisoned and sustained them. They ate with their hands, unguarded, unrestrained—sharing food as they shared this moment, laughter mingling with the crashing tide.

When the last bones had been tossed into the fire, the ceremony of abundance gave way to the ceremony of tribute. They surrounded the bride, radiant in a Hawaiian gown woven from Laguna straw, her dark eyes reflecting the flickering flames. One by one, they stepped forward, showering her with offerings—not gold or jewels, but something rarer. Luminous pearls, caught from the island's hidden depths, scattered like droplets of moonlight across the sand. Feathers from birds of paradise, their colors defying nature itself, drifted onto her shoulders as if the sky had bent low to crown her.

Surely, no beach in the world had ever witnessed such splendor. But it was not the pearls or the feast or the woven gown that made the night unforgettable. It was the sound that followed—a declaration, a warning, a mark upon the world.

Four rifle shots cracked through the sky. Loud. Sharp. Defiant.

The jungle held its breath. The sea swallowed the echoes.

And somewhere, in the unseen distance beyond the waves, the world was made to listen.

The newlyweds, mounted atop their buffaloes, set off along the shore for their honeymoon. The waves licked the sand in a hypnotic rhythm, glowing with bioluminescence, flickering like fallen stars. The sea shimmered, deep and endless, a mirror to the night sky. And the sand, warm and soft beneath them, was no softer than Kitra's sun-kissed skin.

Two years passed, each day carved into the memory of the island as surely as the careful notches on the bamboo pole that marked the passage of time. Seasons ebbed and flowed, bringing storms and calm, harvest and hunger, yet life endured—flourishing in ways none of them could have imagined when they first washed ashore.

One afternoon, under the golden light of a waning sun, a small but momentous event unfolded. Mr. Burns's firstborn, a sturdy little boy with his father's steady determination, took his first wobbly steps across the packed earth of their courtyard. His tiny fingers clutched at Moramay's, the older girl guiding him with patient encouragement, her laughter ringing like wind chimes in the warm breeze. The child tottered, stumbled, then found his balance, and with wide, triumphant eyes, he took another step. And another.

It was a simple thing. A child learning to walk. And yet, for those who had lived through shipwreck and exile, who had built their world from nothing, it was proof of something greater. This island had not just taken them in; it had given them a future.

That evening, Belén stood at the heart of their gathered circle, the firelight dancing in her eyes. Her expression was unreadable at first, but the steady set of her shoulders, the way she clasped her hands before her, told them she had something important to say.

"I have an announcement," she said, her voice carrying over the quiet murmur of the group. "Another wedding is to take place."

There was a hush. A glance exchanged between the men, a flicker of curiosity among the women.

She let the moment linger before continuing. "José María Pérez—Guazuncho—has asked for permission to marry Kandy."

A murmur ran through the group, but Belén wasn't finished. She let her gaze settle on Kitra, the mother of the young bride-to-be.

"But he did not come to you, Kitra," she said, her voice steady. "He came to me."

Kitra's dark eyes narrowed slightly, not in displeasure, but in understanding. She had always known that Belén, more than anyone, was the true matriarch of their small world. It was she who had shaped its laws, she who had kept order, and she who held the trust of every soul on the island.

Slowly, Kitra nodded. There was no protest, no need for one. If Belén had accepted Guazuncho's request, then there was nothing more to say.

Across the fire, Guazuncho straightened, his jaw tightening with nervous anticipation. And beside him, Kandy—no longer a child, but a young woman whose beauty was rivaled only by the quiet strength in her gaze—lowered her eyes, a faint smile playing at the corners of her lips.

The wedding would happen.

And once more, beneath the vast and indifferent sky, vows would be spoken, binding two lives together in a world where love, like everything else, had been carved from the wilderness with bare hands and unyielding will.

Kandy, now sixteen, had grown into a striking young woman—tall, lithe, her beauty carved from the raw majesty of her people. She moved with the strength of a warrior, the elegance of an Amazon, the fire of a spirit untamed.

Belén did not need to ask if she loved José María. She had seen it in Kandy's eyes for years—an unspoken devotion, as pure and radiant as a child's first laugh.

Their wedding was simple, yet solemn in its sincerity. As before, no priest blessed their union, but Belén held firm in her conviction that God, from His high and distant heavens, bore witness to their vows and bound them together for eternity.

And yet, despite the joy swelling around her, despite the laughter, the flickering torches, the scent of salt and earth and roasted meat filling the air—Belén could not quiet the unease threading through her thoughts. It coiled deep within her, a whisper of doubt that refused to be drowned out by celebration.

Had she been reckless? Had she placed too much faith in necessity, in the strange exceptions carved out by fate? Was she bending the rules of God, or merely learning to live within them?

It was Moramay's face that haunted her most in these moments of doubt. Her daughter—born of love, born of exile—growing up on a forgotten island, surrounded by a world Belén had chosen for her. A world that had hardened her, shaped her, given her a life unlike any other.

And yet, was it the life she was meant to have?

Belén had made the choices. She had decided for all of them. It was she who had climbed aboard *The Cormorant* that day, chasing adventure, defying the careful, predictable path of a woman's life. It was she who had refused to let the sea or circumstance break her, who had taken command of an island and rewritten the laws of survival itself.

But if she had ignored that restless hunger—if she had chosen to stay, to silence the call of the unknown—what would Moramay's life have been? A father's presence at her side? A home not built from driftwood and necessity, but from stone and certainty?

Belén had once thought herself perfectly sane. But if she had been mad then—mad with longing, with faith in her own strength—how could she be sure she wasn't still?

The weddings had felt necessary. They had felt right. And yet, in the deep hours of the night, when the tide whispered against the shore and the fire burned down to embers, the question returned, circling her like mist.

What if I was wrong?

Chapter 4: The Swallow Takes Flight

By their sixth year on the island, Belén felt hope slipping through her fingers like sand. She had clung to it for so long—stubbornly, desperately—imagining the moment they would finally leave. She had pictured the sails of a rescue ship, the cries of their saviors, the rush of relief as they set foot on solid ground beyond this lonely prison of trees and waves.

But now, a grim realization had begun to take root. If they waited for a passing ship, they might never be rescued. Their island must be too far from any major trade routes since no merchant vessels ever appeared on the horizon, and many captains likely didn't even know this place existed.

Even the smaller boats that passed through the region kept their distance. The island, marked on old charts as uninhabited, had earned a fearsome reputation. Its coastline was a labyrinth of treacherous reefs, hidden shoals, and unforgiving waves. Few risked coming near, and those who did never lingered long enough to see the thin wisp of smoke from their fires.

For six long years, the pattern repeated itself. Now and then, a distant steamer's smoke would rise like a cruel mirage, always too far to signal. Even when Belén climbed to the highest cliff, waving a white flag until her arms ached, no ship ever altered its course.

Guazuncho, ever watchful with his binoculars, occasionally reported glimpses of small fishing boats on the horizon—but they remained distant, mere specks on the endless sea. They never dared approach the island's perilous shores.

No one is coming.

The thought hit her like a blow to the chest, knocking the air from her lungs. She had clung to hope for so long—like a sailor clutching the splintered remains of a wreck—telling herself that rescue was inevitable. A ship would appear. A mast on the horizon. A sign that the world had not forgotten them.

But seven years had passed. Seven years of waiting, of watching the endless stretch of ocean, of chasing the faintest wisps of smoke in the distance only to be met with cruel disappointment.

She turned to Mr. Burns, searching his face for answers. He had once spoken of escape, hadn't he? Of building another boat after theirs was lost?

By now, he was a father of three, fully at home in this life of sand and sea, as unbothered by the passing years as the tide itself. If he still longed for the world beyond the horizon, he never said so.

"Didn't you promise me," she demanded one day, her voice edged with frustration, "that after our boat was lost, you'd build another one? That we'd reach the mainland?"

Burns scratched his head, squinting as if trying to remember. Had he truly promised that? Perhaps, in those desperate early days—when the fear of never leaving had been too terrible to admit out loud. But if he had, it was never more than words meant to soothe, a balm for a frightened woman grasping for certainty in an uncertain world.

A promise? No. A fantasy.

"Belén," he said, calmly, "how do you expect me to build a ship with no tools? No hammer, no saw, no nails?"

He let out a dry chuckle, shaking his head.

"What do you want me to do—tie driftwood together with my bootlaces?"

Belén turned away, anger flashing in her eyes.

She wasn't asking for miracles—only for effort. For defiance against the fate that had been forced upon them. For proof that he, that *anyone*, still wanted to leave. Because if no one else cared, then what was she fighting for?

Her whole life had been built on refusing to accept the world as it was. She had bent it to her will, shaped it with her bare hands. But now— was she the only one who still longed for more?

Her nails dug into her palms, frustration burning in her chest.

No. She would not surrender to this prison of paradise. She would find a way. If no one else believed in escape, then she would believe enough for all of them.

"Don't savages build boats without iron tools?" Belén shot back, frustration sharpening her voice. "Haven't they crossed vast oceans in canoes, navigating by the stars?"

If they could do it, why couldn't she?

The island had given them everything—colossal trees stretching seventy feet into the sky, their branches thick and strong enough to carve into the hull of a ship. The forests teemed with fibrous plants, perfect for weaving rope. Even the sea itself had offered up its gifts— resinous pitch from driftwood, wax from wild hives, natural oils that could seal the wood against the relentless hunger of the waves.

The materials were there. The knowledge was what they lacked.

Hadn't ancient explorers once done the impossible, setting sail with nothing but their hands, their instincts, and the whisper of the wind to guide them? She imagined Polynesian voyagers reading the waves, feeling the subtle pull of unseen currents. Viking longships cresting through storm-churned seas. The carved canoes of islanders who had never seen a map but still knew exactly where they were going.

She imagined herself among them.

Could she teach herself to lash timber together, to shape the prow of a boat, to stitch together sails from whatever fabric they could weave? Would she need to hollow out a trunk, burn it smooth from the inside like some lost tribe of mariners?

But then the weight of reality pressed down again.

It wasn't the trees that stopped her. It was the work itself. Cutting them down with nothing but crude axes fashioned from sharpened stone. Splitting them into planks with no saws, no chisels. Bending them into shape without iron braces. Weaving ropes strong enough to hold against the weight of the sea. It was a thousand obstacles stacked on top of one another, a mountain so high that climbing it seemed impossible.

And yet, wasn't this entire life impossible? Hadn't she already defied fate once before?

But how long would she fight against the inevitable?

Even as she stood defiantly on the shore, the truth loomed behind her like a shadow. Hope was shrinking, dwindling to embers.

The years stretched ahead, unbroken and endless, like the tide that carried ships far away—never toward them.

And with every sunrise, Belén felt herself waiting for something that might never come.

Life on the island followed its steady rhythm, an unbroken cycle dictated by the land and sea.

They tended the fields near their home, coaxing life from the earth—native vegetables sprouting in neat rows, breadfruit ripening in the warm air before being ground into flour.

At the river's mouth, they cast their handmade reed nets, their fingers skilled and sure, pulling in whatever the tide was willing to surrender.

In the dense jungle, where shadows tangled among towering trees, they set traps for the wild buffalo—ensuring that their corral never emptied, that their survival was never left to chance.

By now, survival had become second nature, but for Belén, survival was no longer enough.

Kitra and Kandy, ever resourceful, spun fibers from reeds and cacti that grew in thick clusters along the lagoons and mountain slopes, weaving them into ropes as strong as any made in a distant city. Over time, their skill deepened. They built simple looms—much like those used in India—until, at last, they could weave cloth and stitch garments with their own hands.

The island gave generously.

Pigeons and wild chickens added variety to their meals. Sago palms, towering like sentinels, offered their starchy pulp, a lifeline for countless islanders across Oceania. Wild hives dripped with honey, thick and golden, a sweet salvation after years without sugar.

The island was no longer a place they endured—it had become a place they mastered.

Kitra had three children. Kandy had two. And alongside Moramay, they filled their small colony with laughter, with mischief, with life. Despite their isolation, they lacked nothing.

If anyone still yearned for the world they had left behind, it was Mr. Burns. Not for its comforts or its vanities, but for the simple, stinging pleasures—a pipe packed with rich tobacco, the slow burn of a well-earned drink at the end of a long day.

But even those cravings had found their answer.

A broad-leafed plant, dried beneath the island sun and rolled with practiced hands, became a fair enough substitute for tobacco—at least for a man who had long since lost the luxury of comparison. The draw was rougher, the taste earthier, but as the smoke curled into the night air, it was close enough to quiet the longing.

And as for drink? The island had its own kind of alchemy. Honey, left to ferment in water, transformed into something raw, something potent. It wasn't the golden mead of Homer's heroes or the nectar of the gods, but when the warmth spread through his chest, when the world softened at the edges just enough—Burns figured it was close enough. A poor man's whisky, perhaps. But even the poor deserved something to take the edge off memory.

But Belén refused to let their progress be purely material. She made a decree—Sundays would belong to God. No work, no hunting, no fishing. Just a few sacred hours carved out for the One whose protection had been undeniable, whose hand had carried them through the years.

She became more than the island's leader—she became its teacher. The children would not grow up in ignorance, their minds left to stagnate like still water. She would shape them, feed them knowledge, give them the words and prayers that might one day guide them beyond this shore.

Yet, as the island flourished, as its people became more settled, Belén felt the opposite. What the others had come to see as home, she saw as a prison. Her longing to escape burned brighter than ever.

On her solitary walks through the jungle, rifle slung over her shoulder to guard against wild beasts, her eyes were drawn upward—to the titanic trees, ancient and unyielding. She sized them up and tried to calculate their weight.

Belén imagined them as something else—something that could carry her away from here. A boat. A real one. A vessel that could ride the ocean swells, carve through the waves, and take her wherever Jorge was searching for her.

If he was still searching.

Doubt coiled around her heart like a serpent. Had he given up? Had he long since accepted her death as fact and moved on? How weak men are, she thought. How easily they abandon hope, reshape their truths, and even find relief in them.

A woman, though—a woman like me—once she chooses her path, she never lets go. She doesn't bury her memories. She guards them, feeds them, lets them keep hope alive.

Even as the others settled into their new lives—crafting routines, building habits, arranging their days as if they would remain here forever—Belén's mind refused to surrender.

Her thoughts were ceaseless, circling endlessly in her mind. Whenever the weight of it all grew too much, she sought solace on the coast. There, the deep channel split her lush domain like a scar— leading her toward the only place that mattered. The beach. The single patch of golden sand where a ship could land, where escape was possible.

The only vessel she had coaxed from Mr. Burns was a canoe, hewn from a single massive trunk. It was crude, but it was hers.

She had learned its moods. The way it moved, the way the wind caught its small lateen sail, the way the oars felt in her hands when the ocean refused to cooperate. At dusk, she would drift through the labyrinth of what could have been.

That torturous space where the past replayed like a fever dream, whispering of different choices, different endings. She would let the wind carry her toward the shore, toward the place where hope still clung stubbornly to the rocks like barnacles.

Once there, she would anchor the canoe, climb the cliffs, and settle onto a rocky outcrop overlooking the endless, merciless sea.

She never let go of hope—not completely. Not as long as she had her field glasses, scanning the horizon, tracing the endless, merciless sweep of the sea. Always watching. Always waiting.

Then, one evening in the seventh year, something shifted.

A shape. Not a trick of the light, not a phantom born of longing, but something real. Belén's breath hitched, her fingers tightening around the glass. Hands shaking, she lifted it to her eyes.

A ship.

Not a smudge against the sky. Not a fleeting shadow swallowed by the waves. A vessel—sharp, solid, unmistakable.

And it was coming straight for them.

Her pulse roared in her ears. No ship had ever done this before. The others had drifted past, blind to the silent figures onshore, indifferent to the thin wisp of smoke rising from their fires. But this one—this one had set its course for land.

Rescue? Or ruin?

The answer was coming. And it was coming fast.

The evening wind, cool as a whisper from the sea, carried the ship steadily closer. She watched as its sails lowered, their white canvas dimming in the fading light. Then—if her ears weren't deceiving her—she caught the deep, metallic clank of an anchor plunging into the water.

She held her breathe as she scanned the deck. Hope and dread warred inside her. For years, she had clung to the dream that a ship would come for her—that aboard it, she would see the one face she longed for.

But as her gaze swept across the figures on board, her heart sank. The crew wore traditional Chinese garments. Bare-chested sailors, their skin darkened by the relentless sun, moved like ghosts against the ship's lantern glow. Not the rescuers she had imagined.

Belén shrank back into the shadows, instincts screaming. Silent as the tide, she slipped from her rocky perch and hurried to her canoe.

The ship wasn't in a rush. It lingered offshore, sails furled, as though waiting for morning. She couldn't wait. Keeping low, she dipped her paddle into the dark waters, steering inland. The towering trees swallowed her as she followed the channel deeper into the island's embrace. Only when she was safely hidden beneath the dense canopy did she finally release the oars.

She unfurled the sail—woven from rattan fibers by Kitra—and let the current guide her home. For the first time in years, she let herself believe they were going to be rescued.

Even if Jorge wasn't aboard that ship, maybe—just maybe—the captain could be persuaded to take them away from this place. If they could reach the mainland, or one of Oceania's larger islands, they could finally begin the journey home.

That night, under a sky untouched by moonlight, she returned home with new determination. Above her, the stars shimmered like scattered pearls on black velvet—beautiful, distant, full of promise.

Mr. Burns was the first to break the silence, his voice steady but edged with something unreadable.

"Chinese merchant ship," he murmured, studying the vessel as it crept closer. "Probably caught in a typhoon. Might be stopping for supplies."

Belén swallowed hard, her mind racing. If he was right, the crew would be searching for fresh meat, vegetables, young breadfruit buds. They would land. They would explore. And if they stumbled upon the settlement—if they saw the carefully tended fields, the corral full of buffalo and poultry, the smoke rising from their cookfires—what then?

She had once relished the thought of unknown ships appearing on the horizon. In another life, she would have watched from the cliffs, breath quick with anticipation, daring to imagine adventure, danger, even romance. But that was before. Before she knew what it meant to be at the mercy of ruthless men.

Now, she wanted only one thing. Escape. At any cost.

She turned to Mr. Burns. "We need a plan."

They had something to bargain with. Bags of pearls—some no larger than a grain of rice, others big as a thumbnail, glowing like captured moonlight. And the banknotes—weathered but untouched, hidden away for years in the hopes that someday, they might be used to buy passage home.

Would it be enough?

It had to be.

But before they made their move, they needed to answer the only question that mattered.

Who were these men?

And—more importantly—what would happen if the ship found them first?

At dawn, Belén, Mr. Burns, and Guazuncho set out. They moved with practiced silence, gliding their canoe into a thick tangle of mangroves where the roots stretched like skeletal fingers into the water. Hidden from view, they climbed a steep, forested slope, its damp earth crumbling beneath their fingers, until they reached a vantage point high above the shore.

The first light of morning spilled across the ocean, turning the waves to liquid gold, the clouds painted in hues of rose and violet. The island stirred, branches swayed, unseen creatures rustled through the undergrowth, wings fluttered in the canopy.

Then they saw movement below. A boat was being lowered from the ship, dipping into the water with a splash. Oars sliced through the waves, smooth and practiced, manned by bronzed, bare-chested rowers.

It was the passengers that drew Belén's sharpest focus. Seated among them, draped in fine silks, were several men. Different from the sailors. Their robes whispered of wealth, their hands gripped rifles and shotguns. Officers, perhaps. Or something worse. A second boat followed, stacked with empty barrels.

Beside her, Mr. Burns exhaled sharply.

"It's obvious," he murmured, his voice barely above the wind. "The ones with guns are here to hunt. The others are after fresh water."

He turned his keen gaze back to the ship, his mind already dissecting its every detail.

"Well-kept rigging. Fresh sails. Solid hull. I'd say she displaces three, maybe four hundred tons. A ship that size needs a skeleton crew—no more than a dozen men. And we're looking at most of them right here."

They watched in silence as his prediction played out.

The hunters split off, vanishing into the dense forest, their weapons slung over their shoulders. The sailors hauled barrels toward the river, their movements swift and efficient. The ship had come for supplies. But what else had it brought? And more importantly—what would happen when they realized they weren't alone?

One figure stood apart. The leader. His refined clothing and superior equipment marked him as someone of importance. He wore a loose yellow blouse, flowing blue trousers tucked into red leather boots, and a wide straw hat that shadowed his face. Round spectacles perched on his nose, glinting in the morning sun. Despite his stocky build, softened by age, he moved with a hunter's precision.

With long, deliberate strides, he left the others behind, descending into the marshy lowlands where life teemed in every direction. Ducks and herons erupted from the reeds, their wings beating the humid air. In the underbrush, unseen creatures stirred. A deep, guttural bellow echoed through the trees—the call of buffalo, waking with the heat of the rising sun.

To the untrained eye, it was paradise, but Belén knew better. The marsh was a graveyard. It looked solid—green moss blanketing the surface, reeds swaying gently in the breeze. But beneath that deceptive skin was a thick, suffocating clay that swallowed anything foolish enough to tread too far.

She had seen it claim a life before. One careless step, and a young buffalo had been lost to the depths. She and Guazuncho had watched in horror as it thrashed, its terrified bellows turning to silence as it vanished beneath the moss. From that moment on, they had never dared to cross it.

But the Chinese hunter had no such knowledge. Drawn by the sheer abundance of prey, he strode forward, boots sinking slightly into the damp earth. He raised his shotgun and fired. A clean shot. Ducks plummeted, their bodies limp in the reeds.

He smiled, pleased. Took another step. His foot sank. Annoyed, he shifted his weight, convinced firmer ground lay just ahead. But the clay held fast, sucking him down inch by inch.

He tried again. This time, his boots disappeared into the mire.

From their hidden perch, Belén and the others tensed. He was in serious trouble.

A second passed. Then another.

Could they risk exposing themselves? On the other hand, their collective consciences couldn't let them just stand by and watch him disappear.

When they heard a single, desperate cry—one sharp, panicked shout as the hunter realized the land beneath him wasn't land at all, Belén, Mr. Burns, and Guazuncho ran. They wove through the underbrush, feet barely touching the damp earth, dodging low-hanging branches and startled herons that exploded into flight.

They sprinted for the marsh, toward the man sinking deeper with every heartbeat.

The mud clung to the hunter like a living thing, wrapping around his legs, his waist, his chest—pulling with slow, merciless strength. His rifle had vanished in seconds, swallowed without a trace. Now, every desperate movement only dragged him deeper.

He tried to retreat, lifting one leg—only to feel the other plunge further. The thick, sucking clay drained his strength, his muscles burning with exertion. Sweat slicked his skin, his breath coming in ragged gasps.

Stay still, he told himself.

He forced himself to stop, lungs heaving. Maybe if he didn't struggle, the sinking would slow. Maybe his crew would notice his absence. Maybe they would come looking.

But the only answer was the sharp, mocking cries of herons circling overhead.

Beyond the marsh, the jungle carried on as if nothing was amiss. The steady thud-thud of axes echoed through the trees as sailors hacked at firewood. The soft murmur of waves kissed the distant shore.

Mosquitoes swarmed his face, biting at his sweat-drenched skin. He dared not even blink.

Stillness wasn't helping.

To his growing horror, he realized he was still sinking— slowly, steadily, relentlessly. An inch every five minutes, then faster.

Too soon, the mud was up to his waist, then is chest. His feet, now lost in an even softer, more fluid layer beneath, seemed to be pulling him down like hands gripping his ankles.

It was getting worse. The panic he had tried to suppress exploded.

"HELP! HELP!"

His voice cracked as he thrashed, arms flailing. He quickly found out this was a big mistake. The motion sucked him another two inches down.

Behind him, voices rose from the shore, and he twisted to look— another mistake. His body dropped another two inches.

Terror shattered the last of his composure. He screamed for help in every language he knew—Chinese, Javanese, Japanese, Malay,

Portuguese, English—words tumbling over each other in a frantic, desperate stream.

Then, cutting through the rising panic—a voice.

Calm. Steady. A woman's voice.

"Stay still. Keep calm. Help is coming."

His chest hitched. Someone had heard him.

A moment later, Mr. Burns emerged from the trees. A long bamboo pole—freshly cut—dragged behind him, its end trailing in the undergrowth.

"Grab this!" Burns shouted, throwing it toward the sinking man.

It wasn't long enough and landed two, maybe three meters short.

The hunter thrashed, his arms clawing at the empty air as the marsh tightened its grip around him. Every desperate motion only dragged him deeper, the thick, clinging mud swallowing him inch by inch. His breath came in ragged gasps, panic rising like a tide. If they didn't reach him soon, there would be nothing left to save.

Guazuncho arrived, hauling the mast from his canoe, planting it firmly in the ground, but even that wasn't enough. The combined reach of the pole and mast still fell short. The hunter was sinking fast, his shoulders now disappearing beneath the muck, his wide eyes wild with terror.

There was no time to think.

Belén acted on instinct.

She seized the bamboo pole in one hand, the mast in the other, and stepped forward, her boots vanishing instantly into the marsh.

One step. Two. Three. The ground beneath her shifted, treacherous and hungry, the cold grip of the mud tightening around her ankles. She could feel it pulling, threatening to claim her the way it had so many before. But she forced herself forward.

The hunter saw her coming and lunged, fingers locking onto the pole in a vice grip. His weight yanked hard, nearly pulling her down with him.

"Pull!" Belén shouted, bracing herself.

Mr. Burns and José María heaved with everything they had, muscles straining, veins standing out against their skin. The hunter's body barely budged. The mud clung to him like a second skin, resisting, refusing to let him go.

The minutes dragged into an eternity of gritted teeth and raw determination. Sweat dripped from their brows, their breath coming in short, ragged bursts. Their hands burned from the strain, slipping against the smooth surface of the mast.

Belén felt the mud climbing higher on her legs, creeping past her knees, cold and relentless. The weight of it threatened to drag her under, but she planted her feet, anchored herself as best she could, and pulled with every ounce of strength she had left.

"Again!" Mr. Burns bellowed.

The hunter gasped, the mud slurping loudly as he was wrenched an inch higher. Another pull. Then another. A final, agonizing heave—

And suddenly, he was free.

The force of it sent them all stumbling backward. The hunter collapsed onto solid ground, coughing, choking, his body caked in thick, suffocating layers of mud. His limbs twitched feebly, weak and useless, like a newborn foal struggling to find its footing.

Belén barely registered the moment before her own body gave in. Her legs buckled, her vision blurred, and then—nothing.

When she woke, the world was spinning. A fire crackled nearby, sending flickering light against the trees. The damp earth was cool beneath her, but a blanket had been draped over her shoulders. She turned her head and saw the hunter still lying where they had pulled him, his chest rising and falling in shallow, uneven breaths.

She had done it.

They had done it.

And as she let exhaustion finally claim her, one thought echoed in her mind—

Not today, marsh. Not today.

Chang-Chu was no ordinary sailor.

He was a wealthy merchant, his empire stretching across Oceania. He traveled between his businesses aboard one of the ships in his fleet— the *Swallow's Nest*, which now sat anchored offshore, gleaming in the morning sun.

When Belén regained consciousness, she found him sitting cross-legged on the grass, engaged in lively conversation with Mr. Burns. To her surprise, his English was flawless.

Fifteen minutes earlier, Chang-Chu had been sinking into the marsh, his fate sealed by the merciless pull of the earth. Now, he was very much alive—caked in mud, aching in every limb, but breathing. And he knew exactly who to thank.

The woman who had risked herself to save him wasn't just fearless— she was unlike anyone he had ever met. Sharp-witted, unwavering, beautiful in a way that wasn't delicate, but powerful. A woman like that deserved something grand.

And so, in the only way he knew how to repay such a debt, Chang-Chu made his offer.

"Marry me."

Belén blinked, caught off guard, but before she could reply, he continued with utmost sincerity.

"I am a widower. I am wealthy beyond measure. I could give you a life of comfort, anything you desire. If you have no other plans, then why not?"

For a long beat, Belén simply stared at him, searching his face for any trace of jest. There was none. He meant every word.

A lesser woman might have been flustered. Another might have laughed outright. Belén? She merely smiled, slow and knowing.

"How generous of you," she mused, eyes glinting with amusement. "But I'm afraid I do have plans."

She left it at that, rising gracefully, brushing the dried mud from her sleeves as if the entire conversation had been nothing more than idle chatter.

Chang-Chu watched her go, both impressed and—perhaps for the first time in his life—thoroughly outmaneuvered.

She had only one wish—to secure passage for herself and her companions. A ship that would take them to any port in Asia or Oceania, from where they could find passage to Europe or America.

Chang-Chu nodded, then leaned back and began his own tale. His ship had set sail from Amboina, the capital of the South Moluccas, its cargo hold packed with spices and tobacco bound for Batavia. But the ocean had other plans. A monsoon.

One moment, they were sailing smooth waters. The next, they were like a dove caught in a hawk's claws. The storm had tossed them like driftwood, hurling them across the Sunda archipelago. A hundred times, they had barely escaped disaster—dodging jagged coastlines, coming within a breath of capsizing.

To survive, they had been forced to jettison two thousand sacks of cargo—spices, silks, fortunes worth of goods—along with their water barrels and every last piece of firewood.

To another man, it would have been ruin. To Chang-Chu? Nothing more than a tree losing a leaf. He was still rich. Now, all that remained was to restock, make repairs, and sail once more. This time, with Belén and her companions aboard, taking them wherever they wished to go.

The *Swallow's Nest* was no ordinary ship.

A masterpiece of Eastern craftsmanship, she was sleek and swift, built not for war but for speed, comfort, and endurance. At 400 tons, she was the fastest vessel registered in Amboina, a ship that could dance with the waves rather than fight them. Her dark, lacquered hull gleamed like obsidian under the sun, her sails—woven from the finest Javanese canvas—billowed with the confidence of a bird in flight. Unlike the cumbersome Western ships that lumbered through the waters, the *Swallow's Nest* moved with uncanny grace, slicing through the sea like a blade honed to perfection.

She had never ventured far beyond the labyrinth of spice islands she called home, never tested herself against the boundless, open ocean. But if her captain willed it, she could go anywhere—across the seven seas, past the edges of the known world.

And now, she had a new course to follow.

Belén had no doubts when she made her request. Australia. A land close enough to civilization, far enough to ensure their escape. From there, they would find their way back to the world they had left behind—to Europe, to Argentina, to whatever fate awaited them.

Chang-Chu did not hesitate. With a flourish, he agreed, as if the decision had already been made the moment she stepped onto his deck.

The *Swallow's Nest* would carry them away from the island that had been both their prison and their kingdom. And beyond the horizon, destiny awaited.

Mr. Burns—at last armed with a proper plane and a well-honed saw— oversaw the repairs with a craftsman's satisfaction. The *Swallow's Nest* transformed under his watch, its sturdy decks reinforced, its sails trimmed for the long journey ahead. The crew, swift and disciplined, worked tirelessly to accommodate their unexpected passengers, fashioning three small but comfortable cabins, each a fragile promise of the new life awaiting them beyond the horizon.

Preparations were meticulous. Enough buffalo and poultry were slaughtered, their meat salted and dried under the relentless sun, stored in woven baskets alongside sacks of sago and breadfruit. Every provision was a safeguard against the uncertainty of the open sea, a final offering from the land that had sheltered them for so long.

And then, on a clear morning, just before sunrise, the time came.

They stood at the water's edge, gazing back at the island that had been both their sanctuary and their prison. The jungle loomed behind them, dark and unbroken, the towering breadfruit trees swaying as if whispering their farewells. The wind carried the scent of the earth they had tilled, the salt of the waves they had fished, the smoke from the fires that had once been their hearth.

For years, they had fought against the island, resented it, dreamed of leaving it behind. And yet, as they prepared to step onto the waiting ship, the weight of parting settled deep in their bones.

Kandy clutched her mother's hand, her dark eyes unreadable. José María pressed his palm to the wooden stockade they had built with their own hands, as if leaving a piece of himself behind. Even Mr. Burns, a man who claimed to have no use for nostalgia, stood in silence, his fingers running absently over the knife at his belt, as though carving one last memory into the island's skin.

For Belén, it was different.

She had long since severed her ties to this place, her heart fixed on a single destination. And yet, as the first golden rays of sun crested the cliffs, she felt the pull of the past—the years spent in exile, the battles fought, the life she had carved from nothing.

A life that was now ending.

The island had shaped them, hardened them, given them a world they had never asked for but had, in the end, conquered.

Now, they would return to a world that had forgotten them.

A few last glances, a few lingering breaths of the air that had once been home. And then, one by one, they turned away.

As the *Swallow's Nest* unfurled her sails and cut through the water, the island shrank behind them, swallowed by the endless sea.

There were tears, but hope burned brighter.

For the first time in years, Belén was no longer trapped. She was sailing toward something real. Toward the one person she had sworn never to stop searching for.

The *Swallow's Nest* drifted into Perth's harbor, its hull slicing through the quiet morning waters. The city stretched ahead, sun-washed and unassuming, the docks lined with merchant vessels, their masts rising like a forest of bare branches.

Belén stood at the railing, her binoculars sweeping over the anchored ships. The wind tangled her hair, the briny air clinging to her skin, but she barely noticed. She was searching—though for what, she wasn't sure. Then—

Her breath hitched.

A name. A name she never expected to see again.

Painted across the stern of a ship, stark against its weathered black hull: *The Innocent.*

A chill coiled down her spine. The world seemed to tilt, the weight of memory pressing hard against her ribs. She lowered the binoculars with slow, deliberate movements, but her fingers trembled as they curled into the railing.

"José María."

Her voice was calm—too calm. A taut thread stretched to its breaking point.

José, standing nearby, turned at once.

"You have sharp eyes," she said, her gaze locked on the ship. She lifted the binoculars and passed them to him, nodding toward the vessel. "Read that name."

José raised the glasses, squinting against the glare of the rising sun. The moment he saw it, his entire body went rigid.

"The Innocent," he said, voice flat.

Belén's grip tightened, knuckles white. The name sat like a stone in her throat.

She inhaled slowly, forcing the words out.

"Do you remember that black ship?"

José's fingers clenched around the binoculars. His stance shifted—braced, wary.

"Yes, ma'am."

She swallowed hard. The dock swayed beneath her feet, though the sea was calm.

"Is that the one?"

José didn't hesitate.

"Yes, ma'am." His voice was steel.

It was the same one.

The ghost of a nightmare, returned.

They summoned Mr. Burns. The old sailor lifted the binoculars to his weathered eyes, his grip steady but tight. He took a long, measured look, then let out a slow breath that reeked of unease.

"It's the same ship," he murmured, his voice a dry rasp. "And it looks like no one's touched it in seven years... not even to scrub off the blood."

As the *Swallow's Nest* crept past its port side, all doubt rotted away. It was Big Ben's ship. The very vessel that had once sailed in the shadow of Carne Cruda—that butcher of men who'd been obliterated when José María's bomb sent the *Cormorant* screaming into the depths, dragging its crew of monsters with it.

Yet this ship—*The Innocent*—had pursued them like a curse, a shadow on the waves. They had watched it vanish, swallowed whole by the howling fury of the Banda Sea storm.

And yet, here it was. Risen.

Its hull, battered and splitting, seemed to fester beneath the weight of years. Its rigging sagged like the tendons of a corpse. The ropes hung in frayed nooses. Filth clotted the deck. Its black paint, peeling in long, curling strips, revealed the pale rot beneath—like skin sloughing from dead flesh.

A thin tendril of smoke writhed from the galley chimney, as if something inside still breathed. A whisper of life. A warning.

But the real question clawed at them like unseen fingers—what had become of Big Ben?

Was he still at the helm of this drifting carcass?

They wouldn't have to wait long to find out.

When the *Swallow's Nest* dropped anchor, Captain Chang-Chu sent a boat ashore.

Belén—now clad in something far more appropriate than her Hawaiian straw gown—turned to Mr. Burns.

"Scout first," she said. "Make sure it's safe before I set foot on land."

Mr. Burns needed no convincing. Dressed as a simple Insulinda sailor, he gladly accepted Captain Chang-Chu's invitation to share a whisky—the first he'd had in seven years—and to savor a long-awaited pipe in the first tavern they came across.

A place fittingly named *The First and Last*—the first bar to welcome sailors after long voyages and the last before they stumbled back to their ships. Inside, the air was thick with smoke and secrets. The floorboards groaned beneath their boots. The murmured conversations of men long at sea swirled in the dim, yellow light.

Chang-Chu ordered tea. Mr. Burns ordered whisky. The first sip sent warmth through his bones. He let it settle, slow and deep. Then, as his eyes adjusted to the gloom, they landed on a broad, hulking figure slumped at a corner table.

His breath stilled. That back. That massive, unmistakable back. Big Ben.

Though it was still morning, the man—who clearly hadn't returned from any journey—was already drinking, nodding off between sips of liquor.

As soon as Mr. Burns recognized him, a thought slithered into his mind. Things always come in threes.

First, he had spotted *The Innocent* anchored in the harbor. Now, its wretched owner sat, half-conscious, in a tavern chair.

Something else—something just as troubling—was bound to reveal itself next. Unless, of course, the saying was wrong.

It wasn't.

The third revelation struck when Mr. Burns let his gaze drift to the tavern's smoke-darkened walls, where layers of tattered notices clung like ghosts of forgotten stories. One, in particular, gripped him.

Yellowed with age, its curled edges whispering of neglect, it was a bounty poster—issued long ago by the defunct *Swan Line*, the shipping company that had once owned the ill-fated yacht *Cormorant*.

The reward was £200 for any information regarding the vessel, believed lost in the Banda Sea.

But it wasn't the bounty that made Mr. Burns' stomach twist. Beneath the main text, the accusations stood out like a curse carved in stone.

Captain Rawflesh was accused of piracy and murder. His alleged accomplices were the Marquis of Balcázar and his wife, Belén de Bazán.

The order was chilling in its finality—if found, they were to be arrested at once.

A flicker of motion at the edge of Mr. Burns' vision broke his trance. Big Ben had drained his drink. The hulking man cast them a murky, drunken glance, then heaved himself up from his chair and stumbled out the door, vanishing into the humid night.

Behind the bar, the keeper had been watching. He sauntered over, a knowing grin tugging at his lips.

"That one," he said, jerking a thumb toward the door, "is my best customer. Been living in Perth seven years now, aboard a ship that never leaves port—waiting for someone who never comes."

He chuckled, as if amused by the sheer absurdity of it. Then he leaned in and gave them the rest. Years ago, in Singapore, Big Ben had gone to the authorities, pinning the entire affair on Raw Flesh. With no one left to contest the claim—because they were all either missing or dead—the infamous captain took the fall.

Belén and her husband had been accused alongside him, but with no trace of them, the case faded into obscurity. The bounty posters had been plastered across every seedy port from Manila to Melbourne, but no new leads surfaced.

Everywhere except Perth, that is—where one barkeep still remembered. Thanks, of course, to Big Ben's unwavering patronage.

Mr. Burns wasted no time. He had to get back to the ship. Belén needed to know—immediately.

There was no doubt. They had to disappear.

Chang-Chu had already offered to take them anywhere they desired, and now, with the shadow of arrest stretching toward them from every port, Belén made her choice.

"Buenos Aires," she said.

A near-impossible voyage for a ship scarcely larger than a walnut shell. Ten thousand miles. One stop at the Cape of Good Hope. Three months at sea—*if* the weather showed mercy.

But Belén, who had endured trials beyond imagination, now feared only one thing: standing trial for crimes she had never committed. A nightmare that could drag on for years, in a foreign courtroom that would relish her downfall.

She preferred to gamble on Chang-Chu's gratitude. He would ask no questions, require no papers.

For the next few days, they moved in the shadows of Perth, gathering supplies and proper clothing. Through Chang-Chu's web of business contacts, Belén sold some of her pearls, securing enough money for a fresh start in Buenos Aires.

Chang-Chu refused payment for the voyage. Instead, he proposed marriage again…twice. Just in case she hadn't been paying attention, he then proposed a third time.

"Should you ever find yourself widowed," he told her, "know that my offer still stands."

Three months later, *The Swallow's Nest* sailed into the port of Buenos Aires.

Chapter 5: The Eyes of Moramay

Father Gazapo had survived three harrowing years in Madrid during the civil war by sheer ingenuity and, at times, audacity. He had disguised himself as a militiaman, led a gang of cutthroats - purely for survival, of course - and spun a web of deception so elaborate that it sometimes startled even him. He had lied, schemed, and played the part of a hardened assassin to protect his fellow friars, who still whispered Mass in the shadows each morning.

But somewhere along the way, he had picked up the habit of swearing like a battle-weary soldier. Not the usual profanities, mind you. His were far more creative, invoking the wrath of forgotten deities and summoning the ghosts of history's most infamous villains. To hear him curse was to be lashed by a verbal storm of Greek mythology, Roman treachery, and the occasional French Revolution reference, all wielded with the precision of a schoolmaster's cane.

Though the war had ended, his sharp tongue had not. Even among his fellow Eastern Catholic Missionaries—men who practically radiated saintliness—Father Gazapo was known to let loose a thunderous, scandalous outburst now and then. His confessor, a man of delicate constitution, had imposed severe penances for such offenses, which Father Gazapo accepted with a sheepish nod and promptly forgot by the next provocation.

Determined to reform, he made a valiant effort to curb his tongue. It was an uphill battle, but by the time Belén entered his life, he had whittled his swearing down to every other day.

And then came Belén. With her, all progress unraveled. The questions this woman asked! For the love of Mohammed's beard! What devil had sent this penitent to torment him with theological labyrinths and maddeningly intricate hypotheticals?

Even her simplest inquiries—like whether the two marriages she had arranged on the island were valid—made his head pound. But it wasn't enough for her to simply accept his reassurance. No, she pressed further. Had the Church always recognized such unions? Could he cite the precise canon law that validated them? And when he didn't answer quickly enough, she demanded to see the Code of Canon Law herself.

Father Gazapo had dealt with many things in his time—armed radicals, secret police, inquisitive bishops—but an insistent woman determined to rifle through canon law was a trial he had not prepared for.

Ah! But the ordeal was not yet over. Determined to get her answers, Belén paid an uninvited visit to the convent hall, a most unwelcome intrusion.

Once inside, she immediately asked about the priest who celebrated the six o'clock Mass—and whether she could meet him. Father Gazapo, already nursing a headache, had given her only a name - Father Teofano.

"Strange last name," Belén mused.

He nearly bit his tongue in exasperation. *It's not a last name at all!* It was a pseudonym, a necessary precaution to protect a young priest who had reasons to remain hidden. But was he obliged to explain this to her? Absolutely not. So, he didn't.

Instead, he let the conversation die there, though Belén's curiosity clearly had not. She had already asked about him more than once. That, to Father Gazapo, was a problem.

Luckily, the priest wasn't home.

Belén—let's finally call her by her real name—had been ready to press the issue further when Father Gazapo, desperate for an escape, darted into the library and returned moments later with two hefty tomes bound in fine English paper. With a flourish, he dropped them into her hands.

"Here you go, daughter. Just what you wanted."

Belén eyed the books suspiciously.

"What's this, Father?"

"Exactly what you asked for—the *Code of Canon Law*, in good old English, thank God! Because you wouldn't understand a word of it in Latin. And let's be honest, you're not going to understand much of it in English either."

He let out an exasperated sigh.

"By Nero's tormented soul! This is too heavy for delicate stomachs like yours, daughter. No offense intended. Saint Paul himself said we should feed children milk, not solid food. But no, you insist on swallowing something you'll never digest… Agrippina's womb!"

Who knows how long his rant would have continued if Belén hadn't cut him off with a single, steady request.

"Could you just tell me the number of the canon I'm curious about? Just to put my conscience at ease?"

Father Gazapo groaned.

"Now you've got scruples. Great timing, daughter! And you really want to read that canon? Fine. It's 1,098—like it's nothing. And just so you know, the Code has over 2,400 of these. Care to read them all? Curious women! Here, give me that book! I'll show you exactly what you need to know… *Not to know more than one should,* as the Apostle says…"

"No need, Father! I've got it!"

Belén, triumphant, flipped straight to the canon in question and read it for herself.

It was there, clear as day. The Church permitted marriage before two witnesses when no priest could be found. Her conscience was finally at peace. But as she traced the ink with her fingertip, absorbing the weight of those words, something else happened. Her curiosity grew. She turned back to the index—eager, relentless, and chasing down a truth she had yet to name.

Father Gazapo squirmed in his cassock, tugging at the stiff collar as though it were a noose. Muttering under his breath, he unleashed a series of curses—not the usual kind, but the ones only he could conjure, full of forgotten emperors and mythological calamities.

"Nosy people. Always asking questions. Can't leave well enough alone…"

"It's not that I want to know *everything*, Father," Belén replied sweetly, still flipping through the heavy tome, her finger tracing the fine print with the precision of a scholar. "Just a few clarifications… Oh! Look at this!"

She suddenly straightened, as if she had just stumbled upon some long-lost treasure. A slow, knowing smile crept across her lips. "I bet, for all your knowledge, you don't remember *this* canon, do you?"

Father Gazapo sighed theatrically.

"Let's see, daughter. Anything's possible. My memory is weaker than King Herod's good intentions. Let me take a look."

Belén ignored his dramatics and, with a teasing glint in her eye, began to read aloud.

"Canon 132: If a married man receives holy orders in good faith, but without apostolic dispensation, he cannot lawfully exercise them."

She shut the book with a soft *thud* and tilted her head.

"What does that mean, Father?"

The effect was instant. Father Gazapo's face turned a deep shade of crimson, his hands twitching as though longing to fling the book out the nearest window. His sputtered response came in a string of exclamations so bizarre, they could have summoned the ghosts of Rome.

"By Pluto's coals! Proserpine's bunions! Saint Paul was right, wasn't he? And with good reason, too!"

Before Belén could react, the old missionary *snatched* the book from her hands as though it had burned him.

"Listen well, daughter!" he bellowed, shaking the volume like an agitated schoolmaster. "Saint Paul did *not* suggest—he *ordered*—that women should keep quiet in church!"

He slammed the book shut, gesturing wildly as if that in itself were enough to silence her.

"In other words, stop meddling in things beyond your understanding—things about *laws* and *canons!* It's indecent and shameful, as the Romans put it! And for the love of heaven, Madame Guernizo, don't go mixing things up when you *clearly*—" he threw his hands toward the ceiling *know nothing about them!*"

Belén—usually unshakable—blinked in surprise. The priest's outburst had been spectacularly disproportionate. And that, of course, only made her all the more curious. Why such a violent reaction to such a simple question? Unless…

Could a man have been ordained in *good faith*—truly believing his wife was dead? A thought like that could rattle the very foundations of someone's world.

Belén studied the priest, weighing her words carefully. But no, this wasn't the time. She had pried enough for one day. With the grace of someone who knew exactly when to retreat, she thanked Father Gazapo, bid him farewell, and left without revealing a flicker of the questions now swirling in her mind.

Whether he noticed or *pretended* not to notice was another matter entirely.

A few days later, her doctor arrived with good news.

"You're fully recovered now," he announced with satisfaction. "And with Buenos Aires enjoying such lovely spring weather, you can finally get up early and attend that six o'clock Mass I had strictly forbidden."

Belén blinked.

"Oh. Right," she replied absently.

She had forgotten all about that restriction. If she was being honest, she had no intention of attending that early Mass anymore. At one time, she had been desperate to go. But now it just didn't matter anymore.

The Missionaries had rearranged their schedules, and the six o'clock Mass was now led by an elderly, near-sighted priest who had neither the energy nor the mystery of the one she had hoped to meet.

Father Teofano. Where had he gone?

No one seemed to know. Some whispered he had been reassigned to the convent's private chapel, where only the cloistered religious attended. A convenient disappearance. Belén had wanted to meet him. She had sensed something unusual about him—something *hidden*. A quiet heroism. An untold story. She had imagined that, somehow, his life might hold answers—perhaps even a path worth following. Perhaps he was even a *saint.*

But now? After noticing Father Gazapo's barely concealed *suspicion* whenever she asked about him, she decided to wait. She wouldn't force the matter. A better opportunity would come. It always did.

In the meantime, Belén enrolled her daughter in the parish's girls' school, where one of the Missionary priests became the child's spiritual director.

The little girl was preparing for her First Communion, set to take place on December eighth—the Feast of the Immaculate Conception.

A child born on an island in the middle of nowhere, who had been baptized by a shipwrecked carpenter. She had her mother's golden hair, but her eyes—dark, deep, and unfathomable—held the mystery of tropical nights over the Insulinda seas. Despite the shadowy depth of those eyes, she was the most joyful, innocent creature in the world.

One afternoon, Belén took her daughter to meet Father Gazapo. The old missionary, who had spent a lifetime witnessing both war and miracles, took one look at the child and felt something stir.

He studied her face intently as his brows knit together in thought.

"Where have I seen eyes like hers before?" he murmured.

Belén's voice was soft as she said, "They're her father's eyes."

And just like that, something passed between them—unspoken yet *felt.*

Father Gazapo's fingers curled slightly over his cassock. His face remained impassive, but a new thought took root in his mind. For the first time since meeting Belén, he wondered if he had misjudged something very important. He prayed for a revelation…one that he wasn't sure he *wanted* to receive.

"Ah!" Father Gazapo exclaimed, gnawing on his nails with an air of theatrical exasperation. "And here I was, thinking nonsense again. Why is it that every time I see you, my daughter, my brain starts running in circles?"

Belén gave him an angelic smile, eyes glinting with mischief.

"I really don't know, Father," she replied modestly.

Then, tilting her head, she added, "But are you sure you *only* think nonsense when you see me?"

The priest threw up his hands in defeat.

"No, daughter. Even when you're *not* around, I still find myself tangled in nonsense—just remembering you, your stories, your endless, maddening *questions.*"

He wagged a finger at her.

"You have a way of stirring things up."

Then, narrowing his eyes, he asked, "So? Any news from your husband?"

"Yes, Father," Belén answered smoothly, lying without so much as a blink. "His employer sent him to Alaska to buy blue fox pelts. It's going to be a long separation."

Father Gazapo grumbled, unimpressed.

"Hmph. Not right, if you ask me. *Let no man separate what God has joined together.* Want me to say it in Latin for you?"

"No need, Father, thank you," she said with a disarming smile. "Hearing it once is more than enough. Though, speaking of Church law… one day, we really *must* discuss another canon…"

"Thunder and lightning on Parnassus!" he groaned, rolling his eyes toward the ceiling. "And here I thought you were finally *done* with theology!"

"Oh, I could never be done, Father," she said sweetly. "And when you're not too *angry*, let me know. I have a very important question about…"

"*Which one?*" he interrupted, suddenly wary.

His eyes narrowed suspiciously. "*Not* Canon 132, I hope?"

"That's the one!" Belén clapped her hands together in delight. "How did you remember?"

"*By Balaam's talking donkey!* Of *course* I remember!" He clutched his forehead dramatically. "You read it to me yourself one day! And here you are again, dredging it back up! By all the torments of Tartarus, *who even imagines such absurd scenarios?!* A *married* man receiving *holy orders* in good faith? Impossible! Madness!"

"But it *could* happen, Father," Belén insisted. "Would you like me to explain *how*?"

"*That's all I need!*" Father Gazapo groaned, throwing his arms up in despair. "*You* come to me with questions, and *I* end up giving you a full theology lesson!"

He shook his head, muttering, "Blast it all to Cyclops' single eye… May the Lord grant me patience…"

Then, sighing heavily, he turned to the little girl standing beside Belén.

"And *you*, cutie," he said, softening, "prepare yourself well for the most important day of your life."

Father Gazapo bent down and kissed Moramay's forehead gently, murmuring, "Most pure!"

As he straightened, something lingered in his expression—something unreadable. His gaze flickered back to the child's eyes. A strange sensation stirred inside him.

It's the first time I've seen this girl… but… strange… it's not the first time I've seen those eyes.

The thought nagged at him all the way back to his room, circling his mind like a vulture over carrion. Finally, frustrated with himself, he muttered under his breath, "One fool makes a hundred, as the proverb says. That woman—Madame Guernizo—sometimes she seems mad, and other times she knows more theology than I do. She'll either drive me insane or turn me into a greater theologian than Saint Thomas… Burnt goat's horn!"

Spring rains had washed the city clean, and the bright Pampero winds had swept away the heavy humidity, leaving Buenos Aires fresh, fragrant, and luminous.

On the morning of the Feast of the Immaculate Conception, the day when thousands of children traditionally received their First Communion—the city itself seemed to glow, as if graced by the divine.

From early dawn, the streets filled with six to ten-year-old girls dressed in pristine white and boys in navy-blue suits, their arms adorned with delicate white bows. Some clutched their oversized missals, proud yet slightly overwhelmed by their sacred duty.

Moramay, a student at the Sisters of Charity school, arrived with her mother.

Belén was uncharacteristically silent. There was something about this day—something deeper than sentimentality—that pressed upon her chest, stirring a feeling she could not name. Scripture said that some voices *speak louder than watchmen on a mountain.* Today, she *felt* them.

Lately, she had visited Father Gazapo less often. But that didn't mean she had stopped thinking—dreaming—*waiting*.

The nuns had invited parents to receive Communion alongside their children, a rare gesture, though it was not customary for fathers and daughters to approach the altar together.

One by one, the girls stepped forward, their hands clasped, their eyes lowered in reverence as they moved toward the communion rail. Then came the adults, following in quiet procession.

Moramay knelt beside her mother. She was radiant—her golden hair glinting in the candlelight, her face alight with an innocent joy, though her dark eyes held a deeper mystery.

Today, something unseen was stirring within the child's soul, like an ocean shifting beneath a misty sky. Belén, kneeling a few feet away, watched with glistening eyes, unwilling to miss a single moment.

Father Gazapo had been scheduled to celebrate the Mass. But given the sheer number of children, another priest had joined him to help distribute Communion.

Belén had positioned herself carefully—far right, hoping to receive the Eucharist from Father Gazapo's hands.

Few sights in the world are as tender as a child's First Communion. The young girls, their white veils fluttering like angels' wings, knelt in hushed rows, whispering prayers after a nun's gentle lead. Hot tears streamed down Father Gazapo's weathered face.

What on earth! Me! he thought, stunned by his own emotions. Me! The tough guy from Madrid—the one who fought alongside militiamen—now melting into a puddle over a bunch of little girls in white dresses!

He turned to the congregation, his voice trembling with raw affection.

"My little daughters… My beloved little daughters…"

He couldn't say another word. His throat closed, choked by something too deep for speech. But those simple words, broken and unadorned, stirred the congregation more than any sermon could.

Wiping his eyes, he lifted the ciborium, turned to the altar, and spoke the sacred words before stepping down to distribute Communion. The children moved in quiet groups to the altar rail. Some knelt on the right, where Father Gazapo awaited them. Others knelt on the left, where a second priest had just emerged from the sacristy, carrying another chalice filled with consecrated hosts.

Belén, lost in her daughter's moment, didn't notice the new arrival at first. Her gaze was locked on Moramay, watching as she opened her mouth to receive the Eucharist—the Bread of Life.

But then something shifted. A breath caught in her throat.

The priest placing the host on her daughter's tongue—the hands that had just traced the sign of the cross. It was him!

The soft gasp which escaped her lips was lost amid the whispered prayers and bowed heads.

She froze. Her vision narrowed to that one lone figure. It was *impossible,* and yet, there he was.

As her turn approached, her heart pounded. Father Gazapo? Or *him*?

The choice lasted no more than a heartbeat. She stepped forward and knelt on the right before Father Gazapo.

And as the priest placed the Eucharist on her tongue, she kept her eyes down; but her entire body, her *soul*, was reaching for the one standing just beyond.

The one who shouldn't be here.

And yet, he was.

Chapter 6: The Woman in the Confessional

Jorge heard the cry just as he placed the sacred Host onto the tongue of a young girl whose dark, radiant face shone with grace. The anguished sound shattered the church's solemn hush, cutting through the air like a blade. It was raw, desperate—less a cry than the final, flailing gasp of a drowning soul.

For a moment, something deep within him stirred, a sensation like the tug of a half-forgotten memory or an unseen hand pulling at his robes. But he smothered it. A mother's grief, nothing more. He forced himself to push it aside, and, in time, he forgot.

Until that night.

In the silent hour when heaven often whispered its clearest inspirations—and when earth, too, sometimes murmured its most painful ghosts—he heard it again.

The cry.

It coiled around him like an unseen specter, slipping through the cracks of his carefully guarded mind. Even as he packed his modest suitcase, preparing to leave Buenos Aires for good, its echo clung to him, like the scent of something burning, something lost.

Jorge had already secured permission from his superior to go. But he had never spoken of the true reason for his sudden departure. He had not confessed to the weight which had shadowed him for years—the shame of his father's reckless marriage to a woman from the slums of Madrid, the indelible stain on his noble name. Instead, he asked to be sent to Chile, offering a practical excuse - to establish a new residence for the Eastern Catholic Missionaries.

More than anything, he wanted to disappear.

He had pleaded with Father Gazapo for secrecy. No one must know where he was going. More importantly, he must be allowed to shed his name like a snake discards it's skin.

The old missionary, trusting in the discretion of his young coadjutor— and eager to expand their mission into fiercely Catholic Chile— granted his request without hesitation.

In just a few days, Father Manrique would cease to be Jorge de Balcázar y Manrique. He would be gone forever. But what had driven him to flee so suddenly?

A chance encounter. Too cruel. Too perfectly timed. As if the devil himself had orchestrated it.

It happened on a holiday, when a fire erupted in a packed theater during an afternoon performance by an English operetta company. The flames moved fast. Panic spread faster. Several performers were injured, rushed to the hospital, their costumes singed, their voices hoarse from screams.

One among them—a young singer, barely clinging to life—suddenly recalled the faith of her childhood. With what breath remained in her, she begged for a priest to hear her confession. The hospital chaplain was nowhere to be found. Desperate, two of her colleagues ran into the street, searching for salvation in the city's indifference.

By sheer chance, they spotted a priest. A missionary, returning to his convent. They pleaded with him. He followed without hesitation.

Inside, he knelt beside the dying woman, whispering the words of absolution, offering the only comfort he could.

She passed moments later.

The priest never asked her name. Never thought to ask. He had only done his duty.

But among the gathered onlookers, one woman knew exactly who he was. Not Father Manrique. Not the new name he had carefully chosen to bury his past. She knew Jorge de Balcázar y Manrique.

Her name was Teodora Cordero. Lead soprano of the operetta troupe. Famous for her beauty. Infamous for her cunning. As her dark eyes locked onto his across the candlelit hush of the hospital room, Jorge knew his past had caught up with him.

Jorge worked swiftly, his hands steady even as the woman beneath them slipped away. Teodora, standing just beyond the bed, said nothing. She only watched.

And waited.

She waited until she was sure—absolutely sure—of who he was.

Then, she slipped into the corridor and positioned herself where she knew he'd have to pass.

When Jorge finally emerged, ready to return to the convent, she stepped into his path.

"Father," she said, her voice deceptively soft, edged with something sharper. "What's your name?"

He met her gaze without flinching.

"Father Teofano."

A slow smile curled across her lips—one that had nothing to do with warmth.

"No," she murmured. "I've been looking for you for half an hour."

She leaned in, lowering her voice to a near-whisper.

"So… back from the dead, are you? Clever trick, dressing as a priest."

Jorge went rigid.

She tilted her head, watching him like a cat might study a wounded bird.

"Tell me, Jorge… are you really a priest? That absolution you just gave—was it valid?"

His jaw tightened.

"Madam," he said, his voice cool and clipped, hands curling into fists at his sides. "I don't know what you're talking about. Now, please—step aside."

"Oh, I will," she said lightly, though the glint in her eyes told him this was far from over.

She stepped to the side, her gaze never leaving his.

"But we'll meet again, dear. And when we do…you'll tell me everything."

The exchange lasted barely two minutes.

And yet, when Jorge returned to the convent that night, her words weighed on him like chains.

She hadn't called him Father Teofano. She hadn't used the name he had carefully chosen to bury the past. She had called him Jorge. That meant she knew.

He had only given her his priestly name, hoping to make it harder for her to track him down. But Teodora was sharp. She was bold. And given time, she would find a way to use what she knew.

He couldn't allow that. The thought of blackmail, of scandal—of his entire life unraveling—was unbearable. So, he acted first. He begged his superior to send him away.

The encounter had taken place just days before Moramay's First Communion.

That night, Jorge dreamed.

The Bible speaks of dreams as messages—whispers from God, warnings carved into the dark.

In his dream, he saw Belén—his Belén—but she was far away, lost in a vast expanse, searching for him with a desperation that clawed at his soul.

He saw himself, standing tall in his priestly robes, hands steady as he laid brick after brick, erecting a wall between them. Each stone was another vow, another renunciation, another barrier meant to keep her out.

It was the only way, wasn't it? The only way to remain faithful. The only way to honor his calling.

And yet, she fought.

Her small, delicate hands—hands he had once held, hands that had once reached for him in quiet, stolen moments—were now torn and bloodied, nails broken as she ripped at the stones, prying them loose, refusing to let him go.

He wanted to call out to her. To stop her. To pull her through.

But the wall grew taller, thicker. Impenetrable.

Jorge woke with the weight of the dream crushing his chest. His breathing was ragged, his body damp with cold sweat. Sleep had abandoned him, leaving only the gnawing ache of something irretrievable.

As dawn's first light bled through the cracks of his chamber, he rose, murmuring a verse from the Psalms, his voice hollow:

"I lay down full of anxiety. The sons of men have teeth like weapons and arrows, and their tongues are sharpened like swords of steel."

He crossed himself, whispered a prayer that felt thin, powerless, and went to celebrate the six o'clock Mass.

The main altar was occupied, so he took a side altar instead, whispering the Mass for the soul of his beloved. His lost Belén.

But deep in his heart, a terrible truth gnawed at him.

She didn't need his prayers.

She was already among the saints.

And he—he was the one who had been left behind.

After Mass, he made his way to the confessional. He had been absent from his usual morning hour for some time, and so, the usual penitents were nowhere to be seen.

The church was still, its vast interior bathed in dim light, only a few early risers kneeling among the pews. Jorge settled onto a bench beside his confessional, reciting his breviary by the glow of a single lamp. The confessional was behind him. He always knew when someone approached—the faint shuffle of shoes, the rustle of fabric as they knelt before the screen.

But this time, there was no sound. Nothing at all. He only became aware of her presence when the silence was broken by a single, stifled sob.

Turning his head, he saw a woman kneeling in the alcove, her head bowed before the small bronze crucifix.

Slowly, Jorge sat up. He reached for the wooden panel and slid it open and waited.

Through the heavy grate, in the dim shadows of the church, he could not see her face.

She should have spoken her name as was the custom, but she did not. Instead, silence stretched between them, thick as the walls of the confessional. Then, at last, she spoke.

Her voice was hushed, unsteady, carrying the soft, familiar cadence of his homeland. But there was something else in it, something distant—like an echo returning from too far away, shaped by years spent apart.

He had heard many voices falter in the confessional. Voices trembling with grief. Voices thick with regret. Voices hollowed out by the weight of sin.

But as she began to speak, he knew she was not here for absolution. She was here for the truth.

"Father," she whispered, barely above a breath. "Suppose a young couple suffers a terrible accident while traveling. The woman is believed to be dead, and the man, thinking himself a widower, enters religious life and becomes a priest. Years later, the woman returns—alive. Does she have the right to go to her husband and ask him to come back to her?"

A stillness filled the space between them. When he finally spoke, his voice was steady. Unshaken.

"Yes."

He could not see her face, but he felt the tremor pass through her. Yet she did not stop.

"And the man?" she pressed, her voice quieter now, as if she feared the answer. "Knowing his wife is alive… is he obligated to return to her?"

Another pause. Another simple, unwavering answer.

"Yes."

For a moment, silence reigned. Then, suddenly, her voice shifted—urgent now, her words spilling out faster.

"And, Father—if someone who holds authority over them both learns the truth… would it be right for that person to keep silent?"

This time, the pause was longer. He knew why. This question was different. Finally, after a moment's thought, he spoke.

"It is not permissible."

A soft, trembling sigh escaped from the other side of the grate.

"Thank you, Father," she whispered, her voice barely carrying through the grate. "What you've told me has brought me great comfort. Please… pray for me. I will need your prayers very much."

Then, without another word, she rose and drifted away, her silhouette swallowed by the dim light of the church.

Father Manrique remained still, listening as her footsteps receded, fading into the vast silence. Yet the echo of her voice remained—lodged in his mind like a thorn. Something about this encounter unsettled him. The questions she had asked. The urgency in her tone. The way her voice, though soft and uncertain, had felt eerily familiar.

It was only when he stood—only when he stepped out of the confessional and into the quiet corridors of the convent—that the realization struck him. It had been a trap. A test. And he had walked straight into it.

The woman had not come seeking forgiveness. She had come for something far more dangerous. Not absolution. Confirmation. Teodora. It had to be her. Somehow, she had found him and uncovered what he had spent years burying. And if he knew anything about Teodora, it was that she would not rest until she had turned that knowledge to her advantage.

Outside, Buenos Aires lay bathed in the golden light of late spring. The convent garden, ancient and still, pulsed with life—birds darting between the trees, the scent of wildflowers thick on the air. Beneath the sprawling shade of a great acacia, an old stone bench stood waiting, his usual place of refuge.

He went there now, breviary in hand. But his fingers remained still on the pages, his prayers unspoken. His mind was too restless. Too alert to a danger that had only just revealed itself.

Teodora would not wait long. He knew that much. This was only the beginning. A warning. A whisper of what was to come. And the next time, she would not be so subtle.

He needed to leave. Immediately.

His request for transfer to Chile was still pending, tangled in the slow-moving bureaucracy of the Church. But there was no more time to wait. He had to vanish before she struck. Before she had the chance to twist the past into something damning. Because she would.

And once the first whisper of scandal took root, it would not only destroy him—it would stain everything. His entire Congregation.

He would rather die a hundred times than let that happen. His priesthood was everything. Not a refuge, as cynics might sneer, but a calling—a deliberate, sacred choice. He had chosen this life. He had chosen God. And yet, for the first time in years, a thought slipped through the armor of his conviction. A whisper of something buried.

In another life, could he have been a husband? A father? Could he have loved and been loved in return?

No. That path was closed to him. And Belén…she had understood that better than anyone.

Now, as he sat in the hush of the garden, Father Manrique felt certain of one thing—Belén was watching over him still.

Because love—true love—never dies. Not in this world. Not in the next.

He had answered the deepest calling of his soul, surrendering his life to God. To be torn from that path now would feel like a tragedy. And yet, as birds trilled from the treetops and wildflowers swayed in the soft afternoon light, an unseen current stirred in the air.

Something was shifting. The quiet forces of love had begun their slow, inevitable work, already pressing against the fortress of his resolve.

Belén had not gone to confession that morning—not because she lacked grace after receiving Communion the day before, but because she feared the truth. She feared the weight of what he knew. Instead, she had cloaked her past in a veil of hypotheticals, asking questions to measure her place in the world.

And to measure his.

Hearing his voice again after so many years had filled her with an aching sweetness—a cruel, exquisite kind of pain. She had always known she might be standing in the way of God's will. And yet, she needed certainty. She needed to hear, with her own ears, the truth of where she stood. Jorge's duty. His obligations. And even the hand Father Gazapo played in it all.

Father Gazapo saw it clearly. Too clearly. He had spent his life guiding lost souls, but now, he found himself faced with a dilemma no scripture could untangle. Father Manrique was one of the most devoted missionaries he had ever known. A man who had given up everything to serve. To lose him now—over a woman's stubborn insistence on reclaiming a past that should have remained buried—felt unthinkable.

And yet, canon law was absolute.

If Belén was alive, if she still claimed him, then Jorge's priesthood was invalid.

There was, however, a way to fix it. If Belén took religious vows, Jorge could remain a priest.

God performs miracles, Gazapo thought, though doubt gnawed at him.

A woman like Belén—so poised, so commanding—was not the sort to lock herself away behind convent walls. Still, he would try; but there was another complication.

The child.

Moramay.

A girl with eyes that mirrored Father Manrique's so perfectly that no explanation, no convenient lie, could refute the truth.

The first time Gazapo met the child, any lingering doubt he might have clung to vanished. This was no ordinary mess. This was an impossible knot, tangled by fate, by choices made long ago, by love that refused to fade.

And so, that afternoon, as the sun stretched long across the mission courtyard, Belén arrived.

Father Gazapo had been waiting for her. Restless with determination. If ever there was a time for confrontation, it was now.

She entered with quiet grace, her beauty untouched by time—regal and untamed, like the Shulamite of the Song of Songs, dazzling as a queen, yet distant as a legend.

Gazapo, a man not easily shaken, felt something shift in his chest.

She unsettled him. This was a woman who had lost everything. A woman who had searched the world for the man who was meant to be hers. And yet, as she stood before him now, she did not come as a warrior. This time, the lioness had no claws.

Belén had spent the last day making peace with the truth—her rights, Jorge's obligations, and even the delicate role Father Gazapo played in this tangled fate. But one thing was certain. She would force no man's hand.

If Jorge hesitated, if even a shadow of doubt crossed his mind, she would let him go. She didn't know what the future held for her, but she knew what she would not accept—a man who stayed out of duty rather than love.

Gazapo, though he hid it well, felt a quiet relief at her words.

"Go ahead, Father," she said evenly. "Tell him. I know my catechism as well as he does. But I won't have someone at my side who comes to me out of obligation. You'll find the right words—or perhaps I should do it myself?"

"No, no," Gazapo cut in, too quickly. "You'd ruin everything if you went to him now, in your current state."

Belén arched a brow.

"My *current state*?" Her voice was sharp now, edged with impatience. "You expect me to believe he doesn't know I'm alive? Tell him— however you must. Just don't let him *die of joy*," she added, her tone twisting with something bitter.

"He doesn't know," Gazapo said firmly. "We've considered every angle, and we haven't said a word."

Belén exhaled, shaking her head.

"Incredible," she murmured. "He didn't recognize me this morning. Not even when I spoke of his own life."

Gazapo studied her carefully. He still had one final card to play.

Canon law was clear. If she took a vow of chastity, Jorge could remain a priest. But could he convince her?

Belén, catching the flicker of calculation in his gaze, gave him a knowing look.

"I leave it to you," she said at last. "Tomorrow, I'll return to hear what my—"

She hesitated, just for a moment.

"What *Father Teofano* decides."

Gazapo frowned. "Calling him your *husband* is harsh."

Belén met his gaze without flinching. Her voice, calm and unwavering, cut through the quiet.

"Call him what you like." She turned toward the door, her posture regal, unshaken.

"Tomorrow, we meet face to face."

Chapter 7: A Name in the Dark

Meanwhile, Father Manrique remained blissfully unaware of the storm gathering around him. He was too busy packing. The letter from Chile had arrived that morning, granting him permission to travel and assess a potential site for a new mission. It was a welcome escape—a door opening just in time.

If he left now, he could still outrun whatever trap had been set for him. His mind kept circling back to the voice from the confessional to the woman whose identity had eluded him. The more he replayed the exchange, the more convinced he became that she had been hunting for legal leverage—a way to twist Church law against him and his Order, to blackmail them under the looming threat of scandal.

How clever she had been. How patient. She had studied her theology well before stepping into that confessional, weaving her words with precision, luring him into a snare of his own making.

Ah, *Teodora, Teodora...* he thought with grim amusement. *Your knowledge of canon law might one day land you in prison—may God save you from worse than that.*

The devil himself must have led her to him. How else had she found him in Buenos Aires, of all places? But she wouldn't get another chance. Tomorrow, he was gone. If he had to, he'd flee beyond Chile—to the ends of the earth, to Shanghai, to any place where her shadow couldn't follow.

He worked feverishly, placing in his suitcase everything he needed to celebrate Mass—no matter where he found himself. A missionary priest required no grand church, no altar, no congregation. He had vowed never to miss a day of offering the Holy Sacrifice—not until the very last one. The one that would be said for his own soul.

He was carefully folding his chasuble when he heard a distinct, yet familiar knock.

"Come in, Father," he called, recognizing the rhythm of the knock before the door even opened.

Father Gazapo stepped inside, his sharp gaze sweeping over the half-packed suitcase, the neatly folded vestments, the quiet determination set in the younger priest's face.

He let out a slow sigh.

Then, with a sad smile, he said, "Don't tire yourself, Teofano. Leave those sacred items for now. You won't be needing them."

Jorge froze, his hands still on the fabric.

"What do you mean, Father?"

Gazapo exhaled, his expression unreadable.

Then, almost to himself, he murmured, "Only God knows for how long. Maybe never again. *Amen.*"

A chill traced its way down Jorge's spine.

He had seen his superior angry before. Frustrated. Even scandalized. But never like this.

"Would you mind explaining that to me, Father Superior?" he asked carefully, setting aside his half-packed belongings and motioning for Gazapo to sit.

The older priest did so, flipping through the book he carried, his fingers moving with quiet purpose. Finding the passage he sought, he handed it to Jorge.

"Read this."

Jorge looked down.

The words on the page struck him like a blade.

It was the very passage from the Code of Canon Law that the woman in the confessional—the one he now suspected to be Teodora—had pressed him to recall.

A slow, sinking weight settled in his chest.

"Read it aloud," Gazapo said.

Jorge obeyed.

"Canon 133, paragraph 3: If a married man receives higher orders in good faith but without an apostolic dispensation, he is not permitted to exercise them..."

The words hovered in the air between them, heavy as iron shackles. Father Gazapo shut the book with deliberate finality, his sharp blue eyes locking onto Jorge's.

"Is that clear to you, son?"

Jorge nodded slowly.

"Yes, Father Superior… but I don't understand why you're showing me this now."

Gazapo studied him, his expression unreadable, the weight of what he knew pressing down on the space between them. Then, at last, he leaned forward, lowering his voice.

"You'll understand soon enough, my son."

The way he said it sent a ripple of unease through Jorge's chest.

"When you came to me in Shanghai seven years ago, asking to join the seminary… you told me you were a widower, didn't you?"

Jorge met his gaze, suddenly aware of the tension creeping into his shoulders.

"Yes, Father," he answered carefully.

"But you never told me your wife's name."

Jorge's jaw tightened.

"She passed away," he said quietly. "I preferred to keep her memory alive through my prayers—nothing more."

Gazapo's gaze didn't waver. His next words came like a thunderclap.

"And what would you say, my son, if I told you she's not dead? That I know her name, I know her, and—more than that—without even realizing it, you gave your own daughter her First Communion?"

Silence. Jorge did not flinch. His expression remained calm. Too calm.

Gazapo clenched his fists.

"You fool! How can you sit there like that after hearing this?"

Jorge exhaled, his voice smooth, unwavering.

"Naturally, Father Superior, because everything you've been told is complete nonsense."

Gazapo recoiled as if struck.

"What?! Are you saying María de Guernizo is lying?"

Jorge's brows knit together in mild confusion.

"I don't even know who María de Guernizo is."

The superior's patience began to crack.

"Then tell me, who is your wife?"

Jorge's lips pressed into a firm line. Then, with measured certainty, he answered.

"The only woman who has ever claimed to be my wife is Teodora Cordero. And she has been a source of trouble more than once."

Gazapo stiffened.

"Teodora Cordero?"

"Yes. In fact, she came to me this morning in the confessional, feigning innocence, asking about the rights and duties of a spouse."

Gazapo's pulse quickened.

"And you're telling me she's *not* your wife?"

Jorge let out a bitter chuckle.

"Absolutely not, Father. She's an impostor."

Gazapo sat back, stunned.

"Unfortunately," Jorge continued, "she possesses certain documents that would *appear* to prove we were married in Madrid. But it was a *false* marriage—one arranged under desperate circumstances, solely to save my father, who was on the brink of suicide over a terrible misfortune. It's a painful story I never shared because I never imagined it would matter. But now, Father, I will tell you—so you understand just how far wicked, godless people will go to destroy us."

For the first time in his life, Father Gazapo sat through a long story without interrupting.

He listened—his mind reeling, his breath shallow—as Jorge unraveled the truth of his past.

A past that had now come crashing through the doors of their holy sanctuary.

When Jorge finished speaking, Father Gazapo did something he rarely did. He pulled him into a firm embrace.

"Son, you've lifted such a weight off my heart!" he exclaimed, gripping Jorge's shoulders as if to steady himself.

Then, after a pause, he added, "So this 'Madame Guernizo'—"

"I have no idea who she is."

Gazapo frowned.

"But the woman claiming to be your wife—"

"That's Teodora Cordero," Jorge said with quiet finality. "She's a fraud. A schemer. She's manipulated me before, extorted more money than I care to count, and now—by sheer, wretched misfortune—our paths have crossed again. But she won't get away with it this time."

His voice darkened, "You must not believe a word she says."

Then, softer, his expression clouded with something far more painful, he added, "My *true* wife—the one God joined me to—was taken from me by Him. She was as brave as Joan of Arc, and she suffered more than anyone should. I have no doubt she is in heaven now."

He exhaled sharply, forcing himself to shake off the weight of memory.

"May I finish packing, Father Superior?"

Gazapo clapped him on the back, his relief palpable.

"Yes! And I'll help you—so you can get as far away from that scoundrel as possible."

And so he did.

That very night, without a word to anyone, Father Manrique boarded a train to Mendoza. From there, he quietly caught a flight to Chile, disappearing into the dark, leaving nothing behind but silence.

Meanwhile, poor Belén knew nothing. The instincts that had guided her through her long, painful journey—the quiet certainty that souls could reach for one another beyond time, beyond distance—failed her now. That night, exhaustion claimed her. She slept dreamlessly, only waking when the great bell of the Missionaries tolled at dawn.

She dressed quickly, wrapping herself in the quiet resolve of morning, and made her way to the six a.m. Mass. She hadn't expected to see Father Teofano today. By now, surely, Father Gazapo had told him that he was no longer permitted to exercise his sacred duties. And yet...

Even knowing he wouldn't be there, she longed to be close to him somehow. Had she made a mistake? She had relied on intermediaries, sent messages through men with their own agendas—when she should have spoken to him herself. That would change. She *would* speak to him. She would not let another day pass without looking into his eyes and saying what should have been said long ago.

But as she knelt in the pew, hands clasped, another thought haunted her. Why did she feel afraid? Would he hesitate?

Even if he had forgotten her—seven years believing her dead—surely seeing her now, standing before him, and *meeting their daughter* would be enough.

Certainly, he would remember. Surely, he would recognize the law that transcended all others: "What God has joined together, let no man separate."

A tremor passed through her. Tears, unbidden and unfamiliar, welled in her eyes. She rarely cried. She did not allow herself such weaknesses. But here, now—so close to the end of her suffering, standing at the very edge of all she had fought for—her strength was slipping through her fingers.

And what if she had been wrong? What if there *was* no clear path ahead? What if the men around her—so certain in their knowledge, so blinded by their theology—understood far less than she, a woman clinging only to the simple, unwavering truth of Christ's words: *"What God has joined together, let no man separate."*

Despair coiled around her heart.

After Mass, still lost in thought, she made her way back to the house. She found Mr. Burns and Guazuncho in the garden, tending to the flowers outside the old mansion they had worked so hard to restore. But for the first time in years, Belén felt as though something inside *her* had come undone.

The house had stood for half a century, its outdated architecture a relic of another era. But the land it rested upon—once barren and neglected—had been transformed by two tireless men into a flourishing sanctuary of life. Mr. Burns and Guazuncho had poured their sweat and strength into the soil, shaping it into something beautiful, something lasting. They had purchased the property not just as a home, but as a refuge—a place where the three families that Providence had brought together could finally live in peace.

Belén worked alongside them, her hands moving methodically, her mind elsewhere. Always elsewhere. Her own family was still incomplete. Still missing its head.

When Mr. Burns mentioned Jorge, she gave him the same answer she had been repeating for days, "Soon, I'll have good news about him."

And nothing more.

She kept her search to herself, guarding it like a fragile flame. The pain of disappointment had been too great before—she would not risk another.

But now, with the hour of reckoning so near, her heart pounded with something beyond hope. A quiet, relentless anxiety pressed down on her, thick as the humid December air. She could barely wait for evening, for the moment she would stand before Father Gazapo and hear Jorge's response at last.

As the day dragged on and the heat of the sun finally relented, she left the house and made her way to the Missionaries' convent. She knocked at the door, anticipation coiling in her chest like a held breath. A lay brother answered, his expression unreadable.

"I'd like to speak with Father Gazapo," she said, her voice steady.

He barely spared her a glance.

"He's gone out."

Something in his tone unsettled her, but she clung to her patience.

"Then may I speak with Father Teofano?"

At that, the lay brother's entire demeanor changed. He turned his back on her with a huff of irritation.

"He's not here either, ma'am! *No one's here!*"

The words hit like a slap.

For a moment, she stood frozen, confusion and disbelief twisting in her stomach. The coldness in his voice—the blatant shift in how they treated her—was like a door being slammed in her face. Why? She had always been received kindly before.

Her strength, stretched thin by years of searching, was running out. Once, she would have fought back, demanded answers. But now, she found herself unable to move, unable to think. Dazed, she turned and walked away, her heart sinking with each step. That night was the longest of her life.

Sleep came in restless fragments, broken by waves of anxiety and a sorrow too deep for words. She lay in bed feeling small, powerless, *abandoned*. She wanted to cry but the tears never came.

When dawn finally broke, she whispered a silent *thank you* to God. At least now the waiting was over. She crossed herself, murmured a prayer, dressed hurriedly, and reached the Missionaries' church before the doors had even opened. A handful of early risers lingered nearby, casting curious glances at her. She did not look like someone who came to morning Mass.

As soon as the sacristan unlocked the doors, she stepped inside, her pulse quickening.

"Will Father Gazapo be hearing confessions this morning?" she asked.

The answer struck like a dagger.

"Father Superior won't be coming down today."

A sharp inhale. She swallowed the unease creeping into her throat.

"Then… what about Father Teofano?"

This time, the response shattered her completely.

"Father Teofano has *left* Buenos Aires."

The words blurred in her mind.

"He's *left*?" she repeated, her voice barely above a whisper. "Where did he go?"

The sacristan shrugged.

"I don't know, ma'am. Ask someone else—though I doubt anyone here knows either."

He let out a dry chuckle.

"We never seem to know anything about anything…"

A shiver crawled down her spine. She was being lied to. She could feel it.

The Mass that followed was a blur. She struggled to concentrate, her mind clouded by the same devastating question—*Where was Jorge?*

She took Communion without confessing. There was nothing on her conscience except the love that had kept her alive, that had given her purpose. Afterward, she approached one of the priests, her desperation growing.

"Please, Father," she said, her voice tight with restrained emotion. "Can you tell me where Father Teofano has gone?"

The priest, unfamiliar with the convent's affairs, only gave a dismissive shake of his head.

"Ma'am, I'm here to hear confessions, not to give out information."

By the afternoon, frustration and desperation burned inside her like a fever. She *had* to know. She marched back to the convent and knocked again, harder this time.

When the porter opened the door, she fixed him with a glare.

"How is it possible that *no priest* is available?" she demanded. "Have they all left at the same time?"

The porter merely shrugged, unimpressed by her fury. Then, without a word, he turned his back on her. The door closed. And with it, so did her last thread of hope.

When she refused to leave until a priest came to speak with her, he reluctantly rang a bell. A few moments later, a tall, dignified priest appeared—his presence commanding, like a soldier trained for battle. He stood before Belén as if he had been expecting her, his face unreadable.

She explained again that she needed to see Father Gazapo or Father Teofano regarding an urgent matter. The priest listened patiently.

Then, leaning in ever so slightly, he whispered coldly, "Don't come back here, ma'am. Those Fathers are no longer in Buenos Aires, and no one else wants to be involved in their affairs."

"I don't understand," Belén murmured, bewildered.

"You *will*," he said sharply.

Then, leaning even closer, he delivered the final blow, "*Impostor.*"

Belén staggered back.

"*Me?* You're calling *me* an impostor?"

"Yes. I don't know anything about your situation, nor do I care to. But I was instructed to give you this message by someone who knows you far better than I do. Now go—and may God forgive you."

Without another word, he turned and walked away.

Stunned and heartbroken, Belén drifted away from the convent like a sleepwalker, her mind in a fog. As she turned a corner, she saw the church doors open and slipped inside, like a wounded doe seeking shelter in the hollow of a rock to wait for death. She *felt* as though she would die. Her hope had been crushed under the weight of that one word—*impostor.*

She slumped into the darkest corner of the church, too numb to pray, her heart drowning in a sea of despair.

Impostor! The accusation echoed endlessly in her mind. Was *that* truly the only message Jorge had for her after seven long years? *Her* Jorge?

The church darkened as evening fell. She barely noticed the sacristan's slow, deliberate footsteps as he moved through the empty space, the jangle of his keys preparing to lock up for the night. By then, her mind had quieted. She whispered a single, hesitant Hail Mary. And from the silence, a thought surfaced:

If this were just about winning back my husband, it wouldn't be worth it. No man is worth fighting for. But my daughter deserves her father... That's all that matters.

Belén took a slow breath, steadying the storm inside her. This wasn't over.

She would return. She would demand to be heard. She would not be dismissed like a shadow, like some nameless, faceless woman swept aside by bureaucracy and indifference.

There had to be a mistake—one she didn't yet understand, but one she would unravel, thread by thread, if necessary.

Yes, she had given a name that wasn't hers. But did that make her a stranger? Did ink on paper carry more weight than the flesh-and-blood truth standing before them?

She didn't need papers for Jorge to recognize her.

Once he saw her—truly saw her—and, more importantly, saw their daughter, no lie in the world could stand against the truth. No rule, no priest, no decree scrawled in an office would erase what they had been, what they still were.

And if Jorge had left Buenos Aires?

Then she would find him. Wherever he had gone, she would go.

She had not crossed oceans, braved humiliation, and fought against the weight of years just to be turned away by the likes of Father Gazapo.

He would not stop her. No one would.

Because her right—before God, before the Church, before heaven itself—was undeniable.

And she would *not* be denied.

And once Jorge saw and heard her, she would accept whatever he decided. Whatever he asked of her would be, for her, *the voice of God*.

She had no intention of fighting against His will. With that thought, she drifted into an exhausted sleep, promising herself that she would obey Jorge's decision—no matter what. Even if it meant sacrificing her own freedom.

Belén woke up different. Stronger. Determined.

No longer would she let herself be crushed by doubt or driven into despair by the selfishness of one man. *God's will could not be twisted to serve a single person's convenience.* Father Gazapo couldn't avoid her forever. Eventually, he would have to face her. He would have to explain why they had labeled *her—her!*—an impostor.

At nine in the morning, she entered the church and positioned herself outside the superior's confessional. She was prepared to wait as long as necessary—an hour, a day, a year. Whatever it took. But she didn't have to wait long.

Less than an hour later, Father Gazapo emerged unexpectedly. As he stepped into the church, his gaze landed on her. He hesitated, shifting uncomfortably despite his usual confidence. After a brief pause, he sighed and walked toward her. Clearly, he had decided it was best to confront the matter head-on.

"If you insist on talking to me," he said, lowering his voice, "we'll do it in the parlor—not here, in a holy place. Go wait for me there while I rinse out the dirty laundry of these parishioners. Then we'll scrub yours down with plenty of soap... *by Caiaphas' beard!*"

Belén turned and made her way to the convent's front gate. The porter glared at her with open hostility, but she met his gaze steadily. He had no choice but to let her in. She waited in the parlor while Father Gazapo finished with his morning penitents. When they finally sat face-to-face an hour later, *he* looked more nervous than *she* did. Belén was the first to speak.

"A tall, broad-shouldered priest... I don't know his name—"

"Father Atlante," Gazapo muttered.

"Yes, that must be him."

"Of course it's him—I sent him."

"Then I need to know something. When he called me an impostor, was that your message, Father Gazapo? Or was it Jorge's?"

"Jorge?" Gazapo scoffed. "I don't know any Jorge."

"The one you call Father Teofano," Belén said, her voice steady. "That's Jorge. *My* husband."

Gazapo's face darkened.

"*Garlic and onions from Egypt!*" he exploded. "Listen to you! So casually, like it's nothing—*Father Manrique is my husband!* Why not claim *I'm* your grandfather while you're at it? It'd be just as believable as you calling yourself María de Guernizo! Can you even prove that's your real name?"

"I can't," Belén admitted calmly. "Because it isn't."

Gazapo blinked.

"So, you *admit* you lied?"

"I had my reasons for using that name," she continued. "But my real name is—"

"*Don't bother!*" Gazapo cut her off. "*I'll tell you what it is!* Let me prove to you that we *didn't* slander you when we sent that message. Half from Father Manrique, half from me."

A realization hit Belén like a flash of lightning. She leaned forward.

"He hasn't *seen* me, has he? And *you* barely know me."

Her voice dropped to a whisper.

"What name do you and Father Manrique believe is mine?"

"What name?" Gazapo scoffed. "*Your real name*, of course—the name of a famous actress, though not exactly from high society."

"Well? Say it."

"Father Manrique knew *exactly* who you were—*he's* the one who exposed you. So come on now, *Teodora Cordero* from the *New Zarzuela Theatre*, why did you try to pass yourself off as this imaginary 'Madame Guernizo' to me and the nuns?"

He leaned back, smug in his certainty that he had shattered her. He watched, waiting for the inevitable collapse—for the tears, for the shame, for the humiliation that should have followed his words like an avalanche.

But Belén didn't break.

For a moment, she pressed her hands over her face—not in despair, but as if steadying something vast and overwhelming inside her. A moment passed. Another.

Then she lowered them.

And when she did, her expression wasn't one of defeat. It was radiant.

Hope—blinding, undeniable, intoxicating hope—lit up her face, rushing through her like breath after suffocation, like light spilling into a room sealed in darkness for far too long.

Her chest lifted with the weight of sudden, crystalline clarity.

"Now I understand everything," she said, her voice steady, brimming with something fierce and new.

Jorge—or Father Manrique, if that was who he had become—had believed she was someone else.

Teodora.

The woman who had haunted his steps for years. The woman who was in Buenos Aires right now.

But she wasn't Teodora.

She never had been.

Gazapo's smugness faltered. Suspicion crept into his narrowed eyes.

"You're not Teodora?" he asked, his voice quieter now, less certain.

"No."

He scoffed, but there was something hollow in it now. A crack in his confidence.

"Oh, how convenient!" he sneered. "And why should I believe yet another lie?"

Belén met his gaze without flinching. For the first time, she wasn't begging. She wasn't pleading. She wasn't defending herself.

She was simply stating what was true.

"I'll prove it to you," she said calmly. "Do you receive newspapers here?"

Gazapo, caught off guard, hesitated.

"Yes, we get them," he admitted. "They're in the convent library—though, honestly, who has time to read more than a few headlines?"

"Then take a little more time," Belén said firmly. "Check *last Sunday's* paper. There's a large advertisement for the Zarzuela

Teodora Cordero is currently performing. Look at her photo, then come back and tell me if she looks *anything* like me. You've judged me too harshly, Father Gazapo. You *owe me* this."

Gazapo shot to his feet without another word, his chair scraping violently against the floor. A cold sweat pricked at his temples as he hurried upstairs to the convent library, his fingers trembling with urgency.

Please, God, let the Sunday paper still be there.

He rifled through the pile of old newspapers, his breath tight in his chest. There. He seized it, his hands shaking as he flipped feverishly through the pages.

And then—he froze.

The world seemed to tilt around him.

Teodora Cordero's portrait stared back at him, clear as day.

And she looked nothing like Belén.

A slow, suffocating horror wrapped around his ribs, squeezing tighter with every passing second. The blood drained from his face. His mouth went dry.

What had they done?

They had accused this woman—this woman who had come in good faith, seeking only truth—of deception, of manipulation, of being an impostor. And yet, the real impostor was not here at all.

A mistake.

A terrible, unforgivable mistake.

But as the weight of his error settled, another, deeper horror gripped him.

This wasn't just about Belén.

This was about Jorge.

Gazapo's stomach twisted violently as the realization crashed down upon him. Jorge Manrique was not simply a mistaken priest.

He was never meant to be a priest at all.

His breath came in sharp, uneven gasps as he ran a shaking hand down his face.

A telegram. It had to be sent immediately.

Father Manrique—Jorge—would have to be stripped of his priestly duties at once, placed under investigation. Because according to canon law…

Gazapo exhaled sharply, gripping the edge of the table as nausea threatened to overtake him.

"Our Lady of Miracles, my dear," he thought bitterly. *"We've really made a mess of things, haven't we?"*

Dragging himself back downstairs, his steps slow and heavy, he re-entered the parlor.

Belén sat where he had left her, unshaken, composed—a woman who had endured humiliation and injustice and had somehow risen above it.

For the first time in years, shame burned through him.

Silently, he lowered himself back into his chair, his throat tightening around the words he never imagined himself saying.

Then, in an uncharacteristic gesture of humility, he reached out and gently patted Belén's hand.

His voice, when it finally came, was rough with regret.

"We're a pair of fools—him and me," he admitted, shaking his head.

Then, with a small, weary smile, he added, "And you, my dear… you're a saint."

Belén's voice softened.

"Can I see him now, Father?"

Gazapo lowered his head.

"No, my child… he's a thousand miles away by now."

Belén's breath caught.

"Did he… run away from me?"

"No," Gazapo sighed. "He ran away from *Teodora*."

"Then he'll come back?" she asked, hope flickering in her voice.

"Not yet," he said. "We have to sort things out first. There's this canon law… Oh, which one is it? *I can't even remember because of you!* But it says that married people can enter religious life only if *both* husband and wife take vows. He's already taken his. Now it's *your* turn, my child. You're a saint already—why not make it *official* and inspire the rest of us poor souls?"

Belén met his gaze with quiet intensity.

"We'll talk about that later, Father Gazapo. Right now, I just want him to come back and meet his *daughter*."

For the first time, Father Gazapo realized he might have lost this battle.

Chapter 8: A Battle of Wills

My Dear Teofano,

If swearing weren't a sin, I'd swear that not even in the blistering heat of my beloved Shanghai have I suffered as much as I am now—thanks to your dear wife, Belén.

Yes, my son. *Your wife.*

There's no doubt about it. *Lord have mercy on us both—she's alive.* The very force of nature that once drove you to the brink of madness is here, in the flesh, and just as relentless as ever. Honestly, had she remained where we *thought* she was—enjoying the beatific vision in heaven—it would have been better for everyone.

Better for *her*, because she'd be basking in God's eternal glory, as Saint Thomas Aquinas so beautifully describes. And better for *us*, because without her, you and I could be building the Chilean mission—your great dream.

Well, my son, that dream has gone straight to hell. Or, more precisely, it has fallen into the hands of the woman who, despite turning our plans to dust, just might end up a saint—if she listens to me. I can already picture it: Belén in a convent, a solemn novice professing her vows, a new Teresa of Ávila in the making.

Though, I must say, she'll be the most *formidable* saint the Church has ever known. She's wild, stubborn, and completely untamable. (*Where on earth did you find this woman, poor Teofano?*) Not that she's wicked—far from it! In fact, *I fear for you*, because you could lose your mind over her *again*. She's the most captivating woman I've ever met—capable of stealing heaven's grace and shaking the gates of hell with a single glance.

She reminds me of Ay-Fa-Chung, the wife of that Chinese mandarin who tormented her husband for years, only to later repent and found an order for reformed women in China. *God forbid Belén takes a similar path!* But knowing her iron will, nothing would surprise me. She's determined to undo everything I've built—but mark my words, she might end up *building something greater*.

She doesn't know where you are—whether you're across the ocean or still hiding in Buenos Aires—but she's determined to find you. And she's not coming with chains.

She's told me again and again that she won't *force* you into anything. She doesn't want you bound to her like a galley slave. She says that once you've spoken to her, *you* will decide what to do—and she will accept your decision.

But my son, there are only *two* ways this can end according to God's law:

1. You return to her, leaving behind the altar and your priestly vocation.
2. She renounces you and enters a convent.

There is no third option.

She *cannot* remain in the world as she is. Yes, canon law allows a wife to take a vow of chastity and live in the secular world while her husband becomes a priest. And honestly, I *do* believe Belén would honor such a vow.

But would it be *safe* for her? No.

A woman with her fire should be *enclosed* for the greater glory of God. We must consider carefully *which* order might suit her best. A Carmelite? A Benedictine? Something stricter, perhaps?

I will do everything in my power to convince her. If she is as strong-willed as you have always said—and as I have now seen for myself— then perhaps, just perhaps, she could become a saint.

A *formidable* one, no doubt.

Pray for me, son. Offer a Mass for this intention—

No, wait! What am I saying? *You can't celebrate Mass!* Or hear confessions. Or perform any priestly duties. The only thing you can do is fast on bread and water, pray, and beat your chest in repentance. Because as long as this woman claims you as her husband, you belong to *her* more than to the Church.

Do you see, my son?

God forgive me, but sometimes I wonder if our Lord Jesus Christ was being *too idealistic* when He said, *"What God has joined together, let no man separate."*

Oh, Lord, what a blasphemous thought—I take it back! I *take it back!* I leave it here only so you can see how even *I* am not immune to the devil's whispers.

I pray that I will have better news for you soon.

Ah, before I forget—

The little girl. *Moramay.*

She had measles, chickenpox, and even a touch of whooping cough, but she's fine now. And *adorable*, I must admit.

I confess, I didn't *fully* believe this entire story until I saw her eyes.

Because my son…they are *identical* to another pair of eyes I know all too well.

Dear Father Gazapo,

When I returned from my journey, eager to lay the foundation for a new Eastern Catholic Missionaries house in Chile, your telegram struck me like a thunderbolt.

Yes—that's the only word for it.

Your message was brief, but it shattered everything.

"Do not celebrate Mass. Do not hear confessions."

The weight of those words was enough to tell me everything. Enough to unravel the fragile order of my priestly life. Enough to confirm the painful truth I had never dared to imagine.

I was not a widower. Not as I had believed all these years.

At first, when you mentioned *Madame Guernizo*, I dismissed it outright. It had to be Teodora—I was sure of it. I knew she had arrived in Buenos Aires, and I knew what she was capable of. I have always been wary of her, always braced for her tricks.

But you were right, and I was wrong.

The moment I received your telegram, I stepped away from the altar, from the confessional, from the sacred duties that had shaped my existence. I placed this impossible, incomprehensible situation in God's hands.

Now, I must speak honestly with you, Father. You may think that my first reaction to your news was despair. Or fear. Or even grief. But no.

When I learned that Belén was alive—*alive*—and searching for me, something else surged within me. Something undeniable.

Joy.

A joy so deep, so overwhelming, that it filled every corner of my soul before I could fight it back.

For the first time in seven years, I allowed myself to remember. *Truly* remember. Not in the way one recalls a name from the past, but in the way one relives a life—breath by breath, heartbeat by heartbeat. I saw her again as she was. The way she smiled, the way she laughed, the way she fit so perfectly at my side.

And I could not help but wonder—*if things had gone differently*...would I have been a happy man? A good husband? A devoted father?

But fate—or perhaps the will of God—tore me away from the woman who was meant to be my life partner, the mother of my children. And that loss led me back to my first calling. The priesthood.

Now, once again, my future stands at a crossroads. But this time, the anguish is far greater. Because this time, *the choice is not mine to make.* It is *hers*. My fate rests in Belén's hands. And if I am to be completely honest with you, Father Gazapo—if I am to strip my soul bare before you—then I must admit something. Even though I have felt every fiber of my being drawn to the priesthood—ever since that first, sacred moment when I heard those words, *"You are a priest forever,"* I was *not* filled with sorrow at the thought that Belén might choose the path that would take me away from it.

No, I did not feel sorrow, and that, Father, *is what shames me most of all*. I am ashamed of my own weakness. Ashamed of my divided heart. *"The spirit is willing, but the flesh is weak."*

And so, I went to the only place I could go. I knelt before the Blessed Sacrament and remained there for an hour, *begging* the Lord to show me the way.

When I finally rose, my prayers had calmed me but there was something else. A strange, lingering sweetness that clung to my soul—one that felt less like *consolation* and more like *temptation*.

Still, I continued my prayers, searching for clarity. Today, as I opened my breviary, my eyes fell upon these words, accompanied by the commentary of Pope St. Gregory, "Whoever leaves home, brothers, sisters, father, mother, wife, children, or lands for my sake will receive a hundredfold and inherit eternal life."

And then, as if my own guardian angel had turned the pages for me, my gaze shifted to Psalm 16, *"The Lord is my portion and my cup; You hold my lot. The boundary lines have fallen for me in pleasant places. Indeed, I have a beautiful inheritance. I bless the Lord who gives me counsel."*

But Father, I must confess something to you. Once, those words filled me with peace. Once, they were sweet upon my tongue. Now, they feel distant. Hollow.

Pray for me, Father. I need it now more than ever.

After reading Teofano's letter, Father Gazapo let out a slow breath, rubbing his temples as if he could knead the frustration from his skull. If he wanted to keep Father Manrique in the Congregation, he would have to fight on *two* fronts now. And one of them was a battle against a woman who was relentless as a storm and just as impossible to contain.

That afternoon, the missionary felt an overwhelming urge to swear— a habit he had been *trying* (with limited success) to avoid. Worse still, he found himself questioning the divine wisdom of certain aspects of creation, despite Scripture's clear instruction.

All the works of the Lord are good; we must not say: this is better than that, for everything will be recognized as good in its time.

But still—*still*—he thought, wouldn't creation have been *better* if God had simply *left that rib inside Adam*?

Hadn't He said, 'It is not good for man to be alone' out of *pity*? Well, look where that had gotten them.

Clenching his fists, he muttered under his breath, "Blessed be every word from Your mouth, Lord, but if You ever decide to create *another* world, take my advice—make it for *men only*. It might be less beautiful, but it'll save You—and us confessors—a *great deal* of trouble. We spend our days untangling earthly messes that You have to sort out in heaven. *Amen.*"

As if to punctuate his unorthodox prayer, a sound echoed down the tiled hallway—the unmistakable shuffle of worn-out slippers against stone.

Here he comes, thought Father Gazapo. *Closer… closer…*

Knock, knock, knock!

The door creaked open before he could respond. The lay porter, his shaggy gray head peeking inside, wasted no time delivering his message.

"She's here."

That was all he said. He didn't need to say more.

The lay brother, having absorbed his superior's exasperation with *her*, no longer referred to Belén by name. She had simply become *"her"*— a vague, exasperated pronoun for the woman who refused to vanish.

Father Gazapo, still clutching Father Manrique's letter—the letter from the *husband of her*—sprang up from his chair.

"Show her into the parlor."

Then, under his breath, he muttered, "Saint Teresa of Jesus, *inspire me*! Help me find the right words to convince this *troublesome* girl to become a saint. She's got *what it takes*—either to shine like a star in heaven or burn like a firebrand in hell…" He exhaled.

"Well? *What are you waiting for?*"

The lay brother hesitated, shifting his weight from one sore foot to the other.

"Well, uh… since I *know* how much her visits irritate you, I… um… sent her away."

Gazapo went rigid.

"WHAT?!"

The lay brother winced.

"Yeah… she's probably halfway home by now."

The old priest's face turned an impressive shade of red.

"Man of God—or the devil! Who *told you* her visits bother me?! *Go! NOW!* Find her, bring her back—I *need* to talk to her!"

The lay brother didn't wait to be told twice. He bolted down the hallway, his worn slippers flapping against the floor, his sore feet barely keeping pace with his newfound sense of urgency. He burst past the convent's screen door, squinting under the harsh afternoon sun as he scanned both sidewalks.

Gone. His heart sank.

Just as he was about to give up, a flicker of movement caught his eye—a familiar dress, disappearing into the church.

There she is. Muttering something that was *probably* a prayer but *might* have been a curse, he hiked up his robe and hurried toward the entrance.

The church was nearly deserted in the stillness of the afternoon, the hush after siesta wrapping the vast nave in an eerie calm. The faint scent of wax and incense lingered from the morning Masses, clinging to the air like a ghost of prayers already spoken.

Only one soul knelt before the altar. The very woman he had been sent to find.

Belén.

She was bowed low before the Blessed Sacrament, her golden hair catching the candlelight, her shoulders trembling with silent, unrestrained tears.

The old friar stopped in his tracks. Something stirred within him—an unfamiliar twinge of remorse. How many times had he dismissed her? Brushed her off as a nuisance, an intruder in a world she had no place in?

And yet, looking at her now, he felt a sudden and disquieting thought slip into his mind.

Who's to say that beneath the silk of her elegant clothes, beneath that golden hair and radiant beauty, she isn't holier than me? Me—with my gruff manners, my dusty cassock, my endless job of sweeping cobwebs from corners no one notices? How would my pride and her devotion weigh on God's scales?

He swallowed hard, then stepped closer, his voice hushed.

"Ma'am," he whispered. "Forgive me. Father Superior sent me to call you—he wants to speak with you."

Belén lifted her face, streaked with tears, and for the first time in days, something flickered in her eyes. A glimmer of hope.

The friar's heart clenched.

Poor girl, he thought. *If she's crying like this, she can't be all bad. Blessed are those who weep.*

She wiped her tears quickly, whispered a quiet *Ave Maria,* and rose to follow him.

The porter's lodge was cool, a welcome relief from the summer heat. Its thick stone walls held the chill of morning, and the red-tiled floor—often splashed with water by the lay brother to keep the dust at bay—gave off the scent of damp earth.

Belén stood alone as the friar went to fetch Father Gazapo. To her right was the parlor where she had been received before. But to her left there was another door she hadn't noticed before.

It bore a simple sign that read *Cloister.* A single word, but one heavy with meaning. In houses of God, such doors marked the sacred boundary—the line no outsider could cross without violating the laws of the Church itself.

A woman could not pass through unless she was royalty. A queen. The wife of a head of state. *Or,* Belén thought, *the wife of a man who now stands on the other side of it.*

She stared at the threshold, her breath shallow. Beyond that door, somewhere in the silence of that hidden world, was the man whom God had joined to her—now separated from her by human laws that dared to defy divine command.

How many times had she read and reread the words that filled her with hope?

"What God has joined together, let no man separate."

Since that day—since the moment everything changed—Belén had been searching.

The day of Moramay's First Communion was when she had seen him again. After all these years, one glance was all it took.

Time had tried to disguise him—the long missionary beard, the weight of a new life draped over his shoulders. It should have made him unrecognizable, but she knew him. Instantly. Unshakably.

And since then, she had searched.

At first, the hunt had been frantic. Days spent wandering streets, watching church doors, listening for whispers of his name. But Buenos Aires was vast, and Jorge—or Father Manrique—had vanished like smoke.

Had he left the city? Fled to another province? Was he already half a world away?

She didn't know. No one knew. Yet—strangely, profoundly—her search no longer felt desperate. The feverish urgency had given way to something quieter, deeper, more unshakable than before, because now, she understood.

She wasn't chasing a man or simply trying to reclaim a husband. She was seeking clarity. She needed to know where she stood—where *he* stood.

She needed to understand her rights as a wife, and he—he needed to understand his obligations as a priest.

There was no more begging, no more pleading with fate. She would find the truth. She would make him face it. And whatever came next…

So be it.

Belén had scoured every book she could find on the indissolubility of Christian marriage. She had devoured their arguments, memorized every doctrine, traced the logic of theologians through centuries of ink and conviction.

Now, she was certain—absolutely certain—there was nothing left to learn. She was ready.

Not just to face Father Gazapo with his fiery exclamations and labyrinthine metaphors, but to stand before an entire council of theologians, if need be. Let them test her. Let them challenge her understanding of the words she could now recite from rote memory, *What therefore God has joined together, let no man separate.*

There was no doubt in her mind. She had every right—every sacred right—to demand the return of her husband. And yet…

That husband—Jorge—was now something else. A priest. A man who, among all men, had been set apart. A man who had been marked, sealed, transformed into a mediator between earth and heaven. His hands, consecrated by sacred oil, held a power greater than that of angels. He could summon the presence of Christ Himself. With a word, with a whisper, he could turn bread and wine into the Body and Blood of God. He could stand at the threshold of eternity and cleanse souls, binding and loosing on earth what would be bound and loosed in heaven.

And she—she, a mere woman—was going to ask him to *give it all up*? To leave behind his priesthood, his calling, his mission? To set aside the crown of his sacred vows for the simple title of *husband*? To step down from the altar and become an ordinary man—just because she could not bring herself to renounce him?

Her confidence wavered.

She had told herself—sworn to herself—that she would accept whatever Jorge decided.

But what if his answer echoed Father Gazapo's? What if he took her hands, praised her goodness, looked at her with that kind, steady gaze of his—and told her she should *become a nun*? What if he said that was where her holiness lay? That she should embrace sacrifice, not for her sake, but for others? As if the world needed *her* to set an example.

The thought filled her with unbearable sorrow, because she knew the truth.

Jorge had never belonged to her. Not fully. Not in the way a man belongs to a woman. He had always belonged to God.

And if she were truly honest—*if she were stripped bare of every selfish longing, every hope, every dream*—she would have to admit it. That had always been his true calling.

Her fists clenched, nails biting into her palms, as she fought back tears. How *far* she felt from sainthood. Her soul was fire and ice, light and shadow—never settled, never still.

Her heart, fragile and fierce, sometimes rang like a golden chalice, and sometimes shattered like a clay pot.

Two unshakable marks had sealed Jorge's fate.

One was *hers*—the mark of their love, given and received, etched into the very marrow of their existence. The words of the Song of Songs echoed in her mind, words she had carried with her through every mile of searching, through every year of loss, "Set me as a seal upon your heart, as a seal upon your arm; for love is as strong as death, and jealousy as fierce as the grave."

But jealousy? She felt none. Who could she be jealous of—*God*?

No.

If she *demanded* Jorge from Him, He would return him to her. Had He not already promised as much? And yet…

There was another seal upon him. One just as permanent. His priesthood.

She knew from her catechism that holy orders left an indelible mark— one no force in heaven or on earth could erase. Not time. Not human will. Not even the fires of hell itself. Jorge had been consecrated for eternity.

Yes, his priesthood had been born of a mistake—an error of fate, a trick of destiny. He had believed himself a widower when he was not. But his ordination was *valid*.

He could no longer serve as a priest while she lived. But if she were to die… or if she were to take the veil and vow perpetual chastity…he could return to his vocation as if nothing had ever changed.

She understood this all too well. Knowing the weight of his dignity, the depth of his sacred vows…how could she ask him to cast it all aside?

To become not a *man of God*, but simply a *man of one woman*?

No.

She would not *drag him down* into a half-life, bound to her by chains of obligation.

If he came back to her, he would come willingly. If not—she would close her door to him forever. She would live as a widow.

But even if she accepted widowhood for herself, she could not accept it for *her daughter*.

Moramay deserved her father. She had searched the world for him, not just for herself, but for the child who bore his name, his eyes, his very soul. Could God—*truly*—have established a law so harsh that it would tear families apart? That it would leave a daughter fatherless, a child an orphan while her father still lived?

She had built her case on scripture. On doctrine. On law. But now, as she stood on the edge of certainty, as the weight of human love and divine law pressed against her heart, she faced the one question no book had ever answered.

Would God ask this of her?

Would He *truly* demand that she walk away?

Overwhelmed by the storm of thoughts crashing within her, Belén turned once again to books.

This time, she sought out everything she could find on priestly celibacy. She read indiscriminately. She poured through Catholic texts, secular arguments, anything that might shed light on the rigid, unyielding law that now stood between her and the man she loved.

But instead of clarity, she found only deeper confusion.

The more she read, the more tangled her thoughts became. Was this law truly unbreakable? Was it divine will, or merely the product of men—men who had debated, rewritten, and enforced it for centuries?

Her exhaustion mounted, her heart restless with every page.

And like many who drift too close to the edge of heresy, she convinced herself that her case—her *unique* case—deserved nothing less than the Pope's personal intervention.

A bold thought took hold of her. *What if her case set a precedent? What if she could prompt the Church to reconsider—just as it had for Eastern Rite Catholic priests, who had been allowed to remain married since the 7th century? Why should Jorge's priesthood be an unbreakable chain, when for others, it was not?*

The whirlwind of arguments, canon law, and historical exceptions filled her mind until she felt armed—*invincible.*

Surely, even Father Gazapo would have to acknowledge the strength of her case.

She would not go to him merely to plead. She would go to *fight*. Not just for herself but for the countless others who might one day find themselves caught in the same cruel snare.

Visiting hours at the Eastern Catholic Missionaries were long over, but Belén hardly cared.

She dressed carefully, selecting a new design of her own making—printed fabric in bold, striking colors. It was a dress that demanded attention, as much a statement as a shield.

Then, with her head held high, she marched to the Mission.

At the gate, the porter barely looked at her before delivering his cold verdict.

"Father Gazapo cannot see you."

Belén's stomach twisted. *Not again.*

The silent walls, the closed doors, the way they always tried to push her away—it felt like a conspiracy.

Or worse—*a verdict already passed against her.*

Frightened, disheartened, but too proud to plead, she turned and left.

As she passed the heavy doors of the church, she hesitated. Where else could she go? Where else would she find refuge now, except in the one place that had always been open to the lost?

The doors creaked as she stepped inside. The cool darkness of the church enveloped her. Candles flickered in their golden stands. The scent of incense still lingered in the air.

Without thinking, she sank to her knees. She did not pray. She simply knelt. In that moment of stillness, all the weight, all the doubt, all the sorrow came crashing over her.

She did not hear the soft footsteps approaching until Brother Gorgonio gently placed a hand on her shoulder.

"Come," he said. "Father Gazapo wants to see you."

Father Gazapo arrived in a whirlwind, his robes rustling as he swept into the porter's lodge. He had been waiting for this.

He found her standing in the middle of the hall, radiant in her summer dress, red as fire, scattered with white and blue prints of sailboats, seagulls, and anchors.

For a moment, something flickered in him. Something dangerously close to admiration. Then he noticed the pattern. The tailor had sewn it all without care for orientation, leaving seagulls flying upside down, sailors standing on their heads, ships floating keel-up, and anchors dangling uselessly from the sky.

"A perfect symbol of its owner," he thought wryly. "She turns everything upside down. God help us if we let this Shulamite charm us."

But he quickly recovered, clasping his hands behind his back as he leveled her with a look of detached authority.

She extended her hand in greeting. He took it, but barely.

Then, with cold politeness, he said, "So, my child, what nonsense have you come to tell me today?"

Belén hesitated. Brother Gorgonio was still in the hall, oiling the old iron lock of the gate a few steps away. She did not want an audience. Only when Father Gazapo gestured toward the parlor did she step forward, following him inside.

The convent's parlor was as austere as she remembered—wooden chairs lined the walls, their seats worn smooth by years of use. A couple of small tables stood scattered with *Propagation of the Faith* magazines, their pages curling at the edges. A statuette of a Guardian Angel stood on one of the tables, its large blond head slightly oversized, its porcelain face frozen in a gentle smile. At its belt hung a piggy bank slot. Belén knew the game.

She reached into her red leather purse—also decorated with those *impossibly* upside-down sailors and seagulls—and pulled out a single gold coin. She dropped it into the slot.

The Guardian Angel bowed deeply in thanks. For a brief second, she almost smiled then turned and took a seat.

Father Gazapo sat across from her, separated by a small wooden table—his expression one of patience, but also something else. A readiness. A waiting.

Belén had come armed with arguments but so had he. The battle was about to begin.

Chapter 9: Would You Like that in Latin?

"Three weeks ago, Father Gazapo, something happened to me—something so unimaginable, so *impossible*—that even in my wildest dreams, I never could have foreseen it."

The old priest tilted his head, already bracing himself.

"What happened, my child?"

"You haven't forgotten, Father."

Her voice was steady, but the weight behind it was unmistakable.

"I haven't stopped thinking about it for a single moment. And I've come to speak with you because it doesn't just affect my past, it *defines* my present. It may very well determine my entire future, too."

Gazapo sighed, shaking his head.

"Dramatic as always. Listening to you, one would think you had come face to face with the Antichrist—who, by the way, is destined to be the most terrifying figure in human history."

"I came face to face with my *husband*, Father," Her voice sharpened. "who is now a *priest*. And I watched him place the Eucharist into the hands of *our daughter*."

She leaned forward.

"Does that seem insignificant to you?"

Gazapo fell silent for a moment.

Then, rubbing his chin, he muttered, "Insignificant? Not in the slightest. That might be one of the strangest situations I've ever encountered."

"Then tell me," Belén pressed. "What do we do *now*?"

"Ah! *That* is the great question, isn't it?" He spread his hands dramatically. "What *do* we do?"

Then, with a pointed look, he added, "But you already know what *I* think you should do."

She stiffened as he continued, his voice growing more solemn.

"The Lord has called that heart—one that was always meant to be *His*—and freed it from the earthly distractions that once led it astray."

Her breath caught.

"Don't say that, Father," she whispered. "Don't you realize how much that *hurts* me?"

Gazapo sighed, relenting.

"Alright, alright, no offense meant, my child. But let's not fool ourselves here—you, with your sailboats, sailors, and seagulls, turned his whole world upside down."

"I am *his wife before God*," she countered, her voice ringing through the small parlor.

"I don't doubt it," Gazapo admitted. "But he has also heard an *eternal* voice—the voice of the Gospel, in Matthew 19—telling him, *'Whoever leaves wife and children for My sake will receive a hundred times as much and inherit eternal life...'*"

Belén's eyes flashed.

"But when he heard that, Father, he *wasn't free* to leave his wife and child!"

Gazapo opened his mouth, but she didn't let him interrupt.

"Long before that—forty centuries before, to be exact—he heard *another* word from God."

Gazapo hesitated.

"And what word would that be?"

Belén leaned forward, her voice unwavering.

"The word from *Genesis*, Father."

She held his gaze as she recited, slow and deliberate, *"'It is not good for man to be alone,'* said the Lord after creating Adam. *So He made Eve as his companion and gave this command, 'For this reason a man shall leave his father and mother and be united to his wife, and the two shall become one flesh.'"*

Silence fell between them. Gazapo drummed his fingers on the arm of his chair, his mind racing for a counterargument. But Belén wasn't finished.

"And the Lord also said to them," she continued, her voice steady, "'*Be fruitful and multiply; fill the earth...*'"

She arched a brow.

"Would you like me to say it in Latin?"

Gazapo's composure cracked.

"Ta-ta-ta!" he spluttered, waving a hand. "Where did you *learn* all this, my child?"

Belén allowed herself the smallest smile.

"It's in the *Holy Bible*, Father."

Gazapo scoffed.

"I *know* that, daughter. But who's been whispering these things in your ear lately?"

Belén folded her hands primly in her lap.

"Who?" she echoed. "No one but myself."

She tilted her chin, her eyes gleaming with defiance.

"These past three weeks, I've read *every* book I could find on the matter."

Gazapo exhaled sharply, rubbing his temples.

Lord help him.

This was going to be a *long* conversation.

"Well, it's clear you've read *more* than you should," Father Gazapo grumbled, rubbing his temples. "Saint Paul *warned* us about this in his second letter to Timothy. He spoke of those who, caught up in the contradictions of so-called knowledge, have lost their faith. And in his first letter to Timothy, he commands *women* to remain silent, to listen in submission, and not to assume authority over their husbands."

Belén lowered her lashes in mock humility.

"Oh, I know that letter well, Father."

Her voice was syrupy sweet, the dangerous kind of sweetness.

"But if you turn just a little further in the same letter, you'll find another passage that says, *'Deacons must be husbands of one wife.'*"

She paused, then, with a knowing smile, she added, "Would you like me to say it in Latin? *Diaconi sint unius uxoris viri...*"

"*Snakes and frogs of the Red Sea!*" the missionary roared, his face darkening. "Who taught you Latin, you *little menace*?!"

Belén only tilted her head, meeting his glare with a gaze as piercing as a dagger.

Then, softly, she asked, "Father, is my husband a *deacon* or a *priest*?"

"He's a *priest*, child! A *priest!*" Gazapo threw up his hands. "Oh, poor woman, do you even realize the depths you're sinking into? He is a priest *forever*, according to the order of Melchizedek!"

"Then," Belén continued smoothly, "there's *another* passage from that same letter that fits him even better. The one that begins... Would you like me to say it in Latin?"

"*Enough, you wretched girl!*" Gazapo shouted, practically leaping from his chair. "There's a passage better suited for *you* in the second letter to Timothy! Let me spare you the Latin and say it in *plain English*, 'In the last days, difficult times will come. People will be lovers of themselves, arrogant, blasphemous, and disobedient... They worm their way into households and captivate *weak-willed women, who are always learning but never able to come to a knowledge of the truth.'*"

His voice rang through the small parlor, bouncing off the walls like a thunderclap.

"This *endless curiosity* of yours, this obsession with things beyond your understanding—it's proof enough that the end times are near!"

Belén sat perfectly still. The storm of words crashed over her, but she remained untouched, unmoved. And *that*—more than anything— unnerved Father Gazapo.

He expected a reaction. A flinch. A scowl. *Something.*

Thinking he had finally silenced her, he allowed himself one last jab, laced with mockery.

"Well?" He leaned forward. "Would you like me to say *that* in Latin too?"

Belén blinked once, twice.

Then, with a glimmer of amusement in her golden eyes, she asked, "Tell me, Father, if the Holy Catholic Church allows Eastern Rite priests to marry, why doesn't it grant the same privilege to those in the Western Rite?"

Gazapo opened his mouth. But before he could speak, she pressed on, relentless.

"Aren't they just as much priests as the others? Don't they have the *same* power to consecrate the bread and wine, transforming them into the Body and Blood of Our Lord Jesus Christ? Don't they also have the *authority* to forgive sins in confession? And if both Eastern and Western priests share the *same sacred duties*—don't they also share the *same human needs*?

Didn't *God Himself* say, 'It is not good for man to be alone'? And doesn't His command to 'be fruitful and multiply and fill the earth' apply to *all* men and women equally?"

A charged silence filled the room.

Then, with a playful smile, she added, "Would you like me to say it in Latin?"

Father Gazapo groaned, dropping his head into his hands.

"*For the love of God, no!*" He exhaled sharply. "Once is *more* than enough, my child. Just—just *get it all out now.* Every last bit of nonsense these books have stuffed into your head."

He waved a hand, already exhausted.

"Speak it, shout it, *sing* it, or bray like a mule if you must—I'll listen! I *swear* I'll answer every one of your questions. But Lord help me, I may mutter a few curses under my breath while I do."

Belén chuckled, entirely unbothered by his exasperation. She had him exactly where she wanted him.

"Alright then, Father," she said, settling in comfortably. "Let's begin."

She folded her hands in her lap, the very image of patience.

"I've read that until the Council of Trent in the 16th century, priests in the Latin Rite were allowed to marry. Is that true?"

Gazapo's nostrils flared.

"Say *everything* you need to say, and *then* I'll respond."

His jaw was clenched. His forehead was beaded with sweat. He bit his lip—*hard*—to keep from shouting the words burning in his throat. Not since his days leading a militia patrol during the English Civil

War had he felt such an overwhelming urge to curse someone into oblivion.

All for the love of God... he thought bitterly.

Then, trying *desperately* to keep his temper, he sighed, "Speak, daughter of... the *Milky Way!*"

Belén smirked.

"Very well," she said smoothly. "I also read that it *was* Pope Gregory VII who prohibited priests from marrying in the 11th century…"

Gazapo inhaled sharply. Lord *help* him. This was going to be a *long* afternoon.

"Wait, wait, wait!" Father Gazapo threw up his hands. "Was it the *16th century* or the *11th*? Even *you* can't keep your own facts straight!"

Belén lifted her chin.

"Some authors say one thing…"

"And others say another!" Gazapo shot back. "So, what do *you* believe?"

"Nothing, Father," she said sweetly. "I'm asking *you*. And I'll believe whatever you tell me."

Gazapo exhaled sharply, rubbing his temples.

"Well," he muttered, "as you've no doubt discovered in your *mountain* of books, critics of the Church have all sorts of theories. Some claim priestly celibacy was a rule imposed by Pope Gregory VII in the *11th century*. Others blame the Council of Trent in the *16th century*. And there are even those—though I doubt you've read *them*—who say celibacy was just a tool to keep the clergy under Rome's control."

162

He narrowed his eyes at her.

"But *they all forget one thing*—celibacy wasn't some bureaucratic rule cooked up by popes or councils. It was *Christ Himself* who introduced the idea of virginity and celibacy."

Belén crossed her arms, waiting.

Gazapo leaned forward, warming to his subject.

"Seven hundred years before Christ, Isaiah prophesied that the Messiah would be born of a *virgin*—an *unthinkable* concept for a world that prized fertility above all else. Then came *John the Baptist*, Christ's forerunner—*also* a virgin. And the Apostle John? The beloved disciple? *Another virgin*—the only one who rested his head on Jesus' chest at the Last Supper."

Belén arched a brow, unimpressed.

"And when Jesus spoke about marriage," Gazapo pressed on, "when He *forbade divorce*—which Moses had allowed—the disciples were *so shocked* that they said, 'Then maybe it's better not to marry at all!'"

"And what did Jesus do?" he challenged. "He *did not* correct them. Instead, He *praised* celibacy, saying it was a higher calling *for those given the grace to accept it.* His final words on the matter were: *'Let anyone who can accept this, accept it.'*"

His voice softened.

"Not everyone *can* accept it, my child. Few truly *understand* the value of celibacy. But the Church has known it from the very beginning. In those early days, it wasn't *easy* to find men willing to give up marriage entirely—so the Church accepted married men into the priesthood…"

He held up a finger.

"But *only* under one condition: that they would live as *brothers and sisters* with their wives. They had to give up their marital rights for the sake of their sacred duty."

Belén saw her opening and took it.

"But *Saint Paul* calls marriage a *great sacrament*," she said smoothly.

"Of course it's a great sacrament!" Gazapo snapped. "Yet *Saint Paul himself* remained celibate! And in his letter to the Corinthians—where he lays out the *very foundation* of Catholic teaching on marriage— what does he say? *'I wish that all of you were as I am (celibate), but each has their own gift from God.'*"

His voice rang with triumph.

"And he makes it *even clearer* when he says: *'The unmarried man is concerned with the Lord's affairs—how he can please the Lord. But the married man is concerned with the affairs of this world—how he can please his wife—and his interests are divided.'*"

Belén nodded, as if she agreed.

"But just before that," she said sweetly, "Saint Paul *also* says—and I *know* Your Reverence won't contradict me—*'Are you bound to a wife? Don't seek to be free. Are you free from a wife? Don't seek a wife.'*"

Gazapo shot up from his chair.

"Thunder and lightning from Mount Sinai!" he bellowed. "What version of the Bible are you even reading?! It must be some Protestant translation!"

Belén's face was the picture of innocence.

"Is it *wrong*?" she asked. "I can read it to you in Latin, if you prefer. It's from the translation by *Monsignor Straubinger*, a *Catholic* professor at the Seminary of La Plata. Are you saying *he* is incorrect?"

Gazapo clenched his jaw.

"No, no, it's *not* wrong," he grumbled. "Too *accurate*, actually—*suspiciously* so. The problem isn't with the text. It's with *you* and your—" he gestured wildly "—your *infuriating* memory, twisting scripture to suit your argument."

Belén tilted her head.

"I'm *listening*, Father."

Gazapo huffed.

"I brought up Saint Paul's letter to show you that priestly celibacy *wasn't invented* by Gregory VII or the Council of Trent. It existed *from the beginning*."

Belén's eyes gleamed.

"But *that's not the issue here*," she said.

"No, *that's not the issue at all!*" she went on, her voice gaining strength. "The *real* issue is this - if priesthood is a *permanent* sacrament and marriage is *indissoluble*, then when someone like my husband finds himself in this situation—" she took a breath "—the *only* solution is for the Church to allow him to *live with his wife*."

Gazapo nearly choked.

"*Vipers of Gilboa! Judas' own noose!*" he gasped. "Go on—go on, you *rose of Jericho*! Finish your argument, and *then* I'll answer."

Belén leaned forward.

"If a priest's ordination can't be undone," she said, "and if his vows to his *wife* can't be undone either, then why shouldn't the Church allow him to *fulfill both?*"

Her voice was steady, relentless.

"Just like the *holy patriarchs* did—like *Melchizedek*—the great priest *you yourself* mentioned—who was also a *husband* and *father.*"

Her gaze burned.

"If the Church allows *Eastern Rite* Catholic priests to *marry*, why not extend that *same privilege* to those in the *Latin Rite?* Wouldn't it be *fairer?* More *reasonable?*"

Gazapo was glaring at her, but he didn't interrupt.

Belén pressed on.

"Men who constantly work closely with *women and children* in their ministry—shouldn't *they* have a stable home? A wife? *Children of their own?* Wouldn't that give them *greater wisdom* when advising others? Wouldn't it *protect* them from temptation—or even from *false accusations?*"

Gazapo let out a strangled noise, somewhere between a groan and a prayer, but he *still* didn't stop her.

"Didn't *Saint Paul* say that *bishops* should be 'the husband of *one wife*' and should *manage their households and children well?*" Belén continued. "And didn't he say the *same* about *deacons?* Doesn't that mean the Apostle *actually preferred* married men as bishops and priests?"

Gazapo clasped his hands as if in prayer.

"Balaam's donkey, you who once debated with a prophet—please save this girl from her nonsense!"

Belén frowned.

"Did I say something *foolish*, Father?"

Gazapo sighed.

"No, child. You didn't say *something* foolish. You said *many* foolish things."

And as he rubbed his temples, Belén simply smiled.

The debate had only *just* begun.

"More importantly," Father Gazapo pressed on, his voice firm, "since the time of Saint Paul, there has been an unbroken tradition—married men who became priests, especially bishops, would make a solemn agreement with their wives to live in *complete* continence. They renounced marital relations, dedicating themselves fully to God's service.

"This has been the rule since Christ Himself walked the earth. Do you recall, my child, when Saint Peter asked Jesus what reward the apostles would receive for leaving everything behind to follow Him?

"Jesus' answer was clear: *'Anyone who leaves home, brothers, parents, wife, or children for My sake will receive a hundred times more and inherit eternal life.'*"

Father Gazapo leaned forward, seizing the moment as Belén fell silent.

"So, if we were to twist Saint Paul's words as *you* are doing, then neither Saint Peter, who *left everything*, could have been Pope, nor Saint John, who remained *unmarried*, a bishop."

Belén didn't respond, and for the first time since the conversation began, she hesitated. Sensing an advantage, Gazapo pressed on.

"Besides," he added, his tone softening slightly, "even if married priests were once allowed, the Church has *every right* to establish new disciplinary rules. Laws change with time, culture, and necessity. Every society, every government *adapts* its laws—why should the Church be any different?"

"But don't you think, Father," Belén interjected, "that a married priest might be *better* equipped to counsel his parishioners? Wouldn't having a wife and family give him wisdom in guiding others? And wouldn't it *protect* him from temptation?"

Father Gazapo let out a sharp breath, shaking his head.

"Belén, this isn't a matter of doctrine—it's *discipline*. We can *debate* priestly celibacy without falling into heresy, *yes*. But understand this—the Catholic Church may allow *some* priests to be married, but only *before* ordination."

"Is there really a difference?" she asked, eyes narrowing.

"A *huge* one," Gazapo shot back. "In the Eastern Catholic Churches—Greeks, Melkites, Ruthenians, Romanians, Armenians, Syrians, Maronites, even the Chaldeans in India—young men preparing for priesthood can marry *before* receiving major orders. But once they take those vows, *they cannot marry*. And if their wives die, *they cannot remarry*. Even in their system, bishops must be *celibate*."

"But still," Belén insisted, "priestly celibacy is a *disciplinary* rule, not a *dogma*. What's stopping the Pope from extending the Eastern Church's privilege to the Latin Rite? He *could*, couldn't he?"

Gazapo sighed.

"Technically, yes," he admitted. "But he *won't*. And he *shouldn't*. Even in the Eastern Catholic Churches, the number of married priests is *shrinking*. Centuries of experience have proven the *wisdom* of priestly celibacy.

"Obedience. Chastity. Poverty. These are the pillars that protect the Catholic Church from the chaos of heresy. Look at the Protestants—

hundreds of splintered sects, all breaking apart because their ministers are tied down by the burdens of family, ambition, money.

"When a priest *abandons* his vocation, what does he do first? He renounces his vows. He finds a wife. And soon, he's chasing after material wealth."

Belén sat back, silent. The fire that had fueled her arguments flickered. She had come here believing she was armed with unshakable reasoning, but one by one, Father Gazapo had dismantled them. Sensing her wavering, he leaned in for the final strike.

"You've brought up the Eastern Churches more than once, my child," he said, his voice low but firm. "So, listen carefully. This 'privilege' they have—or rather, this *burden*—has been a slow poison draining the life from them for centuries."

Belén frowned.

"You mean their priests' marriages?"

Gazapo exhaled.

"This wound runs deep," he began. "Its roots trace back to a troubled council in the Byzantine Empire at the end of the *7th century*. A dark time—war, heresies, confusion. The Church was under siege, often from within. The Roman Empire had split—one emperor ruled in Byzantium, another in Rome. While the Pope in Rome held *true* spiritual authority, the Byzantine emperors *resented* it. They wanted a *puppet* Church—one that *they* controlled.

"In 691, Emperor Justinian II—obsessed with theology but *blinded* by politics—convened a council of bishops from his empire *without* Rome's approval. This gathering, the *Quinisext Council*, wasn't universal. It was *regional*. The Roman Church had *always* upheld priestly celibacy. But the Byzantine bishops, eager to assert independence, *rejected* this tradition. They decreed that married men *could* become priests and continue living with their wives—though bishops had to remain celibate. No priest, however, could marry *after* ordination. This single decision planted a *weakness* in the Eastern Church's discipline—one that has *never* healed."

Belén smirked.

"Then why," she asked, "has the Pope *continued* to accept this 'flawed' council? If it was so illegitimate, why not *reject it* and enforce the same celibacy rule everywhere? That would end the hypocrisy—*one Church, one rule*."

Gazapo sighed.

"That, my child, is the *wisdom* of the Church. Doctrine never changes—but *discipline* must take into account time, place, tradition, culture. The Church is like a *mother*—merciful to weakness, never ruled by *pride*. The Eastern Church had been cut off from Rome for centuries. When some branches finally returned to obedience, the Popes, in their mercy, allowed them to *keep* certain customs rather than drive them away again. And what is the result? Even in the East, more and more priests are choosing *celibacy* on their own. Over time, the *discipline* is correcting itself."

Belén inhaled deeply. Her mind spun with arguments, counterarguments, contradictions. But she *couldn't* give up. This wasn't just about doctrine. This wasn't about *church politics*. This was *about Jorge*.

"We've strayed *again*, Father," she said, voice unwavering. "This isn't about Eastern or Latin rites. It's not about celibacy or the confessional seal. This is about *my husband*."

Gazapo groaned.

"*By the patience of holy Job!* There you go again!" He rubbed his temples. "Haven't we *established* that a Latin Rite priest *cannot* have a wife?"

Belén's eyes darkened.

"Well, *he does*."

"*Did,* my dear," Gazapo corrected tiredly. "*Did.* But he left her behind to answer a *higher* calling. He followed the voice of God. And she— well, she *agreed* to let him go."

"I *never* agreed to that!" Belén shot back. "*No one* asked me! Because *everyone* thought I was dead! I wasn't in heaven, Father—I was *here. Alive!*"

For once, Gazapo hesitated.

Then, muttering under his breath, "Forgive me, child, but honestly, it wouldn't have been so bad if— Oh, what am I even saying?!"

Belén's brow arched.

"I'm wondering the *same* thing, Father."

They locked eyes—a silent duel, neither willing to retreat.

Finally, Gazapo exhaled.

"Tell me, child. What is it you *want*? What is your *plan*?"

Belén's fire dimmed just slightly.

Quietly, she whispered, "What should I do, Father?"

Gazapo softened.

"It is not *I* who will show you, my dear, but the *Master* Himself. *'I am the Way, the Truth, and the Life.'*"

Belén's hands clenched. She *knew* what he meant. She just *wasn't ready* to accept it.

Chapter 10: A War on Two Fronts

About twelve miles from Buenos Aires, where the great Paraná River branches out into the sprawling Río de la Plata estuary, stretched a vast expanse of low-lying land—wild, untamed, and prone to flooding. With every torrential rain, the river swelled beyond its banks, spilling muddy waters over the fields. Yet, what seemed like destruction was also creation. Over centuries, those same floodwaters had left behind a legacy of rich, fertile soil—earth so dark and deep that it promised prosperity to anyone bold enough to tame it.

But taming it was no small feat.

To wrest a living from this land, settlers had to build embankments, dikes, and drainage channels—an unending battle against a river that refused to be mastered. It was here that a determined group of southern Italian immigrants—mostly Calabrians and Sicilians—had made their home. Drawn by the promise of abundant harvests, they endured the relentless cycle of creation and destruction, watching helplessly as their fields flourished one season, only to vanish beneath floodwaters the next.

Still, they persevered.

With their backs bent and their hands stained with the rich Argentine soil, they transformed the region into a thriving agricultural haven, supplying Buenos Aires with an endless bounty of fruits and vegetables.

Though they called themselves Italians, their roots reached further back—to Greece, to the time of the Byzantine Empire. Their ancestors had crossed the sea to Sicily and Calabria centuries before, bringing with them not just their language and traditions but the fierce endurance of Eastern cultures. They clung to their Byzantine Catholic faith, practicing their rites and rituals even when no priest was there to guide them. Their customs, their prayers, their way of life—these were things no flood could wash away.

And where there was land, there was always wine.

The love of vineyards was in their blood, inherited from the sun-drenched hills of their forefathers. One day, an enterprising farmer looked at the ridges formed by the drainage ditches—scraps of land considered worthless for crops—and saw opportunity. Instead of leaving them barren, he planted grapevines along the mounds. The vines took root, stretching their tendrils deep into the soil, thriving where nothing else had.

Soon, the colony was producing wines to rival those of the Old World—barrels upon barrels of deep, ruby reds as rich as those of the Rhône Valley, and golden, honeyed whites as sweet as the wines of Cyprus. What had once been dismissed as unworkable land became the heart of a flourishing vineyard, a testament to the settlers' ingenuity and resilience.

Beyond the farms and vineyards, the region had other riches to offer. The nearby Delta teemed with fish, flocks of wild ducks skimmed the water at dawn, and groves of fruit trees stood heavy with ripening harvests. For those who loved the land, who found joy in the rhythm of nature, this place was paradise—an untamed world, shaped not by the powerful but by the stubborn hands of those who refused to yield.

As Mr. Burns wandered the countryside with Kitra, he found himself struck by a strange sense of familiarity. The landscape—vast, fertile, and dotted with waterways—reminded him of another place, another time. It was like stepping into the echoes of his past, back to the archipelago where he had met his wife, where his first children had been born, where the rhythm of land and sea had shaped his life.

That resemblance ignited something deep within him. A longing. A vision.

He wanted to claim a piece of this land as his own, to till its soil with his own hands, to build something lasting.

For months, the dream consumed him.

Belén, always ready for a new adventure, encouraged him with boundless enthusiasm. José María, restless and weary of searching for work that could match the strength in his hands—hands once accustomed to plunging deep into the sea, harvesting pearls—saw in it a chance to regain his purpose.

But the locals shook their heads. Buying land here? *Impossible.*

Generations of farmers had spent their lives battling the river, reclaiming the land from the floods, shaping the wilderness into fields, orchards, and vineyards. This land was their legacy. Their pride. Farms were passed down like family heirlooms, guarded fiercely, never sold to outsiders.

But Mr. Burns was not a man to abandon a dream once it had taken root. The Irish were known for their relentless spirit—so much like the Basques in their stubbornness—and he had inherited every ounce of it. Even if years passed and the world forgot, *he* would not. He would wait. And when the rarest of opportunities finally presented itself, he would strike.

And then, like fate had been listening, the impossible happened. One of the finest properties in New Syracuse—the name given to the Italo-Greek colony—suddenly became available. Its owner had died without heirs, and by law, the estate passed to the School Board. Instead of keeping it, they decided to auction it off.

It was a dream of a farm—250 acres of rolling orchards, young vineyards brimming with promise, lush alfalfa fields, and a thriving dairy operation. The land was among the most coveted in the region, not just for its fertility but for the wealth it could generate.

The price? *400,000 pesos.* A fortune, yes—but one *within reach.*

For men and women who had once carved their living from the pearl-laden waters of Insulinda, who had amassed wealth from the sea and held fast to it with the wisdom of those who knew what it was to start with nothing, this was an investment worth making. There was no hesitation.

Belén, Mr. Burns, and José María pooled their resources, sealing a pact that bound them together—not just as business partners, but as pioneers of their own destiny. This land would be *theirs.*

They would farm it with their own hands, cut out the middlemen, ensure that every ounce of profit went into their own pockets—not into the hands of strangers who had never felt the sting of labor, or the satisfaction of a harvest well earned. On the land where no one believed they could set foot, they would build a future—one harvest at a time.

The air inside the auction hall crackled with tension. Belén, Mr. Burns, and José María had already fallen under the spell of the land—*La Alquería,* a jewel of orchards, vineyards, and pastures, its soil rich with promise. But they weren't the only ones determined to claim it.

Across the room, a coalition of Italian-Greek families had gathered, bound by a single purpose - to keep the estate within their own community.

It was a battle neither side could afford to lose; and if there was one thing Belén thrived on, it was a battle.

She stood at the center of it all, her unwavering confidence matched by two equally determined allies—men willing to risk everything at her command.

The bidding war erupted the moment the auctioneer announced the opening price of 400,000 pesos. At first, their opponents played cautiously, inching forward in careful steps, raising their bids by increments of a thousand pesos.

But Mr. Burns wasn't here to play safe. He struck back hard, raising the stakes by ten, twenty, forty thousand pesos at a time—a strategy meant to rattle the opposition, to shake their confidence, to break their will before they even realized what was happening.

The tension climbed with every bid.

Five hundred thousand. Six hundred. Seven. Eight.

The hall had become a furnace of whispers and gasps, the weight of each new number pressing down on the room. The rival families exchanged glances, hesitant now, their initial unity starting to crack.

Then, just when it seemed like they were faltering, a voice rang out, bold and unyielding.

"Nine hundred thousand!"

A stunned silence followed.

Mr. Burns and José María froze for a heartbeat, their confidence momentarily shaken. The number was staggering—an audacious leap meant to force them out of the fight once and for all.

But Belén didn't flinch. She stepped forward, her voice cutting through the heavy silence like a blade.

"One million."

A collective gasp rippled through the room. The auctioneer barely hesitated. His gavel slammed down, its sharp crack sealing the fate of *La Alquería*.

Sold!

The news swept through the colony like wildfire. *La Alquería*—one of the most treasured estates in New Syracuse—had been taken by outsiders. The locals could do nothing but watch as Belén, Mr. Burns, and José María walked out victorious.

For the defeated bidders, the only solace in their loss was the belief that the newcomers—reckless, impulsive, and completely unprepared—would run the farm into ruin. They imagined *La Alquería's* orchards overgrown with weeds, its vineyards choked with neglect, and its dairy herds dwindling to nothing. And when the inevitable collapse came, the outsiders would have no choice but to sell—at a humiliating fraction of what they had paid.

What they didn't know—what they *couldn't* know—was who Belén was. More importantly, they had no idea about the strength of the people standing behind her.

Even as she remained consumed by her search for Jorge—her husband so *agonizingly close* yet still out of reach—she found time to do what no one thought possible - revive the farm, move three families, and impose order on chaos.

La Alquería was no ordinary estate. The old wooden house, built half a century earlier on towering quebracho pillars to withstand the river's wild floods, stood tall and proud. Surrounding it, embankments lined with grapevines and shaded by rows of stately poplars gave it an air of quiet strength, as if it had always belonged to the land.

The farm itself was a vast, pulsing organism—a mix of orchards, vineyards, vegetable gardens, a thriving dairy, and pig farming. Laborers lived on the property, their families rooted here as firmly as the trees they tended. Every morning, fruit buyers arrived by barge, their practiced eyes sweeping the orchards, calculating what could be harvested in a day or two. Then, in a whirlwind, they would strip the trees bare, load their cargo, and sail off toward the bustling markets of Buenos Aires.

But *La Alquería's* new owners weren't just fighting against time and nature. The real battle was against their neighbors.

Suspicious, resentful, unwilling to accept outsiders among them, the local farmers did their best to sabotage the newcomers. They whispered threats, stirred up trouble among the workers, and did their utmost to scare off potential buyers.

They wanted to break them before they could even begin.

But they had underestimated Belén. By mid-January—just three weeks later—the farm was fully operational. The orchards thrived. The vineyards were pruned and strong. The dairy and gardens flourished under careful hands.

Little by little, the walls of hostility began to crumble.

The same farmers who had once plotted against them began to realize that the new owners were fair, hardworking, and perhaps even easier to deal with than the farm's previous master—a bitter, miserly old man who had spent six decades hoarding his wealth and keeping the world at arm's length.

For Mr. Burns and José María, the transition was absolute. They rarely left the farm, except for Sunday Mass in a nearby town, where they appeared with their families, solid and steady, a quiet but undeniable presence.

Belén, however, was a woman at war. Every day, she left for the city. Every day, she fought. Not for land. Not for crops. Not for the farm that everyone believed would break her.

No. She was fighting for her husband—locked in an unrelenting battle with Father Gazapo, determined to reclaim the man who had once been hers, and would be again.

This fight—the greatest battle of her life—was dragging on far longer than Belén could bear.

She didn't just want Jorge back—she refused to have him return out of *pity*. She needed to *see* him, to look into his eyes before he even spoke a word.

Because the one thing she feared most wasn't rejection, it was a lie born from compassion.

No, no, no! She would never accept a love built on deception. She would sooner lock herself away in a convent, deceiving the world into believing she had a religious calling, than allow Jorge to sacrifice his vocation for *her* sake.

If he came back, it had to be because he chose to—not because he felt *obligated*.

But Father Gazapo! Oh, how skillfully he had spun his web of arguments and manipulations!

Belén felt trapped, like an animal pacing the same small cage, searching for a way out that didn't exist. She had argued, pleaded, fought—only to find herself stonewalled at every turn.

Weeks passed and still, the letter from Chile that Father Gazapo had promised her never came.

One afternoon, while hacking away at the dry soil of an onion field, Mr. Burns and José María paused to catch their breath. The relentless January sun beat down on them, but their thoughts drifted to Belén. They had both noticed the weight of something pressing down on her shoulders, the restless energy that never let her stand still. They didn't know *everything*, but they had their suspicions.

Burns wiped his brow and spoke first.

"I think," he said, leaning on his hoe, "the lady has picked up the trail of your ship."

José María turned, frowning.

"You mean Don Jorge?"

The old carpenter nodded.

"Ever since he sailed away from her waters, she's never lost hope of tracking his course," Burns continued. "She's like a lookout perched high on the mast, scanning the horizon—watching, waiting. And one day…" he smiled faintly. "She'll shout down to us, 'All hands on deck! Ship in sight!' "

José María let out a long breath, staring across the endless stretch of crops.

"And what do you think she'll find when she does?" he asked, his voice low.

Burns turned to him.

"What do you mean?"

José María hesitated, then spoke the thought neither of them had dared say aloud.

"What if he remarried, thinking she was dead?"

A heavy silence fell between them.

Burns scratched his beard, his gaze distant.

"Well… if that's the case, she'd have to let him go."

"Let him go?" José María scoffed. "She *couldn't* do that. She'd have to find him first—tell him the truth *herself*."

"And what if he doesn't *want* to know the truth?"

José María shook his head.

"Anyone who ever loved that woman," he said, voice unwavering, "could never forget her. Not if she were still alive."

Burns was silent for a long moment.

Then, quietly, he murmured, "No, never. Not in life. Not even in death."

Uncertain of what the future held, Mr. Burns bent down and began tying the onion leaves into neat knots, securing the plants so they could continue growing. The simple, rhythmic task steadied his hands, though his thoughts remained far from the soil.

José María, beside him, drove his hoe into the earth with measured strokes, equally lost in thought.

What would Belén do if she found Jorge married to someone else? Would she fight for him? She wasn't the kind of woman to walk away from a battle—not if she believed she had a right to fight it.

But neither of them could have guessed that the real battle ahead was not the one they imagined.

A sudden, distant hum cut through the still morning air. Mr. Burns straightened and looked toward the house, hidden beyond a grove of trees.

"Ten o'clock," he muttered. "The lady's heading to the city again."

The road ran close to where they were working. As Belén's car approached, she suddenly veered off, pulling to a stop beside them.

She leaned out the window, her expression unreadable.

"What would you say if I had news for you?"

Her voice wasn't bright or triumphant, so they immediately doubted it had anything to do with Jorge.

"If it's good news," Mr. Burns said, wiping his hands on his trousers, "we'll be happy for you. If it's bad, we'll stand by your side and share the burden. Is it about the farm?"

"No," Belén replied, shaking her head.

The sunlight caught in her dark, wind-tousled hair, making it shimmer like a cascading waterfall.

"It's something else..."

She exhaled sharply, as if clearing the hesitation from her mind.

"I won't keep you in suspense," she said, cutting straight to the chase. "I've found my husband."

A stunned silence followed.

"Is he in Buenos Aires?" Mr. Burns asked.

For a moment, Belén nearly snapped—*Seriously? If Jorge were in Buenos Aires, would he be anywhere other than here, with her?*

But she bit back the words, because the truth was, she didn't know where he was. Not for certain.

Thanks to Father Gazapo and his infuriating secrecy, she was left chasing shadows, hitting walls at every turn. The old priest never let even the smallest detail slip, and the other friars at the convent were just as tight-lipped under his orders.

This had to end. Today. Now.

Without another word, she slammed her foot on the gas. The car lurched forward, tearing down the dirt road like a horse released from the starting gate.

"See you later!" she called over her shoulder, as if embarking on a long journey rather than a mere errand.

Then, just before disappearing around the bend, she slowed just long enough to shout, "I'll be back by lunch—with big news!"

And with that, she was gone—a streak of dust and determination vanishing into the horizon.

When Belén arrived at the Missionaries' convent, Brother Gorgonio didn't even wait for her to speak. The poor friar had learned from experience. Without a word, he rang the bell for the superior, adding a special signal to indicate the matter was urgent.

Father Gazapo descended at once, already suspecting who had come to see him. And there she was.

To his relief, today she wasn't dressed to start a revolution. None of her usual bold, head-turning outfits that sent whispers rippling through the convent corridors. Instead, she wore a simple white dress—modest, elegant, and free of any audacious embellishments.

Perhaps, he thought, *just perhaps, a religious vocation is finally beginning to take root in her troubled but devout soul—like the first bud of a delicate flower.*

If so, it was a miracle in the making.

They sat down at the same small table that had witnessed so many of their battles, separating them yet, in its own way, drawing them together.

But today, there was no playfulness in her eyes, no challenge in her tone. She wasn't here to debate. She was here for answers.

"If a priest, ordained by mistake, is caught between two duties," she began, her voice unwavering, "he has to choose one or the other, right?"

"Exactly," Father Gazapo replied, folding his hands before him. "There's no middle ground. Either he remains a priest—pure and celibate—or he becomes a husband and fulfills his responsibilities in marriage."

There was a pause.

Then, in a tone softer but somehow more dangerous, Belén murmured, "A 'great sacrament,' as Saint Paul calls it."

Father Gazapo's gaze sharpened.

He knew this wasn't going to be just another conversation. This was a reckoning. Father Gazapo winced at the subtle jab but kept his composure, responding only with a piercing, unamused stare.

Belén, undeterred, pressed on.

"But if a man chooses the priesthood after marriage, that decision must be made with his wife's consent, correct?"

A muscle in the priest's jaw twitched.

"Yes," he admitted reluctantly.

Belén's eyes gleamed with quiet triumph.

"Because 'what God has joined together, let no man separate.' When Jesus forbade men from dissolving a marriage, He didn't mention women, did He?"

Father Gazapo's gaze darkened. He could see where this was going.

"What exactly are you trying to say, child?"

Belén shrugged, voice deceptively casual.

"I mean… maybe what men can't do, women can."

The priest felt like he had just swallowed a live frog—or perhaps an entire snake. His pulse spiked as he struggled to maintain control. This wasn't just bold—it was heresy draped in silk and spoken with a smile. He took a deep breath, reining in his exasperation. *I can't push her away now. She's too close to surrendering.*

"Go on, daughter," he said evenly, though his grip on the table had tightened. "I'll respond after you finish."

"Don't worry, Father," Belén said smoothly, eyes dancing with mischief. "I'm not suggesting I'll take advantage of some special loophole that lets women do what men can't."

Father Gazapo snapped.

"What am I going to do with you, you onion-headed philosopher?!" he bellowed, throwing up his hands. "When the Bible says 'man,' it means humankind—men and women alike!"

Belén didn't even flinch.

"I'm not arguing, Father. Let's stay on track."

Her voice remained cool, precisely measured, infuriatingly calm.

"If neither men nor women can dissolve what God has united, then how is it that a husband and wife can simply decide—by mutual agreement—that he will become a priest? Doesn't that mean they're undoing what God joined together?"

Gazapo groaned, running a hand over his weary face.

"Ah, forbidden fruit! Tree of the knowledge of good and evil! You are going to send me to an early grave, my child."

He fixed her with a glare.

"Listen carefully. God does not allow married couples to separate simply to chase their own selfish desires. Marriage is a perfect union. But if both husband and wife choose—not to remarry, not to live apart for convenience—but to dedicate themselves to an even holier life, serving God through the priesthood and religious vows, then the Church allows it.

"The Church, as the infallible interpreter of God's laws, teaches that this is His will. Jesus Himself said, 'Whoever leaves brothers, sisters, parents, wife, children, or property for My sake will receive a hundred times more and inherit eternal life.'"

Belén didn't hesitate.

"I don't understand that passage," she said flatly.

Father Gazapo frowned.

"What don't you understand?"

Belén folded her arms.

"If a man truly loves his wife, he wouldn't leave her—not even for a hundred other women. Love isn't a numbers game, Father. And if he *doesn't* love her, then leaving her isn't a *sacrifice*—it's just a selfish trade for a better deal."

Silence.

For the first time in years, Father Gazapo had no immediate comeback.

He simply sat there, staring at the woman across from him, and realized he had underestimated her completely.

"Fire from heaven!" Father Gazapo cried, crossing himself as if to ward off the sheer audacity of Belén's reasoning. "The 'hundredfold' isn't literal, child! It means the spiritual rewards—peace, joy, and countless blessings—that come from dedicating one's life to God. Father Scío, who knows more than both you and me combined, explains it clearly in his commentary."

Belén's eyes burned with unshaken resolve.

"But, Father," she pressed, "I don't even know what my husband wants. Would he really leave me behind for those 'countless blessings'? Or would he return to me, as God Himself commands?"

Her voice, steady yet laced with something raw, seemed to unsettle the priest.

For once, Father Gazapo was silent.

Belén watched him carefully, waiting.

Finally, he exhaled. His expression softened—not with pity, but with something far heavier.

"A priestly vocation is delicate and profound," he said at last.

His voice had shifted, carrying not just the weight of doctrine but something almost personal.

"As the Song of Songs declares, 'If one offered all the wealth of his house for love, it would be utterly scorned.' This love is pure—stronger than death itself. To turn away from it in youth would lead to lifelong regret. And in old age, the soul would yearn, desperate to reclaim what it once cast aside. A vocation is the seal of Christ on one's heart—an eternal mark. Those called by Him, sooner or later, always find their way back to the shore of that calling. They shed every earthly attachment, like a swimmer discarding his clothes before diving into the sea: wealth, ambition, resentment… even love."

Belén's fingers tightened around the edge of the table.

"How can anyone strip away a love as strong as death?" she asked, her voice barely above a whisper.

But Father Gazapo wasn't listening. He was lost now, speaking not just to her but to the weight of a belief forged over decades of priesthood.

"When Christ calls a soul, it must answer. Otherwise, it risks becoming like the guests in the parable who refused the king's invitation to the banquet—one because he had bought a farm, another because he had oxen to test, and another because he had just married and couldn't leave his wife.

"They all traded eternal glory for temporary, earthly concerns."

A bitter smile ghosted across Belén's lips.

"I loved him so much," she murmured, "I would have made him immortal."

The words were soft—an echo of Calypso mourning Ulysses as he left her island for the world beyond.

But Father Gazapo did not hear her.

He pressed on, his voice rising, filled with the conviction of a man who had long since buried doubt beneath devotion.

"Do you know what a priest is, child?" he asked, leaning forward. "He is an eye that chooses blindness to the temptations of the world. An ear that turns deaf to the whispers of the devil. A heart so pure that sin cannot touch it. Once, he was bound—tied by countless chains to the desires and concerns that entangle other men. But the moment Christ calls him, he breaks free. He gives up everything…

"And yet, in ways the world cannot understand, he becomes richer than kings."

Belén did not answer, because for the first time, she wasn't sure which of them had won.

"When the bishop first takes a blade to his hair during ordination," Father Gazapo began, his voice solemn, "the priest speaks words that will stay with him forever, 'Lord, You are my portion and my inheritance.' It is a vow deeper than marriage, more permanent than any earthly bond. When his hands are anointed, they are sanctified—not for labor, not for holding a child, not for the touch of a wife—but for something far greater. Those hands, so human, suddenly wield a power no ordinary man should possess.

"They hold the authority to transform mere bread and wine into the Body and Blood of Christ. They bear the burden of absolving sins, bridging the living and the dead. They carry a power so immense that even angels, even the Blessed Virgin herself, cannot do what a priest does at the altar, in the confessional, in the quiet hours of intercession. And because of this power, the bishop warns him, 'Guard yourself from all temptations of the flesh.'"

Father Gazapo's gaze bore into Belén, searching for any sign that she grasped the enormity of what she was asking.

"How, then, can we ask a man so elevated—so close to God—to *turn back*? To strip himself of his sacred calling and return to an ordinary, *earthbound* existence?"

His voice softened slightly, but the fire in his words did not fade.

"The Church, in her wisdom, gave priests the wings of eagles, freeing them from the burdens of the world. A priest weighed down by marriage becomes a man divided—distracted by the needs of his family, his zeal smothered by financial concerns, his holy authority diminished in the eyes of his flock.

"A priest who belongs to the world is no priest at all. I once heard a Salesian priest in Paris, Father Auffray, say this, and I have never forgotten it, *'A married priest is a compromised ideal—a man reduced to a mere functionary, no longer fully an apostle of God.'* And now, I tell you the same, so you may understand the gravity of what you are asking to undo."

He finished, expecting resistance—another sharp remark, another challenge wrapped in poetry and defiance.

Instead, Belén was silent. She had covered her face with her hands and was crying.

Not a dramatic display, not the loud sobs of someone who wanted to be seen, but quiet, breaking, uncontrollable tears.

Father Gazapo felt a jolt of unease. He had expected an argument. He had not expected this.

"Child…?" he murmured, but the words felt awkward on his tongue.

He wasn't sure if he was supposed to comfort her or brace for yet another duel.

When she finally lifted her head, her tear-streaked face was calm— but the depth of her sadness struck him like a blade. And then she spoke softly. So softly it felt as though the words had been carried from the depths of her soul.

"I, too, once heard God's voice," she said, her eyes distant, lost in memory.

"He binds the generations of humanity together with the same force that holds the stars in place—keeping harmony in the heavens, ensuring life continues on earth. As a child, I knew that my name was written in God's book alongside another. I didn't know whose it was. I only knew that it existed. Until the day of revelation came. Until I saw his face. It was like the sun rising—the only sun that could ever light my life."

Her fingers traced the grain of the wooden table, as if touching something long lost.

"When God spoke to me again, it wasn't through vague instinct. It wasn't a whisper in the dark. It was a command. I belonged to a man. Bone of his bone. Flesh of his flesh. My life changed in that instant, and I believed that sun would never set. I slept beside him… but my heart never rested. He promised me that if he ever had to leave for far-off lands, he would carry me with him—close to his heart, like a shepherd carrying bread for the journey."

Her voice faltered, and when she spoke again, it was barely more than a whisper.

"But then I dreamed that he had gone without me. That he had put miles and miles—and laws—between us. I didn't understand it then. But now, I do. Now that I have heard Your Reverence explain the greatness of the priesthood, I see the wall that stands between him and me. And I see how foolish I was—so blind, so reckless, so desperate—to swear that if anything came between us, I would tear it down with my own hands, even if it left me bleeding."

Her hands clenched into fists in her lap.

"Foolish woman that I am! That's all I have to say."

Father Gazapo sat back, exhaling a slow, deep breath.

Finally, she had seen the truth. She understood and was ready to let Jorge go at last.

A wave of relief washed over him—like a priest watching a prodigal soul return from the edge of a great abyss.

It's over, he thought. He had won. Or at least, he thought he had; but Belén wasn't finished.

She met Father Gazapo's gaze, her voice steady, her words deliberate.

"Just as he returned to his first calling and became a priest," she said calmly, "I will return to mine—so he can be free."

Father Gazapo's brows furrowed. There was something about the way she said it—something too composed, too final.

"Wait." He leaned forward, hope flickering in his eyes. "Did you once have a religious vocation?"

Belén's lips curled into a faint smile.

"No, Father," she said smoothly. "I had a vocation to be a *pirate*. And now, I can finally pursue it freely. I'll go to Montevideo, get a divorce, and let him go. He'll be free—and so will I. Then I'll marry someone more grounded… someone who actually *wants* to be with me."

The priest nearly choked on air.

"Are you out of your mind, child? Or is this some kind of joke?"

"No, Father. I'm perfectly serious."

He studied her face, searching for mischief, for defiance, for anything that would reassure him she was only taunting him again. But there was nothing.

This was not a game.

"Well, you should know," he said gravely, weighing every word, "that it won't change a thing. Divorce doesn't exist for Catholics. Even if Montevideo grants it, you'll still be tied to him in

192

the eyes of the Church. And he still wouldn't be able to serve as a priest."

For a moment, silence.

Then, Belén's voice dropped—soft, eerie, terrifying in its unnatural calm.

"And if he… became a widower? Would he be free then?"

The priest's blood ran cold.

"Yes," he admitted, slowly, carefully. "Of course."

Belén exhaled, her expression unreadable.

"Then," she said quietly, "since I have no calling to be a nun, but I do want to free him to continue his work… I'll just *kill myself.* You can give me a nice funeral."

Father Gazapo bolted upright.

"Horrible thought!" he roared. "What good would a funeral do you in the depths of *hell*, where suicides are condemned?"

Belén tilted her head, considering him with a strange, almost amused detachment.

"Well, since he performs miracles," *she* murmured, her smile bitter as poisoned wine, "maybe he'll perform one more—for the soul of the wife who died because of him."

For the first time in his life, Father Gazapo felt utterly powerless. A moment ago, he had thought he had won. Now, he realized he had been fighting the wrong battle all along.

"No, my child, no," he said, his voice urgent, desperate, pleading. "Go home. I'll bring him back. In five days, he'll be here. It seems God Himself is telling me to give you what you want."

Belén's hands trembled.

"Really?" she whispered. "You're not lying to me, Father?"

Her breath hitched.

"Forgive me for doubting—but after fighting so hard, I can hardly believe he'll actually come back to me."

Father Gazapo softened, his anger, his arguments, his doctrine melting in the face of the raw agony before him.

"Yes, my child," he promised, gently. "I'll bring him back… unless, of course, he finds stronger arguments in his heart than I have in mine."

A fire ignited in Belén's eyes—a fierce, unrelenting certainty.

"Leave that to me," she vowed.

"Will you let me know when he arrives?"

"Yes," the priest assured her. "He'll be here within three days."

That afternoon, Father Gazapo sent a telegram to Jorge.

"Your wife threatens divorce or death. Come by plane. Prepare for a battle worthy of Saint Paul."

Chapter 11: A Lioness at the Gate

Father Manrique unfolded the telegram with steady hands but an unsteady heart. His eyes swept over the words, and a slow, knowing smile curved his lips—a mix of skepticism and something else, something he refused to name.

This has Belén's signature all over it.

Even without knowing all the details, he could see it unfold in his mind like a well-rehearsed play. Belén and Father Gazapo—two forces of nature, locked in a battle of wits and will.

The old priest, sharp as ever, would have unleashed every argument in his arsenal, trying to steer her toward the cloistered life, hoping to keep Jorge bound to the Missionaries. He would have painted the convent walls with golden light, spun visions of sainthood and sacrifice, and made his case with the thunderous authority of a man who had spent a lifetime bending others to his will.

But Belén? Belén was a storm that refused to be tamed.

She wouldn't have come to beg or plead. She would have come to win.

And when words alone failed, she must have done what she always did—forced fate's hand with a move so bold, so reckless, that even Gazapo had been shaken enough to send this message.

Jorge exhaled, shaking his head. It was so like her. Would she truly have threatened to take her own life? He doubted it.

That fearless girl—who had laughed in the face of storms, who had met life's cruelties with fists clenched and head held high—would never surrender so easily.

No, she wasn't the kind of woman to break.

She was the kind who, when trapped between the impossible and the unbearable, would pray to Saint Rita of Cascia—patroness of the hopeless—and somehow make the impossible happen.

And how many times had she done exactly that?

With a quiet sigh, Father Manrique folded the telegram, packed his missionary suitcase, and booked his flight to Buenos Aires.

His soul was at peace—he had placed everything in God's hands.

But his mind? His mind was a battlefield of thoughts.

No matter how much he tried to focus, her face kept appearing before him—not as a distant memory, but as if she were standing right in front of him, challenging him, teasing him, daring him to say something first.

How will she look after all these years?

And then, there was their daughter. Moramay. The child he had unknowingly given her First Communion. Father Gazapo had told him she had his eyes.

Moramay, he thought, rolling the name over in his mind. *Where did Belén find a name like that? A novel, perhaps?*

A quiet chuckle escaped him. Still the same spirited, unpredictable Belén.

But more than anything, Jorge found himself wondering how she had survived. What dangers had she faced? What storms had she weathered? What story would she tell him?

Knowing Belén, it would be nothing short of extraordinary.

If the Lord had not been on her side, he thought, recalling the words of a psalm, *men would have swallowed her alive.*

He knew his own life had been full of unexpected turns.

But hers? Hers must have been like something out of a legend.

In two days, he thought, *I will be face-to-face with Belén again.*

And that thought unsettled him more than he cared to admit.

What will she say?

What will I say?

How do you even begin a conversation after seven years?

She, of course, would speak first. Belén had always been braver than him in matters of the heart—always the first to confess, the first to fight, the first to turn pain into poetry.

And whatever words she chose, they would strike like lightning and never miss their mark.

She wouldn't waste time on pleasantries. She'd tell her story—as thrilling and unpredictable as any tale from One Thousand and One Nights.

And he, powerless against her voice, against the fire in her words, against the way she painted pictures with vivid details and unexpected twists, would sit there for hours…utterly enchanted.

How could anyone not be spellbound by Belén?

And yet, where would they even meet? The convent's reception room?

Too formal. Too sterile. Too public.

Would there be others there—visitors, laymen, strangers whose eyes might pry too closely, whose whispers might coil like smoke in the air?

How strange—how scandalous—it would seem for a missionary priest to sit for hours, alone with a woman like her.

Would he have to stand in the middle of the room and explain himself?

"This is Belén—*my wife*! I thought she was dead, but she's alive! Let her speak and tell me everything she's endured! Let her decide my fate, and may God guide us both!"

No. That was impossible.

Then there was Moramay.

The child whose first communion he himself had blessed, utterly unaware that she was his own flesh and blood.

Why do souls—so mysteriously connected—sometimes fail to recognize one another?

Why didn't I know her when I saw her?

The name echoed in his mind.

Moramay, Moramay… what does your beautiful name even mean?

As the plane descended into Buenos Aires, Jorge watched the city unfold beneath him, its streets twisting like veins, alive with movement.

Every time he saw a girl near Moramay's age, his heart lurched.

Is she like that? Is she taller? Dark-haired or fair? Does she walk with confidence? Does she laugh like her mother?

His mind spiraled with questions, yet the moment it turned toward Belén, the world around him blurred.

In his memory, she remained frozen in time.

She was still the girl on the beach at Fuenterrabía—that windswept afternoon, when the sea had curled at the shore and the wind had tangled her golden hair.

She had stood there, glowing in the sunlight, her gaze following a fishing boat as it slipped into the horizon, her slender arms lifting in a farewell so graceful, so perfect, that it belonged in a painting.

He had never thought of that moment before. Not once.

And yet now, it came rushing back to him—as vividly as if it had just happened.

That morning, at Belén's house, a message arrived from the Eastern Catholic Missionaries.

"Today at 5 PM, Father Teofano Manrique will receive you at our convent."

The words hit her like a punch to the stomach.

Our convent.

His home. The place guarded by a sign that read CLOISTER—a threshold no woman could cross. No woman except a queen.

And he was no longer Jorge de Balcázar. He was Father Teofano Manrique. His home. His name. Two unbreakable barriers standing between them.

Yet—this was what she had fought for. She had demanded this moment, clawed her way to it, shattered every argument thrown in her path. Now, the moment had come.

She would see him. She would speak to him. And he would look at her. *Wouldn't he?* The weight of that uncertainty nearly crushed her.

Only a few hours remained until their meeting. Hours of torment. She wouldn't have wished them on her worst enemy. Belén felt as if she were walking a razor's edge—caught between fierce hope and paralyzing fear.

Because what if Jorge didn't fight at all?

What if he simply stepped into that cold, logical role that Father Gazapo had played so well?

What if she sat before him, poured out her soul, and he answered with nothing but calm, detached reason?

What if, in the end, he spoke the words that would shatter her completely?

She could almost hear them already.

"This is the path I've chosen. Now you must choose yours."

200

Would he then turn—point to the altar, to the church, to the place where he had buried the man she once knew?

Would he expect her to accept a fate she had never chosen, as if it were some fair and equal exchange?

"This is my destiny," he would say. *"Now go and find yours—behind convent walls."*

For days, she had debated, battled, fought. She had torn apart every argument Father Gazapo had thrown at her, wielding her heart like a weapon, defying every cold doctrine meant to cage her.

Nothing had cornered her. Nothing had broken her. But this? This silence—this waiting—this not knowing? It was unbearable. Because what if, in the end…Jorge himself became her greatest defeat?

Belén knew too well that God's ways were never predictable. His plans rarely aligned with human desires, and she had accepted that, time and time again.

But what if this was the moment when His will demanded the ultimate sacrifice—the surrender of her love? The thought gripped her with a terror worse than death.

Yes, she was strong. Despite her delicate frame, she had always been capable of facing storms, of braving dangers without a second thought.

She feared neither the living nor the dead, but now, as the hour of reckoning loomed closer, she trembled like a single leaf caught in a violent storm.

Her mind raced. Who would speak first? What words would be said? Would he call her by name?

She couldn't bring herself to say the name he had taken for his new life. And surely, he wouldn't call her by the false name she had used to find him.

No. She would call him Jorge. And surely, surely, he would call her Belén.

But then a terrible thought struck her—a thought so chilling it seemed to stop her heart.

What if he didn't? What if he called her Madam? Cold. Distant. Foreign. As if they had never shared a life. As if she were nothing but another visitor. A whisper of panic rose in her chest, and she prayed, fiercely, desperately.

"Dear souls in purgatory, I swear I'll have Gregorian Masses said for even the most forgotten among you—if only he calls me Belén and not Madam."

It was absurd. Ridiculous. Yet it felt like everything depended on it. Would he sound like the Jorge she had known? Or would his voice be that of a man who had chosen another world, another life—a man who no longer belonged to her?

She brought Moramay with her, dressing the little girl as beautifully as she could, as if her very presence could soften Jorge's heart.

"Do you remember the priest who gave you your First Communion?" Belén asked.

"Yes, Mama. He was young and had a nice beard," Moramay answered absently, her mind still lost in play.

"Would you like to see him again?"

The girl hesitated, then asked, with disarming innocence,

"Do you think he wants to see me?"

The words nearly shattered her.

"Oh, he'll love seeing you," Belén assured her, forcing a smile. "You're the sweetest and prettiest little girl. I'm sure he'll give you some beautiful holy cards."

Moramay considered this.

"If that's why he'll give me cards, then you'll get even better ones, Mama," she said, her little face solemn.

"You look really pretty today… even though you're so pale."

When Father Teofano Manrique stepped out of the car at the Missionaries' convent, Father Gazapo was already waiting.

Jorge handed his suitcase to a lay brother and followed the superior in silence, knowing there was no need for words.

Inside his room, they embraced—not just as fellow priests, but as a father and son preparing for war.

Father Gazapo settled into his worn friar's chair, leaving Jorge standing.

"My dear Teofano," he said, his voice carrying the weight of something far heavier than words, "prepare yourself like an athlete stepping into the arena. You are about to wrestle with God Himself, just as Jacob fought the angel. Let's see if, afterward, you can say like Saint Paul: 'I have fought the good fight.'"

Jorge listened in silence, his heart already bracing for the impact.

"Do not underestimate the grace within you—the grace you received through the bishop's hands. Guard your soul from the whispers of self-doubt. She is proud, sensitive, and sharp. If she senses even the slightest hesitation in you, she will close herself off like a flower at dusk. Protect her, too, from the wild storms of her imagination… And may God's will be done—not ours."

With those final words, Father Gazapo blessed him.

Jorge bowed, kissed his superior's hand, and turned to leave.

As he did, the old priest's voice followed him, low and urgent.

"Three days ago, she was ready to destroy herself. But I see now—she's ready to fight instead."

Jorge paused for half a breath, then walked away.

Father Gazapo sighed and turned to the porter.

"When she arrives, bring her straight to the receiving room. And notify Father Teofano immediately."

When Belén arrived, Moramay holding her hand, the porter led them inside without a word.

There were no other visitors in the reception hall.

Just the two of them.

Waiting.

Moramay, distracted, swung her little feet over the edge of the bench.

Belén sat stiff, silent, her hands gripping her dress, her breath coming in shallow waves.

Moramay noticed.

"Mama," she whispered, "why are you shaking?"

Before Belén could answer, hurried footsteps echoed down the corridor.

Jorge was coming.

✢ ✦ ✢ —— ◇ —— ✢ ✦ ✢

Jorge searched his mind for the right words.

How useless they were.

How foolish—all those carefully rehearsed speeches, all those nights spent imagining how this moment might unfold.

How do you greet the woman you thought was dead?

What words could possibly be enough?

And then, before he could even think to breathe, there she was.

And he was face to face with Belén.

Seeing her standing there—so pale, so fragile, yet so fiercely alive— Jorge felt something deep inside him break free.

He clasped his hands together, as if in prayer, and whispered, his voice unsteady with tenderness.

"Oh, my Belén..."

The sound of her name in his voice—not distant, not formal, but his— nearly shattered her.

For years, she had imagined this moment.

She had pictured rushing into his arms, feeling the warmth of his embrace, burying her face against his shoulder, and knowing—knowing—that everything had been a bad dream.

But now, standing before him, she couldn't move.

The black cassock felt like an unbreakable wall between them, a sacred barrier she dared not cross.

Her body refused to obey the longing in her heart.

Instead, she reached for Moramay, nudging her daughter forward, as if the child could bridge the distance she suddenly feared to cross alone.

Her voice, usually so strong, wavered.

"This is Moramay..."

And then, barely above a whisper, the question that held the weight of everything.

"Do you know who she is?"

Jorge's breath caught, but his eyes softened as he placed his hands on the little girl's head.

"I know."

His voice held no hesitation.

Then, after a moment, he smiled and asked gently, as if the years apart had never existed.

"Where did you find her name?"

Belén's face flushed.

For all her strength, all her courage, this question made her feel small, like a girl caught revealing her heart too plainly.

Her voice was hushed, as if she were confessing a secret that had carried her through years of darkness.

"I never gave up hope of finding you."

She lifted her chin, her golden eyes shining with quiet defiance.

"When she was born, I gave her a name from the Sinhalese language."

She swallowed hard.

"It means… to hope against all hope."

For a long, aching moment, Jorge said nothing.

He only looked at her—really looked at her—as if trying to memorize every shadow and curve of the face he had lost, the face he had once thought never to see again.

Then, with a smile that reached deep into her soul, he ran his fingers gently through Moramay's dark curls, nodding as if the name itself was a prayer answered.

But Belén wasn't finished.

Her heart pounded violently against her ribs, her throat tightening with emotion. Every fiber of her being begged her to stop, to leave the question unspoken, to protect herself from the answer she both craved and feared. But she couldn't. She *had* to ask. She *had* to know.

Her voice trembled as she whispered, "Her name means to hope against all hope…"

She searched his face, her wide, pleading eyes drinking in every flicker of movement, every shift in his expression. She was desperate for something—anything—that would tell her what lay in his heart.

"Jorge...," she pleaded, barely above a breath. "Should I change her name?"

Silence.

It stretched between them, heavy and unyielding, a chasm filled with memories, regrets, and years of unsaid words. The question hung there like a blade, sharp, glinting, deadly.

Jorge's hands clenched the edge of the table, his knuckles turning white.

He wanted to answer. *God, he wanted to.*

But emotion clawed at his throat, raw and merciless, rendering him speechless. How could he put words to the ache in his chest, to the years of loss and longing? How could he explain what it did to him—to hear that name, to know she had named her daughter after the one thing they had both fought so hard to hold onto?

Belén's breath was unsteady, her fingers twisting in her lap, wringing the fabric of her dress. The silence was unbearable, pressing down on her, threatening to crush the fragile hope she had carried for so long.

"Should I change her name?" she asked again, her voice breaking— like Moses striking the rock a second time for water, as if the first plea hadn't been enough, as if her heart could not withstand the uncertainty a moment longer.

Jorge exhaled, a shuddering breath that carried the weight of too many sleepless nights, too many unshed tears, too many battles fought in silence. His shoulders rose and fell, as though he were releasing years of grief, years of unanswered prayers.

And then, at last, a smile.

Soft. Faint. But undeniably real.

He lifted his gaze to hers, something unreadable—something *deep*—flickering in the depths of his dark eyes.

"Oh, my Belén...," he murmured, his voice thick with emotion. "What a beautiful name you gave her."

And then, as if sealing a vow, as if etching it into eternity—

"No. We won't change it."

She swayed slightly, as if the world had suddenly tilted beneath her feet.

For a moment, she simply stared at him, unblinking.

"Come," Jorge said softly, guiding her to a chair. "Sit here and tell me everything."

Belén hesitated, something flickering behind her eyes—a strange mix of fear and wonder, disbelief and longing.

"My story?" she repeated, almost as if she no longer recognized it.

She lowered herself into the chair slowly, as if afraid the moment might shatter if she moved too quickly.

"I don't remember anything anymore," she admitted, a little breathless.

She met his gaze—so steady, so familiar—and whispered, "All I know is that I have you back... but I don't even know what to call you."

Jorge smiled—a smile filled with pain, warmth, and something unspoken that belonged only to them.

"Call me what you've always called me."

His voice was barely above a whisper.

"You seem shaken and nervous. Are you really that afraid of me?"

Belén tried to laugh and brush it off, but a sob caught in her throat before she could stop it. She pressed her hands against her face, shoulders trembling.

"No...," she finally managed. "Not now."

And she wept.

Moramay, unnoticed, had wandered toward a large birdhouse in the courtyard.

She child knew nothing of fate, nothing of the weight pressing down on her parents' souls. She only knew that the priest from her First Communion had kind eyes…the same kind eyes that watched her now.

And so, without a word, she quietly slipped away, leaving them alone with their past…and their future.

Jorge watched Belén through the quiet, letting her cry, letting her pour out seven years of silence, of searching, of sorrow.

Then, at last, she looked up, wiped her tears away and smiled.

Belén took a deep breath, forcing herself to steady. Then, wiping the last traces of tears from her face, she straightened in her chair and gave him a half-smile—half defiance, half relief.

"Alright," she declared. "That's enough. The worst is over."

Jorge watched her, his face still pale but composed, his dark eyes steady.

"I think this is the first time you've ever seen me cry," she admitted, a hint of surprise in her own voice.

"That's true," he replied.

For a moment, neither spoke. The weight of seven years apart, seven years of loss, searching, and waiting pressed between them. But then, gently, he prompted,

"Now that the bad spell is over, your memory must be coming back. Tell me everything you've been through, everything you've dreamed."

He hesitated, tilting his head as if realizing just how much there was to tell.

"No, wait—it's probably too long a story, isn't it?"

Belén let out a quiet laugh, one that carried both exhaustion and the first traces of joy.

"Very long," she agreed. "I'll tell you everything… later."

Jorge nodded.

"Better that way. But when?"

She lowered her gaze, suddenly shy, her fingers twisting the fabric of her dress.

Then, softly—so softly he almost didn't hear—she answered, "When you come home."

And then—the question that would define everything.

"Are you coming home?"

Jorge didn't hesitate.

Not for a second.

"Yes," he said. "That is God's will."

Belén's breath caught, but something in her still wasn't satisfied.

"Nothing else?" she pressed.

Jorge's voice remained steady.

"And that is my duty."

A shadow flickered across her face.

"Nothing more?"

She rose to her feet as if ready to run—as if terrified by the possibility that he had spoken from obligation, not love.

Jorge saw it immediately and reached out before she could slip away.

"My poor Belén!" he murmured, his voice warm, half-chiding, half-tender. "You haven't changed a bit—not even your impulsiveness. Don't you realize that, dressed like this, I can't speak to you any other way?"

She exhaled, the tension easing slightly from her shoulders.

"You're right," she whispered. "Forgive me."

And before he could stop her, she knelt—not in submission, but in reverence—and pressed her lips to the consecrated hands that had once been hers alone, the hands that now belonged to God.

Just then, voices and footsteps echoed in the hallway. Visitors were arriving.

Belén straightened, masking herself instantly.

"Father Gazapo knows my whole story," she said, her tone suddenly cool, distant. "Ask him to tell you everything today."

Jorge blinked, caught off guard by the sudden change in her.

"Should Moramay and I come back tomorrow? Are there… are there a lot of formalities?"

Jorge sighed. Of course there were.

"Yes," he admitted. "You'll have to request official dismissal letters from my superior in Madrid, Father Conejo, and the case must be processed through the Holy See in Rome."

Her brow furrowed.

"They won't object, will they?"

"Almost certainly not," Jorge reassured her. "My situation is unusual, but it's one of the easiest to resolve. Still… it will take time."

"How long?"

"Two months."

Two months.

After seven years of fighting against impossible odds, two months should have felt like nothing, but still… it felt unbearably long.

Belén nodded in acquiescence.

"Alright."

She turned and called for Moramay, who had been playing quietly.

Jorge placed a gentle kiss on his daughter's forehead, then looked carefully at her beautiful, innocent face, trying to memorize it until he saw her again…soon.

He was suddenly jolted by the feeling of looking into the depths of his own soul, seeing how peaceful and simple the answer to this quandary of theirs was, but not quite understanding it, and this left him frustrated. He didn't dare tell Belén what he was feeling though…not since she had spent so long and fought so hard to find him after all these years.

He forced himself to tear his gaze away from Moramay's unreadable expression and looked over at his wife. With one last glance at him, Belén led their child away with a smile.

From the convent gate, a pair of sharp eyes watched them leave.

The lay brother, the one who had opened the door, shook his head as he muttered to himself,

"She'll be a saint when she dies… but while she's alive… well… huh!"

As he shuffled back into the convent, he muttered Latin phrases he had picked up over the years from overhearing the learned friars.

A roaring lion, just as Saint Peter had written. A lioness, prowling, ready to strike.

A woman who had fought to the ends of the earth for what belonged to her—and who would fight until the very last breath to bring her family home.

Chapter 12: Between Heaven and Her Arms

Twice in his life, Jorge de Balcázar had navigated the intricate process of dimissory vows—once to enter the priesthood and once to leave it. He had pledged himself entirely to the Congregation of the Eastern Catholic Missionaries, taking solemn vows of poverty, chastity, and obedience. And yet, years later, he found himself seeking release from the very commitments that had once defined his existence.

The first time, his path to ordination had taken him to Shanghai, a journey requiring permission from the bishop of Madrid-Alcalá, under whose diocese he was officially registered. This was no straightforward affair. To avoid scandal in Spain—where friends and family might react with shock or scrutiny—everything was handled in secrecy. His case was already extraordinary: a nobleman with a marriage that had seemed like an adventure and a widowhood that left skeptics whispering. The Church, ever cautious, wished to avoid drawing unnecessary attention.

The bishop of Madrid's official authorization for the bishop of Shanghai to ordain the Marquis of Balcázar was what canon law refers to as dimissory letters.

But there exists another kind of dimissory letter—one not of entrance, but of exit. When a member of a religious order, despite having taken lifelong vows, becomes irreconcilably at odds with his community—whether due to misconduct or irreparable differences—his superiors may dismiss him. The process is not immediate. It involves a formal investigation, followed by three official warnings urging the individual to change his ways. If he remains unmoved, he may be expelled. Yet even then, the Church does not release him completely. His obligations do not vanish, and the vow of celibacy remains binding, whether he continues in ministry or not.

In some cases, a priest himself may request release, citing valid personal reasons. But regardless of how or why he departs, the rule stands firm: a man who was ordained cannot marry. If he was widowed before ordination, he cannot remarry.

There is, however, *one* rare exception—a loophole so uncommon it borders on the miraculous. If a man believed himself to be a widower when he entered the priesthood, only to later discover that his wife was, in fact, alive, the Church recognizes the mistake. The indelible mark of ordination remains upon him—he is still a priest—but if his wife truly passes away or takes a vow of continence, he may return to his clerical duties without the need for reordination.

In such cases, obtaining dimissory letters is neither dishonorable nor particularly difficult. It is simply a matter of verifying facts through an official investigation, submitting the findings to the Order's General, and forwarding them to the Apostolic See in Rome. There, the Sacred Congregation for Religious—the body appointed by the Pope to oversee such matters—reviews and grants final approval.

Belén immersed herself in these laws the moment she returned home. With fierce determination, she pored over every chapter and clause governing the process of laicization, eager to understand how Jorge could be freed from his vows. But no book could tell her the one thing she truly wanted to know: *how long* it would take.

Bureaucracy moves at a glacial pace, and Vatican bureaucracy even more so. First, Jorge's file had to be compiled in Buenos Aires, then sent to Madrid, then to Rome, then back again for finalization.

Palace affairs move slowly, the saying goes.

For the sake of propriety, Jorge withdrew to Chile, where he lived in near seclusion. It was a quiet exile, meant to avoid scandal. He did not hear confessions, did not celebrate Mass, did not preach. He merely prayed, read his breviary, and helped two fellow missionaries establish a new religious house, men who knew of his unusual circumstances but spoke of them to no one.

Each week, two letters arrived. One from Belén, growing increasingly impatient with the delays. The other from Father Gazapo, who did not share her frustration.

"As long as the soul is in the body," Father Gazapo would remind him, "one must never lose hope."

But what, exactly, was Father Gazapo waiting for?

Nothing. And everything.

He was waiting for grace. For a divine flicker of understanding in Belén's heart. For a moment of clarity that, at the crucial juncture, he believed had been absent. If that moment came before the case was finalized, everything could be undone. Belén and Jorge could turn back. Father Manrique—the man Jorge had once been—could return to his sacred calling.

"Lord, Lord!" Father Gazapo prayed. "Let a ray of Your grace strike that woman! Just one ray, Lord..."

But grace did not come. The file returned from Rome, stamped and approved.

With a heavy heart, Father Gazapo sent a telegram to Jorge. He kept it brief, wasting no words on what was already lost.

"Come."

Nothing more.

Spring arrived in the Río de la Plata, spilling golden light over the labyrinth of islands and lush riverbanks. In Nueva Siracusa—the Greek-Italian colony nestled along the waterways—months had passed since the last harvest, and preparations for the next planting season were well underway.

At first, the settlers had watched the newcomers at *La Alquería* with quiet skepticism. Surely these outsiders would fail, or at the very least, grow bored of farm life. But by winter's end, it was clear they had been mistaken. The estate was thriving under its new owners, who worked tirelessly from dawn to dusk, showing no sign of regret or weariness.

Belén, once a frequent traveler to the city, now spent most of her time on the farm. That is, until one particular afternoon, when she returned from Buenos Aires—this time, accompanied by Jorge de Balcázar himself.

Jorge was a different man now. No longer bound by his priestly vows, he had shed the black robes of the Eastern Catholic Missionaries, trading them for the attire of a gentleman. Without his thick missionary beard, he looked younger—almost as he had in their youth. He handled the carriage with ease, guiding it through the winding roads as if he had been born to this life, rather than the one he had left behind.

Here, in the quiet countryside Belén had deliberately chosen for them, there was no one who knew their true story.

The Greek-Italian settlers, once wary of the strangers in their midst, had softened. Jorge and Belén were not the type to seek out social gatherings or meddle in local affairs, but they were always polite when crossing paths with their neighbors. And when an opportunity arose to offer help, Belén took it, slowly winning them over—not with words, but with kindness.

Time, she knew, would do the rest.

For now, their world was *La Alquería*, and they rarely left it. Only on Sundays and religious holidays did they venture beyond its borders, traveling to Buenos Aires or a nearby town to attend Mass.

Their servants and farmhands, however, never accompanied them. They were Byzantine Rite Catholics, their traditions and liturgical calendar differing from those of the Roman Church. It was this, more than anything, that caught Jorge's attention. With the delicate touch of a surgeon tending a wound, he began to reach into the hearts of these people—people who had no idea how spiritually starved they had become.

For generations, they had lived like shipwreck survivors, stranded on an island without a priest to guide them. The faith of their ancestors had not vanished, but it had been reduced to fragments—echoes of rituals whose meanings had long been forgotten.

They had no churches, no formal worship, and over time, their great religious festivals had faded into little more than tradition. When they celebrated, they did so out of habit, with no understanding of the mysteries behind their customs.

Of the seven sacraments, only two remained: baptism—performed by elders in the old Catholic tradition; and marriage, which they blessed themselves, believing it valid in the absence of a priest. And indeed, Jorge agreed that such marriages *were* valid, given the circumstances.

Beyond these remnants, their faith had withered. Their devotions were reduced to crossing themselves before images of the Virgin and a handful of saints—not out of true belief, but out of superstition.

Deprived of the sacraments—the lifeblood of grace—they had slowly drifted into a quiet, unspoken atheism. Some among them still clung to a vague belief in God, but Christ had become a distant figure, barely remembered. The rest lived as practical atheists, concerned only with the needs of the body, their souls as dry and lifeless as the cursed mountains of Gilboa, where neither rain nor dew ever falls.

"These poor people," Jorge murmured one afternoon, staring out at the vast, sun-drenched fields. "They live and die as if the Redeemer never set foot in this world. Imagine their shock when they stand before Christ and don't recognize Him—because they never learned to love Him! But is that entirely their fault? Or does the greater guilt belong to those who could have lifted them from this spiritual darkness but never tried? Those who ignored them out of convenience, selfishness, or simply a lack of conviction?"

Belén turned to him sharply.

"And who exactly are you blaming?"

"Their priests," Jorge answered without hesitation. "Or rather, the men who should have been their priests."

"But they don't have priests," she countered.

Jorge's voice hardened.

"They don't have them because they didn't want them. Are we really supposed to believe that, in all these years, not a single young man among them felt the call? No, Belén—any vocation that may have risen was crushed. Perhaps by parents who saw the priesthood as a waste. Perhaps by a community too indifferent to nurture it. Like a seed choked by weeds before it even had a chance to grow."

Belén usually avoided conversations about abandoned vocations, but something in his words struck her. She exhaled sharply.

"Then what we need here is a saint," she said. "Someone who can work miracles."

Jorge let out a quiet, skeptical laugh.

"People don't want miracles—at least, not unless it benefits their health or their fortune," he said. "Remember what happened in Saint Matthew's Gospel? Jesus was preaching and casting out demons. He freed two possessed men, but the demons entered a herd of pigs, which then rushed into the sea and drowned. And how did the townspeople react? Did they rejoice that their land had been freed from evil? No. The entire town—every last one of them—begged Jesus to leave. Why? Because they cared more about their pigs than their souls. They would rather live alongside demons than suffer even the smallest loss."

Belén frowned.

"So you're saying there's nothing we can do for these people?"

Jorge's expression softened, and his voice grew firm.

"Of course not. The day one soul can no longer help another, the world will come to an end."

Belén's eyes suddenly lit up.

"Then I have an idea!" she exclaimed. "Let's convert them to the Latin Rite! That way, they can attend Mass at our churches!"

She expected Jorge to agree immediately, but instead, he shook his head.

"No," he said simply. "That's not allowed. The Popes have forbidden Roman Catholics from trying to convert Eastern Catholics to the Latin Rite—for centuries, in fact, and under severe penalties."

Belén's excitement faded into confusion.

"Why?"

Jorge sighed, knowing this would not be a short answer.

"You have to understand," he began, "the Eastern rites are over a thousand years old. They've taken deep root among simple, tradition-bound people who are naturally suspicious of outsiders trying to change their ways. Whenever Roman Catholics tried to impose the Latin Rite on Eastern Christians, it backfired. The Crusaders tried, and instead of strengthening the faith, they created resentment. The Easterners saw it as an attack on their very identity, rather than a call to unity."

He paused, watching her expression shift from curiosity to deep thought.

"More importantly," he continued, "the Eastern Catholics who returned to communion with Rome are descendants of the Byzantine Church—the same Church that now calls itself Orthodox. Today, there are about 150 million Orthodox Christians, all of them heirs to the Greek schism that broke away from Rome in the eleventh century. They rejected the Pope, and over time, they fractured into countless sects—just like the Protestants."

Belén fell silent. The weight of history, of lost souls and shattered unity, settled between them. There were no easy answers, no simple solutions.

And yet, Jorge's words lingered in the air, carrying a quiet but undeniable truth…the day one soul can no longer help another, the world will come to an end.

Ironically, after centuries of schism and division, many of these sects had begun finding their way back to Catholicism. And yet, every time Rome welcomed them home, it never forced them to abandon their ancient rites. Instead, the Church allowed them to keep their traditions as a sign of respect, understanding that faith, when stripped of its heritage, often withers rather than flourishes.

"To force them to give up their customs now—after finally bringing them back into communion—would only push them away again," Jorge said.

Belén frowned.

"But they didn't just keep their rites," she pointed out. "They also kept some customs that would scandalize us."

Jorge nodded.

"Exactly. But the Roman Church, in her wisdom, has treated these returning brothers with both charity and patience. She has never compromised on doctrine—our faith remains untouched. However, she has shown flexibility in liturgical customs and certain aspects of Church discipline. Take priestly celibacy, for example."

His voice took on the tone of a man who had spent years reflecting on this very subject.

"Celibacy is an apostolic tradition—it dates back to the time of the Apostles themselves. But at first, it wasn't an absolute command, merely a counsel for those striving for the highest level of evangelical perfection. In the Western Church, this counsel became a firm and unchanging law. But in the Eastern Church, it never took hold in the same way. By the late eighth century, a council in Constantinople had established the rules they still follow today."

Belén leaned forward.

"I know those rules," she interrupted.

She had read every book she could find on the subject.

"Then you know that Eastern clerics are allowed to marry—but only before they receive the diaconate. Once they are ordained, there's no turning back. If a married priest becomes a widower, he cannot remarry. And bishops—" Jorge paused, "—bishops must either be lifelong celibates or, if they were once married, take a perpetual vow of continence before their consecration."

Belén tilted her head.

"Has the Western clergy ever tried to gain the same right? To marry before ordination?"

Jorge shook his head.

"Every time a Latin priest has pushed for an end to celibacy, it has signaled something deeper—a weakening of his vocation, a collapse of his true calling. Even in the Eastern Churches, as their seminaries grow and their vocations strengthen, more priests are choosing celibacy of their own free will. The holiest among them dedicate their hearts entirely to God, just as the Apostles once did."

Belén watched him carefully. There was a light in his eyes, a fire that still burned—a fire she knew too well. It unsettled her.

She quickly sought to change the subject, regretting that she had even brought it up. Instead of steering the conversation away, her next words only made things more complicated.

"So, if we want our neighbors to turn away from their atheism and return to the faith," *she said slowly,* "we'll have to send for priests of their rite from Europe…"

Jorge sighed deeply.

"Yes… there's no other way."

A heavy silence fell between them.

Then, just as she thought the matter was settled, Jorge added, almost absently, "Unless…"

Belén's breath caught. She turned to him sharply.

Jorge stopped himself. But she had already heard it—the hesitation in his voice, the weight behind that unfinished thought.

She stared at him. He met her gaze.

For a long moment, neither spoke, as if they had both arrived at the same forbidden idea—a thought neither dared to say aloud, not even in the secrecy of their own hearts.

Finally, in a quiet, almost fragile voice, Belén asked, "What were you going to say before you stopped yourself?"

Jorge hesitated.

Then, after a moment, he answered carefully, "I was going to say that in Europe, North America, and even Brazil—where there are large communities of Eastern Catholics—some Latin priests, including Jesuits, Assumptionists, and Redemptorists, have asked the Holy See for permission to transfer to the Eastern rite so they could serve those communities. And they've been granted that permission."

Belén's eyes widened.

"And these Latin priests—once they switch to the Greek rite—can they marry?"

"No, of course not," Jorge said firmly. "Because they were already priests when they made the switch. And once a priest has received the subdiaconate, which is the point of no return, he can never marry."

The unspoken thought still hung in the air between them.

Jorge had answered her question but not the one she hadn't asked.

A thought passed between them—too subtle to be spoken, too fragile to be given form. To say it aloud would have been impossible. Perhaps even dangerous.

From that moment on, the unspoken thought became something Jorge carried in quiet meditation and something Belén turned over in the silence of her heart.

For a time, the demands of the farm kept them both distracted. The grape harvest arrived, followed by the main harvest, and there was no space for restless contemplation. The land had been generous that year, rewarding their toil with abundance. And so, they worked—day after day, season after season—until the cold winds of winter crept in and everything slowed.

That was when the thoughts returned.

To escape the damp chill of the Delta—where the heavy clouds from the estuary hung low over the water—they spent their evenings near the warmth of the fireplace, burning carob wood until the room glowed with heat and light.

It was on one such gray afternoon, in the second half of the year, that a messenger arrived with somber news.

Miguel Damianos—the ninety-year-old grandfather of their foreman—had died of pneumonia. He passed away in the home he built decades ago on a small plot of land bordering *La Alquería*.

Without hesitation, Belén and Jorge went to offer their condolences to his widow, Doña Basilia—a woman who had borne twelve children, all now grown with families of their own in Nueva Siracusa.

Despite her age, Doña Basilia was thin, sharp-eyed, and restless, a stark contrast to her late husband.

Inside the dimly lit house, she knelt beside Miguel's body, which lay on a simple cloth she had woven herself back in Calabria. Her grief did not come in soft whispers or silent weeping. It poured out in raw, unfiltered words, spoken to no one and to everyone.

"My poor Miguel has died like an ox beside the plow! And now they will bury him like an ox. We spent sixty years working this land, always dreaming of going back home… but he has died here. And I will die here, just like him. This land is good for planting—but terrible for dying. Because here, we die far from God."

Again and again, through the long night, she repeated her lament, her voice thick with sorrow.

Belén struggled to follow her words. She had never fully learned English, despite arriving in Argentina as a young woman. She spoke a rough, tangled mix of Calabrian and Albanian, the ancient language of her ancestors.

But Jorge? Jorge understood *everything*.

And as he walked home at dawn, beneath the cold glow of winter stars, he couldn't shake the feeling that this illiterate, grieving old woman had spoken a truth—a truth that her twelve educated children had long chosen to ignore.

She couldn't read but she saw the world more clearly than they ever would. The lands they had settled on—the fertile, generous banks of the Paraná—were perfect for sowing. But they were terrible for dying.

A few weeks later, word spread that Doña Basilia, unwilling to meet the same fate as her husband, had sold her land. She had convinced one of her granddaughters to accompany her, and together, they had set sail—determined to reach a place where, when her time came, she could die under a priest's blessing.

People laughed at her for it.

"The old woman has lost her mind," they scoffed. "She won't even survive the journey."

Her children consoled themselves with the thought that they had been generous—that they had *allowed* her to take half the value of the land in exchange for her departure.

But to Jorge, Doña Basilia's so-called madness was the only true wisdom he had encountered among these people—people who had spent their lives breaking the earth open, only to forget the sky above them.

And Belén? She felt Jorge slipping away from her. It was as if he were a great eagle, soaring higher and higher—far beyond what she could reach with just the flight of her heart.

The hope that had once carried her was slowly, inexorably, turning into despair.

Jorge rarely visited the Eastern Catholic Missionaries at their convent. He feared the whispers—the sideways glances, the murmurs in the pews.

Who is he now? A priest? A layman?

Questions he wasn't yet ready to answer.

Instead, he met privately with Father Gazapo, his former superior, in the priest's home in the city—the very same house where, years ago, Jorge had heard the confession of a dying woman in a purple turban.

It was during one of those quiet evenings, surrounded by the scent of old books and candle wax, that Jorge finally gave voice to the unease that had been gnawing at him.

"I live among these settlers of Nueva Siracusa," he admitted, "and I see their spiritual desolation. I feel I must help them, but I don't know how."

Father Gazapo, a man whose travels had taken him from the palaces of Rome to the villages of the Far East, thought carefully before answering.

"In Rome, I met several professors from the Pontifical Greek College of Saint Athanasius. It's a seminary that trains priests for Italo-Greek communities of the Byzantine rite. You should write to them. Ask if they have any newly ordained priests who might come here."

Jorge did as he suggested.

Months passed before a response finally arrived. But when he opened the envelope, he found only a single line from the Gospel...*The harvest is plentiful, but the laborers are few.*

A polite refusal. A reminder that even in Rome, where priests were trained in the very heart of Christendom, there were never enough to meet the growing need.

Still, Jorge refused to give up.

He cast his net wider, writing to two other seminaries that trained priests in the same rite—one in Lungro, southern Italy, and another in Palermo, Sicily.

This time, only one frustratingly vague response came.

"If the twenty young seminarians who entered this year complete their ordinations, we may be able to send you two priests."

Belén read the letter over Jorge's shoulder, then let out a dry laugh.

"This is like the story of the old woman in purgatory," she muttered, "who was told she would be freed from the flames with the first Mass sung by her grandson—who had just been born on earth."

She tossed the letter aside. But even as the frustration lingered, a thought struck her—so sudden, so complete, that she felt as if she had stumbled upon an answer that had been waiting in the shadows all along.

And it was *she*—not Jorge—who saw the solution.

Latin priests had transferred to the Greek Catholic rite before. In Europe, in North America, in Brazil, men from various religious orders had done so to minister to their Eastern Catholic brethren.

So why couldn't the Eastern Catholic Missionaries do the same?

Where else would they find a better place for their apostolate than right here—just a few leagues away—among a people who had been left without spiritual guidance for generations?

Could it really be possible that, in Buenos Aires, people could live as far from God as those in the remote villages of China or the deserts of Africa?

The idea consumed her.

Without hesitation, she rushed to Father Gazapo, despite the growing suspicion that, over time, the priest had developed a certain dislike for her.

She barely had time to explain before—*thud!*—his large, hairy hand slammed down on the table with the force of a thunderclap, as if swatting away some invisible insect.

Belén froze mid-sentence.

"What...? Did I say something foolish?" she asked hesitantly.

"No, my dear, no!" Father Gazapo boomed, his eyes gleaming with rare excitement. "For the first time, you've spoken like a book. Go on, go on!"

Emboldened, Belén pressed forward, laying out her case with precise logic, citing historical examples, drawing on the theological knowledge she had absorbed over months of relentless study.

She had barely finished when the priest let out a deep sigh and murmured,

"It's clear. Everything you've said is as clear and true as if the Holy Spirit Himself were speaking through you… which, I must say, is quite unusual—since He doesn't normally speak through a woman."

Belén smiled triumphantly, pleased with his approval. She kept talking, her voice rising with enthusiasm as she outlined the countless spiritual benefits of her plan—

"Enough, daughter, for God's sake!" Father Gazapo interrupted, throwing up his hands. "Now listen to me... What you're saying is absolutely right. It's almost as if God Himself has dictated it to you. But here's the problem—it's not in my hands to make it happen."

Belén's expression darkened.

"Not in your hands? Then… whose?"

The priest fixed her with a knowing stare.

"Yours."

Her breath caught.

"Mine?"

"Yes, by Saint Athanasius! I don't have a single priest in all of America—where three Missionary houses are already struggling to manage their work—who is free enough to take on the mission of ministering to the Italo-Greeks by changing his rite. But you, my dear... you have one in your own house."

The words struck her like a blow, and she went pale.

"I do?" she stammered, slowly rising to her feet.

Father Gazapo leaned forward, his voice quieter now but no less certain.

"Yes, yes! And you know exactly who I mean."

Jorge.

"You owe him this reparation," he continued, "Never in my life have I encountered a vocation more profound, a faith more solid. He was ordained a priest, but he had to leave the altar to fulfill other obligations. And now, you yourself—oh, the mysterious ways of God! —you yourself have found the solution. If he were to transfer to the Catholic Byzantine rite, he could return to his priestly ministry— without abandoning his duties as a husband and father."

The room seemed to close in on her.

Belén left in despair, her heart sinking under the weight of the very solution she had unwittingly set in motion. The bitter irony of it gnawed at her.

She had fought for so long to reclaim Jorge; and now, with her own hands, she had placed him back upon the altar.

Chapter 13: The Seed That Grew in the Dark

When the seed is planted, it begins to grow—even if the sower forgets about it.

When Belén returned home, troubled by her conversation with Father Gazapo and more than a little frustrated with herself for so carelessly bringing up the subject of the Eastern clergy, she spoke with Jorge. She dismissed their friend's idea as absurd, trying to brush it off.

But in doing so, she planted a seed in Jorge's heart—the heart of a former missionary from the East.

From that day on, Jorge's thoughts, and even hers, had a clear path to follow.

And follow it they did—relentlessly, day and night.

Sometimes, Belén would wake in the middle of the night, when the fields lay still under the starlit sky, wrapped in a silence so deep that even the crickets didn't stir.

Lying there, she felt as though she could hear her husband's thoughts. His breathing was so quiet, it was clear he was only pretending to sleep. In reality, he was just as awake as she was.

She saw the struggle in his pale, drawn face and in the sadness that never seemed to leave him. But the worst part was that in watching him, she was also watching herself—spying on her own heart. And she realized she was losing ground.

They never spoke about it, but one glance between them was enough to understand what the other was thinking. And those thoughts, eating away at them like termites hollowing out a wooden beam, could be summed up in one simple question:

Why not?

After all, Jorge had turned away from his original calling—for love, for duty. But now, wasn't it in her power to lead him back to God without losing him entirely? Wasn't that the very sacrifice Father Gazapo had suggested?

One day, Jorge returned from the city carrying a bundle of books sent to him from Europe. As Belén flipped through them, she noticed they were all written in Greek and looked like religious texts.

Ancient Greek was the liturgical language of the Italo-Greek Catholic Church. Jorge had learned it at the seminary, so it wouldn't be difficult for him to understand these books—the very ones used by the priests of that rite in their ceremonies.

Once again, Belén caught her husband drawing the plans for a building.

"What's that?" she asked.

Blushing, he replied, "It's the design for a Greek church. Sooner or later, the priests from Sicily who promised to come will arrive, and they shouldn't find themselves without a place to serve."

Then, looking at her intently, he added, "Don't you think it's time we set aside part of the blessings God has so generously given us to build Him a house?"

"And you know how to do that?"

"I'm trying to understand. Churches of this rite follow a simple design—shaped like a Greek cross, with four equal arms. The altar is placed on the eastern side, and the entrance is on the opposite end. That's all there is to it."

"That's all," Belén repeated softly, but with sadness in her voice.

That night, she had the same sorrowful dream she had many years before: she saw her husband walking away down a long road, while she followed, struggling through countless obstacles. And when she finally reached him, she found an immense wall he had built—one she had to tear down, stone by stone, with bloodied hands.

She had done it once before.

In the end, what was meant to happen, happened. The small, unintentional seed that had been planted took root in their hearts, grew, and bore fruit.

At last, they spoke openly. With a mix of resentment and disappointment, Belén agreed to let Jorge begin the process of returning to the Congregation of the Missionaries—the order he had once left. However, this time, he would change rites, allowing him to serve as a priest without leaving his wife.

The Congregation's superior had embraced Father Gazapo's idea of establishing a branch of priests who would follow the Eastern rite. Many Eastern Catholic communities lacked priests and had been without religious guidance for years.

According to Canon Law, *"A change of rite cannot take place without permission from the Holy See" (Canon 98).*

They applied for the necessary approval, and the request passed through countless offices, moving from Argentina to Spain to the Vatican. Months dragged into years. But by the time the permission was finally granted, the Greek church of New Syracuse was already complete. The townspeople, who had been eagerly awaiting the arrival of the priests, rejoiced at the sight of the finished church.

By then, Moramay had grown into a young woman. With kindness and determination, she pursued her studies at the Vincentian convent school for most of the year, spending her summers among the vineyards and canals of New Syracuse. The lush landscapes reminded her of the island where she was born—an island that Belén, Guazuncho, and Mr. Burns seemed to have left behind in their memories.

But not Kitra and Kandy. With them, Moramay often spoke about those distant days—days that felt more like a story from another lifetime than a memory of her own past.

Her mother had never given her the little brother she had always wished for, but Kitra and Kandy each had several children, whom Moramay adored and loved teaching new things.

As the time approached for sacred ceremonies to begin in the new church, it became necessary to explain to Moramay a unique aspect of Eastern priests: they could celebrate Mass, hear confessions, and perform all their priestly duties while being married and living with their wife and children.

For someone with a Latin mindset like Moramay—shaped by her convent school education and her English heritage—celibacy seemed like an inseparable part of the priesthood. She simply couldn't grasp the idea her parents were trying to teach her.

It had already been difficult enough for her to accept that Father Manrique had left his religious order, become her father, and taken the name Jorge de Balcázar.

That chapter of her life felt like a strange dream from her childhood. She had only made sense of it because her parents had carefully explained the circumstances that had separated them—how her father had genuinely believed her mother was dead, making it reasonable for him to think he was a widower and allowing him to be ordained as a priest.

They had also explained that once the mistake was discovered, he could no longer continue in the priesthood and had a duty to care for his wife and daughter.

Moramay understood all of this perfectly. She also knew that priestly ordination was permanent—her father might not serve as a priest anymore, but he was still, in essence, a priest of the Most High. Every night, before kissing him goodnight, she would gently kiss his consecrated hand.

Over time, she had stopped thinking about these explanations. But that summer, she saw her father overseeing the construction of a Greek church.

"Dad, what's a Greek church?" she asked.

Seeing her curiosity, her father used the opportunity to teach her a chapter of Church history that few people ever learn—or, if they do, rarely remember. He explained the schism of the Eastern Church, which began in the fifth century with the heresy of Nestorius, the Patriarch of Constantinople. It deepened in the ninth century with Photius and became irreparable in the eleventh century under Patriarch Michael Cerularius, who severed the last fragile ties with Rome.

Then, he told her about the parts of the Eastern Church that later returned to obedience under the Pope and how the Roman Pontiffs, with charity and tolerance, allowed them to retain certain traditions—including the unusual practice of permitting married priests—in order to make their reunion with the Church easier.

Moramay understood all of this—so long as it remained a theoretical concept.

But when she was told that the Greek-rite priests from Sicily wouldn't be arriving for another three or four years, and that in the meantime, her own father would take their place—celebrating Mass, hearing confessions, giving Holy Communion, and then, at the end of the ceremonies, simply closing the church and coming home to his wife and daughter—suddenly, she didn't understand at all.

No! Her English soul rebelled against it. She couldn't understand.

How could a priest, who in the morning heard confessions and consecrated the bread and wine—transforming them into the Body and Blood of Our Lord Jesus Christ—spend the afternoon and evening as her father and her mother's husband?

It even felt like they were trying to make a joke out of something sacred.

The worst part was that Belén felt the exact same way. She had no trouble understanding the charitable reasoning behind the Pope's decision to allow Eastern clergy to keep their customs and rites when they returned to the Catholic Church, as long as those traditions didn't contradict dogma. After all, they had existed for over a thousand years.

But that was theory. When it became personal—when it was her own husband—it was a different story. She couldn't shake the deep resistance in her English heart, a heart raised to revere priestly chastity.

Who were these reckless men who had once argued that, within the Roman Catholic Church, priests should abandon the very virtue that set them apart from other men? That they should become husbands and fathers without stepping away from the altar?

Now, Belén didn't just understand the Latin Church's reasons for defending celibacy—she *felt* them, not in her mind, but in her very being. She felt the weight of the battles the Church had fought, the struggles it had endured, to preserve this sacred calling among its ministers.

While his church was being built and the official decision on his transfer to the Greek rite was still pending, Jorge immersed himself in learning its intricate liturgy from his books. He also trained two young settlers from New Syracuse to assist him, preparing them to serve as his apostles.

At last, the day came for the church's dedication. It was placed under the patronage of St. John.

Jorge celebrated his first Greek Mass, assisted by Melkite Catholic priests who had traveled from the province of Santa Fe—priests whose rites closely resembled those of the Italo-Greek tradition.

Not a single settler of New Syracuse, young or old, missed the occasion. Some came out of curiosity, drawn by the novelty. Others, stirred by a movement of divine grace, felt a deeper call to faith. With the patient endurance of their people, they sat through the long, elaborate ceremonies of a Greek Mass, sung in a language they barely understood.

Belén, Moramay, Mr. Burns, Guazuncho, and their families were all there.

And when Belén saw her husband—her Jorge—standing at the altar, performing the miracle of consecration, lifting the Sacred Host high for the people to adore, she felt a sharp pain pierce her heart.

At that moment, she understood.

She saw the undeniable logic and restraint behind the Protestants' decision: once they had abolished priestly celibacy, it was only natural that they would abolish the Mass itself.

She recalled the words she had once read in *The Imitation of Christ.*

How pure must be the hands that consecrate the Body of Christ and distribute it to others! How undefiled his mouth, how holy his body!

No—those hands could no longer belong to an ordinary man of flesh and blood. They had become something more sacred, more exalted than even the hands of an archangel.

That day, after Mass, she fled to a quiet corner of her home, avoiding the people who searched for her and shutting out the foolish comments she knew would be made.

Meanwhile, some of the older settlers of New Syracuse shared stories with their children and grandchildren—memories of their home villages, poor rural hamlets where faith was simple and deeply ingrained.

In those places, priests had rarely attended formal seminary training. Especially in small villages, the faithful themselves would choose a priest whenever there was a vacancy that needed to be filled.

They would seek out a well-respected peasant—a man known for his integrity, preferably young and quick to learn the ceremonies of worship. If he agreed to dedicate himself to the Church, the community would cover what could best be described as an apprenticeship, though not actual studies.

Typically, after three months of training in another parish, he was considered ready for ordination. A bishop of their rite—a Catholic bishop—would then ordain him.

And just like that, he became a priest. According to Catholic doctrine, he possessed all the faculties of the priesthood: he could celebrate Mass, hear confessions, administer last rites, and perform all the sacraments except for Confirmation and Holy Orders, which were reserved for bishops.

But if Latin-rite priests—men who spent fourteen or fifteen years in rigorous study and devoted themselves entirely to their ministry—struggled to reach people in societies eroded by liberalism, materialism, and class resentment, then what could these simple, self-taught peasant priests hope to achieve?

How could they, men who remained tied to their families and their fields, who had learned nothing beyond the formal rituals (whose deeper meaning often escaped them), possibly take on the weighty responsibility of being curates of souls?

Curates of souls! Have you ever truly considered what it means to be a priest of souls?

A great poet once captured the essence of a true priest in words of immortal truth. If any priest does not see himself reflected in this portrait, the fault lies not with the description or the artist—but with himself.

The incomparable Lamartine, that profound poet of yesteryear wrote, "There is a man in every parish who has no family of his own, yet belongs to every family. He is called upon as a witness, a messenger, an actor in all the most solemn moments of life. No one is born or dies without him. He is there to receive man from the womb and to leave him only at the grave. He blesses or consecrates the cradle, the bridal chamber, the deathbed, the coffin. He is a man whom children learn to love, to venerate, and to fear; whom even strangers call 'Father.' He is the one before whom Christians pour out their most intimate confessions, their most secret tears.

"He is, by his very calling, the consoler of all suffering—both of soul and body. He stands as the bridge between wealth and poverty, seeing both the rich and the poor knock at his door. The rich, to leave their secret alms; the poor, to receive them without shame.

"He belongs to no single social class, yet he is part of them all. He walks among the lower classes through the simplicity of his life and, often, his humble origins. He moves among the upper classes through his education, his knowledge, and the depth of feeling that religion inspires and commands.

"He is a man who knows all, who has the right to speak all, and whose words fall upon minds and hearts with the weight of divine authority and unwavering faith.

"That man is the priest."

How can we expect a man who has been called by heaven—who has felt that undeniable vocation—to dedicate himself not only to the sacred duties of priesthood but also to being a good father, managing business affairs, securing an inheritance for his sons, and arranging good marriages for his daughters?

Would he have the time? The health? The heart to take on two missions of such magnitude—each of which is enough to consume an entire lifetime?

And wouldn't he lose some of his spiritual authority if, instead of carrying his breviary into the parish house, he brought his account book? Or if he sat at the dinner table beside his wife and children, still wearing his priestly stole or rochet?

A husband calling the barber to shave his tonsure—a priest sending the sacristan home with a message for his wife—isn't there something deeply contradictory in that?

Can we picture St. Francis Xavier, traveling to India to evangelize the pagans, with his wife and children in tow?

Could we imagine Don Bosco as he was—a father to hundreds of abandoned boys—if we knew that, at the end of the day, he had to leave them behind to go home, kiss his own children goodnight, and comfort a wife who had been waiting for him all day?

These were the first dilemmas that Belén saw Jorge struggle with. He had once lived in an almost mystical state, hearing voices from heaven, but now, suddenly, he felt the weight of earthly responsibilities pulling him down.

For someone with a Latin upbringing, this contradiction was jarring. On one hand, he was a priest at the altar, devoted to his parishioners. On the other, he was a husband, a father, a wealthy landowner with a business to run. How could he balance both?

Would he throw himself fully into his priestly mission, making his parishioners his only love, his only family? Or would he, as Moramay's father, as Belén's husband, as the master of an estate that required his attention, find himself too entangled in worldly concerns—allowing his fire as a priest, his passion as a missionary, to fade away?

Jorge was determined to fulfill both roles completely.

He refused to let his family—who had the first claim on his heart— feel neglected. He refused to let Belén, who was already uneasy about his return to priestly duties, find her fears justified.

And so, he pushed himself harder than ever, striving to be the best father, the best husband, and at the same time, the best priest he could possibly be.

Belén watched him closely, pained but silent, sensing his determination not to give her even the slightest reason to complain— anything that might sound like a reproach.

With the kind of youthful idealism that sees every challenge as simple and every impossible plan as achievable, he divided his life into a strict schedule, one he heroically imposed on himself.

"I'll wake up at five, winter and summer. I'll recite my breviary in advance. At seven, I'll go to the church, open it myself, and sit in the confessional. I'll wait there until it's time for Mass. These people have lost the habit of confession, but I'm certain I can restore it. At eight, Mass. Then I'll spend some time in thanksgiving, and if no one comes for confession, I'll return home by nine for breakfast. From nine to ten, I'll talk with Belén and Moramay. By then, I'm sure someone will be waiting for me in the sacristy or the church with questions, so I'll go see if I can help them. I'll stay there for a while before heading to the farm and vineyards to check on the work.

"That will take a couple of hours—Burns and Guazuncho are talkers. I'll be back by noon and always have lunch with the family. I'll stay home until two, and in the summer, a little longer. Then I'll return to the church for an hour of meditation and my full rosary, if I can. If anyone wants to confess or seek guidance, they'll know where to find me until six in the evening.

"Before heading out, I'll visit the Blessed Sacrament, then go through the parish, checking on those who are sick in body or soul. I won't wait for them to come to me—I'll go to them, like the Good Shepherd searching for his lost sheep."

And so, every hour of his day was planned, right up until eleven at night, when it was time to sleep.

But—*alas!*—not a single day went as planned.

His parishioners, unaware of his schedule, didn't come to the church at the appointed times. Instead, they sought him out at home—during meals, at dinner, in the few hours he had set aside for rest.

Many nights, he was woken from sleep to tend to the sick, spending the whole night by their side, only to start the next day again at five in the morning.

He never turned anyone away.

No matter how exhausted he was, he never skipped Mass, never neglected his breviary, never abandoned the confessional or his meditation. Even when he hadn't slept a single minute, he pushed himself through every duty.

By the end of the day, he was often so drained that it was painful to watch him force himself to sit at the family table. More than once, Belén was tempted to tell him to skip dinner, to send him straight to bed with nothing but a cup of broth.

But she never did.

She didn't want him to know that she saw his struggle—that she could see how impossible it was for him to hold both lives together.

The father of a family is a man. The priest is something more—there are moments in his life that even the angels envy.

But in the constant climb toward holiness, always followed by the inevitable descent back to the world, Jorge wore himself out—both body and soul.

According to Church law, Latin-rite Catholics are allowed to attend the ceremonies of Eastern Catholic churches, and they can fulfill their Sunday obligation by participating in one of their Masses.

Many Sundays, Belén and Moramay chose not to go into the city. Instead, they attended the Greek Mass that Jorge celebrated, having learned its unfamiliar liturgy over time.

In the church of New Syracuse—a church they had seen built at their own family's expense—they experienced a kind of devotion that was both touching in its simplicity and stirring in its ritual poverty.

Because of the lingering influence of the ancient Iconoclast heresy—which had once led to the destruction of religious statues on the grounds that their veneration was idolatry—Byzantine churches, whether Catholic or Orthodox, have no sculptures like those found in Latin churches.

Most of these churches have only a single altar, where only one Mass is celebrated each day.

The crucifix on the altar of New Syracuse wasn't sculpted in relief but painted on a wooden cross. To one side of it, a small altarpiece held an image of the Blessed Virgin; on the other side, one of St. John the Baptist. Suspended from the ceiling, illuminated by a flickering oil lamp, hung a silver dove—the tabernacle where the consecrated Eucharist was kept.

The walls, without niches for statues, were adorned with images of saints painted against a gold background in the distinctive Byzantine style—rich and ornate, meant to captivate the imagination of the faithful, moving them to prayer with the simple, unpretentious faith of the Eastern tradition.

A few times, Belén and Moramay decided to receive Communion there. Though the church felt cold and foreign to their hearts, they hoped to stir in it some of the fervor of their English souls.

It is well known that the Italo-Greek Catholic churches, which preserve very ancient customs, have strict rules regarding Communion for women. According to tradition, women must wait until after Mass, when all the other faithful have left. The priest then administers Communion to them through a small opening in the screen that separates them from the men—much like in a cloistered convent.

But Jorge chose to modify this practice, recognizing that such a custom would be unsettling in the towns of America, where no one finds it strange that men and women attend Mass together and approach the communion rail side by side.

With the approval of his superiors, he gave Communion to his wife and daughter according to the Greek-rite ritual—under both species—

placing a small piece of the consecrated bread, soaked in the consecrated wine, onto a silver spoon and offering it to them.

They received Communion *out of devotion,* as the canon law permits for Latin Catholics attending a Greek Mass. But they also did it to set an example for the settlers who filled the church on Sundays.

Yet, despite their efforts, very few followed their lead.

Jorge began to realize that the Eastern Catholics' lack of enthusiasm for the Eucharist largely stemmed from their reluctance to confess beforehand—a requirement for receiving it.

Time and time again, he noticed people coming to the confessional— not to confess their sins, but simply to seek his advice or discuss personal matters. Once they had finished their business, they would leave without ceremony.

He found this deeply disheartening. Each time it happened, it felt like a failure in his mission as a priest.

Determined to change this, he preached tirelessly about the immense spiritual grace that comes from receiving the sacraments frequently. The most he achieved, however, was persuading a few who had never confessed before to approach the Eucharistic table.

And yet, he had no choice but to give them Communion, praying silently that God would not hold their unworthiness against them— that He would instead see their ignorance and good intentions.

But this resistance to confession had another root.

Somehow, the idea had spread among the parishioners that absolution from a married priest was not valid. The real issue, however, was something more personal—an unwillingness to confess their deepest faults to a man who lived with a wife. They feared that, like any curious woman, she would eventually pry those secrets out of him.

This, more than anything else, seemed to explain the widespread reluctance to go to confession in many Byzantine-rite churches. No matter how much a married priest insisted that he was bound by the sacramental seal—even to the point of death—some people simply didn't trust him.

This was evident even in churches where Eastern priests, trained in European seminaries, had taken perpetual vows of chastity. In those places, the faithful flocked to them, unburdening their souls without hesitation.

And so, in New Syracuse, despite Jorge's tireless efforts to teach sound doctrine, religious life never went beyond Sunday Mass, baptisms, and weddings—ceremonies that often became little more than an excuse for worldly celebrations.

Belén, with her sharp intuition, understood the reason before Jorge did. Without explaining it to him, she asked one day,

"Do you know when the priests you requested from Italy will arrive?"

"No," Jorge replied. "I keep hoping for them, and I need them. The harvest here is ready to be gathered—it is plentiful."

"And the workers are few," Belén added, completing the Gospel passage. "You should ask them to send you unmarried priests."

"I already have," Jorge said with a sigh. "And I'll keep insisting."

At last, the two young priests arrived—freshly ordained at the Seminary of San Benedetto Ullano in Calabria.

It was a day of celebration for the entire colony. Not only were these men of the same heritage, but they also spoke the unique dialect of their people, which was still in use in New Syracuse.

With the enthusiasm of new missionaries, they threw themselves into the work of supporting Jorge, and soon, a revival of faith spread through the community—among both men and women.

But what brought Jorge the greatest joy was the sudden increase in Communion, and with it, a rise in confessions.

Yet, the penitents weren't coming to *his* confessional.

They were flocking to his two assistants. And not just those who spoke their dialect—even those who didn't understand a word of it were choosing to confess to them instead.

That night, as Jorge discussed the matter with Belén, she could hear the sadness and humiliation in his voice, no matter how much he tried to hide it.

Stung by his pain, she didn't hold back her own resentment.

"I noticed it too," she said bitterly. "They don't trust you—because you're married."

A silence hung between them. Then, after a moment, she let out a quiet, anguished confession, "I have always been a burden to you."

And with that, she broke down—not in soft, tearful weeping, but in raw, choking sobs, like the first violent gusts of a storm, announcing itself without the relief of rain.

Jorge, startled and shaken by this sudden outpouring of anguish—an anguish he had never fully seen before—reached out to console her. He used the same gentle caresses and firm, unwavering words that had once won her heart.

"My silk petal... my child—more of a child than our own daughter! Do you think we were put on this earth to follow our own will? The ways of God are not the ways of men..."

"I know that," she said bitterly. "And you should know it even better—because He did not want what you gave Him. You sacrificed yourself, and you sacrificed me. And now, you see it—you were never meant for this. You built your nest on a rock too high."

"Woe to him who, after putting his hand to the plow, turns back!" Jorge answered. "Yes, I have given everything. I have burned myself—my life—on the altar. And worse than that, I have burned my love, which was you, my Belén. But it is not true that God has rejected what I have offered Him. And it is not true that my sacrifice has been wasted. One day, we will see how every drop of my sweat, poured into the furrows, has borne fruit. You and I—we are the wheat of Christ. If the grain of wheat, cast into the earth, does not die, it remains useless. But if it dies, it brings forth much fruit."

She looked at him, her dark eyes brimming with pain, a quiet storm raging behind them.

"What are you trying to say?" she asked, though deep down, she already knew.

"That without sacrifice—without surrendering everything we are, everything we have, everything we long to hold—we labor in vain," Jorge said, his voice steady, unwavering. "We may never see the harvest, Belén, but we must be the wheat sown in this soil, buried so that others may live."

His words were heavy, each one pressing down on her like a stone.

"I heard a voice calling me to follow," he continued, his eyes burning with an unshakable fire, "but it never promised me anything. No comfort. No reward. Only the call. And we must obey, even if it means tearing apart our deepest loves, even if it means breaking our own hearts." He exhaled, his voice nearly reverent as he murmured, "'I have not come to bring peace, but the sword.'"

The sword.

His gaze locked onto hers, full of a devotion so fierce it felt like a living thing between them. "The sword, Belén—to sever the things that bind us most to this world. To cut away love. To cut away desire. To make us wholly His."

Belén's breath caught in her throat as she listened. In that moment, Jorge seemed almost luminous, his face glowing with an almost inhuman fervor, as if a halo of conviction had settled upon his head. He spoke of sacrifice with such certainty, as though the pain of it did not terrify him, as though he welcomed the agony.

But she did not.

She listened in silence, waiting to feel the same divine fire. Waiting for something within her to bend to the weight of his truth. But there was nothing—nothing but the slow, unshakable realization that she could not, would not, follow him into this abyss.

"Your doctrine is too harsh for me," she whispered at last. Her voice was quiet, yet it trembled under the weight of all she could not say.

Jorge studied her carefully. "And if one day you were called to it?"

Belén's heart clenched. She knew the answer she was expected to give. She knew the answer he needed to hear.

"Then I would obey," she said, forcing the words past the ache in her throat.

A slow, sad smile touched his lips. His hand came to rest against her cheek, and for a moment, the fire in his eyes softened. "Then, my Belén," he whispered, "I will pray that you hear the call."

He gathered her in his arms and kissed her, tender and reverent, as though he were already saying goodbye.

But as his warmth pressed against her, Belén suddenly understood—*this* was the sword.

Not a weapon of steel, but something sharper, something crueler.

It was tearing through her, splitting her soul apart. The sword of Christ had begun to cut what Christ Himself had once joined.

A wave of fear swept through her, cold and relentless. If she stood still, if she let herself be swallowed by this path, she knew what lay ahead: a life bound to sacrifice, to suffering, to a love that would never be hers.

No.

Something deep within her rebelled, wild and desperate. She refused to be cut away, to be reduced to the chaff while others reaped the harvest of her loss.

She would not be the wheat.

And in that moment, with his arms still wrapped around her, with his lips still warm against hers, Belén made her choice.

She would escape her fate.

Chapter 14: The Archangel's Bride

Belén was born in the wrong century. She should have lived in the days of Saint Teresa, riding mule carts across Spain to found convents under threat of the Inquisition. Or in the age of Maria Reed and Anne Bonny, those fearless women who commanded pirate ships and ruled the high seas.

Belén had once dreamed of being like them. She had imagined herself at the helm of a ship, her banner fluttering over the waves, her name whispered in the same breath as Tortuga—the infamous pirate haven where men fleeing from Philip II's galleons or Queen Elizabeth's swift warships found refuge.

Even Sir Francis Drake, that notorious English pirate who should have ended his days hanging from a mast, had instead become an admiral and a noble of the realm.

But Belén was born four centuries too late. Now, at thirty-five and beyond, she still wandered through life like a caged messenger pigeon, wings intact but trapped nonetheless.

"I have not come to bring peace, but a sword."

The words passed Jorge's lips almost in passing, but to Belén, they were a bolt of lightning, illuminating something she had always known deep inside.

God calls His people in different ways. Some are meant to kneel in prayer, offering devotion at all hours. Others are meant to take up the sword and fight in His name.

She had never been one for silent, contemplative faith. She had been made for war, but there was no war left. The world had declared peace—an eternal peace, or so it claimed. No battlefields to run to. No cause to serve. So, she turned to another battlefield—the one waiting for her in the world of wealth and power, the life that had been stolen from her by time and circumstance.

As the rightful heir to Don Casto Aguinagalde—the founder of the Bank of Utrera, with its twenty branches and two hundred million in assets—she had every reason to reclaim her noble birthright. Yet, through a twist of fate, the English government had seized her inheritance, believing it to be unclaimed, unaware that Don Casto had left behind a single heir.

After that fateful conversation with Jorge—where she had felt, for the first time, like a rebellious soul telling God *I refuse to serve!* Belén made up her mind. She would go to Spain.

Jorge listened, sadness darkening his gaze, but he did not object. He knew his wife too well. There was no stopping Belén once she had set her sights on something. And besides, there was nothing wrong with her reclaiming what was rightfully hers. Perhaps, he reasoned, part of that fortune could even support their mission—the work they had begun, which always seemed to need more resources.

Moramay, on the other hand, was heartbroken. She had been in her final years at the convent school, a place she loved. Now she was being uprooted, torn from everything familiar—her father, the vineyards and canals of Nueva Siracusa, and the families of Mr. Burns and José María. It pained her to leave the nuns more than anything. Their disciplined, hard-working way of life seemed to her the happiest existence one could have on this earth.

Physically, Moramay was the mirror image of her mother. But in spirit, they were worlds apart. Belén was impulsive, passionate, restless—a woman built for adventure, as honest and sharp as a polished blade. Moramay was serene, disciplined, and detached. She shared her mother's purity but had no curiosity for the unknown. She was charitable but reserved, as if she lived in a higher realm and touched the earth only out of duty or kindness.

At sixteen, she was a reflection of the young Belén who had once roamed the streets of Fuenterrabía—except without her wild streak, without the spark of rebellion. And yet, when they walked together, it was still Belén who turned heads. Time had softened her beauty, but it had not diminished her presence. She had the kind of allure that went beyond youth, a force that commanded attention without asking for it.

From the moment she first arrived in Buenos Aires, she had lived under the name María Aguinalde de Guernizo, claiming that her documents had been lost in her strange adventures. Now, carrying that name, she arrived in Spain as *Mrs. Guernizo* and, through sheer will and clever maneuvering, reclaimed her true identity, her noble titles, and—within a year—full ownership of the Bank of Utrera.

She moved through the circles of power with effortless grace, navigating the English court like she had been born to it. She never had to tell the full truth. People knew she was married to Jorge de Balcázar, the Marquis of Manrique. Their marriage was confirmed in the records of one of Madrid's most prestigious parishes—the motherhouse of the Eastern Catholic Missionaries—where she had been wed by Father Conejo, who, fortunately, was still alive.

But no one knew what had become of her husband. That handsome young man who once dreamed of the priesthood—until *she* crossed his path. People speculated, and she let them. They assumed he lived in America or Asia, managing vast estates so valuable that he could not leave them, not even for a short visit.

And Belén, with her undeniable skill, had no trouble managing her own fortune—along with the small portion of Jorge's estate that remained in Spain. She held a notarized power of attorney from Buenos Aires, stamped and sealed by various foreign ministries, granting her full control over their affairs. She had done what she always did. She had taken what life had given her, turned it to her advantage, and refused to be defeated. But for the first time, as she stood on the threshold of her greatest victory, surrounded by wealth and power, she could not shake a single, persistent thought.

Why does it feel like I have won everything—except the one thing I truly wanted?

Oh, what Belén could have done if she had been born a man in the 16th century! And what she might have accomplished in the 20th—if only she hadn't fallen so hopelessly, so tragically, in love with an archangel.

In Madrid, in London, in Paris—wherever her wealth and restless imagination carried her—there was no shortage of suitors. Some vied for her daughter's hand, others, bolder or more foolish, set their sights on her. Some assumed she was a widow. Others, mistaking her elegance for loneliness, thought she was waiting to be claimed. But neither Belén nor Moramay let anyone in.

Moramay, still untouched by love, had no interest in romance. And as for Belén—her heart was too pure, too unyielding, to be occupied by passing fancies.

Belén was born four hundred years too late! Nothing in her own century could have truly satisfied her. Banking? That was the work of Lombards and Jews—practical, lucrative, but utterly uninspiring. The amusements of high society? Frivolous distractions, dull and meaningless for a woman who had once watched her own ship explode, dived for pearls in the Aru Islands, and hunted sharks beneath the blazing equatorial sun.

So, she turned to travel. With Moramay by her side, she crossed the northern reaches of Europe to the icy desolation of Spitzbergen, then journeyed south to the Cape of Good Hope—the very place where, years ago, she had once dreamed of landing with her young husband, fleeing from the infamous Raw Meat, captain of the *Cormorant*.

And yet neither adventure nor business nor travel could fill the void inside her.

The realization came slowly, creeping in like an unwelcome shadow. She was growing weary. Belén, who had once craved movement, who had once thought that life itself was motion, had begun to feel the weight of constant travel pressing on her. Before she could admit it—even to herself—Moramay spoke first.

"I want to go back to Buenos Aires."

Belén studied her daughter carefully.

The reasons Moramay gave were practical, almost rehearsed. She wanted to finish her business studies, to prepare for a future in banking—her destiny, as everyone had told her. But something about her tone was off. It was too determined. Too final.

And suddenly, Belén, who prided herself on knowing her daughter's heart, began to suspect there was something more. An unspoken reason. A hidden love.

Just as *she* had once forced her uncle to send her away, all because of a forbidden romance—so long ago that it felt like another lifetime. Back then, the solution had been to send her to a Brighton school, to keep her far from temptation, to cure her of her fickle heart. What a cure that was! It was in Brighton, reminiscing about her summers in Fuenterrabía, rereading the mysterious letters of Jorge de Balcázar y Manrique, that her great, noble, and tragic passion took root. A love that would consume her, body and soul, for the rest of her days. And now… was her daughter falling into the same fate?

Something's off here, she thought. *There must be a boy involved…*

Oh, the supposed clairvoyance of mothers! The way they believe they can read their children's souls like an open book, as if every heartbeat, every secret, every hidden longing were written in ink upon their faces.

But whatever the reason, Moramay's wishes aligned with Belén's own; so, they returned to Buenos Aires. Not by sea, though. Never again. She had enough of that after her time aboard the cursed *Cormorant*. Instead, she chartered a plane—one of those high-speed marvels that could cover five hundred kilometers per hour, completing the journey in just a day and a half.

In true Belén fashion, she refused to take the usual westward route. No—she went east instead. She crossed Asia, Oceania, the vast and countless islands of the Pacific—including one where, so many years ago, she had fought against fate itself for a love she refused to lose.

The invincible hope of her youth was fading. She tried to distract herself with movement, with the outside world—anything to drown out the storm inside her. She, who had once loved the sea, freedom, motion, now had moments when she despised them. More and more, she found herself drawn to things that resembled stillness. Captivity. Restraint.

During her long absence, Jorge had written often. His letters were full of his mission—the slow, steady work of bringing Catholicism back to a people who had nearly lost it. These were Italians, once devout, but their parents—too busy "making it in America"—had never even taught them how to cross themselves. Now, with two assistants, Jorge worked tirelessly. So tirelessly, in fact, that he had proposed to his superiors the idea of founding a seminary in Nueva

Siracusa. A place where young men could be trained in the Greek rite, ensuring that the faith took root in the community once more.

The idea was approved. And Jorge, who never let time go to waste, immediately began building it. By the time Belén returned, the seminary was complete. Six young men had already entered, eager to pursue the priesthood.

Belén read Jorge's letters and imagined him there, overseeing the construction, guiding the young seminarians, losing himself in his mission.

For the first time that she could remember, Jorge's once-empty confessional—where people used to come seeking advice rather than absolution—was now filled, day after day, with true penitents. They weren't just looking for guidance anymore. They came to confess, and Jorge knew why. Without Belén by his side, without the ever-present reminder of his other life, the people of Nueva Siracusa saw him only as a priest. Their trust in him grew, and with it, his ministry flourished.

So, whenever the nights stretched long and the silence of his empty home weighed heavily on him, he reminded himself of this—that his sacrifice had borne fruit. And with a sigh of resignation, he thanked heaven for this strange, bittersweet blessing.

One day, Jorge received an unexpected call from the Buenos Aires airport.

The moment he answered, he heard her voice—falling from the heavens like a meteorite.

And then Moramay's.

Jorge nearly dropped the receiver. Had it been part of the Greek liturgy, he might have ordered the church bells to ring. Instead, he barely took a moment to collect himself before announcing to his assistants, "I'm leaving for Buenos Aires. Ten days, maybe more. You'll have to manage without me."

The seminary, the church, the sick who needed tending—he left it all in their hands. His duties as a husband and father called to him now and he could not resist. He had permission to wear civilian clothes, and since he had never adopted the Eastern tradition of a priestly beard, all it took was a simple change of wardrobe for him to look like a man untouched by the burdens of the altar—a man who might have lived another life entirely.

He set off in his own car, his excitement barely contained. God, who knew the depths of his heart, understood. There was no sin in this— no fault in his clean-shaven face, no guilt in his eagerness. It was natural. Human. Even virtuous.

But his assistants, watching him depart with the lightness of a man in love, were less forgiving. They exchanged uneasy glances. And though they said nothing aloud, their thoughts echoed the words of the disciples who once spoke to Christ about the weight of marriage…*If this is the case, it is better not to marry.*

And again, they heard the voice of the Divine Master…*Not everyone can accept this, but only those to whom it has been given... Let the one who can accept it, accept it.*

Jorge, oblivious to their doubts, sped toward Buenos Aires, his heart childlike in its joy, though not without a flicker of embarrassment.

I feel the same way I did back then, he thought. *When Father Gazapo wrote to me in Chile, telling me that Belén refused to leave me, I should have been alarmed. But all I felt was… happiness.*

He had always known what he should feel, and yet, time and time again, his heart betrayed him.

A short time later, he arrived in Buenos Aires.

There, waiting for him, was Belén. The moment he saw her, he pulled her into his arms, holding her tightly against his chest. And in a voice low enough for only her to hear, he whispered the same words Adam had spoken in Genesis—the very first declaration of love in human history. Words that, forty centuries later, Christ himself had repeated to the Jews.

"A man will leave his father and mother and be joined to his wife, and the two shall become one flesh."

Jorge's lips brushed her ear.

"I have no father or mother," he murmured. "I have only you, my Belén. And you are everything to me…"

But Belén, ever quick with a mischievous smile, corrected him.

"You have me… and your parish."

Jorge, still dressed as an ordinary man not a priest, not today, had no interest in discussing the souls of Nueva Siracusa.

"They're fine," he said shortly. "They send you their regards."

And then, swiftly changing the subject, he added, "But I'm taking a break—ten days, maybe fifteen. A real vacation. Tell me about yourself, Belén. About you and Moramay."

Belén grinned.

"I'll tell you about Father Conejo."

Jorge chuckled.

"You saw him in Madrid?"

"Oh yes," she said. "An extraordinary old man—holier than Father Gazapo, if you ask me. Though judging by their names, they must come from the same family."

Jorge smirked.

"And what did Father Conejo have to say about me?"

"Do you really want to know?"

"I asked, didn't I?"

Belén leaned in, eyes gleaming.

"He disapproves."

Jorge raised an eyebrow.

"Of what, exactly?"

"Of you becoming a Greek priest. He has no problem with Greek priests—so long as they're single. But he's not too keen on the ones dragging a wife around with them."

Jorge sighed.

"Of course," he muttered. "He's defending his work. He was the one who married us, after all. Do you think he regrets it?"

Belén tapped her chin, as if genuinely considering the question.

"What I'm not so sure about," she said slyly, "is whether you even *could* have married me back then."

Jorge frowned.

"What do you mean?"

Belén's smile turned wicked.

"Well, for one," she said, "you were already married."

Jorge blinked.

"Married?"

"To Teodora!" she teased, giving him a playful nudge. "Admit it—I saved you from her, Jorge. Where would you be now if I hadn't walked into your hotel that morning in Madrid, just as she was about to trap you?"

Jorge rolled his eyes.

"You've gone completely mad. I hope Father Conejo didn't put these ideas in your head."

"Of course not," she said, grinning. "But there's another reason I think you couldn't have married me back then."

Jorge raised an eyebrow.

"Oh? And what's that?"

Belén crossed her arms.

"Because," she said slowly, "even though you had *two* women in your life…"

"Two?"

"Teodora and me," she winked. "The truth is, you never really had a calling for *either* of us."

Jorge scoffed.

"Oh, now you're an expert on my vocation?"

"Listen," Belén continued, tilting her head as if in deep thought. "If you didn't truly choose… then your consent was invalid. And if your consent was invalid, then our marriage…"

Jorge groaned.

"You theologians are all the same," he muttered. "Always looking for loopholes."

Belén smirked.

"You should thank God we didn't have a canon lawyer at the wedding."

And for the first time in a long time, Jorge laughed.

A real, full-bodied laugh—not the polite, measured chuckle of a priest, but the unguarded laughter of a man with his wife. The wife who had stolen his heart. And who, no matter how much heaven tried to claim him, refused to let him go.

Jorge couldn't tell, but Belén's nerves were unraveling, betraying emotions she fought hard to suppress. She longed to remain composed, but it was a losing battle. A word, a thought—anything—could set her off. This time, it wasn't his presence that unsettled her, nor even their long-awaited reunion. No, it was the way he stood before her, dressed in elegant civilian clothes instead of his Greek priest's robes. He looked good in them—too good—but the sight infuriated her. It felt like a mockery. A man ordained for eternity should not be able to shed his vows so easily, no matter how many councils sanctioned it or if the Pope himself decreed it permissible.

Yet, here he was. Her husband; and her husband was that priest.

Belén lingered on her feet for a moment before abruptly dropping into a chair, covering her eyes. When she finally spoke, her voice was hurried, forced—too much so.

"Did you know I crossed Asia? And my seas?"

"Your seas?" he echoed, brow furrowing. "What do you mean, *your* seas?"

"When I was a girl, I believed they would all be mine one day—either because I'd become a pirate or because I'd marry one." She let out a bitter laugh. "What a foolish dream. I've always had foolish dreams. And in the end, I married... a Greek priest."

"Belén!" His voice was sharp, wounded. "That's unfair, and you know it. You cut me deep. And you have no right—I came here full of love…"

"Shhh."

She pressed a hand against his lips. The touch was both tender and unyielding.

"You can say whatever you want after I finish."

Jorge fell silent.

"I crossed Asia, and I reached my seas—the very waters where the *Cormorant* once sailed. But you weren't there anymore. The bandit Raw Meat, our dear captain, had left you stranded on a deserted island… so he could keep me for himself."

Jorge sighed.

"How many years ago was that?"

His indifference stung.

"I don't know," she snapped. "A thousand years could pass, and to me, it would still feel like yesterday. Oh, how I loved you, Jorge! And you…admit it! If it had been Teodora instead of me boarding that ship with you, she would have settled in just fine with Raw Meat, and you…" her eyes flashed "…you would be saying Mass in Shanghai right now."

"Or in Chile," he added, amused.

"And the *Cormorant* would still be carving through the waves of Polynesia. And she, Teodora, would be the queen of one of its ten thousand islands, just as I was. Because I was born to be a queen—of an island or of a heart."

Jorge exhaled, rubbing his temples.

"You're rambling, Belén."

"That's exactly what I was talking about," she shot back. "I flew over my seas, and in the middle of the night, I recognized my island."

"How could you possibly recognize it?"

"Because the waves around it glow, as if they're made of liquid phosphorus. When they crash against the cliffs, they burst into light— like flames."

Jorge nodded.

"I know. That glow is caused by tiny crustaceans, native to those waters."

"My island," Belén continued, her voice softer now, "looked like a black saint or an Ethiopian queen. Against the dark expanse of the sea, it was crowned in a halo of stars—born from the waves themselves. From my plane, silent and fleeting like a shard of mother-of-pearl, I recognized the voice of those breakers. The same ones I listened to for seven years while my heart never tired of waiting.

"I was the one who clung to hope, foolish as it was. I believed, against all reason, that I would find you again. And I did. But now... now I wish I had never left my island. The place where Moramay was born. The place where I was queen.

"Three nights ago, the stars watched me pass over it once more. And I saw again the endless, restless waves crashing against its shores— the same wild energy I carry within me. Waves like flames of light, moving with the untamed rhythm of the sea... just like my soul."

She had spoken with such intensity that her words seemed to hang in the air, shimmering like heat on distant horizons. Then, as if something inside her had finally broken, the storm within her quieted. The tears came, but softly now—no sobs, no tempest. Just a gentle rain.

Jorge did not try to argue.

Moramay, sensing the weight in the air between them, had slipped away unnoticed. When Jorge finally realized she was gone, he reached out, his touch featherlight as he brushed a strand of Belén's hair away from her damp cheek. It was a gesture so familiar, so achingly tender, that for a moment, she almost let herself lean into it.

"Come on," he murmured. "Tell me about Moramay."

Belén lifted her face, weary but steady, her expression unreadable. She held his gaze for a long moment, as if measuring whether or not she truly wanted to say the words. When she finally spoke, her voice was quieter but laced with something resolute.

"I have some news for you," she murmured. "You might actually like it."

Jorge's brow lifted slightly, his curiosity piqued.

"Oh? What is it?"

She swallowed, inhaling as though steadying herself before taking a step into unknown territory.

"Moramay wants to be a nun."

For a moment, Jorge said nothing. He only looked at her, his dark eyes searching hers. Then, slowly, a small, knowing smile touched his lips.

"She always has," he said simply.

Belén let out a breath that was almost a laugh, though there was no humor in it—only disbelief, only the weight of a truth she had long been unable to accept.

"You knew?"

"Not in words," he admitted. "But I've seen it in her. Haven't you?"

Belén lowered her gaze, as if afraid to meet the answer written in his face. Because *yes*, she had seen it—seen it in the way Moramay had always been different, even as a child.

While other girls had stolen glances at boys and whispered about love in the quiet corners of the market, Moramay's eyes had never wavered from something higher, something unseen. When she was only a child, Belén had found her awake in the early hours of the morning, praying in the candlelight, her small hands folded with a devotion that made her mother's heart ache.

"She was born with her eyes turned toward God," Belén murmured, almost to herself. "Even when she was just a baby, she would look past me, as if she were searching for something beyond my arms, beyond this world. I tried to hold onto her, but…I've always known she was never truly mine."

Jorge listened, his expression gentle, understanding.

"She is not leaving you, Belén," he said quietly. "She is only following the path that was always meant for her."

Belén let out a breath, shaking her head.

"Do you know what it is to be a mother, Jorge?" Her voice trembled, but her words were steady. "To give your heart to someone knowing that one day, they will walk away from you? To love so deeply that even when you see it coming—even when you know from the beginning that they are not yours to keep—you still find yourself unprepared when the moment arrives?"

Jorge exhaled, reaching for her hands.

"I know," he murmured. "Because I once had to let you go."

Belén closed her eyes at his words, swallowing hard against the sudden lump in her throat.

For a moment, neither of them spoke. The silence stretched between them, heavy with all that had been lost, all that could never be reclaimed.

Then, Jorge squeezed her hands gently.

"She will be at peace, Belén," he said, his voice firm yet full of tenderness. "Moramay has chosen freely. And if you love her, truly love her, you must let her go with the same love that you raised her with."

Belén let out a slow, shuddering breath. She had always feared losing Moramay, feared that the day would come when her daughter would walk a path she could not follow.

And now, that day had arrived.

But as much as it hurt, as much as it broke her heart, she knew— she *knew*—that Moramay had never belonged to her.

She had always belonged to God.

Chapter 15: The Sword and the Sanctuary

The day before they arrived in Buenos Aires, as the plane soared high above the endless expanse of the Pacific, Moramay sat in quiet contemplation, her gaze fixed on the distant horizon where the island of her birth had long since disappeared. The vast sky and sea stretched out before her, infinite and unbroken, as if daring her to remember what had been left behind. Then, without warning, she turned to her mother.

Belén, lost in her own thoughts, had been staring at the same unending sea, drifting through a labyrinth of memories and possibilities—what could have been, what should have been, what might have been if fate had twisted in a different direction… or if certain things had never happened at all.

"Mom," Moramay asked, breaking the silence, her voice as gentle as the wind outside, "have you ever regretted leaving your island?"

The question startled Belén. Had her daughter's thoughts been circling the same ghosts as hers? She hesitated before answering, her voice low, almost as if speaking to herself.

"There are times when I miss it... when I wish I had never left."

"Would you like to go back?"

Belén gave a soft, bitter laugh.

"That's impossible now. Too many things tie me to this world."

"Do you love the world that much?"

"No!" The vehemence of her answer surprised even her. "I hate it. I spend my life trying to escape it, but it seeps into every part of me."

Moramay watched her mother carefully, her young eyes searching for something deeper.

"If you could leave it behind, would you?"

Belén exhaled, shaking her head.

"I can't anymore. The world would follow me wherever I went. When you're one of the richest women in Europe, you realize you've lost the best part of your freedom. Wealth is a chain you can't break. No matter where I went, it would go with me. The only way to be free would be to lose everything—to ruin myself completely."

Her voice dropped to a whisper.

"Ah, if only I lost it all… then I could leave the world behind. I could go back to my island, and no one would follow me."

"Not even Papa?"

Belén hesitated, a rare flicker of tenderness crossing her face.

"I think he would follow me anywhere," she admitted. "But I would never allow him to abandon his work just to chase after me. And that is why I don't run away."

"Mom!"

Belén turned toward her daughter.

"What?"

Moramay leaned in, lowering her voice to a near whisper, as if the next words were meant only for her mother and the angels above. They were alone in the cabin—aside from the crew, who were occupied with their duties—so there was no need to keep secrets. And yet, Moramay's next question was one that could only be spoken in hushed tones.

"Mom… if you became a nun, would the world still follow you into the convent?"

Belén froze.

The words hit her like a stone flung from the past. Suddenly, she was back in the days when Father Gazapo had tried to convince her she had a religious calling. Depending on her mood, his insistence had either made her laugh or infuriated her. Now, hearing something so similar from her own daughter, her first instinct was suspicion. Had Father Gazapo written to Moramay? Had he somehow manipulated her into bringing up this absurd idea again?

Her voice sharpened like a blade.

"Don't tell me Father Gazapo put this nonsense in your head!"

Moramay's expression darkened, her lips pressing into a stubborn pout.

"I swear he hasn't written to me—not even a single line!"

"Then where did you get this ridiculous idea?"

Moramay didn't flinch. Instead, she met her mother's gaze with unwavering certainty.

"Why do you call it ridiculous?" she challenged. "To turn away from a world you despise and give yourself to a God who deserves everything—and who is calling you?"

Belén's face softened, the sharpness in her eyes dulling into something sadder, something heavier.

"No," she murmured, shaking her head. "God is not calling me in that way…"

Moramay took a breath, steady and slow.

Then, in a voice barely louder than a whisper, she said, "Well, Mom, I'll confess something to you."

Belén looked up.

"He *has* called me," Moramay said. "And I've already answered."

For a moment, the world inside the cabin seemed to spin. Belén snapped out of her own spiraling thoughts, her heart tightening with something dangerously close to panic.

"What are you saying?" she asked, her voice sharp with disbelief, as if she had just been yanked from a dream she hadn't realized she was dreaming.

She had been so sure—so *certain*—that Moramay's eagerness to return to Buenos Aires was because of some secret romance. She had imagined a young man, a love story unfolding in the shadows. But now, faced with the exact opposite, she felt like the most foolish woman alive. What a brilliant psychologist *she* had been—completely misreading her own daughter.

Moramay exhaled, her expression calm, unwavering.

"It's not exactly news," she said slowly. "More than three years ago, I felt the calling to be a missionary."

Belén let out a sharp, bitter laugh.

"Oh, wonderful! A missionary—just like your father, who ended up as a village priest!"

Moramay remained calm.

"At first, I thought so too…"

Belén rolled her eyes.

"Let me guess—then you decided you wanted to be a Vincentian Sister?"

"No, Mom." Moramay shook her head, her voice steady. "I studied with the Vincentians, and I admire them deeply. I love the work they do. But my calling is different. It's not something I inherited from you, that's for sure. In fact, I know this is the last thing you'd ever expect from your daughter."

Belén narrowed her eyes.

"Just say it already. Do you want to be a Sister of Charity?"

Moramay didn't hesitate.

"No, Mom," she said simply. "I want to be a Trappist."

Belén felt her stomach drop as the plane seemed to dip, the vast ocean below rising to swallow them, the bright sky above turning black and infinite, as if the universe itself had collapsed into an abyss. The roar of the engines dulled, drowned beneath the rush of blood in Belén's ears. It took her a long moment to steady herself, to realize the plane was still gliding smoothly through the sky, that nothing had changed—except everything. Then she saw Moramay, smiling softly, wrapping her arms around her as though comforting a frightened child.

"Forgive me, Mom," Moramay whispered, resting her cheek against her mother's shoulder. "But this is the best thing for someone like me—someone who hates the world and only wants to serve God. I've felt His call in the silence of the night for a long time. At first, I was afraid. But one day, while reading the Bible, I came across the story of Samuel. He was thirteen when he heard God's voice for the first time. That's when I finally knew how to answer."

Belén, still trembling, whispered, "And what was that answer?"

Moramay's voice was calm, unwavering.

"Samuel was asleep when he heard a voice calling his name. 'Samuel! Samuel!' Thinking it was Eli, his master, he ran to him and asked what he wanted. But Eli told him he hadn't called him and sent him back to bed. It happened again. And again. Until finally, Eli understood— it was God who was speaking. So, he told Samuel what to do. The next time Samuel heard the voice, he got up and said, 'Speak, Lord! Your servant is listening.'"

Belén stared at her daughter as if seeing her for the first time.

"And you've heard that voice?"

"Yes," Moramay said with quiet certainty. "Almost word for word. Many times. And when I finally understood who was calling me, I answered—just like Samuel."

Belén let out a shaky breath, her heart twisting.

"Oh, my Moramay!" she cried, pulling her daughter close. "And I've raised you all these years… only for you to leave me now? When I'm alone in a world I hate?"

"That's why I asked you before if you wanted to take refuge on your island," Moramay said gently.

"On my island, yes," Belén said quickly. "Because there, I would still be free—to hunt, to fish, to sail. But in a convent…?"

"In a convent, you would have something greater than the freedom to hunt and fish and sail," Moramay said softly. "You would have the freedom to love God alone."

"And what—forget you? Forget your father?"

"You wouldn't forget us," Moramay assured her softly, eyes gleaming with an otherworldly wisdom that could only have come from the Divine. "You would love us in God."

Belén shook her head, pressing a hand to her forehead as if trying to hold herself together.

"Moramay, you're mad." She exhaled sharply. "If you had told me you wanted to be a Sister of Charity, or a Vincentian, I might have been able to make sense of this insanity. But you said *Trappist*!"

She spat the word like a curse. There were many who, while not outright enemies of religion, still sneered at its stricter orders and mocked those who truly dedicated their lives to it. These were the same people who praised certain nuns—the ones who nursed the sick, fed the hungry, and lived among the poor—only to turn around and deride the ones who withdrew from the world entirely. The Sisters of Charity, the Daughters of St. Vincent de Paul—those nuns were seen as useful. They moved through hospitals and city streets, tending to both the wealthy and the destitute. Society respected them.

But the cloistered? The ones who left everything behind, who shut the world behind them as if locking a door heavier than a gravestone? Those were the ones people despised. They were treated like selfish recluses, as if their very existence was an affront to humanity. Belén wasn't one of those liberal hypocrites—she had no use for their shallow moralizing.

But *still*…a Trappist? A Trappist, who buried herself alive behind convent walls, where speech was forbidden, where silence reigned heavier than chains? A Trappist, who never left—unless she shattered her vows, unless she was cast out, excommunicated?

To Belén, it was unthinkable. A horror beyond words. And yet, this was exactly what Moramay had chosen. The idea was so extreme, so alien, that Belén could barely comprehend it. Where had it even come from? Moramay had never met a Trappist. Their convents were rare, their presence almost mythical.

Books. It must have been the books. Belén clenched her jaw, her thoughts racing. If her daughter had fallen in love with some reckless young man, she would have known exactly how to handle it. But this? How did you fight against God Himself?

Just as she had once fallen in love with pirates—without ever meeting one, without even knowing if they still roamed the seas—simply because she had read about their daring escapades, their courage, their triumphs, and their suffering… Moramay had now fallen in love with a far stranger, harsher fate. A destiny of silence. Of sacrifice. Of total renunciation. No. This was nothing more than a passing obsession. A fever fueled by books and letters. Once she was cut off from them, once she was separated from the voices that whispered these ideas into her mind, the madness would pass.

And to think—Belén had once believed those letters, arriving from distant corners of the world, were from *friends!* Letters that, in reality, had been written by spiritual directors, feeding the fire that these wretched books had ignited. She even found two of them - *The Life of Rancé, Abbot of La Trappe* by Chateaubriand, and another massive tome by Gallardin simply titled *La Trappe.*

As soon as she reached Nueva Siracusa, Belén devoured them herself, determined to uncover what sorcery lay hidden within those pages— what strange force had managed to sink its claws so deep into her daughter's soul. But their return to Nueva Siracusa did not happen after ten days, or twelve, or even the two-week vacation Father Manrique had initially promised his assistants.

It happened on the *third* day after their arrival in Buenos Aires. Jorge could not endure it any longer—the charade of civilian life, the pretense of being nothing more than a husband, a father, a man with no higher duties. An entire sea of responsibilities awaited him back home, and he could no longer ignore its call. And Belén? She had no objection to leaving either. She was *curious*. Curious to see just how much progress her husband's parish had made.

It *infuriated* her to think she had once ruled an island—a true queen in her own right—only to trade it all away to become the *wife* of a Greek Rite parish priest. She, whose spirit was as English as the open sea, as Latin as Queen Isabella herself! And as if fate had not already filled her life with contradictions, now her only daughter—who, by birth and fortune, was meant to be one of the great noblewomen of Spain—wanted to become a *Trappist nun!*

Jorge, of course, had taken the news with much more composure. Unlike Belén—who had been too consumed by emotion, too blinded by rage to get a straight answer—he had managed to *talk* to Moramay. To understand.

While still in Europe, buried in the pages of books that devoured her mind the way books of chivalry had once consumed dreamers of old, Moramay had discovered an order unlike any other. The Trappists. Their absolute austerity captivated her. And as fate would have it, they had just founded a new convent in Argentina, seeking the kind of solitude and silence that had become impossible to find in the Old World. After long negotiations with the Church, the Trappists had finally secured permission to establish two monasteries in Argentina—one for men, one for women. A small group of monks and nuns had already arrived, hoping the foundation would soon inspire local vocations.

A remote but fertile valley had been chosen for the convent, deep in the foothills of the Andes, near Tilcamarca. The monastery stood hidden in a hollow, surrounded by stark, towering hills—accessible only to eagles and condors. The mountains played tricks on the light, shifting from red to green to deep blue, like the woven ponchos of the indigenous people. Beyond the valley's farmland, the surrounding land was so desolate that only the highland natives passed through—people who lived with an almost unthinkable level of hardship. They survived on nothing more than a handful of corn and coca leaves, moving as their ancestors had since biblical times, herding their sheep, goats, and llamas across the barren landscapes.

Moramay had learned all of this while still in Europe. She knew that nearly twenty nuns had already settled in the convent, tended to spiritually by priests from a nearby indigenous mission—a mission that, until now, had barely clung to existence in what was still considered a land of unbelievers. She also knew that young women from some of Argentina's most distinguished families had already requested to join the order. And that the first solemn habit-taking ceremony was set to take place on December eighth—the Feast of the Immaculate Conception. There were still many months to go, but Moramay was certain. She wanted to be among them. She wanted to stand beside those women as they took their vows, renouncing the world for a life most would call unnatural. A life of silence. A life of solitude. A life of sacrifice so absolute that even the most devout shuddered at the thought of it. To the world, it was a death sentence. To Moramay, it was *freedom*.

She had always been different. A girl with a deep interior life. A soul drawn to the infinite. A spirit too restless for this world, but yearning—aching—to find its place in another. She had a divine longing, a love for prayer and solitude, a heart that felt like a small sea stretching endlessly into the vast, unknowable ocean of eternity.

So, when Belén and Jorge finally confronted her—after a long and exhausting conversation—Moramay did not shrink beneath her mother's scorn. She did not flinch at her sarcasm, nor did she falter under the weight of her father's objections. She stood firm. At the end of it all, Jorge turned to his wife and spoke plainly.

"This is not a whim. It's not some foolish fantasy inspired by what you call 'spiritual chivalry books.' It's a true and holy vocation. And to fight against it would not only make her miserable—it would be fighting against God's will."

Belén *cried*. She wept in fury, in helplessness, in the burning frustration of betrayal. *My priest.*

That was what she called Jorge whenever they argued—spat the words like a curse. And now, here was *her priest*, siding against her. Not even in this would he stand with her, so she retaliated the only way she knew how.

The very next day, she transferred Moramay to a different school— one run by nuns of an entirely different breed. Cunning, pragmatic, modern women of the Church, who understood the world and knew how to mold young minds. They were given clear instructions… fight her vocation. If they could not *destroy* it, then at the very least, they were to *redirect* it. Steer it toward something practical. Something modern. Something *useful* to society.

Whether those nuns spent the following months subtly coaxing Moramay toward their own congregation, we can safely assume an attempt was made. Belén had finally accepted that her daughter would become a nun. But she would *not*—under any circumstances— join the Trappists.

What kind of life was that?

To shut herself away in the mountains like a ghost, never seeing another human face except for her twenty or thirty silent companions—whom she could not even speak to because their Rule forbade it under pain of mortal sin? To work the land like a farmhand half the day, and spend the rest of it in endless silence, her voice swallowed by prayer and meditation like a hermit? And all the while, her parents would grow old and die alone. Their family line would end. The world would change. It would unravel, explode, burn, *live*— and none of it would matter to a Trappist nun. Their Rule demanded detachment. Indifference. A heart unshaken by the joys and tragedies of the outside world.

To Belén, they were nothing more than selfish ghosts. Jorge, however, met her fury with nothing but calm.

"There's a scene in the Gospel I'm sure you haven't forgotten," he said. "The Lord visits the home of Martha and Mary, the sisters of Lazarus. Martha, ever the practical one, immediately begins preparing food, tending to the house, making everything ready for her honored guest. Meanwhile, Mary does nothing. She simply sits at Jesus' feet, her hands folded over her heart, her eyes locked on his face, drinking in every word he speaks. To Martha, this is *unbearable*. She is the one doing all the work, and yet Mary just sits there, absorbed in devotion, as if the weight of the world is no longer hers to carry. Frustrated, she turns to Jesus and says, 'Lord, don't you care that my sister has left me to do all the work alone? Tell her to help me!'"

Jorge paused. Then, he turned to his wife.

"And what did Jesus say to her, Belén?"

She *knew* the answer. She knew it *well*. But Jorge spoke it aloud anyway.

"He said, 'Martha, Martha, you are anxious and troubled about many things. But only *one* thing is necessary. Mary has chosen the better part, and it will not be taken from her.'"

Belén's lips pressed into a thin, defiant line.

"Are you saying," she demanded, "that *Moramay* has chosen the better part? That what she is called to do is *greater* than what I do? *Greater* than your work?"

She narrowed her eyes, her voice laced with venom.

"Because let's not forget—you abandoned your wife to devote yourself to your *sheep*."

Jorge met her gaze evenly.

"I'll answer you," he said, "with the words of Jesus himself. 'In my Father's house, there are many mansions.'"

He let the words settle between them before continuing.

"There are different gifts, as Saint Paul says. Each of us must devote ourselves to the gift we have been given by God—the source of all perfect things. And Moramay has found hers."

"And blessed is the one," Jorge said, his voice steady, "who, like Moramay, has been given the rarest gift of all—the calling to prayer. A gift so misunderstood in our time, growing rarer with each passing century."

Belén scoffed, crossing her arms.

"Oh please. I've heard that work itself is a kind of prayer. Didn't Pope Pius IX say something like, 'I prefer a convent where they work hard and pray little, to one where they pray much and work little'?"

Jorge shrugged.

"I don't know what Pius IX said," he admitted. "But I do know this— no Pope would ever dismiss an order whose Rule commands them to devote themselves to work. Teaching, preaching, hearing confessions—every duty is an act of service. A friar or nun who abandons the work of their Order under the excuse of prayer would be in the wrong."

Belén's eyes narrowed.

"And isn't it even worse," she shot back, "to join an Order where prayer is everything?"

Jorge shook his head.

"For one thing," he said calmly, "the Trappists do plenty of manual labor. The same people who call them idle wouldn't last a week doing what they do—not even for a high salary. And yet, they do it… just to feed and clothe themselves with the work of their own hands."

Belén snorted.

"If they work that hard, how much time do they even have left to pray?"

Jorge smiled slightly.

"The same amount of time we waste on idle chatter, entertainment, distractions. If you added it all up, you'd see how much of life is spent on things that don't matter."

Belén frowned. To her, real action—tangible work—was prayer. Sitting in silence, lost in contemplation? A waste of precious time. The idea that her daughter would give her life to such a thing made her stomach tighten.

"But tell me this," she challenged. "Wouldn't they be more useful to the world—wouldn't they bring more glory to God—if they worked more and prayed less?"

Jorge didn't flinch.

"Ah, work," he mused. "Producing things that can be counted, measured, weighed. There will always be people doing that—for pleasure, for profit, even for charity. But that alone does not balance the scales of God. Some things cannot be measured. Because anything material—anything that earns praise or reward—carries its own satisfaction. But someone must offer up what no one sees. Someone must place upon God's scale—already weighed down by the sins of the world—the immeasurable weight of unseen sacrifices: self-denial, silent offerings, obedience, poverty, chastity… and above all, prayer."

For the first time, Belén hesitated. Despite herself, she was intrigued.

"Go on," she said. "I'm listening."

Jorge leaned forward.

"Think of the people you know," he said. "Good people, by the world's standards. People who don't steal, don't kill, don't commit any obvious wrongs. People who take great pride in their morality. But tell me, Belén—does God mean anything to them beyond a vague idea? A distant philosophy debated by idle scholars?

"If God did not exist, would they invent Him? No. They would never create Him—because they do not need Him. They have never worshipped Him. Never thanked Him. Never sought Him in suffering. And when death comes for them, they do not wish to see Him at all.

"They have not rejected Him out of hatred, but out of indifference. To them, God as a Father is irrelevant. They believe they are children of science, of evolution. Their prophets are Darwin, Büchner, Haeckel, Spencer. If the existence of Christ, the Virgin Mary, and the wonders of Catholic faith had depended on them, none of it would exist at all."

Belén exhaled sharply.

"I know plenty of those so-called 'moral' people," she muttered. "And you're right—if it had been up to them, Christ would never have come into the world."

Jorge's eyes darkened.

"Exactly. Now, tell me this—what will happen when those same people, who never wanted God, never thought of God, never cared for God… suddenly find themselves face to face with Him?"

Belén was silent.

Jorge prodded, "Imagine it—the moment they stand before Christ. The Christ they never desired. The Christ who would never have been born, if it had been left to them. What hope do they have? The ones who dedicated their lives to science, or business, or politics? The ones who obsessed over books, paintings, rare stamps, fine wines? They always knew they would die one day. Yet they never once seriously considered the one thing that truly matters—what happens after death. And now, standing at the gates of eternity, do you think the God they ignored, the Heaven they never longed for, will welcome them as His beloved children?"

Belén swallowed hard. A long silence stretched between them. Then, finally, she sighed.

"No," she admitted quietly. "Certainly not."

Belén shook her head, her voice thick with frustration.

"But if that's true, then their virtues will have been for nothing," she said bitterly. "All their charity, their philanthropy, their righteous way of living—it will all have earned them nothing in the end. That isn't fair. They'll have made just as bad a bargain as the worst sinners, who at least had the pleasure of enjoying their vices."

Jorge met her gaze, steady and unshaken.

"No," he said simply. "God does not ignore even the smallest act of kindness. Not even a cup of water given in charity goes unnoticed. Their virtues will have earned them a reward—but only in this life. Because they never desired anything beyond this world, their reward will have been here, among the things of this world. Wealth, comfort, admiration. All given, all received. And then, when they stand before God… their hands will be empty. They will have brought nothing with them into eternity."

Belén's voice dropped to a whisper.

"Then… will they be damned?"

Jorge exhaled, his voice softer now, almost reverent.

"The mysteries of God are beyond us," he murmured. "But I will say this—people like that need a miracle to be saved. A miracle of grace that breaks through at the last moment, that forces open the eyes that have refused to see the light. Only then can humility and repentance be born in them. But miracles do not happen in a vacuum. Someone must ask for them. Someone must pray—unceasingly—for those who have never once thought of God, which is an even greater tragedy than rejecting Him outright. There must be souls, pure souls, who dedicate their lives to prayer. Souls who ask for nothing in return, who receive no reward for their sacrifices except the conversion of those who never prayed for themselves."

Belén was quiet for a long moment. She stared at the floor, lost in thought, then slowly repeated a phrase that had struck her like a revelation.

"It is necessary… that someone throw the imponderable weight of weightless things onto God's scales."

Jorge smiled, pressing a gentle kiss to her forehead. In that moment, he believed he had won. That at last, she understood. That she would finally stop fighting and allow Moramay to follow her calling—just as a river naturally finds its way downhill.

But Belén had not surrendered. The battle raged on. She clung to her daughter, as if Moramay were the last piece of her world still within reach. Her husband was already gone. She could not bear to lose her daughter too.

Nueva Siracusa became her refuge. She threw herself into work, into distractions, into friendships with people who, though they never said it aloud, anxiously watched the turmoil within her soul.

Every day, she attended Mass at the church of one of Jorge's assistants, Father Basilio Cadi. Sometimes, she even took Communion from his hands, allowing herself—if only for a moment—to be carried away by the mysticism of it all. And then, for hours, she would bury herself in books about the Trappist Order, trying to understand what had drawn Moramay to such a life.

But she never attended Jorge's Masses.

She loved debating religion with him but seeing him in his priestly role unsettled her in a way she couldn't explain. And yet, in one of the many contradictions that defined her, it unsettled her even more when he stepped away from that role to act as a husband or father.

Their arguments were endless. Why did the Church still allow these ancient Orders to exist, unchanged for fifteen hundred years? To Belén, they were relics—frozen in time, their extreme austerity an unspoken rebuke to the more lenient rules of other, equally honorable Congregations.

Take the Trappists, for example. No time for recreation. No time wasted on idle conversation. Every moment of their lives belonged to prayer or work. They woke at 1:30 a.m. to chant Matins in the choir. On Sundays, they rose an hour earlier, because the prayers were longer. On major feast days, the bells summoned them from sleep at midnight.

There was no dressing for bed. They slept in their habits, on straw mattresses laid over wooden planks. No sheets. No pillowcases. No undergarments. The rough wool of their robes chafed against bare skin—a torment at first, but, they claimed, something the body eventually adjusted to. Some even said it became cleaner, healthier. Every Saturday, they washed their habits. It was why the Rule permitted them to own two—so they would always have a dry one to wear. But if a monk's robe became soaked from rain or sweat before then? He had no choice but to let it dry on his body.

This was the life Moramay had chosen. And no matter how much Belén tried to understand it, no matter how many books she read, she could not make peace with it.

Night prayer stretches until 5:30 a.m. on ordinary days. But there is no pause, no moment to rest or gather one's thoughts. As the final word of the night's prayers fades into the silence of the chapel, the monks remain where they are, kneeling in the choir. Prime begins immediately—the first prayer of the new day. Only after this do they rise and gather for a ritual known as "saying the fault." One by one, each monk steps forward, prostrates himself before the abbot, and confesses any faults he has committed in the past twenty-four hours. Not only that—he is also required to report any lapses he has observed in his brothers.

To the outside world, this practice is incomprehensible. Harsh. Even cruel. Critics call it a form of self-inflicted humiliation, an archaic custom that should have been abandoned centuries ago. But those who live within these walls know the truth…the one forced to accuse his brother suffers more than the one being accused. *Let those who can understand, understand.*

At 7:00 or 7:30 a.m., depending on the day, the monks attend Mass— or, if they are priests, celebrate it themselves. By 9:00 a.m., they begin their work, toiling in silence until 11:30 a.m.

The 17th-century reformer of La Trappe, Abbot Rancé, left no room for doubt when it came to labor. He forbade his monks from pursuing academic study or intellectual endeavors, believing such things did little to sanctify the soul and far too much to inflate human pride. Instead, their hands must be roughened by labor. Farming. Tending livestock. Carpentry. Masonry. Shoemaking.

To the modern world, it seems senseless—a waste of minds that could be devoted to theology, to study, to writing. But to the Trappist, it is a matter of discipline, of humility. Over time, the rule has been softened slightly, but the foundation remains firm…work must serve the soul, not the ego.

At 11:30 a.m., they break for half an hour. Then, back to prayer. At 2:00 p.m., another thirty minutes are dedicated to prayer before they resume their tasks. Only at 2:30 p.m. do they finally break their fast. Until that moment, they have not had so much as a sip of water. For the Trappist, the dining table is not a place of indulgence—it is an altar. A place where one of humanity's strongest desires—gluttony— is sacrificed daily. And gluttony, they believe, is not simply eating too much. It is the pursuit of pleasure in food, the desire for taste and variety, the habit of choosing meals for the sake of enjoyment rather than for pure nourishment.

Thus, their first meal of the day consists of eight ounces of bread and two plates of vegetables, cooked with nothing but water and salt. In regions where wine or cider is customary, they receive the drink prescribed by St. Benedict himself—about a third of a liter.

During Lent, even this meager meal is delayed further—until 4:15 p.m. For the next ninety minutes, the monks are free to pray in solitude or read. Then, Vespers. Then, another brief period of silence. At 6:00 p.m., they gather for Compline and sing the Salve Regina in the most solemn manner. Only then comes supper.

Ah, the supper of a Trappist. A mere four ounces of bread and a single "portion" of food—which, according to the Rule, means a small piece of cheese or a handful of cooked or raw vegetables. Beets. Carrots. Potatoes. Nothing more. Even this is considered a luxury by their standards. So much so that during Lent and other fasting days, supper is eliminated entirely. The final act of the day is the recitation of Miserere. The monks stand motionless in their white robes, their hoods drawn over their faces. At a signal from the abbot, they fall prostrate to the ground, lying in absolute silence. They remain there— like souls laid to rest—until a second signal is given. Then, they rise like men returning from death, and in a single voice, they chant the psalm together.

Afterward, each monk kneels before the abbot, who sprinkles him with holy water. It is 7:00 p.m. Their day—of labor, of penance, of prayer—is over. Silently, they return to their simple wooden beds, still fully clothed, hoods pulled over their faces.

And so it continues. Day after day. Year after year. A rule that has remained unchanged for fifteen centuries.

At all times, the monks are bound by a vow of strict silence. To break it is a grave sin. No words may be spoken unless permitted by a superior—and even then, only in cases of true necessity.

Yes, life at La Trappe is hard but dying there is easy. Far easier than dying in a palace, surrounded by wealth and luxury, after a life given over to pride and pleasure.

When a Trappist monk is nearing death, the infirmary nurse performs a simple, ancient ritual. He takes ashes and draws a cross on the cold stone floor. Then, he covers it with straw and lays his dying brother upon it. There is no frantic struggle against fate, no desperate battle to prolong life. Trappists do not rage against death—they slip into it quietly, like lamps running out of oil. Once the monk breathes his last, his brothers carry his body to the cemetery and lower him into a grave—perhaps one he himself had dug, never knowing for whom it was meant. There is no coffin. Only the habit he wore in life, wrapped around him in death. As his brothers chant the Office of the Dead, the earth closes over him. No marker bears his name. And so, no one will ever know whether beneath that unmarked cross lies a former beggar who found his way to the monastery. Or a prince who abandoned his kingdom to seek a greater one. This is the life of the Trappists.

The women's monasteries follow the same Rule—softened slightly, but in spirit, unchanged since Saint Benedict set it forth and Saint Scholastica embraced it for her sisters centuries ago.

Belén sat frozen, the book still open in her lap.

Her daughter. Her Moramay. A Trappist? The word sent a chill through her bones. She snapped the book shut and turned away, as if shutting it could erase the nightmare from her mind.

One day, the superior of Moramay's school requested a meeting with Belén. Belén arrived, hopeful. Surely, at last, Moramay had come to her senses. Surely, the nuns had managed to guide her toward a different future. But no. The news was the opposite of what she had prayed for.

The superior told her that Moramay was the most obedient, diligent student she had ever taught. But in the matter of her vocation? She was immovable. Nothing had changed. She would be a Trappist—or she would live tormented by the guilt of turning away from God's call.

Belén felt the blood drain from her face. This was madness. Furious, she pulled Moramay out of the school immediately, furious that these useless nuns had failed to dissuade her. She threw herself into her work, clinging to the hope that somehow, somehow, she could still win this fight. But deep down, she knew.

After a month had passed, Belén and Moramay traveled together, visiting settlements, walking through orchards, meeting people who had built full, happy lives in the world. There was so much to live for—so much beauty, so much real purpose.

And yet, nothing changed. At last, Belén was forced to say the words she had been running from.

"She's still determined," she admitted to Jorge.

A long silence stretched between them. There was only one option left. If Moramay was so certain, then Belén would take her to Tilcamarca herself. Let her see the terrible, isolated, inhuman life she was choosing. Let her stand before the brutal, jagged mountains that walled the monastery in like a prison. Let her look upon the desolation of that place and ask herself—is this truly what you want?

Rumors had reached Belén about the unbearable solitude of Tilcamarca. About the silence so deep it crushed the soul.

Maybe—just maybe—seeing it with her own eyes would be enough to shake Moramay's resolve.

There were still two months before December eighth, the Feast of the Immaculate Conception—the day the first novices would take their vows. Time enough for one last fight.

And so, Belén and Jorge set out for Tilcamarca, with Moramay beside them. Before leaving, Moramay said her goodbyes to everyone as if she would never return.

A few days later, Jorge returned home alone. Belén had stayed behind, fighting the final battle for her daughter's soul. Unless God Himself intervened, it seemed inevitable.

On December eighth, Moramay would take the Trappist habit.

Chapter 16: Valley of the Angels

Tilcamarca was the end of the line—the final train stop for anyone traveling to the secluded convent of the Trappist nuns.

A picturesque town, nestled in the folds of the Andes, it seemed almost too beautiful to be real. Those who visited spoke of it only in hushed tones, as if fearing that one day its charm would attract too many outsiders, bringing with them the ruinous tide of tourism. The mountains loomed like silent sentinels, their jagged peaks painted in breathtaking hues by the shifting sunlight. The air was impossibly fresh, crisp with the scent of pine and wild herbs. The water—pure, abundant, untouched by the contamination of cities—rushed in icy streams through the valleys.

It was a place where time moved slowly, where the traditions of the past still lived undisturbed. A perfect refuge.

But beyond Tilcamarca, past its quiet streets and shaded courtyards, the road vanished into the wilderness. From there, a journey of twenty leagues lay ahead—a grueling trek through treacherous mountain trails that led to the legendary Valley of the Angels, where the doves had once defied the eagles and made their home.

There were no roads. No carriages. No easy passage. The only way to cross the vast, unforgiving landscape was on muleback or by riding a sturdy mountain horse. Even for those accustomed to the journey, it was two full days of relentless travel, with only a single resting point along the way. There could be no delays—no time to slow down, no second chances. The mountain winds were merciless, howling through the ravines with a bite so sharp that even in the height of summer, it could chill a person to the bone.

Yet, for those who dared to make the journey—whether in faith or curiosity—there was one reward…the night sky.

The stars over this forgotten path burned with a brilliance unseen in the outside world, their cold fire lighting the way from Tilcamarca to the Valley of the Angels. A sight so breathtaking that it silenced even the most restless of travelers. And when they arrived—when they stood at the gates of the hidden monastery—they understood.

The Trappists had chosen their refuge with perfect precision. It was a place cut off from the world, yet closer to God than anywhere else. According to the ancient records of La Trappe, the valley had been foretold long before it became a sanctuary.

Many years ago, in an English monastery, there had been a monk unlike the others—a man who had roamed the world before taking his vows. A traveler who had crossed mountains, deserts, and endless miles on horseback and foot, seeing lands no other monk had seen. Before leaving behind the world forever, he wrote his memoirs. A guide for his brothers.

And in those pages, the restless traveler-turned-monk had left a prophecy.

If ever war and revolution drive La Trappe from its home, let them go to the Valley of the Angels. There, surrounded by desert and stone, lies water enough to sustain them, meadows rich with life, and forests of cedar and wild walnut. It is a refuge unlike any other—a place untouched, where only the faithful will dare to go.

Years passed. The world changed; and then, his words came true.

When an English convent needed to relocate, the superiors of the Order remembered the monk's forgotten prophecy. They sent someone to seek out the Valley of the Angels.

But the land was not as he had described it. The desert was no longer endless—railroads had begun slicing through the wilderness, towns had risen along the tracks. Yet even with these changes, the valley remained far beyond the reach of ordinary travelers. The roads **were** impossibly rough. The mountains formed a natural wall, shielding it from the creeping hand of modern civilization. It was still a place of silence, sacrifice, and solitude.

During autumn and winter, the valley became a prison of ice, buried under thick snow that did not thaw until early spring. Even the Indigenous people, who descended from the highlands in the rainy season to tend their crops, stayed away.

The valley had its guardians. Two Redemptorist priests, sent from a convent in Salta, had made it their mission to care for the souls that passed through. They lived in a simple stone hut, built for them by the locals who had come to rely on their visits. Every year, the priests returned, offering not just spiritual guidance but also tools, medicine, and aid. Over time, their presence became permanent.

A parish was built, bringing with it the final piece needed to establish the Trappist convent. And so, the prophecy was fulfilled.

The Valley of the Angels became what it was always meant to be…a sanctuary for those seeking God—and a grave for those leaving the world behind. This was the world that greeted Belén and Moramay as they arrived at the gates of the inn attached to the convent.

For centuries, monasteries had followed the same sacred tradition to offer shelter to travelers. It was an act of mercy, an unspoken rule woven into the fabric of monastic life. That was why ancient monasteries always had a guesthouse, a place where the weary could find food and a bed—at no cost. But to call it an "inn" was generous. There was no comfort to be found here, only necessity. The walls were bare, the bedding coarse, the food simple. But after twenty leagues of punishing travel, even the roughest linen felt like silk, and the simplest soup tasted rich.

No one came here lightly. Whoever dared to reach the Valley of the Angels was not driven by idle curiosity. They did not come for luxury or for adventure. They came for something far greater.

Belén did not come for devotion. Her journey had another purpose. She had brought Moramay here for one reason only…to show her what she was choosing. To confront her with the cold, silent, merciless reality of life in the monastery. To make her see the loneliness, the brutal isolation, the inescapable finality of it all. To make her understand—before it was too late—that once she crossed that threshold…there was no coming back.

The sting of defeat still clung to Belén, like the chill of the mountain air. But though her battle was slipping away, she had not yet surrendered. The brutal solitude of the road, the rough company of two muleteers who might just as easily have been outlaws—none of it fazed her. If anything, she found the adventure exhilarating.

By mid-September, winter still lingered in the mountains, reluctant to release its hold. Patches of snow clung stubbornly to the rocky slopes, melting into hidden streams that whispered as they rushed downhill. Above them, eagles returned from their unknown winter refuges, their vast wings cutting through the deep cobalt sky. Falcons circled hungrily, waiting for the smaller birds that would soon nest in the shady ravines. For now, though, both eagles and falcons hovered over a far easier prize—the halfway resting point.

Here, in a lonely outpost tucked between the mountains, a well-stocked chicken coop and a small goat herd provided irresistible temptation to the skyborne thieves. At dusk, a young shepherd herded the mules into the corral, but it was never enough to stop the losses.

One day, a hen. The next, a goat. Snatched in an instant, carried away before the barking dogs or the shepherd's stones could do anything to stop it.

A family of semi-Indigenous farmers lived here, tending to this remote waystation, which was little more than a two-room hut—stone walls set in mud, a thatched roof, a fire that never fully went out.

By the time Belén and Moramay arrived, they were half-frozen and starving. They unsaddled their mules themselves, leaving the beasts to the muleteers to lead them to the corral. The room they were given had no bed, no fire, not even a chair to sit on. So, they gathered armfuls of wood and built their own fire on the hardened earth floor, watching the flames lick the darkness.

Before long, the embers were roasting a young goat, born earlier that year. Belén crouched near the flames, turning the spit with practiced ease, while Moramay unrolled their thick woolen saddle blankets and spread them directly on the ground. They layered them with fleeces from their riding gear, building makeshift beds against the cold.

The mountain night was merciless, a cold so sharp it sank into the bones, but wrapped in coats and vicuña ponchos, they were far warmer than Moramay would ever be in her convent—if she stayed.

That thought gnawed at Belén as she watched the flames flicker. Would this be the last journey they made together?

Dawn came too soon. A knock at the door jolted Belén awake. She turned to see their guide standing in the threshold, silhouetted against the fading morning star, its last gleam dissolving into the first hints of sunlight.

Moramay was still asleep, her face peaceful in the firelight. For a moment, Belén hesitated. She had earned her rest. But pity was fleeting. She gave her no extra minute. The journey was far from over, and time was slipping away. She roused Moramay with cold efficiency, barely speaking to her as they prepared to leave. Resentment had made her distant—she was losing this fight, and she knew it.

After settling their payment with the farmers, she gathered what little news there was to hear. No one had passed through in six months. That alone spoke volumes about how truly isolated the thirty or forty women at the distant Trappist convent really were. She also learned that a small community of shepherds had settled nearby, along with two priests who served as curates. But the valley would not remain empty for long. In the summer, a bishop and a host of others would arrive for a special ceremony.

Moramay lifted her head at this. Her heart leapt. She knew what it meant. The celebration would mark the moment when several novices would take the habit, dedicating themselves to Christ forever. Her family's unusual circumstances had granted her permission to shorten her novitiate period. This was it. It was happening.

Belén felt her stomach tighten. She turned away, mounted her mule, and urged it forward.

The road twisted along the rugged mountainside, climbing higher into the barren foothills of the Andes. Then came the descent. A long, winding fall into the valley, where the starkness of the peaks gave way to forests thick with cedar and wild walnut, fed by streams that never ran dry. The path was treacherous, a labyrinth of switchbacks and hidden ravines, guarded by forbidding hills that loomed over them like silent watchers. Only a seasoned traveler could navigate these trails.

At times, the path climbed again, leading them to dizzying heights where the world below seemed impossibly small. Up here, the only living things were the great-winged condors, gliding through the thin air, watching them from above.

For hours, the mules marched in single file, hooves clattering along narrow ledges. On one side, a towering cliff face. On the other, a sheer drop into chasms so deep that even the roaring hidden rivers below could not be seen—only heard, an endless whisper that felt at times like a call. Like the ocean's pull. Like something ancient and unknowable, waiting in the depths.

They stopped only once, at midday. In a small clearing, they changed horses and ate in silence—fire-roasted steak, washed down with a few sips of gin.

Even Moramay, with her pious resolve, accepted the burning-hot bottle from one of the muleteers and took a sip. The strict religious rule forbidding certain drinks had not yet applied to her.

By the time they set out again, night had fallen. Darkness swallowed the landscape, and only the keen instincts of the mules—feeling their way through the void—kept them from veering off the path.

The guides knew the way, leading them forward with unwavering confidence, their cigarettes the only visible markers in the blackness, tiny glowing embers flickering ahead like phantom lanterns. Belén and Moramay followed, wordless. The valley was waiting.

From time to time, Belén glanced at her wristwatch, its luminous hands glowing faintly in the darkness. They should have waited.

The people in Tilcamarca had warned her—the journey was meant to be made when the days were long enough to reach the valley before nightfall. But she had refused to delay. She had counted on the brutal terrain, the biting cold, the exhaustion sinking into their very bones— all of it—to break Moramay's resolve before she had the chance to don the coarse habit of a nun. And yet, as the hours passed, Moramay remained silent, unwavering.

Belén tightened her grip on the Parabellum pistol holstered at her waist. Just in case. The wilderness was unpredictable. Pumas prowled these mountains. And men—some even more dangerous than wild animals—sometimes lurked in the remote passes. If anything threatened them, Belén would not hesitate. She had excellent aim.

Around eleven at night, one of the guides suddenly reined in his mule and pointed ahead. In the distance, through the vast blackness of the valley, a faint flicker of light shone—small, almost unreal, like a dying ember in the night.

The muleteer removed his hat, a gesture of quiet reverence. It was the light of San Rafael, a small shrine placed years ago by missionaries in a hollowed-out walnut tree. Over time, it had become a silent beacon of devotion, marking the path for weary travelers. No one spoke. They rode on, the flickering light guiding them forward.

Not long after, the inn finally came into view—a large, whitewashed house, its outline just visible in the shadows.

One of the muleteers swung down from his saddle and rapped several times on the heavy black door with the handle of his whip.

The echo rang out, swallowed by the emptiness. The other muleteer tilted his head, listening to the solid, resonant sound of the wood. He grinned, almost to himself.

"Good cedar. Well dried."

Then, with a trace of pride, he added, "It's made of cedar wood from here."

Belén glanced at him.

A man born in these mountains. A man who belonged to this wild solitude as much as the trees and the wind.

They knocked again. After a long silence, the door finally creaked open.

First came a small lantern, casting dim golden light against the night. Then, the face of an old man, his beard thick, his clothes foreign-looking, as if he had stepped out of another century.

It was Don Juan, the Catalan innkeeper who had come to this remote land long ago, following the Trappist nuns out of sheer devotion. His wife appeared behind him—a woman no younger than he, her hands as worn and weathered as the stone walls of the house. And beside her stood their daughter, Montserrat—young, but solemn, her dark eyes carrying the quiet weight of someone who had long accepted her fate.

The English convent they had once served had sent them here, and they had never turned back. Of their many children, only Montserrat remained. She had not yet taken her vows, choosing instead to stay behind and care for her aging parents. But once they were gone, she would enter the convent, just like the others before her.

For now, she helped run the inn, tending to the rare travelers who passed through—though that winter, the only guests had been engineers and bricklayers, finishing the construction of the church and convent.

That year, however, everything was changing. Pilgrimages had been announced. Important visitors were coming—relatives of noble young women about to take the habit. Montserrat shared all this as her mother prepared a simple meal and set up their room for the night. Then, suddenly, she paused.

"Just one night?" she asked, glancing at Belén.

Belén lifted her chin.

"No. Many. We are staying in the Valley of the Angels until the day of the feast."

She watched Moramay carefully, waiting.

The girl had endured two grueling days on horseback, a journey that would have shaken even the toughest traveler. Now, Belén was certain—this was the final blow. The realization that she would be trapped in this isolated, lifeless place for weeks would be enough to crack her resolve.

She would start to doubt. She would start to break. But Moramay didn't flinch.

Instead, she simply turned to Montserrat with that same calm, serene smile and said, "But after tonight, you won't need to prepare my bed anymore."

Montserrat frowned.

"No?"

Moramay's voice was quiet but unshakable.

"No. Because tomorrow, I'm entering the convent."

The room fell silent.

Belén went rigid, every muscle in her body tensing like a drawn bowstring. Then, without a word, she turned on her heel and stormed out, slamming the door behind her.

Outside, a single lantern burned in the gallery, its light casting flickering shadows across the worn wooden beams. In the distance, she could hear the voices of the muleteers. They had settled in the kitchen, warming themselves by the fire, their laughter low and easy after a long day's ride. They had seen this valley countless times before. To them, this place was just another stop. But to Belén, it was the end of everything.

María, the elderly innkeeper, carried her sixty years with surprising ease. As she stirred a steaming pot over the fire, she explained the routine of the two priests who served the convent.

"They always retire after dinner," she said, adjusting the coals. "By now, they're surely asleep, preparing to rise with the first light of day."

She glanced at Belén, wiping her hands on her apron before continuing.

"They live in a little pavilion next to the inn. At dawn, they ride to the convent, where one of them celebrates Mass at seven-thirty, assisted by the other, who says another Mass right after. Once that's done, they have the rest of the day to themselves—unless the Mother Abbess calls them for counsel. Then, in the evening, they return for the blessing of the Blessed Sacrament."

Belén leaned against the wooden table, arms crossed.

"And during the day?" she asked.

"Oh, they usually travel on mules through these mountains of God," María said with a small chuckle. "Otherwise, we don't see a soul all day—unless urgent mail arrives from town."

Belén's brow furrowed slightly.

"What are their names?"

"One of them—the German—has been here so long he's practically part of the land. Father Juan Holzer. The other is from Salta—Father Saravia—but I don't know his first name. They're both Redemptorists."

Something flickered in Belén's eyes.

"And when the weather is bad?" she asked, her voice taking on a sharp edge.

María turned, sensing the shift in tone.

"They must get terribly bored," Belén muttered.

"Oh no, madam!" María shook her head with a knowing smile. "When the storms roll in, they're quite happy to stay indoors by a warm fire. Winters here are bitter. They study—they have a whole stack of books. Sometimes, they work in the garden. The vegetables we eat here—they're very good, and plenty—all grown by them, with a little help from us. There's always something to do," she added, lifting the pot from the fire, "and sometimes the days feel too short!"

Then, with a warm but pointed look, she said, "Enough talk. If the lady would like to take her seat at the table..."

She gave a quick glance at the chickens roasting over the fire, then left the kitchen.

Belén followed, but as she passed the muleteers, she offered a polite, "Good night. See you tomorrow."

The men tipped their hats in response, murmuring their farewells.

In the makeshift dining room, where Belén and Moramay would also be sleeping, Montserrat had already set the table. She moved quickly, energized by the discovery that Moramay shared her vocation. Excitedly, she filled the young woman in on everything she knew. From her, Moramay learned that a new stone wall had recently been built around the convent's garden. The nuns worked it themselves, growing their own food, just as their Rule required.

Belén entered just in time to hear this. Her eyes narrowed.

"And if it doesn't rain?" she asked, her tone sharp. "If pests destroy the crops? If the vegetables don't grow?"

Montserrat simply shrugged.

"Then they'll go hungry," she said. "That's all."

Belén's mouth parted slightly. *That's all?* Frustrated, she pressed on, her questions growing sharper.

"And what if one of them doesn't eat vegetables—like Moramay?"

"She will learn to eat them."

Belén inhaled sharply.

"And if one of them gets sick?"

"One of the Fathers is a doctor. He will treat her."

"And where will the medicine come from?"

"God will provide, madam."

Belén clenched her fists.

"And if she dies?"

Montserrat didn't hesitate. "Then she will go to heaven, madam."

That was the breaking point. Belén's voice snapped.

"That's not what I'm asking!"

Montserrat's expression remained calm, her hands still busy clearing away the dishes.

"Then the lady must clarify."

Belén's eyes burned.

She steadied herself, then said coldly, "I mean—if she dies, do they just throw her out into the field like a dog?"

Finally, Montserrat stopped what she was doing. She turned fully to face Belén, her face serene, unwavering.

"No, madam," she said quietly. "They bury her like a saint, in consecrated ground, right there in the orchard."

Her voice was steady, but there was something in her tone— something that made the room feel smaller, heavier.

"Her grave is already dug," she continued, "and as soon as one is filled, another is opened. No one knows who will lie in it next."

Belén turned sharply to Moramay, waiting—hoping—for a flicker of hesitation, a trace of fear, but the girl was still smiling.

Montserrat picked up a pitcher and poured fresh water into a tin cup, speaking as she worked.

"But no one has died yet," she said lightly. "And it will likely be many years before anyone does."

Then, with a small smile, she added, "Because work and vegetables don't kill anyone."

Belén said nothing. She didn't want to respond. She couldn't. And Montserrat, sensing her silence, went on, her voice almost too casual.

"After all, even in the cities, with doctors and medicine, people die like flies..."

She set the cup down with a quiet clink, then met Belén's gaze.

"So why should we fear the idea of living out here?"

Then, with a final, knowing smile, "And if our time comes sooner, as God wills it, all the better. We'll reach the final harbor that much faster."

Montserrat's words, simple yet laced with unsettling irony, cut through Belén like twin daggers. But she was a woman of class, self-control, and unwavering composure. She refused to let herself break—not here, not now. She forced a smile, straightened her back, and accepted Montserrat's invitation with an air of nonchalance.

"Dinner is served, madam. If you don't need anything else..."

"No, nothing else."

Montserrat nodded.

"Then I'll bring the chicken. My mother is an excellent cook."

With that, she disappeared into the kitchen, leaving Belén alone with Moramay.

Belén turned to her daughter, her gaze sharp.

"Did you hear that, Moramay?"

"Yes, Mom."

"And?"

Moramay's smile was radiant.

"I'm thrilled."

Belén scoffed.

"Thrilled? And you're going to eat vegetables? You, who only ever ate pigeons on the island, chickens in Buenos Aires, and fresh silversides at the best cafés? Since when have you touched anything green, my angel?"

Moramay laughed lightly.

"Never, Mom. But I'll learn. If they give me raw carrots, I'll eat them."

Belén's voice dropped into a whisper, her disbelief turning to something closer to horror.

"And will you dig your own grave, too?"

Moramay's eyes sparkled mischievously.

"I'll start tomorrow. That's actually what excites me the most."

That was the last straw.

"Crazy! Crazy! *Crazy!*"

Belén pushed the steaming bowl of soup away as if it were poison. Then, without another word, she flung herself onto the bed, fully clothed, turning her face to the wall.

She did not cry aloud. But silent sobs wracked her body, her chest rising and falling with the weight of her grief, her exhaustion, her growing sense of powerlessness. She barely noticed when Doña María entered, carrying the roasted chicken. The old woman set it quietly on the table, then slipped away, her wisdom telling her not to interfere. The meal sat untouched.

Moramay, undeterred, knelt by her mother's bedside and whispered her prayers. Then, believing Belén to be asleep, she leaned in and kissed her forehead softly, before settling in for the night.

Moramay woke before dawn, restless with excitement. She moved carefully, not wanting to wake her mother.

But Belén, drained from the journey and the previous night's emotions, slept late. When she finally opened her eyes, the golden morning sun had already spilled into the room, bathing the wooden walls in warmth and light. She groggily sat up, feeling the stiffness in her body from sleeping in her clothes.

I went to bed dressed like a Trappist, she thought bitterly.

Then she noticed Moramay, already awake, sitting nearby with a book in her hands—one Belén knew for certain she hadn't brought with her.

Belén narrowed her eyes.

"Where did that come from?"

Moramay looked up, as if expecting the question.

"Father Holzer and Father Saravia came by to greet you," she explained. "They lent me this—sermons by Bossuet, written for noblewomen at the royal court when they took the habit."

Belén immediately sat up, fully alert.

"Where are these men? I want to see their faces."

Moramay laughed softly.

"First, you need to eat, Mom. You fell asleep without touching your dinner. I've got coffee for you—made with goat's milk. It's better than anything you've ever had."

Belén eyed her suspiciously.

"And you?"

Moramay grinned.

"I was up before dawn. I got dressed quietly and went to the convent church—which, by the way, is a masterpiece. I attended both Masses celebrated by the Fathers, one after the other. I confessed to Father Holzer and took communion at Father Saravia's Mass. I was the only person in the church, but through the tiny mesh grating, I saw at least thirty hosts passed to the nuns and novices in silence. Then I came back and found you still asleep. The Fathers arrived later, but they're probably outside now—in the garden."

She flashed a teasing smile.

"Oh, and guess what? As a test, I already ate a raw carrot. Not bad at all! And I even used a hoe. I haven't forgotten what I learned as a child on the island. If I start digging today..."

"My God, Moramay!" Belén interrupted, exasperated.

She sat up fully now, pressing her hands to her temples as if trying to physically contain her frustration.

"I don't blame you. I know exactly where you got that reckless spirit from. But this obsession with trying new experiences? It's riskier than anything I ever did. At least I never made my mother suffer!"

Moramay's eyes twinkled mischievously.

"You never knew her!" she shot back. "But I'm sure that if she had been alive, your honeymoon wouldn't have been so amusing to her."

Belén snorted.

"My honeymoon?" she repeated with sarcasm. "Who even remembers my honeymoon?"

Moramay sighed, reaching for the steaming cup of coffee.

"Come on, Mom, let's not fight. I'm still in the world for one more day."

She softened her tone as she handed the cup to Belén, preparing it exactly the way she liked it.

"Here's your breakfast. And outside, I can hear Father Holzer's voice. I'm going to tidy up so we can let him in."

Belén took the cup, but her hands trembled slightly as she wrapped them around it. She had been prepared to fight her daughter's decision. But how do you fight someone who isn't afraid?

Just then, Montserrat entered, moving briskly as she straightened the beds and flung open the doors and windows. Crisp mountain air rushed in, carrying with it the golden light of morning.

A few minutes later, Belén sat alone with Father Holzer. He already knew—thanks to Moramay—that her mother had followed her here to fight until the very last moment. He had expected resistance, but as he watched Belén settle into her chair, eyes bright with defiance, he sensed that this would not be an ordinary conversation. Belén wasted no time.

"Let me be very clear, Father Holzer," she said, her voice steady, her conviction sharp. "I don't oppose my daughter's vocation because I have anything against monks. How could I, when I'm practically married to one?"

Father Holzer raised his eyebrows.

"I beg your pardon?"

"Exactly what you just heard," Belén said, leaning forward. "I am married to a Catholic priest. And not just any priest—he's alive and well, still serving his parish in Buenos Aires. In fact, if I fail to convince my daughter to leave with me, he'll be arriving here soon. You'll see for yourself, Father. He'll say Mass in your church, and my daughter and I will take Communion from his hands. Imagine that!"

Father Holzer blinked, his composed expression faltering.

"That's… highly unusual."

"Not possible?" Belén challenged.

"No, madam," he replied carefully. "Just… the strangest thing I have ever heard."

Belén laughed dryly.

"Oh, Father, my life is full of strange things. I should have married a pirate, but instead, I ended up with a Catholic priest."

Father Holzer was still processing her words, but Belén didn't wait for him to catch up. Instead, she launched into her story, detailing everything—how she had met Jorge, the impossible choices they had made, the life they had built on the fringes of what was considered acceptable. By the time she finished, Father Holzer understood.

This was, without a doubt, the most unusual situation he had ever encountered. But Belén wasn't finished.

"Well, if you think that's strange, then my daughter's so-called vocation is even stranger," she said, her tone turning sharp.

Then, she laid out her real argument. She despised the Trappist Order. To her, these women—cloistered behind stone walls, detached from the realities of life—were wasting their existence.

Just then, Father Saravia entered. He greeted Belén politely and informed her that her daughter was in the convent garden—digging.

"Digging what?" Belén demanded.

Father Saravia smiled slightly.

"A hole."

Belén shot to her feet.

"Do you see now, Father? She's completely out of her mind!"

The two priests exchanged amused glances. Father Holzer spoke first.

"Madam, religious orders like the Carthusians and the Trappists, which seem detached from the world, are actually the ones living in the deepest reality—the reality of faith. They restore the true meaning of life. It's foolish to believe we can turn this world into paradise, because this world is not meant to be our home. It is a place of trial, a passage. Imagine if the souls in purgatory somehow adapted to their suffering so well that they began to enjoy it—so much so that they no longer wished to leave. Would they not be as misguided as those who cling so tightly to life, trying to fix this world, only to become so attached to it that they no longer wish to die?"

Belén scoffed, folding her arms.

"Well, I have no attachment to life," she said coolly. "And even less so now, when my death would resolve so many things…"

Father Holzer ignored the comment, but he studied her closely. *This woman is made of strong material,* he thought. *But she has been poorly guided.* And so, he continued.

"There are people who settle into this world as if they will never leave it. They go on with their lives—working, eating, celebrating—never thinking about what comes next. At fifty, sixty, even eighty years old, death finally comes for them—something they always knew would happen, yet never truly believed in. And when they die, they die forever. Their immortal souls step into eternity, only to realize they had spent their entire lives thinking about everything—except what truly belonged to them. They spent their days preparing for the journey, but not the destination. They are no different from a man who boards a ship run by madmen, steered by a criminal. Instead of asking where the ship is going, he focuses only on enjoying the ride— and laughs at those who try to warn him. Then, when the ship reaches its final, inescapable destination, he realizes too late—he never thought to ask where he was going."

For a long moment, Belén said nothing. Then, finally, she let out a short, bitter laugh.

"I once took a trip like that," she murmured. "On a ship run by madmen. And I thought I was right."

Father Holzer tilted his head slightly, recalling the incredible story she had told him about the *Cormorán.*

"We all do," he said simply.

Father Holzer had met many extraordinary people in his life, but as he listened to Belén's story, he understood something crucial—she was not the one orchestrating these events. This was God's design, not hers. And so, he spoke.

"Souls have lost their instinct for the divine, because the modern world has erased the supernatural from life. Even priests—who should know better—spend their days trying to make this world as comfortable as possible. We want work to be easy and rewarding. We want our days to be filled with pleasures. And so, we pile up good wishes like talismans—Merry Christmas, Happy New Year, Safe Travels, Great Success! We build a fortress of comfort around ourselves, blind to the contradiction.

"Because if we do not settle our spiritual debts here—through the small currency of hardship, inconvenience, and humiliation—then we will pay for them later, at a far greater cost. If a priest were to discover a way for people to be perfectly happy in this world and never die, the bishops would congratulate him, and Catholic newspapers would hail him as a great benefactor of humanity. But he would, in reality, be an ally of the devil, disrupting God's plan.

"Because Christ never said, *Blessed are the happy.* He said, *Blessed are those who mourn.* That is why these nuns—who do not try to turn earth into heaven, because they know that would go against God's design—are the ones who have truly understood life. They see it through the lens of death, which gives life its meaning and makes it bear fruit.

"Unless a grain of wheat falls to the ground and dies, it remains a single grain; but if it dies, it bears much fruit. Whoever loves his life in this world will lose it, but whoever hates his life will keep it for eternal life."

For the first time, Belén had nothing to say. A truth was settling into her, heavy as stone. She had spent her life chasing adventure, dreaming of being as free as a pirate on the open sea. And now, she was beginning to see—Moramay had chosen an even bolder path.

A path Belén could never take. A path that demanded a sacrifice she could never understand.

That very day, she and Father Holzer accompanied Moramay to the convent. The Mother Abbess, already well aware of their story, received them with warmth and quiet dignity. Belén insisted on seeing the inside of the convent. To her surprise, she found nothing repulsive.

The refectory, though painfully simple, was not as bleak as she had imagined. The dormitory, with its austere wooden bunks, was stark but not miserable.

Even the silence, which she had expected to be suffocating, felt strangely… peaceful.

As she walked through the convent gardens, she watched the nuns tending the earth with quiet devotion. There was no bitterness in their faces. No despair. Just purpose.

The wind rustled the leaves. Birds sang in the branches. The air smelled of warm earth and fresh herbs.

For the first time in her life, Belén felt exhausted—not just in body, but in spirit. It was as if she were wrestling with God Himself. And she was losing.

That evening, when it was time to part, Belén clung to Moramay— her arms tightening around her daughter as if she could somehow hold on to her, somehow pull her back into the world she was leaving behind. Tears spilled freely down her face, the fight finally drained out of her.

"I'll stay in the valley until the Feast of December 8th," she whispered. "And I'll visit you every day until then."

Moramay smiled. She had already won.

For the next week, Belén did as she had promised.

Each morning, she rose before dawn, dressed quickly, and made her way to the church—knowing that Moramay was there behind the grate. She knelt at Mass. She took communion alongside her daughter. And when she returned to the inn, she felt lighter. Something inside her had begun to soften.

But one morning, she turned to Father Holzer and said, "I'm tired, Father. Not just of the coming and going—though I am tired of that—but of the empty hours in between. I spend my days trying to fill the time, and I can't anymore. Would it be possible for me to stay at the convent until Moramay takes the habit? I'll help in any way I can. And when my husband arrives for the feast, I'll return with him to Buenos Aires."

Father Holzer spoke to the Mother Abbess. She had no objections. A vacant cell was prepared for Belén.

That afternoon, she stepped inside the convent and the heavy door swung shut behind her with a deep, resounding thud. The outside world disappeared. Inside, the air was cool and still.

Beyond the walls, spring had fully arrived in the Valley of the Angels. The scent of cedar and wildflowers filled the air. And for the first time, Belén no longer felt like she was fighting a battle. She felt like she was waiting for something.

Chapter 17: Gold Cannot Ransom a Soul

By the time the Feast of the Immaculate Conception approached, the Valley of the Angels was overflowing with visitors. Every available horse, mule, and guide had already been claimed. The bishop had arrived, bringing with him a procession of priests and acolytes.

Alongside them were the godmothers of the young women about to take their vows, their families, and a scattering of curious onlookers—outsiders drawn by morbid fascination rather than faith.

To them, this was not a celebration. It was a tragedy. So many young women—beautiful, educated, full of potential—turning their backs on the world, vanishing behind these walls, never to return. Some whispered that this was nothing less than a mass suicide. That in the twentieth century, such a ceremony should still be allowed seemed barbaric to them. What kind of society permitted a young woman to vow perpetual chastity, forsaking pleasure, ambition, and success?

These same spectators had no issue with young women pursuing fame in the theater or cinema, even knowing that most who tried never made it, that some lost not only their careers but also their dignity, their health, even their lives. But that these women, driven not by love of the stage, but by love of Christ, would choose a life of prayer, solitude, and sacrifice? That, they found incomprehensible.

They ignored the truth—that nuns, despite their seclusion, rarely died young. That few ever left the convent once they had entered, having found a peace the world could never give.

They refused to see that outside these walls, where freedom was supposedly absolute, there were countless tragedies—celebrated actresses, socialites, and singers who had gained the world, only to end their own lives, unable to bear the misery behind the glamour. But no nun had ever died of despair.

Still, the outsiders didn't last long. After the first day, they were exhausted and disillusioned, cursing themselves for coming. Watching was one thing; enduring the journey was another.

Riding a fine horse along a smooth road? Easy. But ten leagues on the back of an unruly mule, under the blazing December sun, across treacherous, snake-ridden mountain paths? Intolerable. And so, one by one, they left, their fascination with the spectacle no match for their discomfort.

Just days before the festival, five notable figures arrived in Tilcamarca. Among them was Jorge de Balcázar, who had been appointed master of ceremonies by the bishop. With him were Mr. Burns and his wife, Kitra, along with José María Pérez and his wife, Kandy—once a wild goat on an island, now a woman with an exotic name and an untamed spirit.

Their arrival was overshadowed by an unsettling question. Why had Moramay chosen Kitra as her godmother, when Belén—who was still in the Valley—could have taken that role herself?

Even Jorge couldn't shake his unease. Did this mean Belén had refused to take part in the ceremony? Was her resentment toward her daughter so deep that she would not even stand beside her as she took the ring of Christ's bride?

Meanwhile, in Tilcamarca, travelers were growing desperate. With no guides, no mules, no way forward, they went door to door, offering gold pesos for anyone willing to take them to the valley. No one answered.

For two weeks, every available guide had been hired, every animal claimed—hauling pilgrims, clergy, supplies, and trunks of ceremonial vestments into the mountains.

On the second day, a Quechua boy appeared—small, dark-skinned, no more than fifteen, quick and nimble as a mouse.

"I was born over there," he said, pointing to the distant peaks. "I know the roads well."

He had just returned with a traveler who had given up, unable to make the full journey. He had two mules available – one to ride and one for supplies.

Jorge didn't hesitate. He accepted the offer and left before sunrise, alone—his four companions left behind, still hoping for another guide to appear.

There is nothing more magnificent than late spring in the mountains after a long, wet winter. The snowmelt had swollen the rivers, feeding the forests until every tree was alive with birdsong, every bush burst into flowers, and the air itself seemed clear as crystal. It was a world singing with new life.

Yet Jorge rode on in silence, heavy with sorrow. He should have felt at peace. But the words of Christ echoed in his mind, the very words he had once spoken to Belén, "I have not come to bring peace, but a sword. I have come to set a son against his father, a daughter against her mother."

He had always known these words. He had believed them, but now, he was living them. They felt unbearably cruel.

Belén had not understood. To her, this doctrine was unbearable. She had fought against it with every fiber of her being. And yet—this was the truth of Christ.

For some, He was peace—His yoke was light, His love a refuge. For others, He was the sword—the only blade sharp enough to sever even the deepest bonds. For some, following Christ meant joy. For others, it meant giving up everything—and even then, knowing only the bitterness of righteousness.

Jorge thought he had already given everything. But now, as he rode through the mountains, as Christ's sword cut deeper than ever, he realized there was still more left to give.

Had he surrendered his daughter? Had he surrendered Belén? The Church—his mother—had been powerless to separate them. Even the Pope himself, with the full weight of the Keys of Heaven, had been unable to unbind him from her. And yet, in order to follow his missionary calling without feeling as though he had betrayed God, Jorge had been forced to create a fragile, makeshift arrangement—a prison of his own design, one that bound them both within it.

But within that self-made prison, both sweet and bitter, they had found no peace. Not then. Not now. And certainly not ever.

Jorge was sure that Belén hadn't found it either. For some time now, he had sensed something off in her letters. A bitterness that was unlike her.

She was still generous, but now with a forced politeness. Still determined, but with growing impatience. Still affectionate but withdrawing further and further from the world—and perhaps, from him.

He had written to her a few times from the Valley of the Angels, always apologizing for his long silences, blaming the difficulty of finding a reliable messenger. Her replies were rare and brief.

And in them, he sensed something worse than anger…distance.

But it was her last letter that unsettled him the most. She wrote that she had been reading a Bible in the convent and had come across a passage.

"Then the Lord called to Samuel, and Samuel answered: 'Here I am, Lord, for you have called me. What do you want of me?'"

She said nothing else. She didn't explain why she mentioned it. She simply left it there.

Jorge's hands tightened on the reins. Now, he remembered. He had once spoken those very words to her, long ago—when his apostolic zeal had burned like a flame, before it had been tempered by sorrow and contradiction. He had promised her, with absolute conviction, that he would pray for her to receive a divine calling— just as he had. And now, in a horrible flash of shame, he realized—he had never dared to pray for that at all. Because the thought of her receiving such a calling had terrified him. He had feared finding himself alone, buried under the weight of his priestly duties, stripped of his greatest happiness—her. And yet, no matter how he tried to hold onto her, she had been slipping away from him for years. Was there anything of her left that still belonged to him? Or had he already lost her completely?

"Let that day never come, Lord! Let it be true for me as it is for all: What God has joined together, let no man separate!"

The spring air was cool and fragrant. The mountains, illuminated by the late afternoon sun, shone with a wild, untouched splendor. Jorge noticed none of it.

His young guide, tireless as a mountain goat, trotted alongside the mule, chewing coca leaves mixed with ash, a sharp and bitter paste that kept exhaustion at bay. From time to time, the boy would set aside his coca leaves he had been chewing and replace it with a mixture of boiled corn salt. With that and a strip of jerky, dried meat tough as leather, he needed nothing more to sustain him. Whenever they reached a stream, he would crouch by the water, pushing aside the thick clusters of watercress, and drink alongside the mules, as naturally as if he were one of them.

They spoke little, only enough to mark how far they were from the day's end.

By nightfall, they reached a post station, where Jorge was able to hire ten mules and two guides to ride back to Tilcamarca and bring his stranded companions.

He doubted that Mr. Burns—who had never been trained for long rides—could cover twenty leagues in two days. And it seemed even less likely that Kitra and Kandy would be able to endure the grueling journey. But Guazuncho, at least, had worked as a ranch hand in his youth—he might have enough strength and stamina to make it.

Even if the group had to move slowly, they would arrive in time for the ceremony. Kitra would be there to stand as Moramay's godmother. That was the plan.

But Jorge's mind was already drifting away from logistics, away from practical concerns—toward the question that wouldn't leave him alone.

Why had Belén refused to stand beside Moramay at the most solemn moment of her life?

Why had she chosen to remain absent, when the bishop would ask, "Do you wish to be blessed, consecrated, and married to Our Lord Jesus Christ, Son of the Most High God?"

And when Moramay would answer, "I do."

Then, suddenly a new and even more troubling thought struck him. What if Belén wasn't standing among the godmothers...because she intended to stand among the novices? What if—without waiting for his consent— she had already requested to enter the convent herself?

His heart stopped. Would the abbess, or anyone else who knew his story, not assume that he would approve of such a decision? Would they not think that this was what he had always wanted—for her to finally free him from this impossible situation, to let him dedicate himself fully to his priestly calling?

Oh, the contradictions of the human heart!

Hadn't he once prayed for her to hear the call of God? Hadn't he feared it at the same time?

And now, faced with the possibility that his prayer had been answered, why did it feel like a death sentence?

Once, he had believed this was impossible. Once, Belén had fought like hell to remain bound to him, to hold on to what they had, no matter how fragile, no matter how forbidden. And in those days, he had convinced himself—lied to himself—that he wanted her to choose a religious life.

Lies.

All lies.

He had never wanted that. Not truly. He had been a hypocrite, a coward—and now, he regretted every moment of his weakness, because he was caught in the very illusion he had created.

No, no, no! She couldn't have done this without his consent. And he would never give it. Not out of selfishness—he told himself—but out of loyalty. Out of a love for truth.

But even now, he was lying to himself again. He pretended—so he wouldn't have to fully admit his own weakness—that he knew Belén's heart better than she did. And because he knew her, he could swear that if she had chosen to follow in Moramay's footsteps, it was not because of divine grace.

No—it was a whim. A matter of wounded pride, not faith. Her so-called vocation was false—a passing illusion she would soon regret, with disastrous consequences. Instead of simplifying their tangled, impossible situation, it would make it even worse.

Because Belén—his Belén—could never be a nun. Not for life. And certainly not a cloistered one. Not trapped in perpetual silence, buried behind stone walls, vanishing from the world forever.

There was still time. He could still stop this. And when people questioned him—the bishop, the Mother Abbess, Belén herself— when they wondered why he was rejecting what he had once claimed to desire, he would tell no one the truth. Not the Church. Not Belén.

He would never admit that he was against her becoming a nun because he knew—without a shred of doubt—that she had no true calling.

He would simply say, "No, and no!"

Let them think whatever they wanted. There was still time to save her. His thoughts were like a fever, burning, restless, impatient—making his mount's pace feel unbearably slow.

"Can we go any faster?" he asked the boy beside him.

The collita shot him a brief, disdainful glance and said nothing. Jorge gritted his teeth. Later, he tried again—this time with an incentive.

"If we reach the Valley of the Angels before nightfall, I'll give you five pesos."

The boy stopped walking. For a moment, he simply stared at Jorge, his agate-colored eyes unreadable. Then, without a word, he sat down on the edge of the path, pulled a new pair of sandals from the bundle on his back, and tossed his old, tattered ones into the ravine. Once his new shoes were on, he took off like a comet, so fast it seemed as if he had wings on his feet. Jorge's mule had no choice but to keep up.

They arrived just in time—while the last golden traces of sunlight still glowed on the mountaintops, though night had already begun pooling in the ravines, the first stars flickering to life above.

At the inn, they had been expecting Jorge for two days. A room had been prepared for him—one he was to share with a distinguished priest, a man eager to meet the Spaniard who had crossed over to the Greek rite.

Jorge's story had spread through the bishop's inner circle, and the bishop himself had sent word that he wished to speak with him privately. When Jorge received the message, his face went pale—as if he had just been summoned to stand trial. For a moment, he was tempted to feign illness to avoid speaking to anyone—not until he had seen her.

But then came the news that froze him where he stood.

Belén was not at the inn. She was at the convent, and he wouldn't be able to see her until the next day.

With no excuse left, he went to the bishop's chambers and spoke with him at length. Afterward, they proceeded to dinner—a grand affair where the bishop himself presided over a long, overcrowded table.

Despite the many important figures present, none seemed to hold as much weight as Jorge himself. The bishop placed him at his right hand, lavished him with hospitality, and in doing so, stirred jealousy among the guests. Whispers spread like wildfire. Some had already heard his story. Others had only heard rumors. But all of them watched him.

Jorge barely touched his food. He spoke only when necessary—just enough to avoid seeming rude. Because inside him, there was no room for conversation. There was only one thought, beating like a drum.

What had she done?

As he sat there, drowning in his own darkness, a phrase from the Gospel of John flashed through his mind, *You must be born again.* He had just heard those very words from the bishop, and for the first time in his life, he understood what it meant to long for rebirth.

To wish he could close his eyes and disappear—not to sleep, not to escape, but to die completely and return as someone else. But it was impossible. He was awake. He was sleepless, restless, trapped in his own skin. His heart still beat—furiously, stubbornly—refusing to die while its owner still lived.

Then, another passage came to him. Not from the Gospels, but from the prophet Hosea. *But I will allure her, lead her into the wilderness, and speak tenderly to her. There she will sing as in the days of her youth.*

For the first time since arriving, his mind stilled. That verse stayed with him, offering itself as a plan for the day to come.

Chapter 18: The Last Chain Breaks

The bishop, whose authority stretched over the vast and isolated Valley of the Angels, had weighed Jorge's predicament with careful deliberation. The Greek rite was impossible—there were no books, no vestments, no trained acolytes to assist him. And so, with a solemn nod of understanding, the bishop granted him permission to celebrate Mass in the Latin rite instead.

The next morning, Jorge stood before the altar, his voice carrying through the stone-walled chapel as he performed the sacred rite. The nuns gathered behind the iron grille, veiled and silent, waiting to receive communion. Among them, two figures approached the small gate—Belén and Moramay.

It had been over two months since he had last laid eyes on his wife and daughter. Yet, lost in the solemn rhythm of the Mass, he did not recognize them. The novice veils concealed their faces, their presence blending into the quiet sea of devotion.

The church itself was stark but commanding, built from the region's plentiful stone, its arching galleries lined with unembellished brick. Unlike the modest chapels found in other remote corners of the land, this one had a grandeur that stood in contrast to its severe simplicity. No gilded altars, no painted saints, no carvings adorned its walls—such luxuries were impractical here, where mules struggled to carry even the bare necessities.

There were no bells to call the faithful to prayer, though perhaps, in time, artisans could be summoned to cast them. There was no organ, for the Trappist rule forbade music. Silence was the monastery's only melody, deep and resonant as a heartbeat beneath the weight of the valley's solitude.

After Mass, Jorge lingered in prayer, his head bowed over clasped hands. He sought guidance, strength—communing with the One he had just received in the Eucharistic wine. The same God who, as the prophet Zechariah wrote, made virgins bear fruit.

Then, he sent word to the Mother Abbess. He wished to speak with her first, then see Belén and Moramay.

The response came swiftly. The abbess, engaged in discussion with the bishop, could not meet with him now. But he was invited to wait in one of the guest rooms.

The room was large but unadorned, its thatched roof casting uneven shadows over the cool tile floor. Along the walls stood simple wooden chairs with woven rush seats, each one carved by hand. A rough-hewn black cross loomed over the sparse furnishings—a few benches, a heavy table, each piece solid and purposeful, like the faith that governed this place.

Outside, the hush of the monastery was broken only by the occasional strike of a hammer or the scrape of a hoe against the earth. And if Montserrat's tale was more than mere legend, perhaps that hoe belonged to a nun digging a grave—the first to be buried in this desolate valley.

A strange, unexpected emotion gripped Jorge's chest, something vast and unidentifiable, a mix of reverence and sorrow.

Then, footsteps echoed in the gallery. He braced himself, steadying against the wall, willing his weakness not to show.

And there they were.

Moramay was first. He kissed her gently, a father's love untainted by time. Then he turned to Belén, drawing her into his arms, holding her tightly—this woman who was flesh of his flesh, bone of his bone. The one he had feared losing. The one, by some miracle, he now felt he had recovered.

Belén, ever composed, did not resist his embrace. When Moramay slipped away to her duties, she spoke—not hesitantly, not ceremoniously, but plainly, as if picking up a conversation they had only briefly set aside.

"I didn't write to you about what I'm going to tell you now because I needed to be sure of myself first. And once I was, I wanted to tell you in person."

Jorge felt the shift in her tone, a quiet tremor beneath the steady calm.

"I have settled my fortune," she continued. "I spared no effort in bringing a notary here. Everything is gone. I am as poor as a rat."

Jorge's breath hitched, but she went on.

"And just so you know—though I have donated millions to religious and charitable institutions, I haven't given a single cent to your church in New Syracuse or to the nuns here. Because that, in a way, would still be holding on to something for myself."

A slow, creeping dread took hold of him. He turned pale, his mind spinning. Money? What did money matter now, when it felt as though he had just begun to hear a verdict read aloud and was realizing—too late—that it was a death sentence?

Belén spoke with the same gentle ruthlessness, as if unaware that she was dismantling the foundation of his world, brick by brick.

Jorge forced himself to remain still. He burned with silent fury, but he would not falter. He would listen, composed, measured—just as she was. Nothing was final yet. No matter what she said, she could not make this decision alone. Not without him. Not Belén. Not the bishop. Not even the Pope or the Church itself could separate them.

And he—never, never, never—would give his consent. This was the thought he clung to, his last unshakable belief, as Belén spoke of the slow unraveling of her past self. The resistance she had once felt toward religious life—toward the strict enclosures, the asceticism of the nuns—had, over time, eroded.

At first, she had been skeptical, but the quiet, unwavering devotion of the sisters surrounded her, their peace settling over her like a balm. The peace of Christ. A peace the world could never give. And then, at last, she had understood the words Jorge had once spoken to her, 'Moramay has chosen the better part.'

Belén, however, had spent her life chasing something always just out of reach. Until now. And now—suddenly, inexplicably, as if led by an unseen hand—Providence had set her upon the threshold of the most extraordinary journey of all. To become a nun.

Why not? What more could the world possibly offer her that it hadn't already? She had tasted its finest pleasures, seized its most coveted treasures. And yet, hadn't it all, in the end, left her feeling hollow— or worse, repulsed?

Beauty, love, wealth, freedom—she had held them all in her grasp, only to find her soul still aching with an insatiable hunger. What was it? What was this nameless longing that gnawed at her, this restless yearning that felt as if it had existed for a thousand lifetimes? Had she not already lived enough to recognize the emptiness of some things and the exhaustion of others? And if that was true, then what, exactly, had she so despised about the life Moramay had chosen, as if selecting the rarest jewel from a king's treasury?

Digging deep within herself, she finally understood. It had not been the discipline, nor the austerity, nor the silence that had repelled her. It had been the idea of servitude.

She had pitied the nuns, those poor creatures bound to perpetual obedience, yoked to the will of a superior who could command them to do anything—no matter how repugnant, no matter how impossible. She had shuddered at the thought of surrendering even her innermost thoughts to a rule that dictated not just action, but intention.

But then—after days, weeks, months inside these walls, bound to the same discipline, enduring the same privations, granted no privilege, no exception—something happened.

She felt free.

The sweetness of surrendering her own will to follow the will of Christ—expressed through the rule of the order, through the voice of its superior—became a revelation.

If the superior, in giving orders, could err, then she, in obeying, could never be wrong.

That certainty—the unshakable assurance of walking the right path, the quiet security of knowing she remained in grace so long as she obeyed—was unlike anything she had ever known.

For someone like her, someone who had lived recklessly, who had stumbled through life driven by impulse and passion, the clarity of obedience was intoxicating. The thought of never making another mistake—not because she was perfect, but because she was no longer the one choosing—was exhilarating.

It was new. It was sublime. It was exquisite. And in comparison, the so-called freedoms the world had once dangled before her now seemed like nothing more than gossamer strands—thin, fragile illusions of liberty that, in truth, had always been cages.

She knew the world. She knew its promises. She knew its temptations. She knew exactly what it could offer—and, more importantly, what it never could.

It had never given her peace. It had never given her freedom. And it had never, not truly, given her love.

She had loved with a passion so consuming it had nearly driven her to madness. And yet, in the end, she had found herself having to defend that love before the only One to whom she could deny nothing.

By now, she was certain—a thousand times certain—that God was not satisfied with the pieces she had offered Him.

"I do not want your gifts. I want you."

The whisper had echoed in her soul. And she knew. Giving herself to Him meant surrendering completely. Letting go of everything she had clung to, everything she had once fought to keep, everything she had fiercely defended as her right. Even before God Himself.

Well. Now she understood. If she wanted to give herself, truly and fully, she could not hold back a single thing.

Jorge exhaled sharply, the sound halfway between protest and pain.

"All of this—maybe it would make sense if you only had to think of yourself," he said, his voice raw with disbelief. "But didn't you think of me? Did you ever stop to remember me?"

"Oh, Jorge," she answered, almost tenderly. "You were before me at all times. I leaned on you. I even used you to argue with God."

She hesitated, then—her voice softening.

"But my Jorge… your entire life stands as proof against your heart of flesh. And against mine."

He flinched, as if struck.

"One day," she murmured, "I told you, 'I have always been a hindrance to you.'"

"And I protested with all my soul!" he burst out.

"No." Her reply was gentle, but unrelenting. "You protested with all your wits, Jorge. But your soul remained silent. Because deep down, you knew I was telling the truth."

His mouth opened again—to protest, to deny, to plead—but she silenced him. Her hand, still strong, still gentle, still unyielding, pressed lightly over his lips.

"Let me speak now, Jorge."

Her voice was steady.

"Then you can say whatever it is you need to say. You've known many people in your life who were called to religious vocations. But tell me—have you ever met one whose calling was as certain, as unshakable as your own?"

Jorge arched an eyebrow, but before he could answer, she pressed on.

"When you were born, your name was already written among the 144,000—the ones Revelation speaks of, 'those who were not defiled with women.'"

Her voice carried both reverence and challenge.

Then, with a wry smile, she added, "Shall I quote it for you in Latin?"

Jorge smirked, tilting his head slightly.

"No need," he replied. "I'll recite it for you instead. But tell me, where exactly are you going with this? My name was never written among the 144,000 virgins."

Belén's expression darkened, her lips curling with something between sorrow and irony.

"It was," she said bitterly. "But I erased it."

Jorge let out a small laugh, shaking his head.

"How is it that even in a convent, you manage to be so impossibly presumptuous?" he teased, his voice laced with affection.

"You know as well as I do—if a name was written there, it was written from all eternity. And no one can erase it."

She narrowed her eyes.

"Well, my dear," she said, "you're not going to convince me that I didn't derail your vocation. But say what you like later—right now, let me finish."

Jorge sighed, folding his arms in mock defeat.

"Do you remember the letters you used to send me when I was at Brighton College?" she asked.

"If you don't want me to talk, why are you asking me questions?"

"Just answer me—yes or no," she said with a small, knowing smile. "As Christ himself teaches us."

Jorge rolled his eyes but played along.

"Yes, of course, I remember them! I wrote to you every single day. Poured my heart into them."

Belén's smile deepened.

"Well," she continued, "I remember receiving far more letters from other admirers—endless streams of them. And do you know what I did with most of them? Threw them straight into the trash."

Jorge chuckled.

"That bad, huh?"

"Oh, you have no idea. It was an act of charity—not to read the nonsense those poor fools scrawled on paper. The same drivel, over and over—movies they'd seen, dances they'd attended, cocktails they'd discovered. A sea of trivialities."

Jorge opened his mouth to interject, but she cut him off.

"No, don't go bragging about your letters just yet," she said playfully. "If I liked them, it wasn't because they were romantic. It was despite the fact that they were so very... strange."

She paused, watching his reaction before delivering her verdict.

"I'll be honest with you, my dear—I didn't understand them."

Jorge looked almost offended.

"There were too many references to the *Song of Songs,* too much St. Francis de Sales, too much St. John of the Cross—but not enough about *you.*"

She tilted her head, studying him as if the realization still puzzled her.

"They weren't love letters," she said softly. "Not really. They were confessions—but not confessions of love for me. They spoke of something else. A love neither you nor I could fully name at the time. And then, one day, you finally gave me the key to the mystery..."

Jorge leaned back, exasperated.

"You're being unfair to my poor letters! There was nothing cryptic about them. If you didn't understand—"

"Not entirely. Not at first. But later, when you finally admitted to me—and I do give you credit for your honesty—that your first calling had been to the priesthood. That you had dreamed of becoming a missionary at the Institute of Foreign Missions in Paris. That you had spent years in seminary before duty—before the grand, noble weight of your family's name—dragged you away."

Her voice took on a teasing, almost mocking tone.

"The great houses of Balcázar and Manrique. First-class grandees of Spain. *Et cetera, et cetera.*"

Jorge sighed, relieved to hear the sarcasm in her voice—it meant she was regaining her usual confidence.

"When I learned that," she continued, "everything fell into place. Your letters weren't letters at all. They were fragments of a personal journal—written without you even realizing it. Pages torn from the heart of a man who longed for something else entirely. And, foolishly, I became the confidant of a sorrow neither of us truly understood."

Her gaze softened.

"Your oath to your father kept you from the altar. But you still loved that altar more than anything in the world. More than me, your fiancée—whom you unknowingly turned into the keeper of a melancholy I had no business holding."

She exhaled sharply, as if the weight of the past had suddenly pressed down upon her.

"And yet," she whispered, "I still loved you. Oh, my poor Jorge. Because your name had been written next to mine in heaven since the beginning of time."

Jorge smiled despite himself.

"That, I do believe."

Belén's expression grew wistful.

"And then one day," she murmured, "you wrote to me about Theodora. You told me you were unworthy of me. And I—I actually believed you."

Jorge's expression darkened.

"It wasn't a story," he said quietly. "It was the truth."

"Then I believed in that truth," she replied. "And because of it, I broke with everything—my family, my country—and I came looking for you."

She met his gaze, her eyes gleaming with something he couldn't quite place.

"I found you in a hotel in Madrid," she said. "Packing your bags. Getting ready to return to the Seminary of Foreign Missions. Tell me, am I wrong?"

Jorge exhaled, rubbing a hand across his face.

"I don't remember," he admitted, his voice tinged with something like regret. "All I know is that when I saw you that day—so bold, so unlike anyone else—I suddenly realized how deeply I loved you. And from that moment on, I could think of nothing else but marrying you."

A slow smile spread across Belén's lips.

"That marriage," she murmured, "was one of your most brilliant inventions."

Jorge laughed softly, shaking his head.

"What a reckless girl you were, my Belén."

"Be quiet!" she shot back, though there was warmth in her voice. "You're talking more than you should. Let me finish—I still have so much to say."

"Then speak, my love."

She drew in a breath, steadying herself.

"So, by following me, you veered off course from your vocation, and we embarked on our honeymoon. I have no complaints about you— you were the kindest, noblest, most devoted husband this earth has ever known. But then… the *Cormorant* sank, and I vanished.

"You thought I was dead. And with that, you believed yourself free— free to finally answer the calling that had been whispering in your soul from the beginning. And yet, remarriage never crossed your mind, did it? No, your first instinct, your only instinct, was to become a priest. You rushed toward ordination like a man starving for the altar, as if desperate to bind yourself to it forever."

Jorge frowned.

"Father Gazapo guided me every step of the way."

Belén let out a dry laugh.

"Oh, I'm *well* aware of that," she said, a glint of irony in her eyes. "Father Gazapo and I have a few unsettled accounts. He'll have to face me when he's in purgatory, waiting for my prayers to get him into heaven. And believe me, I intend to leave him there for a good few weeks—to atone for what he's done to me."

Jorge chuckled despite himself.

"Father Gazapo is a *saint,* Belén."

"I don't disagree," she conceded. "But even saints aren't exempt from a little time in purgatory. A couple of months should do it— he's *earned* that much, my Jorge."

Jorge shook his head, smiling, but she pressed on.

"They ordained you a priest, and you were the happiest man alive… until I reappeared. And then, I had to fight—tooth and nail—against Father Gazapo, against you, against *everything,* to bring my husband and my daughter's father back home."

Her voice softened.

"And you *did* come back. But your vocation never left you. It gnawed at you like an ache that wouldn't fade. You grew restless, pale, consumed by something you wouldn't name—until you finally convinced yourself that you could find a middle ground between your faith and your family. And so, you turned to the Greek rite, trying to have both."

Jorge exhaled. "Father Gazapo—"

"Enough about Gazapo!" she interrupted sharply. "On the other hand, Father Conejo told me in Madrid what you already knew…"

"Yes, yes," Jorge muttered.

"But even then, you still hadn't found peace. Because deep down, you knew the truth—that a priest who consecrates the Body of Christ, who hears confessions, who distributes Holy Communion every single day, *should not be married.*"

Her words hung in the air between them, heavy and undeniable.

"Yes, the Church permits it in certain Eastern communities—as an *act of mercy* toward them. But history has shown time and time again— married priests never inspire the same reverence in their flock. They lack the *spiritual authority* needed to serve fully. The Catholic priesthood is not like that of the old law. In the Old Testament, a priest sacrificed lambs and doves, but the Catholic priest offers something infinitely greater—the true, living Christ Himself. This priesthood is a *new race,* one born from the Virginity of Christ and His Most Holy Mother, also a Virgin."

She took a step closer, her voice low, fierce.

"It may sound like a contradiction, but history has made it a *fact*. It's a supernatural law built upon something deeply natural: the line of married priests from ancient Judaism has long since disappeared, even though the Jewish people still endure. And what of the married priests in those heretical Christian sects? Spiritually barren. Their churches are lifeless, sterile. But the race of Catholic priests—the men who have renounced *everything*—has flourished for two thousand years, spanning sixty generations, spreading across the entire earth."

Jorge remained silent, listening.

"At the Poles, at the Equator—everywhere, even in places where not a trace of a married priest can be found—there will be a missionary, a parish priest, a monastery filled with men who have forsaken all earthly ties *for the sake of souls.* Because the people *know,* Jorge. They know, deep in their hearts, that a man who has built a family of his own can never *fully* make his entire flock his family."

Her eyes met his, unwavering.

"That's why the confessional of a married priest is always empty. And you saw it with your own eyes. Day after day, you sat in that silent confessional in New Syracuse, waiting… while your parishioners went instead to your celibate coadjutors. Because *instinctively,* they knew."

Jorge lowered his head. His voice, when he spoke, was quiet.

"…It's true."

Belén inhaled sharply, her hands tightening at her sides.

"And I—watching this unfold—knew that I was only holding you back. So, I *left* for Europe, chasing after some illusion—*I don't even know what.* Because we had tried *everything.* I returned like a queen from the Arabian Nights—wealthy beyond measure—but disillusioned, embittered. And the more I tasted the so-called freedom of the world, the more I despised it. And then, with both horror and envy, I realized that Moramay—less experienced than either of us—had chosen the better path."

Jorge let out a small breath, shaking his head.

"I told you so," he murmured. "I reminded you of Martha and Mary."

"Yes, you told me," she admitted. "And your words—*oh, Jorge, your words*—they started to work inside me. Until I could no longer ignore them.

"I had to face my own conscience and ask myself: *If you know this is the better path, what are you waiting for? Why don't you choose it too?*"

A long silence stretched between them.

Jorge's gaze drifted downward.

"For us," he whispered, "it's already too late."

Belén's expression was unshaken.

"It is *never* too late to open the door when Christ is knocking," she countered. "When He *stops* knocking—*that* is when it will be too late."

Jorge looked at her then, his heart caught between sorrow and something far greater.

"You and I," she continued, her voice fierce with conviction, "we may never reach the glory our daughter will have in consecrating her virginity to God. But there is still something left for us.

"Something *even rarer*."

Jorge swallowed.

"And what is that?"

Belén's lips curved, not in triumph, but in certainty.

"On the day of the Final Judgment, while the rest of humanity *stands,* we will be *seated.*

"You and I will be ministers of the Lord as He judges the world."

Jorge frowned, his brow furrowed in confusion.

"What do you mean?" he asked.

The passage she was referring to had slipped from his memory.

Belén, however, had not forgotten. She had read it too many times in recent days, letting the words etch themselves into her soul. And so, with quiet certainty, she recited it. *"The Lord has said, 'Because you have left everything to follow me, on the day of regeneration, when the Son of Man comes to sit on the throne of His Majesty, you will be seated with Him, judging the twelve tribes of Israel. And everyone who has left his house, his brothers or sisters, his wife, his mother or father, his children, or his fields for My sake, will receive a hundredfold and inherit eternal life.'"*

She let the words settle between them before she continued.

"How could you forget this passage, Jorge? *You* were the one who showed it to me once, long ago, when you spoke of your own calling." Her gaze bore into him. "Now tell me—can you truly say that you have left your wife to follow Christ? Can I say that I have left *you*?"

Jorge didn't answer.

"No," she said for him, her voice unwavering. "We cannot. Because it isn't true. We heard the call, but we answered like the man in the Gospel who told the Lord: *'I have a wife, and I cannot go.'* And worse—you tried to *bargain* with Christ. You sought a way to follow Him without displeasing your wife."

Her words struck like a hammer, but before he could protest, she softened.

"Tell me, Jorge… do you remember the story of the disciples on the road to Emmaus?"

His throat tightened, but he nodded.

"Yes. I remember."

"They were walking away from Jerusalem, away from the place where their Lord had been crucified. They believed it was all over. And on that road home, a stranger joined them. He walked beside them, explaining the Scriptures, though they did not recognize Him. When they reached the village, evening was falling. The stranger made as if to continue on His way, but they urged Him: *'Stay with us, for it is nearly evening.'* And He did. It wasn't until He broke the bread at the table that they finally recognized Him. It was Jesus—the Lord who had been walking with them all along."

Jorge smiled faintly, searching for something to say.

"You certainly know your Scriptures."

She didn't smile back.

"Do you not understand?"

"I'm not sure what you're trying to tell me with that story."

She met his gaze and spoke quietly, but her words carried the weight of an undeniable truth.

"I'm telling you that for *us,* Jorge—yes, it is getting late."

She reached forward, brushing her fingers over the silver strands in his hair.

"The threads of time are already woven into you. And in me, too."

She exhaled softly.

"It is getting late."

Jorge lowered his head. The words he had once used to shape her mind, to mold her faith, to justify his own path—now, she wielded them against him with precision. She could even recite them in Latin, just as he once had, refusing to alter the sacred texts.

In every argument they had ever had, Belén had always emerged victorious. And how could she *not* win now—when she was fighting him with his *own* weapons?

Something inside him crumbled, and before he could stop himself, the words slipped out—raw, unguarded.

"So, you want to leave me," he whispered, "at the very moment my daughter is leaving me too?"

Belén's breath caught.

"Have you thought about the loneliness you'll be leaving me in?" His voice wavered. "Without you, my life will be nothing but a desert. *I'm afraid,* Belén… afraid of what my life will become without you."

She looked at him then, her expression filled with something fierce, something almost *tender.*

"*Man of little faith!*" she chided, her voice gentle but unyielding. "Do you not remember the words of the prophet, when he describes the lands where Christ walks? *'The desert will rejoice; the solitude will bloom like a lily.'*"

Jorge swallowed, the verse rising in his memory.

"She will bloom like a lily," he murmured, but his voice was hollow.

Belén's eyes softened.

"And besides," she continued, "who says a priest's life is a *desert* just because he has no wife or children? Who says the spiritual fatherhood of a man called *Father* by all is not enough to bring him unspeakable joy? Who says that consoling the suffering, guiding the lost, defending the weak, forgiving the penitent, opening the doors of grace to the newborn, and *opening heaven to the dying*—who says *that* is not enough to fill the days and years of a priest? To say otherwise is blasphemy."

Jorge closed his eyes. Shame burned through him at the doubt he had spoken aloud.

"You're right," he admitted at last, his voice low. "A thousand times right. And of all people, *I* should never have spoken the way I did. No one has felt more deeply than I the *sweetness*—the *intoxicating joy*— of that Eucharistic wine you spoke of."

But then, his fingers curled into fists.

"*Still*," he said, "even if my life will not be empty, I *cannot* ignore what yours will become. You, Belén—*you*—if you allow yourself to be swept away by a sudden vocation, a calling that fights against your *very nature*... Have you truly thought about it? You, who have *always* loved freedom above all else?"

Her answer came instantly.

"Yes! I *have* loved freedom," she declared, her voice rising with passion. "And do you know the only time in my life I *truly* had it?

"Seven years. Alone on a deserted island. *That* was freedom.

"Everywhere else, I was a *slave*—to society, to its rules, to its fashions, to its obligations, to its *ridiculous* expectations of what a woman should be. I was shackled. I was caged. And only when I was alone— *truly* alone—did I know what it was to be free."

Jorge's breath was shallow.

"And what about the vow of *perpetual obedience?*" he pressed. "Have you really thought about *that,* Belén? You, of *all* people? You, who are so strong-willed, so unyielding—so *impossibly, gloriously independent.* Have you really considered what it means to surrender your will *forever?*"

The air between them was charged, electric.

Belén's lips parted—but for the first time, she did not answer immediately. She exhaled, looking at him with something between tenderness and pity.

"Oh, Jorge… You don't even believe what you're saying." Her voice was gentle, but there was steel beneath it. "You know better than that."

She leaned forward slightly, her gaze unwavering.

"You *know* that when a person chooses to submit to a higher rule, they break the *true* chains—the ones the world has wrapped around them so tightly they don't even realize they're bound. Gulliver, tied down by a thousand tiny Lilliputian ropes, was more of a prisoner than an elephant shackled by a single chain. Nothing makes us more aware of our freedom than the moment we *give it up*—willingly, consciously— to serve something greater. The only ones who *cannot* obey are those who have never mastered *themselves.* Because true freedom—the highest perfection of freedom—lies in obedience."

Jorge remained silent, but she could see the way his fingers tightened around the armrest of his chair. He was listening.

"A religious person submits to a spiritual rule," she continued, "but in doing so, they *liberate* themselves from their most relentless oppressors. From the body, with its endless hungers. From the world, with its crushing expectations, its exhausting demands. Look around you, Jorge—the world is *full* of people who think they are free, but in truth, they are prisoners.

"They are slaves to their comforts, their habits, their indulgences. Slaves to their grudges, their desperate need for distraction. Slaves to

346

their own *curiosity,* always needing to see, to know, to meddle. They think themselves masters of their own destiny, but they are bound by invisible chains. They *must* do what society expects. They *must* speak a certain way, dress a certain way, *think* a certain way. They cannot act freely—sometimes because they fear *ridicule,* sometimes because their bodies, weakened by excess, won't *allow* it."

She let the silence stretch before delivering the final blow.

"The world calls that freedom. I call it a *prison.*"

She stood then, pacing slowly, her voice measured, controlled.

"They *pretend* to enjoy themselves. But tell me, Jorge—who is more free? A queen, adorned with jewels, but watched by a hundred eyes, suffocated by etiquette, *trapped* by the demands of her court? Or a nun, bound by her Rule, deep within the silence of a cloister, alone with God?"

Jorge rubbed his temple, sighing.

"Fine. Let's say you *can* endure the discipline. But what about the prayers, day after day, *hour* after hour? What about the food—weak broth, black bread, never a feast? What about the cold, the sleepless nights? Won't the silence drive you mad? Forgive me, Belén, if I concern myself with such things…"

"Bah!" Belén laughed, waving a hand as if swatting away a gnat. "Jorge, do you take me for some delicate little doll? *I am a woman.* And I have the grace to master myself."

Her voice was almost playful, but beneath it was something fierce—unyielding.

"Yes, there will be moments," she admitted. "I will long to speak when I must remain silent. I will struggle to stay awake in the chill of midnight prayers. I will crave a hearty meal instead of a plate of boiled vegetables. I will miss the softness of sheets when I lie down under a coarse blanket, on a wooden board with no mattress. There will be days when I grow weary of seeing the same faces, hearing the same voices, walking the same halls. I will long—oh, my Jorge—I will *ache* to see you again. I will struggle to obey a superior whose wisdom I doubt. There will be times when silence feels like the greatest torment of all."

She turned to face him fully, her eyes burning.

"But tell me, Jorge—*do people in the world not suffer the same burdens?* How often do we force ourselves to endure what is unbearable—not for *faith,* but for *convenience?* How often do we swallow our pride, grit our teeth through humiliation, wear false smiles out of politeness, out of *fear?* How often do we allow those with power—whether a nobleman or a common officer—to trample our dignity? How many times have men left the grandest palaces, sick with self-loathing, furious at their own cowardice? How many have taken their own lives after suffering an insult they *could not avenge?"*

She leaned in slightly, lowering her voice.

"Suffering exists *everywhere,* Jorge. But the burdens borne in a convent? They are no heavier than the burdens demanded by *ambition, by vanity, by fashion, by pride.* And at least here—here, every suffering becomes *merit.* Every hardship becomes *grace.* But in the world?" She exhaled softly. "Suffering is nothing but ashes and loss."

A silence fell between them.

Then, in a whisper, she added, "Woe to those who *waste* their suffering."

Jorge did not answer. He only stared at her, his face unreadable. But Belén knew she had won. Slowly, she rose from her chair. The dim candlelight cast a golden glow on her face, but she was already radiant with something greater…a light not of this world.

Jorge remained seated, his hands limp on his lap, his mouth slightly open as if there were still words inside him struggling to be spoken.

She smiled softly.

"Now," she murmured, "give me one last kiss—one that will remain on my lips for all eternity."

Chapter 19: The Sword Has Fallen

They arrived in the dead of night on December seventh, just as the brilliant evening star cut across the jagged silhouette of the dark mountain. One of the guides pointed ahead.

"This is the Valley of the Angels. There—see that inn? That's where the pilgrims stay."

The group dismounted at the door and knocked. Montserrat, still awake, answered. The moment she saw the weary travelers, she turned and called for her mother. The old woman groaned.

"Where will I put them? What will I feed them?" she muttered under her breath.

The inn was already overflowing. The only space left was a cramped corner in one of the makeshift huts hastily built to give pilgrims at least a roof over their heads. But that corner had been reserved by Father Manrique for his family members, who were expected to arrive that very night. She had stayed up for them, preparing a simple dinner in anticipation. But if they delayed much longer, all she would have left to offer were cold embers.

"We're the ones you've been waiting for," Guazuncho reassured her.

At once, her face brightened.

"Thank God! Come with me."

The night was breathtakingly clear, the sky pulsating with stars. She didn't even need a lantern to guide them to their designated lodging—a narrow space at the far end of a hut, its walls woven from reeds and its roof a patchwork of straw. The inn had long run out of rooms, forcing them to make do with whatever shelter they could fashion against the elements.

After settling them in, she returned with bowls of steaming soup—and a message from Father Manrique. Kitra and Kandy were to present themselves at the church doors by 7:30 a.m. to serve as godmothers for two novices. The ceremony would begin at eight.

Kitra and Kandy exchanged surprised glances. They already knew Kitra had been chosen as Moramay's godmother—but nothing had been said about Kandy.

"They must have assigned you a novice whose godmother couldn't make the journey," her husband speculated. "The trip is grueling. Some of the women may not have been able to fulfill their commitment."

Kandy nodded thoughtfully. She spoke English more fluently than Kitra, though her presence alone stirred curiosity. Her deep complexion, framed by the soft waves of her hair—the unmistakable mark of the Rodiya people—contrasted with her delicate Aryan features. To most, she could have passed for a Creole of Andalusian descent. Who would have guessed she had been born on the island of Ceylon? Who would have imagined that Kitra—her mother, now the wife of Mr. Burns—had once been a slave, sold like chattel by a ruthless Sinhalese trader?

And yet here they were—Kitra and Kandy, alongside their husbands, Mr. Burns and Guazuncho—standing among the pilgrims gathered in the Valley of the Angels, summoned to witness the solemn festival of La Trapa. The strange, twisting paths of life.

Despite all their careful planning for the grueling twenty-league journey on muleback, exhaustion clung to them like a second skin. They were half-dead from fatigue and lack of sleep. Even Mr. Burns, the sturdy Irishman, looked as though he had been put through a test of endurance. The moment they were shown where they could rest their aching bodies, they collapsed into sleep, leaving the pot of soup that Doña María had so kindly brought them in the capable hands of Guazuncho.

Nothing—not twenty leagues, not a hundred—could wear him down. After polishing off his stew and roast, he shared a hearty meal with the muleteers before finally stretching out to sleep, wrapped in his poncho, using his riding gear as a pillow—just as he had done in his ranch-hand days.

And, as always, he was the first to wake. Stepping outside, he breathed in the crisp, mountain air.

The inn stood atop a small hill, offering a perfect vantage point over the valley. A hundred meters away, the stone walls of the convent began—enclosing a neat, fertile square of land, carved from the rugged mountain slopes. A thin stream wound its way through the meadow, nourishing crops before vanishing into the gorges beyond.

In one corner stood the church, its whitewashed walls glowing faintly in the dim light before dawn. Beside it, the house where those taking their vows that day would live out the rest of their lives.

Already, the valley was stirring. Pilgrims wandered the narrow dirt paths, some alone in quiet prayer, others in hushed conversation, waiting for the ceremony to begin. Most were indigenous men and women, their presence both humble and dignified. The men wore white wool hats, thick ponchos woven in vivid colors, calf-length pants, and rawhide sandals. The women, their dark skirts swaying gently with each step, wore similar hats adorned with a simple ribbon, their shoulders draped in smaller, more understated ponchos.

These were the same families who made this pilgrimage year after year, braving the unforgiving trails to visit the missionaries. Some came to baptize their children, others to see their young wives married before the altar. Their faith—ancient, unshaken, as immovable as the mountains themselves—was woven into the rhythm of their nomadic lives. For them, walking fifty or sixty leagues on foot just to confess once a year was not an inconvenience. It was devotion. It was life.

After their long and punishing journeys, they sat motionless, their backs pressed against the cool stone walls, their bodies wrapped in heavy ponchos. Silent. Still. Chewing their coca leaves in slow, deliberate motions. Their eyes—dark, unreadable—drifted over the scene before them, not with curiosity, not with longing, but with a quiet detachment, as if time itself could pass unnoticed. Who could truly know what lay within their hearts? How mysterious was the justice of God, who alone weighs the burdens of all men, measuring their deeds against the light they were given?

When the moment arrived, José María roused his companions. They shook off the last vestiges of sleep, stretching their weary limbs before accepting the simplest of breakfasts—a bowl of warm goat's milk and a thick slice of freshly baked bread from Doña María's kitchen. No words were needed. The ceremony awaited.

They made their way to the church just as the heavy wooden doors creaked open. By sheer fortune, they were the first to step inside, securing a place at the communion rail—the closest they could get to the presbytery and the altar, where the sacred rite would soon unfold.

At the same time, Kitra and Kandy, following Doña María's quiet instructions, entered through the convent's inner door to take on their appointed roles.

Tradition dictated that each novice be accompanied by two godmothers, but the realities of this remote valley—its harsh roads, its grueling distances—had forced certain adaptations. Not every woman assigned to this honor had been able to make the journey. And so, today, each novice would stand with only one godmother. For Kandy, this meant she would share the duty with another woman.

The nuns had built their church with faith in the valley's future, trusting that, as it had in so many barren lands before, a monastery's presence would bring new life to what had once been desolate. The church itself, though modest, possessed an undeniable presence. Its single nave—spacious enough for the small parish on ordinary days— now strained against the swelling crowd, as pilgrims from near and far pressed into its narrow walls. Devotion, curiosity, reverence— whatever had drawn them here, they had come. And for this one day, this forgotten valley had become a place of national importance.

Built of red brick in the Gothic style, the church stood solemn and unembellished, its towering stained-glass windows filtering the harsh sunlight into a soft, diffused glow. There was only one altar, dedicated to the Holy Virgin. Beside her stood Saint Scholastica, sister of Saint Benedict and patroness of the convent. Her brother, though the founder of their order, had ceded the place of honor to her, standing quietly to her left.

Above them, suspended in the half-light, hung a dark wooden crucifix, its presence commanding yet austere. Six tall candlesticks flanked it, each bearing a wax candle, their flickering flames barely disturbed by the hush that filled the space.

Near the entrance, a simple stone font of holy water stood as a silent sentinel.

Along the nave, unadorned wooden confessionals rested against the walls, facing fourteen small Greek crosses inlaid with mosaic, each marking a station of the *Via Crucis*. Just beyond the communion rail—a smooth balustrade of pale marble—the sacred space began. Most days, the church was stark, unadorned, a reflection of the monastic life within. But today, it had been transformed.

Flowers—more than had ever been seen here before—filled every corner. Lacking enough vases, the nuns had woven garlands, draping them over the pedestals of the statues, twining them around the *Via Crucis* stations, trailing them along the confessionals, and spiraling them up the pillars of the communion rail.

They climbed the windows, wrapped the cornices, spilling color and fragrance into the air like an unspoken hymn of praise.

But the most breathtaking sight of all was the cloister grille. To the left of the altar, the dense iron gate—normally a cold, impenetrable barrier—had been transformed into a wall of living beauty. Daisies, roses, and achiras, freshly gathered from the edges of streams and reservoirs, covered it from top to bottom, softening its stern bars with their delicate blooms.

The lilies had been saved for the altar and the tuberoses and irises— for the crowns of the fourteen brides of Christ.

Behind the reinforced grille, veiled as they were during Holy Week, the entire community of nuns waited in silence. Their presence was a whisper, a breath, a barely perceptible shifting of shadows. Only the faintest sound of footsteps betrayed them—no voices, no murmurs, only the weight of their anticipation filling the sacred hush.

To the right of the altar, directly across from the cloister gate, a small tent had been set up, its closed curtain concealing the final preparations. Behind it, on a long table, lay the novices' garments— folded with care, waiting. Beside each pristine white habit, a belt, a rosary, and a simple cloth to collect the young woman's hair. The scissors. A jug of water. A washbasin.

The moment was near.

Pressed tightly against the communion rail by the surging crowd, Mr. Burns and José María felt both grateful and bewildered. They had secured the closest view of the ceremony, yet much of what unfolded before them remained a mystery.

One detail, however, stood out. Among the fourteen pristine white habits laid out on the altar, one had something extra placed on top—an unadorned gold ring, a crown of roses, and a sheet of paper with a pen and inkwell beside it. A quiet question passed between them.

Why the difference? Who among the novices was to be crowned with roses?

Before they could dwell on it, a stir rippled through the congregation—the bishop had arrived. Three acolytes walked ahead of him, parting the crowd with the slow, deliberate movement of the cross and torches. Beside the prelate walked the master of ceremonies—Jorge Balcázar—though many now called him Father Manrique.

The bishop ascended the altar steps and knelt for a moment of silent prayer. Then, rising, he began to don the vestments of his office. He was an old man, his body frail and bent by time, but in his deep-set brown eyes burned an unshaken fire. The mark of a lifetime of devotion. The purity of a soul that had emptied itself for others. It was said that in his vast diocese—where the highest mountains in the world carved the earth into impassable labyrinths—there was not a single village he had not visited at least once. He had traveled where no carriage could go, crossing lands where only mules and the sure-footed could pass.

But every journey had left its toll. Death had nearly claimed him more than once. And now, as the richly embroidered mantle was draped over his fragile shoulders, it seemed almost impossible that he could bear its weight. Yet he did. Like a reed, bending but never breaking, he stood tall beneath the burden. The final touch was the placement of the miter upon his noble head.

A hush fell over the congregation as the small procession formed. The bishop, flanked by his clergy and preceded by the cross and candlesticks, moved with solemn grace across the presbytery. His path led him to the doors of the cloister, where the ritual would begin.

There, he would knock—formally requesting that the novices be given to him, to be wed to Christ. Three times, the sound of his knuckles rapped against the heavy wood. At once, the veil covering the entrance was drawn aside. The great doors swung open.

The Mother Abbess stood before them, her presence commanding yet serene. A large cross rested against her chest, her superior's staff held firmly in her grasp. Around her, forming a radiant circle, stood the fourteen brides of Christ.

Dressed entirely in white and crowned with tuberoses and lilies. Their beauty so otherworldly, it seemed to summon visions from a time long past. The mind instinctively reached back to the days of Solomon, where only the *Song of Songs* could capture the sight. *"As a lily among thorns, so is my love among virgins."*

The godmothers stepped forward, their presence silent yet steady, and each novice took the arm of the woman chosen to guide her. Slowly, the procession moved toward the altar.

The bishop, leaning heavily on his staff, climbed the steps once more. His face, deeply lined with years of sacrifice, bore a quiet exhaustion. He took his seat, his gaze sweeping over the congregation as the fourteen brides of Christ knelt in formation before him.

In that moment, neither Mr. Burns nor Guazuncho could recognize the ones they sought. They searched desperately through the sea of veils, the flowing white gowns, the faces obscured by garlands of flowers.

They spotted Kitra among the line of godmothers. But where was Kandy? And Moramay? And Belén?

Then, a voice—clear, unwavering—rang through the hush. The first novice had stepped forward, kneeling before the bishop.

"What do you ask for?"

The answer came without hesitation.

"The mercy of God and the grace of the holy habit."

At first, they did not recognize her beneath her crown of lilies. But the moment she spoke, they knew.

Moramay.

She rose and returned to her place, kneeling at the *prie-dieu*, Kitra at her side.

One by one, the other novices came forward, each introduced by the master of ceremonies.

Jorge Balcázar.

His face was calm, composed, but in the crowd, there were those who knew his story. And though his voice never faltered, they watched him with quiet reverence, knowing the weight of what had brought him here.

Then, without shifting his gaze, Guazuncho nudged Mr. Burns urgently.

"There—there!" His voice was barely above a whisper. "Look! *Mrs. Belén*—dressed as a bride! And Kandy, at her side!"

At last, they had found her.

Belén stood at the very end of the line, motionless, poised, her eyes lifted toward the altar.

And as the master of ceremonies approached to lead her forward, she moved with unwavering resolve. Not a tremble in her step. Not a flicker of doubt in her gaze. She had rehearsed this moment in her soul a thousand times.

And when the bishop asked, "What do you ask for?"

She answered in a low, steady voice.

The prayers swelled, carried by the unseen choir of nuns behind the cloister veil. Their voices, woven into the solemn rhythm of Gregorian chant, echoed through the church like a river of sound, pure and unaccompanied, untouched by instruments—stripped of all artifice, purely human, purely divine.

"The Lord is my portion and my chalice...The measuring cords have fallen for me in pleasant places; indeed, I have been given a glorious inheritance..."

And now, the most striking moment of the ceremony had arrived— the moment richest in meaning, breathtaking in its simplicity. The cutting of the brides' hair.

One by one, each novice stepped forward and knelt before the bishop, her godmother standing beside her in quiet reverence.

The master of ceremonies placed the scissors into the bishop's hands and draped a cloth across his knees. Then, with a tenderness that made the moment almost sacred, the godmother removed her goddaughter's crown and veil, guiding her head forward in submission.

And that youthful hair—her *glory,* as Saint Paul had called it—fell in heavy locks beneath the careful snips of the old shepherd, who worked with the gentleness of one shearing a lamb.

The first to kneel was Moramay.

Oh, Moramay—you who had never needed to be born again, as your mother had.

From the first dawn of your life, you had heard the voice of the One who feeds His virgins among the lilies. You had run to Him, without hesitation.

"The patrols that roam the city found me. 'Have you seen the one my soul loves?'"

"And when I found the one my soul adores just a few steps away, I seized him, and I will not let him go until I have brought him into my mother's house, into the chamber of the one who gave me life..."

Moramay's innocent locks fell, and Father Manrique carefully lifted the towel, handing it to Kitra, her godmother. His brow remained somber, his lips pressed into a firm line, yet his every movement was measured, deliberate. He knew the eyes of the congregation were upon him, weighing his every action, searching his face for any sign of weakness.

And so, as the nuns' voices drifted in delicate, unseen waves from behind the flower-draped grille, he whispered along with them, "Who may ascend the mountain of the Lord? Who may dwell in His holy place?"

"He who has clean hands and a pure heart..."

Thirteen young heads bowed beneath the bishop's shears.

Then came the fourteenth. The bishop—so aged, so weary from the weight of his own years and the burden of the moment—let the scissors slip from his fingers.

His breath caught. His voice, weak, faltered.

"I can't continue... Go on, Father, because... Manri—"

Jorge bent swiftly, retrieving the scissors just as the final novice stepped forward—just as that last radiant head bowed in submission.

And then, for the first time, he saw that golden hair. The same golden hair that had once gleamed in the sunlight of Fuenterrabía. That had danced in the wind, dazzling his eyes until he had dreamed of being a painter, just to capture it forever.

That hair was now before him. Awaiting its fate. She was still *flesh of his flesh*. The sword of Christ had not yet severed the bond that no human hands could break.

He grasped the thick, silken strands with his left hand and raised the scissors. For a single moment—just the briefest hesitation, too fleeting for anyone to notice—he faltered.

Then, with hands steadied by something beyond his own will, Father Manrique carried out the task. One snip. Then another. The golden waves tumbled onto the cloth spread across the bishop's lap. The sound of the scissors was neither harsh nor cruel. It was something else—something deeper, something final.

It was the breaking of an illusion. The shedding of vanity. It was eternity, unfolding. And yet, when the last lock had fallen, Jorge rose to his feet—pale, trembling, disoriented. Like an executioner who had just severed the head of his queen.

The chant soared above the silence, "Lift up your gates, O princes, and the King of Glory shall enter in..."

"Who is the King of Glory?"

"The Lord of Hosts, He is the King of Glory..."

One by one, the novices disappeared behind the tent to the right of the altar, where their godmothers helped them remove their wedding gowns and dress in the austere habit. The only garment they would wear for the rest of their lives.

When they returned to the altar, the bishop lifted his frail hands and covered their heads with white veils, the delicate fabric settling like mist over their bowed forms. Into each pair of hands, he placed a candle, the flames flickering in the dim sanctuary, illuminating the faces of the newly clothed brides of Christ.

"Receive this light, so that when the Bridegroom comes, you may go out to meet Him with your lamps burning and be admitted into the heavenly wedding feast."

The first stage of religious life—the taking of the habit—was complete, but the ceremony was far from over.

A rare and extraordinary dispensation had been granted by the Holy See, a privilege rarely seen in the strict discipline of the Trappist order. The decree recognized not only the uniqueness of her circumstances but the undeniable strength of her vocation.

One novice would not wait the customary one or two years to take her final vows. One novice would enter religious life forever, *this very day*.

Near the altar, on the Epistle side, a small table had been set. Upon it lay the symbols of final commitment: a gold wedding ring; a crown of roses; a parchment letter of profession, waiting to be signed; an inkwell and a pen.

Fifteen centuries had passed since this rite was first observed in the Benedictine tradition, of which the Trappists were a branch. And now, the ancient vow would be spoken again.

The thirteen other novices, their habits still fresh upon their shoulders, withdrew into the cloister.

Only one remained.

Belén. The woman we thought we knew.

She stood alone in the presbytery, her white veil framing her resolute face. Beside her, as witness and godmother, stood Kandy.

Then, just as the solemn Mass began, the unexpected happened. The bishop did not continue. Instead, he placed the miter upon his head and, seated in his chair, spoke in Latin—the ancient call:

"Veni. Come."

And this Belén—this Belén whom we had never *truly* known—stood, stepped forward, knelt before him, and answered, *"Statim sequar Te.*I follow You immediately."

The bishop's voice rose, calling her again.

"Veni. Come."

Belén stood once more, took another step forward, and knelt again.

"Statim sequar Te ex toto corde meo. I follow You immediately, with all my heart."

A final time, with greater force, the bishop summoned her—this time adding not just a command, but a reason.

"Veni, filia mea, audi me; timorem Domini docebo te. Come, my daughter, listen to me; I will teach you the fear of the Lord."

And then, for the first time, she did not simply *speak*—she *sang*.

Her voice rose, clear and unshaken, carrying the ancient melody of plainchant. The plea of the prophet Daniel, echoed across centuries of devotion, trembled in the air like incense.

"Statim sequar Te ex toto corde meo... ne confundar... secundum mandatum Tuum et secundum misericordiam tuam. I follow You immediately with all my heart... do not let me be put to shame... deal with me according to Your commandment and the greatness of Your mercy."

The words—spoken for a thousand years by a thousand women, who, on the Day of Judgment, would stand as instruments of God's justice—stirred something deep in the blood of those who *understood* them.

This was it. The moment of the irrevocable promise.

Still kneeling, Belén lifted her hands and placed them in the bishop's. Kandy, prepared beforehand, stepped forward, presenting her with the pen.

Belén rose to her feet. And for the last time, in her elegant script, she wrote the long name that carried centuries of English nobility. Then, turning to the gathered assembly, she read aloud the solemn vow that bound her to Christ—*forever.*

Her voice was steady. Unwavering. With that single vow, she became His prisoner.

According to tradition, the signed letter of profession was to be handed to the godmother, who would then present it to the abbess of the convent.

But Belén *forgot*...or pretended to. Instead, she stepped past Kandy. She crossed the sanctuary and, breaking with ritual, placed the document directly into the hands of the master of ceremonies, Father Manrique.

Their eyes met. No one else noticed. But he knew at once—this was no absentminded mistake.

Belén—whose voice had always been the same yet had never sung the same note twice—had done this deliberately. In that final gaze, she left him a gift. Her last look. A look that held *everything.*

Jorge saw it all—the depth of her decision, the radiance of her happiness. He saw her purity, her courage, her faith, her love, her hope. And something more. At that instant, her eyes shone with the brilliance of a star just before it vanishes. And in that brightness, he saw it—the blue lightning of the sword.

The sword of which Christ had spoken when He declared, "I have not come to bring peace, but a sword."

The only sword sharp enough to sever what no human hands could break. And in that moment, Jorge *understood.*

They were separated.

Forever.

And instead of despair, he felt something unexpected rising within him.

He *blessed* the One who had given him the strength to be reborn at the very moment he gave *her* a new name.

The bishop placed the crown of roses upon Belén's veiled head, the soft petals settling against the white fabric. Then, with quiet solemnity, he slid the ring onto her finger…and the choir sang.

"I am married to Him whom the angels serve, before whose beauty the sun and moon grow pale."

Then, silence. A silence vast and weighty, settling over the assembly like a cathedral dome. The bishop was preparing to speak. But it was not a sermon. Instead, he began to recite the solemn, fearsome *imprecation* that had thundered beneath the vaulted ceilings of churches for centuries—echoed thousands of times on the day of the most sacred vows,

"By the authority of Almighty God and of the blessed apostles Peter and Paul, we solemnly forbid—under pain of excommunication—that anyone should attempt to turn these virgins from the service of the Divine."

His voice deepened, reverberating through the nave, through the stones, through the very bones of those who listened.

"If anyone dares to violate this command, let him be cursed in his home and cursed in the streets, cursed in the city and cursed in the fields, cursed while waking and cursed while sleeping, cursed in eating and cursed in drinking, cursed in walking and cursed in stillness."

"Let his flesh and bones be struck with sickness, and from head to toe, let there be no health in him."

"Let the curse fall upon him, as it did upon the children of iniquity in the days of Moses. Let his name be erased from the book of the living, never to be counted among the righteous."

"Let him be condemned with Cain, the murderer of his brother; with Dathan and Abiram; with Ananias and Sapphira; with Simon the Magician and Judas the traitor; with all those who have said to God, 'Depart from us; we will not follow Your ways.'"

"Let him perish on the day of judgment. Let him be devoured by eternal fire, together with the devil and his angels—unless he repents and atones for his sin."

"So let it be. So let it be."

A single morning. And yet, it felt as though it had been built from stone—massive, immovable, eternal. The weight of the words spoken that day, the ink with which the vows were signed, would remain for centuries upon centuries.

A week later, Mr. Burns and José María were granted permission to say a final farewell to the two Trappists who remained behind—pieces of their very souls, now enclosed behind iron and silence.

By then, Father Manrique had already left the Valley of the Angels.

And in the meantime, something had happened—something neither of them had foreseen.

The Mother Abbess had appointed Sister Esperanza—Belén's new name—as the convent's portress.

In a cloister as strict as this one, only two voices were ever heard, the superior, who gave orders and answered inquiries, and the gatekeeper, who spoke with those who came to the convent's threshold.

Sister Esperanza had been given the rarest of roles. A woman who had once been the center of the world—now, the only one allowed to speak from behind its walls. That morning, she could have spoken freely. The Rule would not have bound her tongue. She could have answered every question, unraveled every doubt.

But she did not. She only listened.

When she finally did speak, her words were brief, deliberate—like the measured strokes of a calligrapher's pen. They had come seeking answers, desperate to solve the mystery that haunted them—the enigma left unspoken by Father Manrique.

Moramay's decision had made sense. She had always seemed destined for the cloister—quiet, humble, contemplative.

But Belén?

Belén, with her boundless imagination, her unshakable ambition, her hunger for the world? Belén, so wild, so willful, so vividly alive? How could someone like her wake up one day and realize she was made of the same stuff as saints?

She encouraged them to speak, pausing her work to give them space. And so, one by one, they poured out their hearts. First, Mr. Burns, his English laced with the rhythm of the sea. Then Kitra, her voice still carrying the quiet humility of her past life. Next, Kandy, the perfect *criolla*, speaking English with the unmistakable lilt of Argentina. And finally, Guazuncho—heartbroken, inconsolable. He would have died for her a hundred times, and now, she was leaving them behind.

Why? Why, Belén? Why?

Sister Esperanza listened, patient and steady as the tide.

When their voices fell silent, she spoke at last. But not with explanations, nor with reassurances. Just a single phrase from the Gospel of John. She could have searched for a year, spoken for a lifetime, and never found truer words, "The Holy Spirit blows where it wills."

She met their gazes with infinite tenderness—then quietly resumed her work. On a small piece of cardboard, in her elegant English script—the same refined hand the nuns at Brighton had failed to change—she wrote a line from Saint Augustine. When she finished, she rose and walked to the crucifix in her porter's lodge. But before nailing it in place, she held it out for them to see.

It read, "Late have I loved You, Beauty so ancient and so new! Late have I loved You!"

She was about to affix it when, suddenly, a thought crossed her mind—one of those delightful, unexpected musings that often found her. She smiled to herself, sat back down, and rewrote the phrase. This time, in the Latin she had once read in an old tome of *St. Augustine's Confessions: Sero te amavi, pulchritudo tam antiqua et tam nova, sero te amavi! Late have I loved you, O Beauty so ancient and so new, late have I loved you!*

Then, as if offering an explanation, she looked up at them with a playful glint in her eye.

"I'm writing it this way just in case Father Gazapo visits—he likes to hear things in Latin."

Her friends left that day knowing this was their final farewell to Belén, but they carried with them the memory of her ineffable smile as she spoke her last words—and, more than anything, the image of her eyes.

Calm, blue, unwavering.

Like the surface of a lake so still, so clear, that one could see all the way to the bottom—where the rock beneath never moves.

The End.

About the Author – Leanne E. Staback, Ph.D.

Leanne Staback is a retired teacher, nondenominational reverend, passionate storyteller, artist, and the President and CEO of Page Turner Books, Inc. With a lifelong love for literature, education, and theology, she has dedicated her career to inspiring minds through engaging storytelling and spiritual exploration.

A devoted scholar of the Christian religion in all its forms, Leanne has spent decades studying the richness of Christian traditions, theology, and history. Her work reflects this deep understanding, weaving together faith, morality, and human experience into narratives that uplift, challenge, and inspire. Whether writing for children, young adults, or those seeking deeper spiritual insight, she brings a unique perspective that blends intellectual curiosity with heartfelt devotion.

Leanne has authored over 20 children's books and three YA novels, crafting stories that entertain, educate, and instill meaningful life lessons. She is also the visionary force behind Page Turner Books, Inc., where she mentors aspiring authors, fosters literacy initiatives, and works to bring fresh, impactful voices to the literary world.

Her latest work, *The Eyes of Moramay*, is a deeply personal project, adapted from Hugo Wast's *Lo Que Dios Ha Unido*. In reimagining this classic work, Leanne blends her love of historical fiction with her profound theological insight, offering readers a compelling exploration of faith, destiny, and the enduring power of love.

When she's not writing, Leanne enjoys exploring new ideas, spending time with family, and fostering a love for reading in the next generation. Whether through literature, education, or ministry, her mission remains clear: to illuminate minds, nurture souls, and turn pages into adventures that resonate across generations.

About Hugo Wast

Hugo Wast (the pen name of Gustavo Adolfo Martínez Zuviría) was an influential Argentine writer, politician, and academic whose literary impact was significant in both Argentina and the broader Spanish-speaking world. His works, primarily written in the early to mid-20th century, combined elements of historical fiction, Catholic morality, and nationalist themes, making him one of the most widely read and debated authors of his time. His literary works were known for his ability to weave compelling narratives that resonated with religious and conservative audiences. Wast's influence was strong in mid-century Argentina and Latin America where his legacy remains debated due to his political affiliations and ideological positions. Nevertheless, his novels continue to be studied as reflections of the cultural and religious landscape of his time.

The Works of Hugo Wast

Novels and Fictional Works

1. Flor de Durazno (1911) – One of his earliest and most famous novels, later adapted into a film starring Carlos Gardel.
2. Ayer fue primavera (1912)
3. Fuente sellada (1918)
4. Ave sin nido (1918)
5. Desierto de piedra (1919)
6. La casa de los cuervos (1919)
7. Valle negro (1920)
8. El jinete de fuego (1923)
9. Myriam la conspiradora (1924)
10. Lucía Miranda (1926) – A historical novel set during the early Spanish colonization of the Río de la Plata region.
11. Tierra de jaguares (1927)
12. Los ojos vendados (1928)
13. Don Bosco y su tiempo (1929) – A novelized biography of Saint John Bosco.
14. El Kahal (1935) – One of his most controversial works, criticized for its anti-Semitic themes.
15. Juana Tabor (1937)
16. Oro (1938)
17. Este mundo y el otro (1942)
18. Lo que Dios ha unido (1944) – A novel about marriage and Catholic doctrine, one of his most widely read works.
19. Autobiografía de un cobarde (1949)
20. Una estrella en la ventana (1953)

Essays, Speeches, and Other Writings

1. Bajo la toca de Nazareth (1923) – Essays on religious themes.
2. La santa de las pampas: vida de la Beata Laura Vicuña (1932) – A biography of Blessed Laura Vicuña.
3. Fiestas cristianas (1934)
4. Pequeñas historias (1937) – Short stories and reflections.
5. Historia de los judíos (1937) – A controversial historical and ideological essay.
6. La Catedral de los pobres (1942)
7. Fiestas de la Iglesia (1945)
8. El automóvil y la carretera (1946)
9. Vida de Santa Teresita del Niño Jesús (1947) – A religious biography.
10. Mensaje en la aurora (1949)
11. Viaje al reino del alba (1950)
12. El libro de mis hijos (1951)
13. Carta a un hermano en la fe (1954)